John ~~Thornton~~ ... ~~and~~ Me

AN AUXILIARY NOVEL TO THE

John Thornton and Margaret Hale

LOVE STORY

~ Loyal Wynyard ~

loyalwynyard.com

Dedicated to

Monica Hall

She leadeth me to the "turn of phrase"
and
Delivereth me from myself

I shall never forget:
~~Start~~ / Begin
~~Maybe~~ / Perhaps

About this Book

Elizabeth Cleghorn Gaskell (1810-1865) has been one of my favored British novelists, known for such works as *Cranford, Wives and Daughters, and North and South.* These accomplished works often reflected areas where she had lived throughout her lifetime. All have been brought to the screen by the British Broadcasting Company. It was my absolute passion for North and South (2004 BBC) that prompted this, my first novel. My apologies to Elizabeth Gaskell for my own simple style of writing.

This book, in no way, attempts to emulate her talented style of writing or proposes to improve on her work of North and South; quite the contrary, as that would be an impossibility. It is because of my love for her story, her characters, and her subject's domain, that I felt I wanted more of it. Loving Gaskell's work in North and South, I started to write auxiliary stories around it, all within the canon of North and South, all of which began small, but eventually birthed this novel. Above all, this novel is written to share and continue the love between John Thornton and Margaret Hale. I apologize to the North and South purists, who may find any additional writings to an Elizabeth Gaskell novel to be ill conceived. To the other readers who want more, as I did, I offer this, my first novel. I hope you enjoy this story.

Long live Margaret Hale and John Thornton in our hearts.

This book begins as Margaret Hale is being borne away in a carriage from John Thornton, as he utters the words, "Look back at me." In this book you will find Margaret uttering the same words.

This is a romance novel. As nearly all novels of this genre, it will include some sensual love scenes.

- Loyal Wynyard

Acknowledgements

Much appreciation and gratitude are owed to some very good friends who put up with me, helped, and guided me through this first novel. I want to thank them for their invaluable assistance and friendship.

The Period Drama Passion Lovers

Lynda Bennett from New Zealand, was the first to read the dreaded first draft, which now only holds a faint resemblance to the original words. Lynda kindly offered her time and opinions, which made me stop and think about some of the directions, I was taking.

Lucie Swiers from Belgium, a new internet friend, who is a budding novelist herself, gave me some wonderful ideas. Lucie was my sounding board on "What Would John Thornton Do." If anyone matches my passion for John Thornton, it is Lucie.

Monica Hall from Canada, a longtime internet friend, who spent many months helping me hammer out my style of writing. She took great pains, in turning the phrases for me until I became more successful at it, but she's still the master. I'll never forget her first comment after reading my first chapter. She said, "What are you doing, writing a tech manual?" I've never laughed so hard, but knew she was right. Monica has rescued me from myself. Thank you Monica, my critique goddess.

I would like to thank all the gals at JustPeriodDrama.com, IMDB.com, (North and South) forum and North and South enthusiasts for keeping the dream of Margaret and John, alive.

My Pinochle Guys

Thank you to my pinochle partners on Thursday morning for putting up with me talking about my book and allowing me to sneak in their names as the gentlemen, they truly are. Thank you, Craig Steen, Paul Cribb and Al Vespoli, in Brevard County, Florida.

Table of Contents

Chapter 1

 *Lost Love*

1851 winter, Milton, N.W. England

"Look back .... look back at me."

John heard his thoughts slip from his mouth, as he stood and watched the coach bearing Margaret away forever. Unknowingly, she carried his heart, his soul, and his future dreams.

Inside the carriage, Margaret dwelled deep within her own misery of lost family, drowning in the solitude she thought her life to be, too absorbed to give a backward glance.

On that snowy day, John's soul froze over; all of his passion fell dormant. With her coach out of sight, he felt nausea sweep over him. He was an empty shell. A large void

1

replaced his heart. He wondered if he wanted to live in a world without her.

John Thornton was a tall, virile, handsome man of thirty one years. He had black hair and ocean blue eyes, and beneath his cravat and black frock cloak he carried a taut muscular, perfectly proportioned body. Years of hard learning had produced a keen mind, and with his mother's guidance, he achieved manhood and became a gentleman. Simmering just beneath the surface was a well managed temper, fueled by great passion, but rarely displayed. He was well regarded by his peers and ladies alike, and though he did not seek it, seemed destined for history and fame.

John never had the luxury of a misspent youth and had little time for sowing his wild oats. Hardship fell early in his life. His father committed suicide, the result of unfortunate business mistakes, and John was forced to support his mother and sister. As a young lad, he worked hard to restore his family's good name and eventually repaid his father's creditors, even though the name Thornton had been written off as a bad debt.

Through pure diligence and hard work, John became a merchant, a tradesman, and a Master and Cotton Mill owner, employing several hundred workers. Milton, the town where he was raised, had birthed the Machine's Industrial Age, and John Thornton was an integral part of it. He, along with other owners, pioneered the manufacturing of cotton fabric and shipped it, not only within country, but worldwide. Cotton was a low profit commercial item for which the world was starting to clamor. With its lower cost and lighter weight, it replaced many textiles such as canvas, fur, velvets, and linen. It was already Great Britain's largest exported product, and because of it, the town of Milton was on the verge of exploding into a very large dot on the map.

John became a leader among his peers in the cotton industry. Inspired by the words of Miss Margaret Hale (since gone from his life), he soon became the solution to the unsolvable wage issues that had kept the workers impoverished.

By 1851, when the worst of the labor issues existed, Margaret Hale, her mother, and father (a disillusioned clergyman turned teacher) and Dixon, their housekeeper had been in Milton for a year. John became acquainted with the family and fell in love with Margaret Hale almost immediately, but differences in customs of the slow-paced south and the industrial north caused a series of misunderstandings between them. Margaret felt John was too crude and forward, certainly not a gentlemen in the genteel south or London tradition. Most of the time, she shunned him. She didn't care for his northern ways.

One eventful day, Margaret visited John's mother, Hannah, at their home situated within the property of Marlborough Mills. While there, a riot broke out among the strikers who were demanding more pay. Barred inside the house, Margaret and John observed the incited crowd from an upper window. Margaret spoke to him, begging him to consider the situation and see it through the eyes of the workers. "They're being driven mad with hunger" she told him, "but they're only human. You must find a solution. Please, go talk to them." John pondered her suggestion for a few moments, then without really knowing what to say, walked outside to speak to them. As Margaret continued to watch from inside, she realized the crowd was growing angrier and she quickly went out to help him. Knowing that they would not harm a woman, she forced herself between John and the rioters and tried to reason with them. John was momentarily caught off guard. Angry, but fearing for her safety, he tried to force her back into the house when suddenly he felt her body slump, lifeless against him, having been felled by a thrown rock intended for him. John carried an unconscious Margaret inside and laid her on the couch. His mother told him to do what he needed to do and that she would care for Margaret. Minutes later, the doctor arrived and declared she had a bad bump on her head but she would be fine. The doctor took her home in his carriage.

Unbeknownst to Margaret, her spontaneous reaction signified more than just concern for John's safety. To the people in the north, she had signaled an interest in John which propriety could not overlook, and although not her intention, it was taken as such by all who witnessed her behavior. Both John and his Mother then felt he was obligated to protect her reputation and ask for her hand in marriage. Marrying Margaret was already in his thoughts, but doing it at this particular time was less than ideal for either of them.

Her rejection of his proposal was a miserable and extremely painful experience for them both, but over time John felt that she was beginning to understand the ways of the north. He remained hopeful that a relationship could be salvaged in the future. Other misunderstandings of lesser significance were also present, but they were nothing more than that, solvable, if time were on their side.

During that same year, Margaret suffered several losses: First, Bessie, the only friend that she made since moving to Milton, then tragically and within a short time of each other, her parents. She was devastated by the death of her father, her only remaining parent, and having lost so many of her loved ones, she felt lonely and bewildered. Margaret secretly wondered what it was within her, or what she had done, to cause such grievous misfortunes to befall her and desolate her life so quickly.

Immediately following her father's death, and even though she was of age, Margaret's aunt took her under her care and swept her away, to live in London. Aunt Shaw never thought Milton was good enough for her sister and her family, so Margaret was quickly forced to adapt to London and its societal lifestyle, a lifestyle that John never felt she totally embraced.

The day she left Milton, Margaret went to say goodbye to John and his family. She gave him a book that had belonged to her father. In that instant, John realized his world had changed dramatically. Moments later, he stood silently watching her coach leave his mill yard. As it passed through the gate, out of sight, John knew Margaret was gone from his life. But, he vowed, he would not . . . could not let it end this way.

I cannot lose her, lest I lose myself.

Chapter 2

 Abandoned Hope

Over the next year, John Thornton became a shell of the man he once was: a thinking human being with no central core, little constancy, adrift in his own life. In an effort to keep his company from failing, he kept long hours at work, trying to lose himself in his mill. Margaret's words, on the day of the riot, continued to haunt him. He recognized that consideration for the human condition of his people was the road to the mill's salvation, but how to accomplish this remained an issue for him and all the cotton masters. Feeling lost, he nevertheless was determined to resolve the wage issue, even if it meant losing everything to do it. And through it all, his faith in Margaret's insights remained intact. Resolute to form a new perspective, John set to work on a solution.

By the end of that first year after Margaret had left, he began to see the benefits of his hard work. He had successfully tightened controls, hired capable, more productive people, and retrained his workers. In order to pay wages, he diluted most of his personal financial holdings. He met with his workers individually, and held monthly meetings so they could air their grievances. Wanting his labor force to comprehend the whole picture, he demonstrated, with slate and chalk, where every pound was going, and helped clear all their financial misunderstandings of the company. His goal was to make them partners in his decisions. Over time, the entire mill came to recognize their newly acquired knowledge (some absorbed more than others), as fair and equal. They had a sense of partnership and they had a purpose: they wanted John to succeed. He wasn't only their boss, he became their friend. In the end, the workers' personal interest in the success of the company, and their mutual pride and dedication to workmanship, produced a finer product.

Before long, John's mill began to reap great rewards; the other mill masters, observing the result of changes he had made, began to follow his lead. Although they didn't always agree with him on his expenditures and personal sacrifices (with regard to the workers), John showed them that sacrifice was at the core of his success. He believed in a new way of thinking: a future vision that embraced the workers' humanity and would ultimately resolve most problems. Recognized as a highly acclaimed merchant within the Cotton Industry, it wasn't long before other burgeoning industries began to take notice of the name John Thornton and the town of Milton. Respect and admiration for his business skills, and absence of dissention among his 300 plus workers, resulted in his fame being spread throughout other areas of commerce. His methods were recorded in trade journals, and he was asked to speak at various functions around the country. John was obliging, but shunned the limelight, and never put himself forward to be admired. He disliked receiving praise for common sense work and he highly undervalued himself. The world, however, saw him differently...

At a time when John was achieving great success and blazing historical trails, his personal life was far from successful, but he kept it well hidden from all but his closest friends. Margaret never wrote to him after her bereavement ended. He had written her two letters, but they went unanswered. This puzzled him. It was most unlike Margaret to be so impolite. Having had no communication from her, and having heard no news of her, he began to worry, sensing she might slip through his grasp.

My destiny cannot be to live without her.

In the second year after Margaret left, John attempted two more courteous letters but received no replies. Now, concerned that something was amiss, he wrote to Dixon, hoping she could shed some light on Margaret's apparent disregard for his letters. Clearly, this was not the Margaret he once knew. He had to find out why.

Late one evening, John returned home from the mill. As he entered the sitting room, Hannah was sitting at the dining table, reviewing Cook's menus for the following week.

"Good evening, Mother. How has your day been?"

Hannah Thornton looked up from her work and smiled fondly at her son. "Oh, a bit tiring..." Lottie came by to gossip for a while and we had tea. Then I wrote a letter, did a little cross stitch... and here I sit working on our meals for next week." Rising from the table, walking to the couch, she watched him, as he removed his coat and cravat and placed them over the back of a chair. "And how was your day, John?"

John walked over to the buffet and poured himself a brandy before responding. Lifting the glass he turned slightly towards Hannah, "Mother?"

"Yes, John, but I would prefer a small sherry, instead. By the way, something came in the post for you today. It's on the dining room table."

Without acknowledging her comment about the post, John continued pouring their drinks. "It was a rather easy day, today. Higgins still amazes me with his capacity for completing all the work I assign him. I can't find the end of the man. He never tires, never complains, good teacher - a perfect overseer. I'm going to get him into the office for some of the financial side of the business." Picking up her sherry, but leaving his brandy behind, John walked to the dining table and retrieved the letter. Crossing the room, he handed his mother her glass. He paused a moment to open the note, quickly scanning for a signature.

"Finally," John said as he walked back to the buffet and picked up his brandy. Walking over to his leather chair in front of the fire, he sat down and began to unfold the letter.

"Who is it from?" his mother asked, watching John's movements.

"It's from Dixon, the Hales' housekeeper. She now works for Margaret."

Hannah looked at him angrily. "John, you didn't! Please tell me you didn't write to her and ask about Miss Hale behind her back."

Raising his eyes to meet hers, John answered, "Mother, I cannot tell you so, because I did write to her. I wrote to Margaret four times in two years and received no response to my letters. I thought a quick note to Dixon, requesting a reply, would let me know if Margaret received them. I have reason to suspect that her family may be censoring her post. I didn't tell you about writing to her because I knew you would go on . . . like you are about to do now . . ." He paused for a moment, letting the weight of his words sink in. His mother's consistent negativity towards Margaret Hale, from the very beginning of their acquaintance, was an ongoing source of frustration for him. "So," he continued, "if you don't mind, mother, I would like to read Dixon's letter now."

As John began reading, Hannah was up and pacing the floor. She was worried about this "re-emergence of the "Miss Hale" story. For the past two years, he had been seeing other women, no one permanently, but she thought Miss Hale was far from his mind. Suddenly, Hannah's thoughts were interrupted as she heard the sound of glass, shattering on the floor. She quickly turned around and saw John, still seated, bent slightly forward with his elbows supported on his knees. He was holding his head in his hands, looking down, staring at the letter that had fallen to the floor.

"What is it, John?" she asked, alarmed by his pale face and empty unfocused eyes.

She watched as he stood up. Without acknowledging her question, and oblivious to the glass fragments on the floor, he walked out of the room, down the stairs, and out the front door with neither coat, nor hat, in hand. Hannah was stunned; he'd never done anything like that before. She hurried to the window, in time to see him walking through the mill gate.

At the sound of footsteps coming from the kitchen stairs, Hannah turned and saw Jane, the housekeeper, entering the room, dustpan, and broom in hand.

"I thought I heard the sound of breaking glass, ma'am." she said, glancing around the room.

Hannah composed herself. "Over here, Jane," she said as she pointed to the floor, "but hand me that letter first, if you don't mind?"

Jane handed her mistress the note and began to sweep the glass. Hannah waited patiently for her to leave, then sat in John's chair and began to read.

Dear Mr. Thornton,

It was nice hearing from you. I do not think Miss Margaret got your letters because I think she would have told me. She and I are close friends. She does not care for London, so we talk a lot about Helstone and Milton. I know she wrote to you once or maybe it was two times, because she asked me if I wanted to add anything. I just wanted to say Hello to you. Did you not receive them?

I don't know if this is good news or bad news for you, but Miss Margaret married her a college professor last month. She is not living here anymore. They live on the school grounds somewhere. I was not allowed to go with her because they have their own staffing.

To be honest with you Mr. Thornton, I don't know if she was happy to be married or happy to be out of here. She's been very sad a long time, but I don't think it is all about her parents dying. She just hates living here and society life being pressed on her. I know she would have been happy to hear from you, because we wondered how you and Mr. Higgins were getting along. I think that is all you wanted to know. Please write again if I can tell you anymore, I like getting letters.

Dixon

By the time Hannah finished reading the letter, tears were rolling down her cheeks, and her heart beat rapidly in her chest. She felt terrible for her son. She decided to wait and have dinner with him, but he didn't return and she could not eat. Feeling unwell, she retired to her room for the evening.

Knowing John was at a very low point, weighed heavily on her conscience, exhausting her even further. She recognized she held some blame in this disaster in her son's life. Originally, she never endeared herself to Margaret, and had since tried to sweep her memory out of the way. John, meanwhile, had been holding on to her tightly, in his heart. "How he must have struggled to tolerate me," she thought," when I was so quick to dismiss any conversation about Miss Hale."

Will he ever forgive me?

Outside, John walked towards nowhere; numb, not caring, and oblivious to everything around him, including the cold and the approaching darkness. His thoughts were incomprehensible; he was inconsolable.

I cannot believe what has happened to my life. It is over.

John had loved Margaret for over three years. Although there had been no communication between them for two of those years, he still had clung to hope. He had dreams and he had plans, all of which just died a horrible death.

Walking with his head down, people stared at him as he passed. He wandered aimlessly out of town and found himself at the cemetery, where Margaret had visited weekly, at the grave of her lost friend, Bessie.

John's insides were churning as he walked around in circles, simultaneously wrestling with anger and sorrow. Tears rolled down his face, as his stomach convulsed with pain, and pure mental agony consumed him.

Margaret . . . my love, my life, why did you marry someone else?

Holding his arms straight over his head, shaking his fist skyward, shouting and sobbing at his maker, John wailed to the heavens, "Why, God . . . why? Why take Margaret from me, again? What have I done to deserve this? . . . God, anything but this!"

John silently cursed his god. For him, God no longer existed. With despondency heavily descending upon him, he slid to his knees and fell backwards on to the cold damp ground. A few moments later he sat up, resting his head on his arms, which were laying across his up-drawn knees. Tears of utter desolation poured out from him. He thought he was watching himself go mad.

"I have loved her for three years, God. Two years ago, my heart broke when you took her from me. I have not looked into her face since then, but have continued to live in hope every day. And today, God, you put a pistol to my head and pulled the trigger. You have taken away my love, my reason for living, my everything. She wrapped herself around my very soul, now you've wrenched her away. You have destroyed me,

God. I am done with you, as you are done with me." John cried uncontrollably, feeling as if he was bleeding to death, and wishing, somehow, that he could.

As the hours rolled by, he sank deeper into despair, and thoughts of ending his own life began to appear, but the recollection of the family's grief, over his father's suicide, kept him teetering on the brink of life. He knew, without a doubt, living in a world without Margaret, in a world without *hope* of Margaret, meant living in a void: a meaningless, senseless life; forever floating, trapped in a world of depression, and ostracized from reciprocated love.

As the pale light of dawn rose over the smoky town, John stood slowly, straining at his stiffness, and decided to go home and try to survive the rest of his damaged life. There were no tears left to shed. He was completely and utterly spent.

Everything is gone . . . lost to me now . . . and I, too, am lost.

Approaching his home, John tried putting on a good face for the early workers wandering the yard, but he knew he looked awful and it matched his mood. Feeling unprepared to face his mother over Miss Hale, again, he mounted the porch steps, took a deep breath, and turned the doorknob. As he came bravely through the door to the sitting room, Hannah looked up from her chair and quietly gasped. Standing before her in muddied clothes, looking totally exhausted, was her son: face swollen, eyes bloodshot and cheeks stained and streaked with tears. He was a broken man and her heart sank for him. *How he suffers...* Without saying a word, she walked over, putting her motherly arms around him. She wanted to tell him she was sorry, but it didn't seem enough, considering her past attitude toward Miss Hale, so, she kept silent on the matter.

"Would you like something to eat, John?" Hannah asked, tentatively, as she stepped back from him.

"No thank you, mother. I'm going to clean up and lie down for a few hours. Would you send Jane to find Higgins and tell him it will be a while before I get to the office?"

Hannah said she would take care of it. Having decided she would say nothing about the letter until he did, she stood silently watching him. Picking up Dixon's letter, John turned and walked to his room, closing the door behind him.

Hannah thought to herself that she had never seen him so dejected. Unfortunately, and all too late, she realized the great love her son had for Miss Hale; so much more than she had ever thought. At last, she fully recognized the understanding John had of Margaret. Hannah knew, for certain, she had misjudged this woman.

In his room, John undressed and bathed, feeling the weight of loneliness descend upon his tired body. Putting on a fresh undergarment he lay down on the bed. Exhaustion overtook him, finally, and he slept fitfully, never finishing Dixon's letter.

He awoke several hours later, bathed in sweat. Throwing his legs over the side of the bed, he sat up, trying to clear his head. He wished he was awakening from a nightmare, but there it was, on the night table: Dixon's letter, spelling out *THE END* to the rest of his life. Reaching over, he picked it up, and began reading where he had left off:

> To be honest with you Mr. Thornton, I don't know if she was happy to be married or happy to be out of here. She's been very sad a long time, but I don't think it is all about her parents. She just hates living here and society life being pressed on her. I know she would have been happy to hear from you, because we wondered how you and Mr. Higgins were getting along.

Suddenly, he stopped. "What did *that* mean . . . *happy to be married or happy to be out of there?*"

John stood, continuing to read, as he paced the floor and ran his fingers through his hair. They were words, *just words,*

14

but ignoring them would haunt him forever. Nothing could be done now; there could be no difference in their permanent separation. But still… he had to know…

Did she marry for love?

It seemed absurd to want to know the answer; what difference would it make? Yet, deep down, burned the desire to feel what might have been. What if she *could* have loved him? That, at least, would be worth something to him.

He knew what he must do… In a few weeks he was due to attend the annual convention for the cotton mill industry, held in London.

"I will visit Dixon while I'm there. I must understand what she meant by those words."

Chapter 3

 A Visit with Dixon

1853 summer

Upon discovering that Margaret had married, John spent the next few weeks trying not to sink through the hole in his heart, until he could visit Dixon and discuss the content of her letter. Still determined to understand the meaning of her statement about why Margaret married, he wrote, requesting a few moments of her time on the day he planned to be in London.

In addition to losing the greatest love of his life, John now feared the loss of his mother. She was growing weaker and more staid, appearing increasingly deficient by the day. It was small comfort to John that she was under Dr. Donaldson's care. She still refused to share her health issues, and John's concern grew. Aware of Hannah's waning strength, Dixon came to mind. She would be ideal; a caring companion for his mother. John had no idea, however, with Margaret married and gone, in what capacity Dixon served the Lennox household. He needed to find out if she was available to tend to his mother, as her fragility progressed.

With sleeves rolled up, John sat slumped over his desk, strewn with scattered papers, graphs, and financial ledgers, immersing himself in concentrating on the upcoming convention. He looked up at the sound of a knock on the door, welcoming the distraction from his tiresome work.

Higgins opened the door and poked his head in, "Can I have a word with you? Oh ... It looks like this might not be a good time. Should I come back later?"

John tossed his feathered pen down onto the papers. "Come in," he said, "I'm not getting very far with this and I could use a rest. What can I help you with? Take a seat."

Pushing his chair out from under the desk, John leaned back with his hands behind his head. Arching his stiff back and stifling a small groan, he waited for Higgins to enter the room.

Higgins stepped inside, closed the door behind him, and removed his cap. He sat down across from John, and not knowing how to start, he began whirling his cap round and round by the rim. John could see Higgins was anxious and worried about something.

"Higgins," he prompted, "I know that look. What's on your mind?"

Shifting slightly in his seat, he began, "Boss, you put me in charge of this mill. And it is for the mill I am speaking to you now. Nearly all of our people, including myself, are sensing a drastic change in your manner. We are all concerned and there is much talk. They are coming to me, asking what's wrong with the Master. Many think the mill might be in trouble. I know that not to be true; I tell them that, but have no explanation to give them about their concerns. You and I work close together and I can see a great sadness that you're trying to hide from everyone. I didn't want to speak about this with you, as it must be personal in nature, but the people are growing more worried by the day; that includes me. They're starting to fear for their jobs, and some have talked about looking for work at other mills. Can you share anything which might relieve their worries?"

John stood, curling his hands into his pockets, and turned away from Higgins. He gazed out the window over-looking the yard where his laborers were working. He'd known all along that his recent behavior would soon be called into question, and he wondered how to broach the concerns about the two women in his life.

Still looking out the window, John began to speak, "Higgins, you put that most delicately. Your leadership skills improve by the day. In the entire world, I think you've been the closet friend to me. Sometimes I look upon you like a brother. I think we're quite alike, you and I. We have the same high standards. We're both honest to a fault; we work hard, and we care for our fellowman. You're not just my overseer. I'm proud to call you my friend."

John turned and faced Higgins. Pausing briefly, he allowed his words to sink in, and then began pacing the room. "I'm going to tell you, and only you, the two factors that have been plaguing my life recently. Part of it is personal, and the other part will be known soon enough."

As Higgins watched his boss pace the floor, sorrow flooded him; he knew it was all going to be bad.

Not wanting to look Higgins in the eye, John turned back to the window and slowly started to speak. "First, and again... this is for you only . . . about a month ago, I learned that Margaret Hale married a college professor. They're living on the college campus in London. I've had no communication with her since she left Milton, although I've tried repeatedly. I feel there's more wrong than right going on there, and I *will* get to the bottom of it."

Feeling helpless, Higgins looked up at John who was still staring out the window. "I'm sorry, Master. I knew of your feelings towards her, so I can only imagine how deeply saddened you are over this. This alone tells me why you've acted the way you have, of late. If I could ask, what do you feel is wrong?"

John turned, facing Higgins once more, and sat down at his desk, clasping his hands in front of him. "I think it's very unlikely that Miss Hale ever received my four letters to her in two years, and I've never received a single response. I finally wrote to Dixon; she doesn't believe she ever got them. I'm going to get to the bottom of this, or go crazy wondering. It's too late for anything to be done, other than to ease my mind that she had not purposely avoided replying. I do feel there has been some . . . some... shall I say, mishandling of her posts?"

John leaned back in his chair, casually twirling his pen between his fingers and spoke before Higgins could reply. "It gets worse." He hesitated a moment before continuing, "I'm now facing the fact . . . my mother does not have long to live. The doctor comes to the house several times a week, but she doesn't wish to confide in me about the seriousness of her illness. So, I've decided, since I cannot be at her side constantly, when I go to London in next week, I'll ask Dixon if she can be her companion and watch over her. I don't believe mother will have any further contact with our workers, since she hardly leaves the house now and never comes to the mill. I think we can be honest with our people and let them know that I'm worried about her health." He paused for a moment, taking a deep breath.

Higgins, be strong for me now.

"As much as I wish to be among our workers," John continued, "I don't want to see the pity in their faces..." then he added softly, "... as I see in yours now. Assure them this mill is in the best financial shape it has ever been, and that we have hopes of building another."

"Master, I'm sorry to hear... "

"Higgins, dear friend," before you try to find the words to say to me just now, I'm going to ask that you don't speak them. I know you're sorry for me. I have no doubt you'll suffer along with me. You yourself have been at this point, with the loss of your daughter, and I can now understand some of what you felt, and perhaps Margaret, too. It's a hardship we cannot help but bear."

"Yes, it is, Master." Higgins said softly, wishing he could give John some words of comfort.

Smiling slightly, John continued, "I'm going to thank you now, for what I will probably lay at your door over the months ahead. As it is, you already do everything here, but I may find myself asking for more. I'm sorry for that, but I know you'll see me right," said John, leaning forward on his desk, looking down at his steepled fingers, avoiding any eye contact, lest he tear up.

"Whatever I can do . . . Master. I wish you all the best getting through this. I'll be here for you. Don't give another thought to the mill. Just handle your personal affairs, and I'll be an ear if you want to talk about anything."

"Thank you Nicholas," John replied, his voice thick with emotion. He didn't rise to extend his hand in thanks but he knew Higgins would understand. "I know you will. You're always there for me."

The following week, having quietly instructed Fanny to keep an eye on their mother, John said good-bye to Hannah. While he was having a few final words with Higgins in the office, he collected the papers of his documented studies, and slipped them into his leather portfolio. Feeling confident that he had done all he could, he departed for the train to London.

His journey lasted almost four hours but was comfortable. He didn't notice any of the other mill owners on his morning train. He used the time to relax, refresh his notes, and go over the conference agenda. Tomorrow he would breakfast with his friends and then attend a short strategy meeting, before the conference, which was scheduled to begin at 11:00 am. A meal would be served around two o'clock in the afternoon, and the conference would adjourn between five and six o'clock. Dinner would be held across the street at the Stag and Whistle pub, with late evening plans differing with every person. But for John, it was the day after the meeting that concerned him the most. He was determined to visit Dixon. After several hours of thinking about the conference and his visit, the swaying train and the sound of its clickety-clack rhythm lulled him into sleep.

An hour later, he was abruptly awakened by the noise of screeching brakes and to the hissing of vented steam. After several stops, his station was called out and John prepared to disembark. Donning his hat, he gathered his travel bag and portfolio then gingerly hopped off the train, before it came to a halt. Pushing his way through the platform crowds, he made his way to the front and hailed a hansom cab. He went directly to his hotel, having decided to sightsee later, should time permit.

That evening, as he entered the large, wood paneled dining hall a few minutes early, John spotted his fellow mill owners. Standing behind chairs at a round table, glass in hand, they were casually engaged in conversation. When the last owner arrived, they all settled into their seats and began discussing the next day's events.

Slickson immediately came to the point. "I think we're well prepared for tomorrow," he said. "We already had our big discussion at Thornton's house the other night, plus, we'll be meeting again tomorrow morning. What do you say we just enjoy the evening, at least not talk about the conference?"

There was agreement all around, as glasses were raised, and the men settled back down into other conversations. The dinner progressed through to the final course. By then, most of the conversation had turned towards the possibility of other factories coming into Milton. Many of the Masters were receiving inquiries from outside merchants, wishing to relocate. It seemed inevitable that, with new businesses flowing in, some type of merchant council or chamber would have to be created, if they were going to maintain a balance of wages. They had to form some guidelines for the influx that would be headed Milton's way. This would ensure the survival of their mills, as well as that of the manufacturers of low profit goods and their wage concerns. The evening ended with everyone in agreement to meet for further discussion when they returned to Milton.

The next morning, as the clock in his room struck seven, a porter, at John's request, promptly knocked on the door announcing the time. John called out "thank you" through the door and the porter left. He had an hour before meeting the masters for breakfast. He shaved and dressed, then collected his notes and headed downstairs to meet the others. Everyone was ready for their morning meal and eager to discover what the day would bring.

The conference lasted until nearly 6:30 p.m. Discussions and debates led the day, with John acting as spokesman for their group. Little was settled, except for small concessions by the shippers, and a promise from the growers to yield more volume. Prior to the meeting, John and the other Milton owners knew that's all they could expect, but it took all day to get to that point. They left the conference satisfied with their small achievement and headed out for dinner, across the street at the pub. With the meal and talk of the day completed, some owners left to catch late trains and others had plans similar to the night before.

Having nothing better to do, John decided to take a carriage ride over by the college, just to see the type of environment where Margaret lived. "It suits her well." he thought. The ivy covered walls and arched doorways seemed warm and inviting, academic, and definitely a world apart from the grand tiers that one might find in London. He hoped she was happy and being treated as she deserved.

Somewhere among these hallowed halls, my true love lives.

Despite going to bed at 10 o'clock, John arose the next morning, suffering from a very poor night's sleep. His thoughts turned to his mother's failing health, and what he would do if Dixon wasn't available. His sadness regarding his mother was tolerable now, because he knew what to expect; what Dixon might tell him about Margaret was causing unbearable anxiety. Time seemed to drag on, as he counted the hours until one o'clock when he would meet Dixon and find out what she had meant in her letter. The thread of hope he was clinging to could very well break today, but he needed to know everything in order to deal with the rest of his life.

It was nearing 11 o'clock when he came down for breakfast, having packed all his things and closed out his room account.

From his pocket, he took an old yellowed piece of paper with an address on it, and asked the registrar if he recognized the area, and how long it would take to get there. The registrar was unfamiliar with the exact address, but knew the area and approximated a 20 minute carriage ride. John checked his pocket watch and calculated that he should leave the hotel by 12:30 p.m.

He ate alone, mostly pushing food around on his plate, and finished his second cup of tea. Pulling out his pocket watch for the third time in half an hour, he noted it was almost midday. He paid the waiter for his uneaten meal, collected his belongings, and went into the lobby where people were talking or reading the paper. Sitting alone, in a far off corner of the room, he allowed his mind to wander. He wasn't too concerned about finding a caretaker for his mother, surely it would be an easy task to accomplish, but finding someone who would put up with her stubborn ways, might prove to be difficult. Having his home on the mill property meant he would be able to assist her, but surely, as she grew weaker, she would need someone to help her with the more personal details.

And then there was Margaret… John wondered what he would do if Dixon told him she believed Margaret married to gain freedom from her relatives. Certainly, they would have encouraged a commonality with the different levels of the London upper class. Marriage to a college professor sounded like an act of escape from a certain measure of the higher social circle. But in other ways, John thought, it did have a ring of truth about it: An educator would be very much to Margaret's liking. Realizing he was becoming more anxious by the moment, he took out his pocket watch once more. Time came to hail a cab.

Five minutes before the hour, John stepped out of the coach. As he paid the driver, he instructed him to return in 20 minutes; if he was going to be any later then someone would come out and pay him to wait.

Arriving at Captain Lennox's home, John looked over the highly ornate, white Regency town home, with its columned front porch and tall windows. Hesitantly, he proceeded forward. He climbed the marble steps up the slight embankment then stepped onto a slate walkway leading to the door. Before he could lift the knocker, Dixon opened the door. Removing his hat, John entered the house.

"Good to see you Mr. Thornton." Dixon said politely, a hint of sadness in her voice. "You can place your hat and things over here." She pointed to a highly polished table in the foyer. The Mr. and Missus are not in, but they know you were coming. If you will follow me."

"Good day to you, Dixon. Thank you for seeing me."

Dixon led John toward the back of the house. "Mr. Thornton, if you would care to go out onto the veranda, I'll fetch some tea."

"Very good. This is a lovely home you work in, Dixon. I've not seen a veranda in many years. I'm sure you remember the air in Milton; it wouldn't suit such a luxury."

As John stepped out onto the wide veranda, he was immediately struck by the large fountain, toward the center of the back garden, spewing water into its trough at the bottom. He had always been fascinated by the water wheel engineering that lay beneath its foundation. Wheels would turn by falling water, raised in turn by other wheels bringing the water back up the center flow. Thinking back on his study of its construction, he was reminded that there would be a hidden chamber where a workman could repair the works from below, if needed.

Before he could have a closer look at its complex design, his senses were suddenly filled with the awareness of her, and then the voice struck his heart like a thunder bolt.

"Hello Mr. Thornton."

Chapter 4

 *Perhaps Someday*

It had been two years since he'd heard that soft lovely voice, now, depressingly fading to a whisper in his heart. Hardly believing the moment, he slowly turned around and *she* was there, standing off to the side on the veranda. Margaret was pulling all the air from his lungs.

John audibly inhaled as he took in Margaret's vision which had been captured in his mind since he first met her. Was there any beauty on earth to match hers? . . . He didn't think so. Margaret, once his entire future, stood before him, and she belonged to someone else. The person who unknowingly took his heart was right there; he wanted to reach out and touch her, to know that she was real.

What do I say to her at such a time?

With a faint smile, John began, "Miss . . . . Mrs. . . . . I'm sorry; I don't know your married name."

"Margaret interceded with, "Reed. But I would appreciate it if you would call me Margaret. I think we've been well enough acquainted for some time to drop the stiff propriety. May I call you John?"

As he walked towards her, he could smell her scent and he struggled to get his words out. John wanted to tell her that she could call him anything, but . . . "Yes, I would like you to call me, John. I'm taken by surprise to see you here. I didn't expect this. You're looking well."

Margaret fidgeted with her handkerchief. "I came by three weeks ago to collect more of my books from my old room when Dixon told me of your letter and the news about your mother." She paused briefly, realizing she was having difficulty looking into his eyes, but couldn't understand why. "Shall we sit, while Dixon brings our tea?"

They walked a few paces over to the more comfortable padded wicker seating arrangement, with its large green and red tropical flower design. Margaret on the settee, sat very primly and John in a single chair to her right sat rigidly, still disbelieving the moment.

Dixon brought out a silver tray with the china tea service. "Mr. Thornton" she said, as she poured the tea, "I have talked with Miss Margaret, and she knows all about your offer to me in helping Mrs. Thornton. She will answer for me, I'll be upstairs if you need me, but I would like to talk with you a moment before you leave."

"That will be fine Dixon." John told her. "And would you watch for a coach waiting out front in twenty minutes, and let me know?"

"Yes, Mr. Thornton, I surely will." With that Dixon took her leave.

"John," Margaret said, now turning slightly towards him, "I am genuinely sorry to hear about your Mother. I know this must be a very hard time for you, watching as her health fails. I really wanted to get to know her better, but as you know I was swept away by my family before I could come to grips with my own life."

"Yes," John said, repressing his anger, "How well I remember that your family forced you to leave Milton, but I guess I can understand it, with your family feeling about Milton, the way they did. I remember there was so much I wanted to say, but the opportunity never arose. I know you've been through a lot, and I'm sorry for that." He couldn't help but ramble; there was so much in his heart, so much left unsaid.

Margaret continued, "Dixon is now an extra staff member in this house, but my cousin was certainly willing to keep her on until she found employment elsewhere, or I found a way to keep her. She's overjoyed to be needed in your home, but saddened as to the reason."

All the while Margaret was speaking, John knew he was staring. He could hardly pay attention to her words; he was gazing intently at her lovely face. Surprisingly, he didn't see the radiance one might have expected in a newly married woman. John slightly shifted in his seat as his emerging arousal caught him off guard. That had ceased being a common occurrence after she left.

"Dixon's already packed and can be in Milton next week," Margaret went on.

There was a moment of silence as John, mesmerized, realized she had stopped talking. "I'll be very grateful for her help." He told her. When the time comes and my Mother is no longer with me, Dixon can remain on as head of housekeeping, which currently, only includes Jane and Cook. She'll be welcomed to stay on forever or until she finds something else she would rather do. I'll not worry about an extra staff member. Jane is young enough to marry any year now, and she might be gone soon."

Not wanting the conversation to stop altogether, John politely inquired," How have you been, Margaret? Well, I hope?"

Margaret cleared her throat, "About my marriage . . ."

She certainly got to the issue immediately.

John promptly stood. He wasn't expecting this conversation to come up so quickly. He was afraid of what she might say. Perhaps she is nervous, too," he thought. Turning his back to Margaret, he looked out over the beautiful landscaped grounds. He was afraid of the emotion that might show itself at any moment now. "Yes," he interrupted, "I must say, it came as a shock to me when I read it in a recent letter from Dixon."

Seeing him turn from her, and feeling surprised at his words and the desolate tone of his voice, Margaret asked, "Did you not receive my two letters and then the invitation to our wedding?"

What? What is she saying? Did she write to me before she married?

"No," he said. "I did not. Not one word did I receive." Turning to face her, he said in an anguished voice, "Nothing. Nothing have I heard from you, since that snowy day you left Milton."

Margaret could see the torment that creased his brow and descended across his handsome face. She had to look away. Suddenly, a small voice inside her said, "*He loves you still, Margaret . . .*"

John sat down in the chair, pinching the bridge of his nose between his thumb and forefinger. He slowly cast his eyes back at Margaret, noticing her dejected posture. "Did you not receive the four letters I wrote to you?"

"Margaret quickly raised her lowered head, and frowning softly, sat staring at John as she tried to take in his words."

"*Your* letters? . . . *Four?* No . . . no . . .," she said while shaking her head in bewilderment. "No, I've heard nothing from you, or about you since that day I brought you father's book and said goodbye. Those few days are still very much of a muddle to me, I hardly can remember them. I . . . I thought I must have really hurt you by saying goodbye so quickly.

29

Eventually, I remembered you with Ann Latimer at Fanny's wedding. I thought, perhaps, the two of you were probably, well . . . you know. And after my two letters went unanswered, there seemed to be no mistaking the fact that you had moved on. And I couldn't blame you, for it was I, unquestioningly, who mishandled our friendship and . . ."

Margaret was startled as John bolted out of his seat, again, taking long strides across the expanse of the veranda, clearly in a state of barely controlled anger. "Margaret, first, Ann Latimer never meant anything to me, ever. It was always you. Can you not see what your family has done to us? Or perhaps it's just me? Margaret, had our communication not been subverted I feel we wouldn't be where we are today. What I can say, for certain, is that having no word from you has irretrievably damaged the course of my life forever. You must know how I've always felt about you." He crossed back to his chair and sat down, watching Margaret as he spoke each word.

"John, had I known that you still held some regard for me, I would have . . ."

Silence was suspended, as Margaret fought to contain the words she knew she shouldn't speak.

There was a pause in the conversation.

"I'm sorry, Margaret." John said, noticing her discomfort. It was improper of me to speak of my feelings, please forgive me. I just can't believe what has happened. If only . . ."

The sound of Dixon knocking on the open door caught their attention. "Mr. Thornton," Dixon said, "there's a coach outside . . . Mr. Thornton . . . ?"

"Yes, thank you Dixon." John said. Nodding his head towards Margaret, he asked, "Margaret, will you excuse me a moment?" And without waiting for an answer, he walked towards the front of the house.

With John out of sight, Margaret turned to Dixon. "Dixon, I've just found out that over the past two years, John wrote me four letters! I'm sure my family has intercepted all of our mail. They don't know what they've done . . ." Margaret's voice trailed off slightly. "Dixon, I think he still loves me, after all this time," she said humbly.

"Miss Margaret, you must be the only one living that don't know that." Dixon scolded her gently. "He thinks no one knows; he tries to hide it and keeps it tucked away, but I see it. I could see it several years ago; I got to think nothing has changed." Hearing his approaching footsteps, she lowered her voice. "He's coming back now. I'll be in the other room if you need me," Dixon passed John on her way back inside.

"Indeed, I apologize for interrupting our conversation," John said, returning to his chair.

"John, I don't know what to say." Margaret began, attempting to resume their conversation. "This is so awkward . . . no . . . this is much worse than that. This is tragic! I'm going to have harsh words with my family and get to the bottom of things. Seven pieces of post cannot just disappear into nowhere. I believe our lives would have taken another path had I known you were still aware of me. Nothing they can do will atone for this. Nothing!" . . . "Nothing," she said softly. Her voice trailed off into a whisper, as the realization that it was all too late to change, descended upon her. "Nothing can be done."

Hearing those words from her lips, John looked up sharply, in awe, emotions spreading through his body like wildfire.

Did she understand what she had just said? Does she truly believe there might have been hope of a future together?

Even though he could not question her about it, her wounded expression spoke volumes to his heart.

Regaining her composure, Margaret said, "John, I'm sorry. I shouldn't be talking like this. As to your question just before you left, Booker is a history professor at the nearby university. Being married to an academic is quite a different world. The social scene is far easier to tolerate than, what I was being encouraged to do, when I lived with my family."

There IT is. The answer. She married more out of convenience than love.

How much more of this catastrophic mistake could he bear to hear? His life lay in ruins and perhaps for her, as well.

"It's a totally academic environment; they seem to stay in their own little world. Lots of debates go on as if it were normal conversation. The books are piled to the rafters. The students come and go from our lodgings; you would think we were living in the dormitories."

John could barely stand listening to much more, but he knew he must. He wanted to smother her mouth with his, so she would stop talking.

"We had a slow and long courtship." Margaret was saying. "I never seemed to want to commit, but eventually I did." She paused for a moment, smiling wistfully at him. "So. . . how about you, John? Is there anyone special in your life, if there is no Ann?"

Looking directly into her face, he softly answered, "There was a special woman in my life, but that seems to be over now." John quickly looked away, embarrassed that he had said such a thing. How ungentlemanly that was, knowing she understood the significance.

"I'm sorry, Margaret. I didn't mean for it to come out that way. Please forgive me. I can't seem to keep my thoughts to myself. I've taken up enough of your time. I hope we can remain friends and perhaps in the future our correspondence will be uninterrupted. Do you think you could call Dixon for me?" He stood to leave.

Margaret stood as well, less than an arm's length from John. Just the presence of him there, his hovering over her, so tall, his tantalizing manly smell, his solid, muscular body, the timbre of his voice, that handsome face and those beautiful hands with long slim fingers . . . everything . . . the all of him . . .

I cannot bear this ache . . . thinking about what might have been.

She began to weep. With John so near, it was then that she recognized her own deep feelings, clawing from within her. Knowing that she could never be closer to John than she was at this very moment just seemed an impossible truth.

Staring at her tears in disbelief, John reached for her hands but Margaret quickly threw her arms around him and lay against his strong chest. She didn't know why she did it; she was drawn inexplicably to him. John represented something to her, but she wouldn't allow the 'why' to take form in her mind. She pushed it away, not wanting the realization to invade the moment.

He hadn't moved. He didn't back away from her unexpected behavior. He was a rock standing there for her. Through his thick clothing, she could feel his heartbeat accelerating, pounding loudly.

His love for me is thrumming in his chest. Dear God, what am I doing?

John gently put his arms around her, and closed his eyes, letting the moment wash over him like a cresting wave rolling onto shore. He knew this was improper, he had no understanding of why Margaret was embracing him, but he was not going to let it stop. "Dearest Margaret," he whispered, grasping her closer. Margaret, so small in his arms, that his hands circled her body from shoulder to shoulder. Kissing the top of her head, he inhaled deeply to capture her scent. "Dearest Margaret," he whispered again. He could hear her muffled sobs and saw the wet tears drop to his sleeve. Loosening some of his own self control, he feathered her with light kisses down the side of her face. Nestling his mouth against her neck, he whispered "Oh God, how I love you, Margaret," as he pressed her more tightly to his rigid body.

God, let this moment continue forever.

He wanted to kiss her mouth, so badly. He began tilting her face up to his, but she backed away with teary eyes and flushed cheeks, she looked up one last time into his face. The moment was gone.

"I . . . I don't know what I'm doing," Margaret said, continuing to back away. She turned to go get Dixon.

John stared at her as she left the veranda. His mind was racing. He knew she wasn't free to express anything, but he had just been given the most precious gift he could ever receive. Never before, had he held her. Finally, he was able to tell her what he had waited to say for so long. She had voluntarily come into his arms, held him, and allowed him to hold her body pressed against him. The passion he was feeling was so intense, he was afraid he might open the cage and release the primitive animal within himself. He thought about carrying her upstairs, and taking her. He had never experienced this . . . this fervor.

"Mr. Thornton?" "Mr. Thornton, you look a million miles away." Dixon was standing in front of him, trying to get his attention.

"I was." John said. "Sorry, Dixon. You wanted to see me before I left?"

"Miss Margaret is upstairs crying, sir. I hope everything is all right?" Not getting any reaction from him, she continued, "What I wanted to ask was when did you want me to be there in Milton?"

"As soon as you possibly can, Dixon. Please check the train schedules, and post me a note about your approximate arrival time, and I will have someone come to collect you and your things. I thank you very much, Dixon. I know my mother will be well looked after and I appreciate your help." Glancing over her shoulder, he asked, "Am I to assume that Margaret will not be down to say goodbye?"

"I don't think she'll be down. I better go to her and see what I can do. Can you see your way out, sir?"

"Yes, Dixon, I can. And would you give Margaret a message for me? Tell her I said, "PERHAPS SOMEDAY." That's all. Goodbye, Dixon."

Chapter 5

 The Ruby and the Diamond

Upstairs, Margaret collapsed across her old bed weeping, soaking herself with tears that wouldn't abate. She felt ashamed and mystified by her sudden emotion for John and her own response to him. She was lost in his embrace until his rigid passion for her became all too flatteringly apparent. Unexpected elation, brought on by his desire for her, had momentarily swept her away. For Margaret, passion had quickly disappeared from her marriage to Brook, and she martyred the guilt of her naivety. She had endured mortifying feelings of inadequacy as a woman but today John did not see her as the failure she saw herself to be, thus dispelling some of the disappointment in her own femininity. His sensual reaction had restored a small part of her womanly self confidence.

She loved her husband . . . so what had prodded her in seeking refuge in John's arms? Nausea had swept over her when she realized their correspondence had been intentionally intercepted, and her possible destiny had been manipulated out of her own hands.

John, almost a stranger for the past two years, had demonstrated his devotion and his passion, neither of which could be found in her new marriage.

Why isn't my own husband showing me this regard?

She desperately wanted to remain in his arms, to feel loved, but eventually she struggled against her newly found sensuality and stepped back. How she despised herself. As she retreated into the house, she saw John drop his arms to his sides, as in defeat. In a fleeting moment, she saw him cross from exhilaration into utter rejection. Every way she turned, it seemed John was feeling some form of refusal from her. She felt sick to her stomach with how she has treated him over the years, and yet, still, he loved her.

Dixon came into the room, rousing her from her dismal reflections.

"Are you all right Miss Margaret? I hope those tears are from happiness and not sadness."

Sitting up, Margaret said, "Dixon, I'm fine, I think. I just became a little melancholy, no more. Is Mr. Thornton still downstairs?"

"No, he left. He told me to tell you two words." He said, "Tell Miss Margaret *'PERHAPS SOMEDAY'*. It don't make much sense to me, but I guess you'd know what he meant."

"Thank you, Dixon." Margaret said, feeling the impact of John's parting words.

He loves me still and carries hope for us even though I am married. What more harm did I just cause to us both?

Thirty minutes later, John stood on the platform waiting for his train. As there were less passengers leaving London than arriving, he soon found himself alone in the coach, stowing his hat and cases over the top, finally settling by a window as the train pulled away.

"Perhaps someday . . ." He was leaving a door of hope open for both of them, for even with her marriage, he could not close his. John had no other choice, now; he would never give up. When he had first learned of her marriage, two months ago, he had lost all hope that she had ever cared for him. But it was different, now. Even though she had married for convenience, and even with another man making love to her, John felt Margaret was reaching out for him through her silence. He could be imagining it because he wanted it to be that way, but he didn't think so. John was prepared to live a life waiting for her. Twenty four hours ago, he had nothing . . . nothing but grief and sorrow. After today, he had a small piece of her heart; he felt sure of it.

When John arrived home, he was surprised to find his mother still awake, for it was past the time she usually retired. He walked over to her sitting on the couch. John noticed she was wringing her hands when he bent and kissed her on the cheek.

"How was your health, while I was away, Mother?" He asked as he straightened himself and began removing his waistcoat and cravat. He sat down in his chair by the fire, clasped his hands across his lap, and stretched his long legs out before him.

Hannah looked over at her son. "My health is fine, but I've been sitting here all weekend," she said, "feeling sorry for my outburst about the possibility of you wanting to see Miss Hale. Your letter to Dixon made me realize that I'm forcing you to hide things from me and do things behind my back because you fear my reaction."

"Mother, I do not fear your reaction for myself. I am capable of taking responsibility for my own decisions, but I dislike upsetting you. You and I have always been of a different opinion when it came to Miss Hale and I try to keep that part of my life away from you, so you will not worry. I'm sorry, but there it is."

"No, John, I will change. I've done a lot of thinking while you were away and I'm completely resigned to the fact that Miss Hale is your real love and always will be. I need to be part of that with you. If she is so deeply embedded into your heart, than she shall be in mine, too. If I could do anything to change the past for you, I would. Whoever you love will be important to me because she'll bring you happiness, which then will be my happiness."

John's eyes narrowed speculatively, "Mother, this is quite a change. It sounds to me that you're more ill than I previously thought." He tried to keep the alarm out of his voice.

"Oh, John . . . it's not that. I know I'm getting older, as it should be, and maybe my time is becoming shorter. That isn't it. It was the letter from Dixon and your reaction to it that opened my eyes to all of my past misgivings. It's not like she had to make me happy, she had to make you happy. Originally, I didn't think she did a very good job, but you handled her rejection and still you loved her."

John rose and went over to the couch. Kneeling down beside his mother, he spoke earnestly, "Your words mean a lot to me. Thank you, Mother. But now that she is married, I fear all your newly found sentiment for Margaret will never see the light of day." He could feel himself on the edge of tears. He couldn't share with her that he would live in hope, waiting out the lonely years. His mother had just made a heartfelt concession, but she would never understand that.

Hannah reached out to him, embracing him was the only comfort she knew how to give, knowing she could never make up for the past.

Hannah grew weaker over the next six months, worrying John. He was powerless to help her and began spending more time with her, even though she objected.

One afternoon, Dixon came bursting through the mill's office door. "The master, where's the master?" She hollered for anyone to hear.

Higgins came out of a back room and said, "Dixon, what is it?"

"It's the Missus. I must find the master right now."

"I'll take you to him; he's in the carding room. Follow me," Higgins said as he grabbed her by the arm and hurried her down the warehouse path to the mill room door. "Wait here, I'll get him for you. I'll be right back."

Higgins slid the door open for only a second and Dixon could see the room full of cotton fluff, cascading down on the master, as he walked his platform, overseeing his workers. In less than a minute, the door opened again and both men came to a halt in front of her. "Oh Master," she said anxiously, "it's the Missus. She had a lay down a while ago, I just checked on her and she seems very pale and is asking for you, Master. I'm afraid she might be . . . be . . ." Dixon couldn't finish her words.

John rounded on Higgins. "Take care of things here," he said quickly. "Send someone for the doctor and fetch my sister." With that, he began running across the yard toward his home. When he reached the main stairway, he took the steps three at a time and ran into his Mother's room. She seemed very comfortable laying there with a peaceful look on her face. John rushed to her side, breathless, and knelt by the bed, holding one hand on the top of her head while his other hand held hers. "Mother. Please hold on. I've sent for the doctor. Can I do anything for you?"

"Nothing. Calm down, John," Hannah whispered softly.

A surreal darkness began to descend upon him, as John sensed he only had moments left with her.

Mother, please don't leave me.

He looked at the translucent skin on her hands and his eyes traveled upwards to her face. She was looking into his eyes. With tears seeping from the corners, he said, "Mother, I love you."

Just then Dixon appeared at the door. John, sensing they were being watched, said, "Leave us, Dixon. Send Fanny in when she gets here and close the door, please."

As the door closed behind her, Hannah said, "You know, John, Dixon has been a wonderful companion to me, Jane has always been a great help and you know how I love Cook. I know I protested at the beginning about Dixon but I really grew to rely on her, she has been a great comfort for me. You will see them right, won't you?" Hannah's voice was so tender; it barely hovered above a whisper.

"You know I will. Mother, please, don't give up," he pleaded.

"John," she said, "let us not waste words now. I have much to say and little time." John caressed her hand firmly, as Hannah continued. "You John, you are the one I worry about. Losing Margaret was your greatest tragedy from which you have never recovered. And I don't think you ever will. I'm so sorry I didn't do more to ingratiate her into our lives. I was a jealous mother, who didn't want to let go of her son. But I see what this has done to you, and I am sorrier than you will ever know. I plan on finding a way to make amends when I pass beyond the limits of this world."

"Mother, please . . ."

"John, let me finish. In my jewelry case, I have an heirloom, a ruby heart pendant on a gold chain. It was passed down to me by grandfather when I was a little girl. I want Margaret to have it. It will be up to you how to present it to her, but I want to give it to her; I want to say *'I'm sorry'* to the woman you love.

Breathless, Hannah paused, tiring from rushing her words.

John, I've loved you all of my life. No mother on this earth could be as proud of her son as I am of you. You took our early hardships and used them to mold John Thornton; to the man you are today. You're not only a successful business man, but I know you are becoming known, far and wide and will be in the history books someday. You are financially set for your future, but you are not emotionally settled. I will ask God to help. He owes my son a favor."

John opened his mouth to speak and found he had no voice. Struggling, he began to speak his final words to her. "Mother, I, have also loved you every day of my life. You have made me what I am today, not I. Your love and strength, your guidance, your endurance and your courage, have been my moral compass all my life. At times I've considered you my conscience and asked myself, 'what would mother do in this situation?'."

Pausing to wipe his tears that were falling onto his mother's shoulder, John continued.

"I will miss you more than I can say, for you have been my constant companion in life, as well as my friend. I shall be lost without you."

Hannah patted his hand with hers, trying her best to assuage him.

"John, you are a strong, intelligent and a loving man . . . and you will get through this. You shall never forget me, and that brings me peace and the only closure, I seek. Please tell Fanny, I love her, too. Smiling weakly at him, Hannah whispered, "John . . . you were always the life in me. You made me so proud of you every single day of your life. I love you, son . . ." And with those words, John heard her final rush of air and watched her slowly slip, peacefully away from him.

Grieving for her with his tears, John closed her eyes and lifted her to him, burying his face to her bosom. As he rocked her slowly and wept at her breast, like a child, he murmured, "This is where I first met you and this is where we will part. I love you, Mother. Thank you for bringing me into this world and for loving me."

He was still holding and rocking her when the door opened and the doctor entered. Walking towards the bed, Dr. Donaldson stopped in mid stride, as he quickly assessed the situation. Not wanting to intrude on John's final goodbye, he quietly backed out of the room.

Fanny arrived at John's side minutes later, and found him still holding their mother in his arms. She leaned over her kneeling brother and softly placed her hands on his shoulders, encouraging him to let go. John gently laid his mother down on her pillow, looking into her face, as he stroked her cheek and kissed her forehead, for the last time. He rose to embrace Fanny. She cried on his shoulder for a moment, then looking up into his glassy eyes, kissed him on the cheek, and finally knelt down beside her mother. No words were spoken as John left the room.

Walking out into the hall, John closed the door behind him and pulled a handkerchief from his pocket to dab his eyes. As he entered the parlor, Higgins walked over to him, clamping his hand on John's shoulder. "I'm so sorry for the loss of your Mother." he said. They stood in silent communion like two brothers, each knowing the pain of great loss. Regaining his composure, John straightened himself, wiped his eyes again, and shook Higgins hand with both of his, saying, "I know you are. Thank you, Nicholas."

Dr. Donaldson, waiting with Higgins in the parlor, stood. Speaking quietly, he said, "My condolences, too, John. I'll take care of everything from here. Take some time for yourself and see me tomorrow about arrangements."

"Thank you," John said, then slowly proceeded to his own room, and quietly closed his door.

John spent the evening secluded in his room.

When morning came, he went into his mother's room and stood, perfectly still in the doorway, and slowly glanced around. He saw the impression of her head, still on her pillow. His heart was heavy as he gazed at her few, worldly possessions. Walking over to her vanity, John recognized the familiar broach she often wore, her favorite silver hair barrettes, and her black velvet jewelry slip case. Looking inside, he saw the heirloom ring that hadn't been worn in many years: A large diamond, shining brightly in a platinum filigree setting. The ring had belonged to his grandmother, who had died before he was born. He slipped the ring into his pocket, thinking, perhaps someday . . . yes . . . perhaps someday . . . it would be used in a wedding. He found the ruby heart pendant and tucked it away in his handkerchief, wondering how he would give it to Margaret. There were other pieces of jewelry John had not seen, but he wanted Fanny to come look through her things. As he sat at her small writing desk, he sifted through her personal papers finding little of much consequence, only a few trade articles about himself that she had cut and saved. He went to her bed and sat, where she had just lain only a day before, and picked up her pillow. Holding it to his face, and smelling her familiar perfume, he mourned into it. Finally, he lay back, holding the pillow to his chest, as he gazed at the ceiling wondering what his life would be like without her. This house was going to feel quite empty, he thought. Every night she had waited for him to come home. He had never previously experienced anything quite like this. His father's suicide was fraught with embarrassment, police investigations, and every sort of confusion regarding his business, but losing his mother was much sadder. It made him think of Margaret and how she could have endured going through such a loss, three times in one year. John thought he could empathize with her misery when she lost her parents, but he hadn't known the half of it. How did Higgins ever cope with losing a grown child? He rose from the bed, placed her pillow back as it had been and walked to the door, casting his eyes back, one last time. Closing the door, he headed off to see how Dixon and Cook were coping.

He found them consoling each other in the warm kitchen. John looked at their sad faces and gestured for them to come to him. Putting one arm around each of them, he said, "We'll get through this." Just then Jane came through the door, already weeping, and John motioned her over to be included in the group.

Moments later, standing back from the three women John said to them, "Ladies, we will all make it through this difficult time. Mother was a strong woman and so must you be."

"Mr. Thornton . . . ," but John interrupted Dixon.

44

"Let me quickly get through with what I have to say, while I'm able. Dixon, as I've said before, you will become head housekeeper, starting now. Cook, your position remains unchanged, unless Dixon or Jane needs to help you from time to time. Jane, your duties will also be divided with Dixon's. I'll be making arrangements today, but we should expect a house full of guests in a few days. Please start planning for that. We will need small sandwiches, cakes, and tea. I'll take care of the liquors. Dixon, I'll ask Fanny to come by, look over Mother's effects, and take what she wants. I will then look myself. Dixon, Jane, and Cook, at that point I would like you to look through the remainder, and see if there is a keepsake you might like of hers. Afterwards, Dixon, you will be responsible to distribute any remaining items, where you see fit. Please set aside any jewelry, monies, or papers for me."

Looking directly at them, John could see by their faces that all was understood, so he continued.

"On the day of the funeral, I would like the food prepared ahead of time; so that way you will be able to attend, if you so desire. I know my mother relied on all of you to do good work, and you never disappointed her. She liked all of you very much, and said as much in her final words to me." Stifled sobs escaped from the women.

"Finally, before I leave . . . I know her loss to you is great, and you know her loss to me is greater. We share the sorrow of each other's loss, so please do not tell me how sorry you are; I already know it. Right now, it is written all over your faces. I'm doing my best to cope, and talking about the sadness will not help me recover. Do not pity me, and do not pamper me, as that will only reinforce what I know I've lost. On behalf of my mother and myself, I thank you all for what you've done for this family." John paused briefly before continuing.

"I will not have breakfast today, but I will return around noon for a sandwich. If any well-wishers stop by today, you may, or may not, choose to talk with them. Tell them I'm not seeing anyone just now, and ask them to leave their card. Get through the day as best you can, and we'll end our workday early this evening. Dixon, make some plans with your gentleman friend, Mr. Granger tonight. I would like to be alone in the house for awhile. Good day." John turned, and headed towards the back door. He had said all that had to be said, but he didn't have the control to let it flow out like normal conversation. He left swiftly, before his emotions could engulf him.

It was still too early in the day to see about the church service and other arrangements, so John went to the carriage house. He decided to go for a ride out into the country, and instead of hitching one of the horses to a small buggy, he saddled Arkwright. He needed to get away from the impending crush of condolences and steel himself against the days to come. The day beckoned brightly to him, as he rode several miles out of town until he found the hill that afforded a nice view of the city. Tethering his horse to a nearby tree, John sat on a fallen log, which had been there since he was a lad. With the billows of smoke down-wind, he had a clear vista of the city where his life had begun. He thought of his mother and how far he had come because of her, all she had taught him, and just how much she meant to him. He smiled over the happy times, but was saddened to think of all the things he wished he had said to her. It pleased him to know she finally came to accept Margaret as the woman he would always love. He shed his tears, once more, as past memories assailed him. An hour later, he headed homeward, thinking about the rest of his day.

Back at the house, Dixon gathered herself together and wrote a brief letter to Miss Margaret about the Missus. She knew the Master would not bother Margaret with his sorrow, but was certain she would want to hear about it.

Three days later, John was taken aback at the hundreds of people who attended his mother's service and burial. She had had only a few friends in her later years, but they were all in attendance. John was quite self-conscious and humbled by the compliment which was paid to him, through the attendance of so many of his business acquaintances from all over the land. He hoped that very few condolences would be openly expressed, as this would cause him great discomfort. He wanted to just get through the day.

The service was beautiful, and even though it was fall, the church was ringed with soft colored flowers. John could not bring himself to give a eulogy, so the pastor read from the notes which John had provided for him. Fanny and her husband, Mr. Watson, sat beside him during the short service. Higgins had previously selected the pallbearers, and included himself as one. As the mourners exited the church, John greeted nearly everyone before they walked to the cemetery. Having already expressed their condolences, many left after the burial. John was relieved to see that most of those remaining were business associates, and they wouldn't dwell on sympathetic words, since they had already expressed them.

Dixon, Cook, and Jane had left immediately to prepare for the unexpected, larger group. John had a carriage waiting for them.

When everyone arrived back at his home, John, offered drinks, mostly brandies, which were accepted heartily. His driver, Branson, filled in as the libations master for the afternoon. The talk got lively and there was polite laughter around the room. Whenever it was appropriate, John joined in; he could feel the heavy curtain of sadness starting to lift. He remembered his Mother once telling him that laughter at a funeral, even by the family, was not disrespectful; it was healing. How he wished he could tell them how grateful he was - he knew they were rallying him back into the world, pulling him from his emotional slide - but men never said those words to other men. In place of any sentimentality, a simple "thank you" was proffered, as they drifted home.

The last of the guests left around 6:00 pm, and the house was finally quiet. John summoned his staff and they hurried to his side. "Thank you, ladies, for what you did today: You served this family with dignity and respect. The food, as always, was excellent, and your service to the guests was flawless. If all the food has been attended to, I want you, Jane and Cook, to go home. Dixon, why don't you get out of the house for a while, and visit Mr. Granger. Please, give him my thanks for his attendance today. Tomorrow, we start a new life in this house. Now . . . please go and rest yourselves." John walked over to the bar and poured himself a Scotch, as soon as the ladies left. Turning to where his mother sat most evenings, he raised his glass in remembrance, offering to fetch her drink, as he had always done. She wasn't there, but John felt as though he could see her spirit smiling back at him. He toasted her a final farewell.

Shaking off that emotional setback, he thought about how his staff had made him proud. John knew they had worked their hearts out so that everything would reflect on their respect for his mother. He wanted for them to leave for their sake as well as his own; John needed just once to be totally alone, and get past the impact of the solitude. He wanted to finally collapse into his emotions and feel the loss of the women he had loved. He had to plunge to the bottom of his existence, and try to find a footing from which to push off, and surface into the rest of his life, wherever it may lead.

The following day, John received a note from Margaret.

Dear John,

I only received word of your Mother's passing yesterday. I am so terribly sorry. I wish there had been sufficient time to attend and be there for support. I know I have been gone from Milton quite a long time now, but I still feel connected there, especially to you, since I know the pain you are bearing. Please accept my most sincere condolences. If ever I can do anything or just listen, write to me. Many times, John, I have wondered how you were, especially after our meeting on the veranda in London. How often that day comes to mind. I wish I could tell you what it meant, but I cannot. Dixon has been keeping me up to date with your great strides in the mill. I always knew you would find a way.

My   most   heartfelt   regards,
Margaret

These were the only words he had heard from her since that day in London. He had not expected any. A strange, almost mystical, revelation enveloped him as he read her letter; one woman lost to him was writing about the other woman lost to him. It felt vaporous; both had disappeared from his life. John folded the note and put it in his coat pocket over his heart. He was comforted by the thought that her penned hand now rested there, as once did her real hand, not long ago.

She thinks of that day often, as do I.

John smiled, thinking back on what his Mother had said about "working on his behalf" when she reached the other side. He had never believed in such things, although his heart wanted to accept the possibility.

But perhaps someday . . . John would come to understand that a mother's love knew no bounds.

Chapter 6

 Dreams, Hopes, Passion

By early spring, almost nine months had passed since that summer afternoon when John had met Margaret in London, a day forever burned into his mind like a glorious epiphany. Coveting that time with her had become his sanctuary, his escape, where he would go to draw from the well of precious moments, to sustain him in his own life

Determined not to draw attention to himself, John invited the company of other ladies, mostly to keep up appearances in his working sphere and to not be perceived as a *loner* or someone to be pitied. He found little solace in their company and couldn't help but compare them all to Margaret. Even with his occasional carnal trysts, primarily outside of Milton, nothing much beyond cordiality inspired him to repeated associations with the ladies of his acquaintance. Women flocked to John, but none could turn his head . . . save one. He was wealthy, important, handsome and a gentleman, all of which attracted women to him. But because of his steadfast love for Margaret, he found that to be more of a hindrance than a blessing.

One day Higgins was sitting in the office, feet propped up on a nearby chair, arms crossed, observing John as he leaned over his ledgers, talking to himself. "So," he began, somewhat mischievously, "according to my daughter, Mary, it seems you're known as *The Catch in* Milton.

John, his head buried in business journals, suddenly realized what Higgins had said. "I'm what?" He asked, laughing, as he sat upright in his chair. Clasping his hands on top of his head, smiling at the joke, he stared at a half-smirking Higgins.

Higgins couldn't help but laugh. "Mary has a friend who works as a lady's maid, she won't tell me who it is, but the maid overheard her mistress talking to another woman about you. It seems you have an *air of mystery* about you, according to the single ladies around town. Much more than you did years ago, I dare say. You're the big fish, apparently; the best catch for a husband. I know you've been seeing more women lately, but what are you doing with them to be creating all this talk?" Higgins was still laughing and kidding with him.

"Well, you must be in a good mood today because you rarely jest with me," John said, relaxing back in his chair, ready to dismiss Higgins' ramblings.

"Well, Master, I thought you'd think that when I told you, but I'm not jesting. It's all true." Higgins was trying to control his humor, but was having a hard time of it. He thought John might find it complimentary, or at least cheerful, but when Nicholas saw that John realized he wasn't kidding, John didn't seem to find it quite as amusing.

"Heaven help me, that's certainly something to which I do not aspire. I have been implicitly careful as to leave no feelings of further expectations with anyone I've seen."

"Maybe that's why you are still *The Catch,*" Higgins suggested, "no one has hooked you. They must be wondering what bait to use next."

"There is still only one lure to pull me in and she sits in London."

In his heart, where Margaret lived vividly, John would still have preferred to remain a very private, obscure man. Being with other women was a way to pass the lonely times and appease his male needs, whenever the offer presented itself to him. As a gentleman, he never initiated such closeness, but it had often found its way into his path. Never knowing if their amorous attentions were casual or serious, the male part of him participated, but his heart never engaged. There had never been any words of love, or future intentions, or disrespect . . . just the opportunity of the moment, nothing more.

By fall, John had built his second mill, spending much of his time modeling it in the Thornton tradition. Prompted by the strength of consistently strong orders, he created a second shift on both sites. Higgins ran both mills, while John trained Higgins' replacements, one for each factory. John had future plans for Higgins. Like it or not, Nicholas was destined for more responsibility as John and his accountant taught him the overall basics of the financial picture. John knew Higgins had arrived at his own mirrored managerial style, when Higgins suggested a small relief staff to give workers regular breaks. This would allow them to leave their looms for a short rest period, while not taking any machinery offline. John embraced this suggestion and was proud of his overseer, whose idea was now being implemented by other owners.

Once or twice monthly, John fulfilled his Magistrate responsibilities at the City Courthouse, presiding over small cases that didn't have to go before a judge and jury. These consisted mainly of infractions where the punishments were clearly set. City growth was now threatening to increase John's bench time in the court system.

One morning as John mounted the steps to the courthouse, he heard the excited sounds of raised voices and a woman crying, so he followed the voices down the inside stairs to the

Chief's office. Arriving on the lower level of the police station, John inquired, "Chief Mason, what seems to be the problem?"

"Sir," Chief Mason said, looking perplexed, "we have a kidnapping. Our first, I think."

"Can I be of any help?" John asked

"Yes, sir." Mason replied, perhaps a little too quickly, "I would appreciate your insights. Thank you, sir."

"Let me have a moment and I'll clear my cases. I'll return directly." John said, as he left the room and headed back up to the entrance level floor toward his magistrate court. Finding his clerk, he inquired about the cases scheduled for a hearing that day, and then instructed that they be rescheduled. "We have a kidnapping case developing," he said, "and I feel I can be of help there. I'll be in Chief Mason's office, if you need me." Turning, he pushed through the swinging doors and headed back to the Chief's office to lend what assistance he could.

When John returned, he noticed a familiar man and woman talking to Inspector Mason. They were discussing a note that their daughter had received earlier in the week. John realized these were the parents of the missing girl, and he, a new manufacturer to Milton. The note said, **I WANT TO KNOW YOU.** It was dismissed as someone who had taken a fancy to their twenty year old daughter, just home from finishing school. After listening to their entire story, along with Mason's thoughts, John suggested that Mason send for someone at the Metropolitan in London, who was familiar with kidnapping cases, and have him at the station by tomorrow. John stayed several hours talking with the parents. He arranged for a ransom, should it be required, as the father, a liquor baron owner was new in town and may not have had all his finances transferred into Milton banks. John assisted in every detail, including the examination of the note itself, which seemed to bear an impression made by something written on the page before it.

"Mason, I think that's all we can do for today," he said. There will probably be a ransom note coming. Make sure the house is guarded. I'll leave it in your hands and check with you tomorrow, or come and find me if anything new transpires and I can be of help." John pulled on his great coat, collected his hat, and said goodbye to Mason and to the parents of the girl, expressing his sympathy for their current situation. Suddenly, a thought struck John: They may be looking at a rapist, or worse, and not really a kidnapper. Waiting until the family had left, he returned to discuss with Mason, the possibility of the second scenario. The investigation into the case, no matter what was intended, would begin the same with what they knew thus far.

Arriving home in the early afternoon, John found Dixon, distressed and crying, at the stop of the kitchen steps. He walked over to her and asked what was wrong. Guiding her to the couch in the sitting room, he sat by her, waiting for her to calm down and speak.

"Master, I just got this short note from Miss Margaret's cousin, Miss Edith." Wiping her tears with her apron, Dixon continued, "Miss Margaret . . . she just lost her husband through a terrible fall from a balcony at his college. She don't say much more except that Miss Margaret is all right. I think one of us should go to the funeral. The problem is that it is tomorrow..."

Surprised, but with no hesitation in his voice, John said, "I will go. I'll leave almost at once and arrive there this evening. Does the note say where the funeral or service will be held?"

"I don't know about the funeral" Dixon said, still obviously distraught, "but the service is being held in the college chapel at 11:00 o'clock tomorrow morning. You'll go then?" She seemed immensely relieved. "Please tell her how sorry I am. She's had so much misery."

John knew that all too well, as every heartbreak she had, had been his own.

"There is some quick business that I need to attend to, before I leave," he said to Dixon. There was a kidnapping in Milton, early this morning. I'll have to write a note to the Chief, telling him where I've gone, as he was expecting me to be at hand. Will you please see that he gets it right away? Get

Branson to take it to the Chief. I will leave for the station immediately after speaking with Higgins."

"Yes, Master. I will see to it, "said Dixon, wiping more tears away. Once again her thoughts turned to Margaret. "I wonder what she'll do now. She can't stay at the college no more. I guess she'll move back in with her aunt or cousin. Oh, how I know she will not like that! I wonder if she'll be wanting me again."

All the time Dixon was talking, John was writing a brief note to Mason. "Thank you, Dixon," he said, grabbing his coat from the back of his chair and handing her the note. "I'm leaving right away."

John hurried into his room and packed shaving accessories, a fresh shirt, and cravat.

Dixon had hardly turned around when she heard John close the front door downstairs.

Briskly opening the door to his office, John hollered, "Higgins! Where is he…? Oh, there you are." Higgins stepped out from a back room. "Higgins, I have urgent news that requires my attention in London. I've just heard about a funeral tomorrow that I wish to attend, so I'm leaving on the next train."

"Calm down, Master. You're all nervous. Whose funeral is it?" Higgins asked.

"I believe his name is Booker Reed."

"Booker Reed?" Higgins questioned, frowning. "I don't think I've ever heard you mention that name."

"Booker Reed was Margaret's husband." John said, watching Higgins' expression as he put two and two together. "It seems he had an accidental fall from a balcony. That's all I know, except that the funeral is tomorrow morning at the college campus. I don't know where I will be staying but it will be at a hotel someplace close to there. I'll travel back home tomorrow."

Being the polite man that he was, Nicholas didn't mention the obvious: This could mean John may eventually find what he's always sought. "Miss Margaret's husband?" he asked.

"How can this poor woman handle yet another death of someone close to her? I feel for her," he finished, sadly.

"She's always been a strong woman," John said, "but even I cannot tell how she will do after all this. I want to go and give her our support."

"Please, give her my condolences." Nicholas added, sincerely. "Good luck, Master."

Seeing Branson come into the yard, headed for the courthouse, John gave a wave for him to stop; John walked out of the door and arrived at the station about ten minutes, before the next train. Milton had grown so large, there were now many trains coming and going through the city. While standing on the platform, he suddenly saw a vision of Margaret in the arms of that other man. Out of nowhere, a three year old memory surfaced...

I hope someday to know who that was.

A Constable arrived on the platform and walked over to speak with John. "Good day, Mr. Thornton. I'm Constable Wilson. It's a privilege to finally meet you, sir."

"And a good day to you, Constable Wilson." John replied, "I assume you are the man that the Chief is sending to London?" He asked.

"I am, sir. I volunteered for this assignment, hoping to gain more insight into criminology, and this seemed a good chance to learn. I fear Milton is becoming a large enough city to be attracting every kind of crime as it continues to grow."

John wanted to speak to that remark but the train was pulling in. "I see you have a book that you undoubtedly want to read, but if you would care to talk a little more, please join me in the same coach."

"I would be honored, sir," the constable replied.

The train came to a stop and both men removed their tall hats and stepped into a comfortable coach fitted with upholstered bench seats, oak paneled walls and an overhead shelf for storage. No one else entered the coach, so both men settled into their opposite seats, speaking very little until the hissing of steam and other loud metallic sounds decreased.

"Mr. Thornton, I'm glad that we are alone because I'd like to talk with you about this case. I've only been on the force for two years and have never seen a kidnapping. What has been your experience, and what likely outcome should we expect?"

"I have always lived in Milton, Constable Wilson, and I have never seen a case such as this in my adult life. I'm sorry to say that I can't give you any firsthand knowledge. However, I have read many judgments handed down on these types of cases, which explain all that has happened." John proceeded to speak about some of the cases that he remembered more clearly. They talked for hours about the current case, including the possibility that it wasn't a kidnapping at all, but something conceivably more dire.

"Thank you Mr. Thornton," Constable Wilson said when they were finished. "This gives me some knowledge of what the Chief is up against." He paused briefly, as he picked up his book. "What they say about you is true," he said.

John was looking out the window, and the statement quickly brought his head around.

"I'm sorry, what did you say?" he asked, with interest.

The Constable explained, "You're said to be a kind and intellectually just man. Not many would have taken the time, like you've done, to talk with me and acquaint me with your experience in law and justice."

"Thank you," Constable Wilson, "that is very kind of you to say. I'm not certain those words make up my character, but thank you anyway." As he didn't care for compliments, John let the subject drop right there. To be respected was enough for him. He never wanted to draw attention because of his actions; these came naturally to him. He felt he was no better or worse than the next man, and he never ceased to be amazed as to why honors should be heaped upon him. Nothing, except for the advances he had made in worker relations, set him apart from the others; at least this was the way he saw himself.

They both fell silent, the Constable picking up his book, while John watched the scenery drift by as he thought about the 'morrow. Unintentionally, he drifted off to sleep... Margaret in his arms . . . standing on a veranda in London...

He was startled into wakefulness by the pitch of the train's whistle announcing its arrival. John opened his eyes to steam spewing past his window and felt the engineer braking the train. Yawning, he pulled out his pocket watch; it was close to their arrival time. "I apologize for dozing off. That was rather rude company on my part. Are we here?"

"Yes," Wilson said, "we are in London, but we have several more stops before ours."

Seeking to fill some time, and because the Constable was an interesting young man, John continued their conversation about the law. "With your interest in criminology and your eagerness to learn more, I think you'll go far in your career. Do you have aspirations of becoming a Chief some day?" he inquired.

"Right now my aim is to become a detective. They are a new and growing specialty within law enforcement. I am sure we will see a detective division in the Metropolitan and in Milton someday. Milton is poised on the brink of becoming a very large city. I want to be prepared to grow with the force and be part of its anticipated expansion."

John was consistently impressed with this young man's vision. He felt he was looking at himself ten years ago. "Wilson," he said, "I hope all that comes your way, as you are certainly preparing to take a leadership role in your career. If you don't mind, I'd like to look in on you from time to time to see how your plans are proceeding. I wish you the best. I'd also like to go with you to the Met and meet the detective."

"Thank you, Mr. Thornton." he replied, more pleased than ever that he had had the good fortune to meet him. "I think this is our stop. Yes, it is."

An hour later, John left the Metropolitan feeling that both the kidnapping situation, and Constable Wilson, were in capable hands. He had wished the detective and Constable

Wilson luck before leaving, and told them he would see them late tomorrow evening.

John hailed a hansom cab, and asked the driver to take him to a nice hotel with a dining hall near the college.

Twenty minutes later, he arrived at a very elegant, ivy covered stone hotel. He proceeded to the dining room which, he noted, still held the style of a hundred years previous. As he sat waiting for his meal, he gazed about the room, with its wealth of Chippendale furnishings (the royalty of antique furniture). An hour later, having finished his superbly cooked dinner, he left the ornately accented banquet hall and headed to the registration desk. He requested the registrar to awaken him by 9:00 a.m. and have a bath ready by 9:30. He then handed his bag to the porter and followed him up the wide winding staircase.

John entered his handsomely appointed guestroom, disrobed to his undergarment, brushed the dust off his clothes, and hung them in the wardrobe. Checking the view from his window, he discovered a nice scene of all the lit gas lamps across London. He opened the window for some cool air. It was past 10:00 in the evening, but sleep did not come for many hours.

Instead, his . . . hopes, dreams, and passion . . . long buried themselves, were seeking to rebuild their home that once was John's heart.

The dream that Margaret would re-enter his life was interrupted by a knocking on the door, rousting John out of his heavy sleep. "Yes?"

The porter exclaimed, "9:00 am., sir."

"Thank you," John replied, throwing off the covers. Rubbing his hands over his face, trying to wipe away the cobwebs, he sat on the edge of his bed and thought nervously about the day ahead. He knew he had to find a way to speak with her. There was so much in his heart that he would want to say, but knew this was not the day to express any of his love that awaited her. Somehow, he would need to convey only words of support and let her lead the conversation where she was comfortable. John wondered how he could prevent his mannerisms from drifting, unintentionally, into a happy environment, while around her.

There had been a few times in John's life when he felt like he was standing on a cliff, and realized that what he did in the next few minutes or hours could determine all that came after in his life. This was just such a day.

Feeling like his stallion, Plato, rearing up in his stall, shaking off his restraints, pawing at his gate that confined him, John knew he had to keep his own eagerness harnessed. He cursed himself for his lack of consideration for the deceased. He knew since the day she had backed away from him, almost a year ago, that this funeral was going to take all the control he could muster. Although he didn't anticipate any emotion from Margaret regarding himself, he felt this was the first day of the rest of his life. There was no doubt in his mind: She would be his one day, sharing his dreams, his hopes, and his passion.

John took his time shaving, bathing, dressing, and dreaming. He closed out his account and left his bag with the registration desk until after the funeral. By 10:00 o'clock, he returned to the stately dining hall for a breakfast of poached egg, toast, and tea. He thought about the coming hours and wondered how Margaret would suffer the day. Wishing he could protect her from the harsh reality of her loss, he steeled himself to seeing her saddened, knowing how much it would upset him.

Finally the time arrived and John walked down to the chapel.

Chapter 7

 She's Not the Margaret, We Once Knew

As the large crowd milled outside, talking, John made his way through to the chapel steps and entered the church. He seated himself near the front, across from where Margaret was likely to be. The organist began to play and the assembly filed inside, quickly filling the pews, until there was standing room only. Searching through the mass of people, John finally noticed Margaret, walking down the aisle. She was accompanied by a man and woman, who could only have been her husband's brother and sister, John thought. Margaret was naturally dressed in black with a netted veil covering her face. But he thought; only Margaret could still look stunning in mourning attire. He gazed intently through the veil at her profile, surprised to find few tears being wiped away. She was composed, as she held her head high, determined to show strength, and still accepting of yet another death in her world of friends and family. The organ music quietly ended and the minister began his words with a prayer to the congregation. It was a nice service and a close faculty friend, an older gentleman, Dr. Trevor Pritchard, who gave the eulogy. But John's attention was steadfastly engaged on Margaret; he was somewhat baffled that she showed little emotion.

She looks withdrawn, as if she has been discarded from life. Odd, that she shows little sadness.

After the ceremony was completed, the minister announced that the short private burial would commence immediately behind the chapel. Booker Reed was being buried in the campus church graveyard. Apparently, John heard murmured around him, this was an honor rarely bestowed. Everyone was invited to remain for refreshments in the dining hall, two buildings over.

Having Margaret near, yet so far away, he decided to attend the private burial, hoping to find a moment to speak with her. The pallbearers bore the coffin out first, followed by Margaret, her family, and the Reed family. The general assembly then flowed out with John being one of the last ones to exit.

Taking full strides with his long legs, he soon reached the party as they neared the burial site, directly behind the church. The college cemetery was very elegant with its filigree ironworks, tall oak trees and intricately carved head stones. About a dozen people attended the private burial, but John, being self conscious of his height since no one could miss seeing him there, slipped behind the few that were standing.

He was encouraged by the fact that Margaret was handling her situation well and had seemingly shed very few tears, yet he was concerned that there could be more behind her apathetic manner. He could sense it; he wondered if anyone else could feel it. Once the final words were read by the Reverend, the mourners filed past the lowered coffin to pay their last respects with a handful of earth or flowers. John watched as Margaret stood over the gravesite for several seconds, tossed her bouquet down to the coffin, then walked away, escorted by her family and followed by the other mourners.

John was the last to leave, and as they all walked toward the front of the church, he was still deciding how he should approach her.

Margaret . . . look back at me . . .

As if she'd heard his very thoughts, Margaret slowly turned her head and, looking back, noticed John's tall stately presence, casting his long shadow.

His breath caught, and he stopped walking, drinking in her vision as she stared at him.

Through our silence, she is looking back at me, as if she has heard me.

John could feel her eyes gazing at him even through her dark netted veil. Knowing she was now aware of his presence, his heart began to hammer against his ribs, reaffirming that he loved her more than life.

Margaret stopped and motioned for the others to pass her then looked back in his direction. The family wondered what had caught her attention. Her cousin wanted to wait on her, but Margaret waved Edith on.

Not taking his eyes from her, John removed his hat and started walking towards her. This was a special moment for him, but out of sympathy he withheld his smile. He was living one of his recurring dreams. He recognized it for what it was - Margaret walking towards him as he walked towards her. He had lived this moment in his mind many times. As she took steps in his direction, the distance between them grew shorter until John touched her extended hand.

Face to face, she lifted her veil.

Someday . . . she will lift her wedding veil to me.

63

Releasing a hushed sigh, John looked into her glassy blue eyes and lost himself in the delicate features of her face. Even at her lowest, Margaret was the most beautiful creature in his world. He searched for words which now seemed stranded deep within him. The silence became awkward. John knew if he forced himself to speak, he would fall over his own words. However, he cherished the fact that she was looking at him intently, unable to speak, herself.

Margaret could hardly believe he was standing before her, so tall and handsome, holding the sun behind him like a monolith. John was the pillar of inner strength she so desperately needed in her life, right now. And, no doubt, had probably needed for several years, she realized.

Thank you, God, for sending him here.

The stalled moment seemed welcomed by them both as their eyes roamed each other's faces, like long lost lovers being reunited. The vision was rapturous for John. Margaret felt every bit the same, however, but she smothered that emotional passion.

Margaret felt like she had been thrown a rope as the high waves were breaking over her, battering her down into the sea. John was from a different world, a world she had missed for many years. She knew he would protect her from the storm which seemed to be swirling about her. Looking into his face she saw his serenity, his strength, and his love, all beckoning her to step into his space.

My arms are your sanctuary . . . reach out to me . . . Margaret

Feeling extremely vulnerable and suddenly weak, she collapsed against him, laying her arms against his chest. What a strange sensation, finding peace and safety even when she was not in any danger. She needed to draw something from John, but what it was she didn't know. There was something about him that made Margaret want to lean on him. For just a few moments, she longed for reassurance that in her own world, Margaret's world, she was not alone. "John . . . hold me . . . hold me close."

He was swiftly overwhelmed, driven by his deep love for her, surrendering his reserve, allowing his eyes to mist. The emotional wall that John had been hiding behind for many years began to crack. He fought his dominant male instinct to sweep her off her feet and carry her away to safety. He ached for her, but gently wrapped his arms about her discreetly, and sheltered her to him. John felt her unleash shivering sobs against his body. She felt so warm and soft in his arms; he almost closed his eyes from the pure tenderness of the moment. Despite the scrutiny of onlookers and how it might be perceived, he threw propriety to the wind and did not interrupt the moment. John held Margaret close to him, weathering her through her storm. He laid his cheek on top of her head to secure her closer, reveling in her scent and the feel of her within his arms. Suddenly, he felt Margaret's weight sliding through his grasp, as she fainted. He grabbed her tightly, swinging his arm under her knees and lifting her easily to his chest. He carried her over to a white wooden bench, nearby.

Margaret's Aunt Shaw and cousin Edith hurried back to see what had happened, and immediately began to fan and fawn over her. "What did you say to her," Aunt Shaw asked, rather haughtily.

"We have yet to speak a word to each other," John replied, somewhat annoyed. "She must be exhausted from the strain and stress of the day." He had no sentiment for these people.

As Margaret's eyes fluttered open, bringing her back into her surroundings, her aunt sighed in relief. "You're going to be all right, Margaret," she said, assuring her as though she were a child. "We'll take you home and you won't have to talk with all these people."

John was buried in Margaret's eyes, watching for *her* awareness of the family's efforts to direct her life. If possible, he vowed, never again would he allow them to make decisions for her.

John spoke calmly but firmly, "Would you please allow Mrs. Reed and I a few moments before she leaves, so that I can express my condolences and those of others from Milton."

Silent glances and frowns were exchanged between Margaret's relatives.

"I must insist on this," John said sternly, sensing their reluctance. "I will bring her to the front of the church directly; please just give us a moment. I have come a long way to say these few words to her and I intend to say them. You have meddled in Margaret's affairs, possibly changing the course of her life, but you will not meddle in mine, ever again. Please, leave us."

Knowing how they had successfully contrived to keep Margaret and him apart, ruining at least one of their lives, John would brook no argument, especially from this family. There was iron in his voice and he remained resolute.

Aunt Shaw and Edith walked away, quite aware of what his underlying reasons had meant.

Rising to a seated position, Margaret apologized to John for the scene she had created and thanked him for his help.

John sat her down beside him and turned towards her, rubbing her hands. "I'm so glad to be here with you. I am sorry for your loss. Higgins, Mary, Dixon, and I all want you to know you have our support."

"How are they?" she asked, regaining her senses. "I miss them immensely."

"As they do you, Margaret" John said. "Please let our friendship help you through the coming difficulties you will face. We will all worry and want to write to you, if you will allow us. I will keep in touch with you no matter how you feel about it. If I receive no response, I will come to London and speak my mind to your family. No one can stand in my way ever again, except you." He gazed at her beautifully sad face with its tear streaks and flushed cheeks, as he handed her his handkerchief.

"Thank you, John," Margaret said, trying to stifle her tears.

"I'm hoping you might think to consider returning to Milton for your mourning period." John said, studying her face closely. "There you will have true friends who wish to support your wishes and not steer you in any direction. The thought of you having to return to your family is almost more than I can bear. Please keep that in mind as you begin your recovery. I could even take you away this very moment, should you wish to escape all this." Seeing her tears increase, he added in a sorrowful voice, "Margaret, I'm sorry. Please forgive me. I thought I was conveying words that would be welcomed."

"I'm not crying from sadness, John." Margaret assured him, "I'm overcome with relief. I have felt so . . . detached . . . from this world for a long time. You have brought an oasis to my desert. How I've longed for friends, my friends,   and . . . and . . . thank you, John, for being here today. I know you never met Booker and this inconvenience to you is for me, alone."

Having sensed something more in her words and actions, and unable to keep his sentiment under control any longer, John said softly, "Margaret, there is no inconvenience here. Never with you."

"Seeing you standing there, John, I thought my guardian angel had come to rescue me. Suddenly, I was safe from the world. I knew everything was going to be all right. You saved me from the whirlpool of faces and condolences. You have lifted me up today. I'm sorry if I embarrassed you."

I want you always to come to me.

"You could never embarrass me, Margaret," he remarked tenderly. "I *am,* and always will be your guarding angel." Please think about the people who want to help you. They all love you, you know."

"As I do them." Margaret hastened to assure him. "Please thank Nicholas, Mary, and Dixon for their sympathy and support. I may yet come to rely on all of you." Margaret looked devoutly into John's face. "Thank you . . . most of all. I'd like to tell you how much it means for you to be here with me, but propriety forbids such admissions." She paused, wondering if she should say more. "I think I should return, now, before we speak beyond our places."

John became aware of a lump in his throat. Her words seemed heaven sent.

Margaret . . . how I love you.

"Margaret, before we go . . . and this is a most inappropriate time but not knowing where your future will lead you, I would like to ask a personal question. I've thought about that night for several years, and if you don't wish to tell me, I will understand."

"Yes, John, ask anything and I will tell you what I can."

"I never met your husband and, although, I think the answer is no . . . was he the gentleman who I saw you with at the train station that night?"

An awkward silence captured the moment, for them both.

Why doesn't she speak . . . I've crossed a line.

"No, John, that man was not Booker."

John knew it was a terrible time to ask a question that he had no right to ask. As Margaret hesitated, he realized he would be at a loss if she didn't continue.

"Margaret," he said, gently, "I never should have inquired into your personal affairs, and I am quite ashamed of how selfish I've been."

"John," she reassured him, "I'm the one who should be ashamed . . . ashamed of not trusting your feelings for me at the time. It has troubled me, as well, for I should have confided in you. Your attitude towards me changed considerably after that night. I knew why, but I couldn't rectify it then; now I feel I can. I needed to keep that secret from you and from everyone, really."

"I don't understand, Margaret. A secret?" He prompted.

"It's a long story for another time, but I will tell you that the man you saw me with that night at the train station, is someone I have loved all my life . . . that man was my brother."

"Your brother!" John repeated quietly, in bewilderment. The realization that the stranger was her brother slowly relieved him of the mystery that had torn his heart out over three years ago.

He was her brother . . . !

"I hope someday to hear the whole story. I know I was harsh and distant and I am truly sorry. I think you remember my feelings towards you at that time. I admit it unsettled me to think you had another gentleman in your life. I dare say it would be no different today. But, as you say, that's for another time. I think we have a lot of - *IF's* - in our past," John continued, somewhat regretfully, "*If* you hadn't run out to the rioters, *if* I'd known he was your brother, *if* our letters weren't conveyed away from us, *if* I'd known you were about to marry, but those are all behind us now. Margaret, dare to free yourself from your past.

"Thank you, John. When we have time to discuss the whole story, you will understand."

He nodded to her, hoping that day would come. John stood; ready to assist her, "Do you think you can stand, now, Margaret?"

"Yes, if you let me take your arm. I'm sure I am steady on my feet, now. The swarming emotions have cleared. When are you returning to Milton?"

"Just as soon as I leave here," John said, as he helped Margaret and curled her arm around his. "Do you know what your immediate plans might be?" He asked as he began to slowly escort her toward the church, not wanting the moment to end.

"I shall be at my cousin's house for a week," she said, "after which I must return to our campus quarters and begin packing the few things that were ours. There are thousands of books to donate to the school's library, and personal items that his family should have. It will probably take a few weeks to resolve all the paperwork. I've not totally decided to move into Edith and Maxwell's home, as is being suggested to me. But, I may stay with them a month or so until I have firm plans. This shall be the last time that I ever depend on them. I need time to take care of all the consequences of Booker's death, including our living quarters. Most importantly, I'll need time to consider my future. However, I do know for certain that I will not stay in London for my entire mourning period. Like you, I feel that going back to that environment is directly in opposition to the life I want to lead. I'm anxious to start a brand new life, on my own.

John, hearing those words, put his free hand over her hand, which was wrapped around his arm, and pressed it tightly. "Will you want Dixon to return to London?" He asked, as they continued walking.

"I want her to stay with you for now," Margaret answered, "until I'm quite assured of my direction. I'm financially independent and I *will* leave London. I will handle my affairs without family intervention. I'll always love them but I can never forgive them for what happened between us, our . . . letters, that is. Thank you for holding your temper back there. Your words were quite valiant and far more effective than mine had been. Right now, I feel I am handling Booker's death quite well; far different from when my parents passed. His family has been very supportive throughout this trying time and want me to continue receiving the stipend that was his rightful inheritance as a second son. They are quite wealthy and quite generous."

They walked a few steps in silence.

You've been without your Mother for almost a year and a half. How are you faring, John?"

"Margaret, I'm managing well. I'll not lie and tell you that I did not grieve a long time after she died, because I did. I owed her much. My life is quite empty with her gone, even with

Dixon trying to 'mother' me. I suppose we will soon have to have words." He smiled, as did Margaret, at the thought of anyone having words with Dixon.

"And you haven't married; I know this because Dixon writes occasionally about you and your work in Milton. Do you have a steady lady in your life?" Margaret asked.

"No, there is no steady lady in my life and never has been since . . ." John caught his own words before he could embarrass himself.

"May I ask why you have not married yet?" Margaret probed gently.

"No, you may not ask, but I think you know . . ." Flustered, he continued, "I am sorry. That was quite inappropriate to say."

God . . . can I not hold my tongue?

"Please, don't apologize. It brings me great comfort." Margaret said, feeling a flush of heat come over her.

I have hurt this man at every turn in our acquaintance, and yet he still loves me after all this time, waiting through my marriage. I do not deserve the attentions of a man such as him. He is a far greater person than I am, and to think that I once thought . . .

John had not missed her blush or her words. As they neared the cemetery gates, John could see family and friends waiting for her. Stopping suddenly, he stepped between Margaret and her family, so his back was to them, shielding her. He was so close to her that he could feel her body heat.

I want to take you into my arms, right now, to kiss you.

"Margaret, I wish your society allowed me to visit while you mourn, but I dare not seek to cross the boundaries of propriety, in London, for your sake." John lifted her hand and lightly kissed the back of it in the London gentleman tradition as he drank in one last look from her exquisite face, burning her vision into his heart.

Leaning down towards her, he murmured softly into her ear, "I miss you, Margaret. Please, come back to us. Don't lock your heart away. Return to me." He looked into her eyes that were staring at him in awe and then hesitantly turned and left, feeling her absence pressing in on him from that first step away. There was a knot in his stomach, but he had done all he could do for now. But was it enough?

Instantly feeling his loss and a great sense of emptiness, Margaret watched as he threaded his way through the crowd. She would never let him walk out of her life.

John Thornton, look back at me.

As he proceeded around the groups of people waiting to see her, he turned back to Margaret one last time and was ecstatic to see that she followed him with her eyes.

She is still looking at me . . .

John noticed that she soon became ensconced by the gathered mourners.

A half hour later, he was seated on the train, re-living every word and each moment of his time with Margaret. How he desperately wanted that hope back! He tried to be objective, but found he could not. Recalling how she had come into his arms once again, in need of a temporary rescue, John knew she had found solace and protection in his embrace. The day had begun to close in on her, but he felt there was more to it than the funeral; something more was underlying her grief. He still sensed she was calling out to him, almost as if she was tired from treading water far from shore. The time was soon coming when he would respond to all of her needs, without the heavy curtain of propriety always hanging between them.

For the four hour ride home, John reflected on his few moments with her, feeling as if his heart would burst if he were left alone with his dreams much longer.

I looked like her guardian angel . . . You were saving me from . . . You lifted me up. . .

As the train pulled into Milton, John shook himself out of his reverie and forced himself back to earth. Once again, his thoughts returned to the kidnapping. Exiting the train, he hailed a carriage and went directly to Chief Mason's office. As John arrived at the courthouse, he could see Mason through the window of the glass door, enmeshed in paperwork. Tapping lightly, he walked in. "Mason, what has happened so far?" He began in an excited tone. "And hello, to you, too, Detective Carlson. Forgive me, I had my mind elsewhere and didn't see you sitting there."

"Good evening to you, sir. Please, no apology needed," the detective responded.

"Sir, I'm glad you're back. There have been some developments in the case. Only hours ago, Lindsey McKeever escaped her abductors and hailed a passing coach for help. She was on Hyde road about 2 miles outside of town. She said she hid along the road until she spotted a decent coach that she could stop. No second note was received and no money exchanged hands. It was obvious, by her condition, that she had been assaulted in some way, starved and possibly tortured or beaten, so I allowed her to be taken home and examined by the doctor. We will interview her tomorrow, if the doctor permits. The house has been guarded. She told us that she remembered being hauled away in her own trap and thought she had walked about two miles before being picked up, so I have men searching the area for her trap. I'm glad that she is alive and safe, but those men are still out there, probably long gone by now, but we won't give up. She thinks there were at least two men, but she wasn't sure, as she was blindfolded the whole time. I plan on going out there tomorrow morning at

10:00 o'clock with Detective Carlson. Would you would care to join us, sir."

"No, I'll leave that in your capable hands. Let me know if I can be of any other help. I'll return tomorrow and read your report. We still don't know if the assault was the original intent or if it was a kidnapping. The note she received, doesn't clearly specify that either way for us. I'm very sorry that this has been as brutal as you may think. I know you will continue to seek these depraved animals." Shaking his head and frowning, John said, "There is no lower form of species on this earth than men who prey on women and children to . . ." He could not finish his sentence.

"I agree, sir. I am sorry you were called away on such unpleasant circumstances, yourself," Mason said.

"Thank you, Mason. No, it wasn't a pleasant time for Mrs. Reed. You'll remember her as Miss Hale. She lost her husband through an accidental fall. It's been a long day for me. I'm just returning now from the funeral and would like to get home." Donning his hat, John turned towards the two men. "If I can be of service, contact me. Otherwise, I'll see you tomorrow afternoon. Goodbye, Mason. Goodbye Detective Carlson," He shook hands with the men and left the office.

Moments later, John entered his coach, anxious to return home and tell Higgins and Dixon about his visit with Margaret.

Chapter 8

The Husband's Secret Life

John arrived home to a waiting Dixon and Higgins. Shrugging out of his coat, he bid them a hello as he hung it on a peg. Dixon handed him a cup of tea. "Thank you, Dixon, I was in need of this, he said, taking the cup from her. "Please sit, both of you. I just want to stand a moment longer; my legs are stiff from the ride. While he drank his tea, John paced the room, wondering where to begin. The day had been a big event in his life, but he didn't want to share everything that happened. His affectionate words to Margaret would remain private.

Higgins and Dixon settled into chairs in the parlor, anxious to hear the news he brought from London. Dixon was fidgeting, while Higgins sat forward with his elbows on his knees, absently tapping one foot on the floor.

"Master, you look tired. How did the day go for you and Miss Margaret?" Higgins finally asked, relaxing back into the cushioned chair, propping an ankle on the opposite knee.

John soon sat down and began relating his day from his arrival at the chapel to his departure from the church grounds. "As much as Margaret appeared brave," he told them, "her perseverance eventually failed her. She was holding herself fast, buffering the sadness, but when she recognized me there, it was like she surrendered her courage. I'm sure she would have reacted the same way, had either of you two, been there," he added, although not entirely sure that was true. "Despite having her own family and her husband's family near to guide her, she displayed a different posturing to me. It was as if I was the only friend she had in her world at that moment, and perhaps we *are* her only friends. And if that news isn't disturbing enough, I had an unsettling feeling there was more, lying beneath the surface somewhere. When I assured her of our support, she referred to it as an *oasis in her desert,* and her relief emerged far more serious than I would have expected, which signaled to me that she was under some strain in addition to the funeral. Something has happened to her. I sense a change, almost like desperation, in her. It was all I could do to leave her today."

John set his tea cup off to the side and stood up. Walking back and forth in front of the fireplace, he took some time forming his thoughts before he continued, "The only thing that I can equate it to, is what it must feel like to be drowning and then suddenly be pulled to the surface. It was as if she had been startled back into life. She appeared very downtrodden; I guess that's what I would call her behavior, before she saw me. Sadly, she is not the spirited Margaret, we all remember. I will stay in contact with her and find the cause of this change, if it's the last thing I do. I will only wait three months before I visit her and it will be unannounced. Something is wrong there, even though she did not speak of any such problems. But, she wouldn't, of course. I want her here, away from London. I will only wait so long before I become very involved in her life, whether her family likes it or not. I won't sit back and wonder what's going on, ever again. I want her here where she is free of outside pressures and free to make her own decisions."

Listening intently and with increasing concern, Dixon quickly interjected, "I cannot even begin to know what she might have on her mind, but I think she was very unhappy in her marriage, almost from the very beginning. I'll write her and ask her to come to Milton as soon as she can. I don't think it matters where she lives during her bereavement period as long as she has the support of people around her." She blotted her eyes with a handkerchief.

"Why do you say she was unhappy in her marriage, Dixon?" John inquired with due concern. "You've never mentioned this before." Looking back, it also would explain some of her reaction to him on the veranda as well as today.

"Master, I would tell you if I knew." Dixon replied. "It just seemed as if all the spark went out of her soon after the wedding. I could feel it before I left to come here, and her letters have done nothing to make me feel different." Of course," she added, "she isn't looking forward to returning to her family, either."

"Yes," he agreed, "and that's exactly what bothers me about her being in London. This news of her unhappiness, while married, may well have had a lot to do with what I was sensing. I had wondered why she showed so little sorrow." John said, frowning at this new disquieting information. His mind was racing with errant thoughts. Suppose he beat her or abused her in other ways . . .? Thankfully, Higgins interrupted his wild exaggerations.

"Master, you can count on Mary and me to write her," he said reassuringly. "We, too, will urge her to return to her friends here. She's always been very dear to my family and me. I have worried along with you, but now I see that we have a chance to reclaim her and we can't waste this opportunity by sitting idly by and letting her heal, or bereave, or whatever you want to call it," he finished, rather profoundly, as he caught the look of unexpected admiration on John's face.

"Higgins," John said, "you have stood beside me for nigh on three years and have never expressed that depth of your feelings for Margaret, as you just have. This tragedy in her life has brought your heartfelt sentiments to the surface. I'm pleased that you feel such a kinship to her, but why am I just now seeing your strength of character in this regard?" John asked in a lighthearted tone.

Higgins looked directly at John, slightly embarrassed. Man to man, as if Dixon weren't present, he told him, "I felt the void, as you did, when she left. Then, as you and I became better acquainted and we talked about personal issues with each other, I became almost as emotionally upset as you were when you spoke of her. I never could speak up; for fear that you might misunderstand my feelings. I love her, too, but not as you do. I'm filled with compassion for her, but not passion for her. She feels like family to me, perhaps she's standing in for Bessie in some regard, I don't know how to explain it. I've missed her insights and our conversations, just as you both have."

John walked over to Higgins and placed his hand firmly on his shoulder "Now I see the firebrand as you were once described to me!"

Smiling fondly at them, John concluded, "Thank you both for expressing your support. Obviously, we all have the same goal for our Margaret. Let's hope for the best."

The room remained quiet for several minutes as they looked down at the carpet, apparently deep in thought over all that had been spoken.

Eventually, John cleared his throat, "I'd like to ponder this more in private, and we will speak again, but in the meantime, please write to her. So…what else is there to discuss? Higgins?" John had detected a slight change in his expression. "You look like you have more to say."

"Yes, I do have something and after telling you of my feelings for Miss Margaret, it better get said, now." Higgins laughed, relieved that his Master had given him an opening. "Aside from all of us wanting Miss Margaret to come back, I would like to announce that I'm going to be married."

"Higgins! This is wonderful news!" John said, walking from the hearth to shake his hand excitedly. Higgins was embarrassed but smiling broadly.

"I cannot believe I didn't see this coming. Do I know the lady?" John asked enthusiastically.

"Master, I do not think so, unless you know her from somewhere else in the city. You may find this interesting, but her name is Margaret, Margaret Randall, but she prefers to be called Peggy. You may know her younger brother, Constable Wilson." The tone of Higgins' words clearly showed his pride in Peggy. "She is widowed with no children, and has been tutoring Tom with his lessons. She is well educated. She comes from a merchant family who had little fortune, so she had to seek her own work. Young Tom has been working with her for nine months, but she and I have been courting for about two months."

"Higgins! You rascal! Courting for two months and not a hint of that to me. Tell me, does the lady know she's engaged, yet?" The two men laughed at John's words of sentiment for his friend.

"We must toast to this happy announcement," John said, glancing at Dixon.

She handed a brandy glass to everyone, giving her Master the bottle, and he poured their drinks.

Glasses raised, John spoke, "To Nicholas Higgins and Peggy Randall. May the best day of your past be the worst day of your future."

"One more thing Master, before I should be going. Would you be my best man?"

John smiled broadly at his friend. "I would have been disappointed if you didn't ask. Of course, I shall . . . with pleasure," and the two men shook hands once again.

"I hope someday to repay the favor." Higgins told him sincerely.

"Yes, let's hope to see that day, Higgins" And when is all his taking place?"

"Well . . . we haven't settled on a day, yet. With my position here at the Mills changing and a new wife coming, I want to acquire a nice cottage which can accommodate all of us comfortably. That will come first and then we will set a date."

"I couldn't be happier for you." John told him again. "Thank you both for sharing this night with me. Dixon has her gentleman, the postman, Mr. Granger. Look how far we've come in half a year. Perhaps, there is hope for us all."

Higgins rose to leave. "We have hope, now, Master. You know I will do whatever I can to see Margaret back in Milton. I'll be going, now. See you tomorrow," he said as he started towards the door.

"Goodnight, Higgins." John said, and finishing his brandy, he turned to Dixon. "The rigor from the day has me quite tired. Please excuse me; I think I'll take myself off to my bed. Good night to you, Dixon." And with a smile and slight inclination of his head, he turned and walked towards the hall to his room.

"Good night Master. We'll all do what we can."

Settling into bed, John sensed his world was straining to right itself. Hope was at least a possibility, where only a day ago it had never existed

God might not have finished with me, after all . . . Mother?

Milton had been covered with a great chill in the air, as the holiday season was fast approaching. John had written a congenial note to Margaret. He had been careful not to pressure her into any hasty solutions, as she pondered the direction her life would take. The three month deadline was nearing and John wouldn't wait much longer before making a brief unannounced trip to London. Reading her response to his letter had lifted his spirits, as she had expressed gratitude for having received correspondence from Nicholas and Dixon, each hoping to see her in Milton soon. As he had predicted, she was not happy to be back with her family. Nothing had changed in their determination to have her embrace London with all its culture. She confided in him that she was getting very close to fleeing London.

This worried John because she had given no indication from her writings which direction she might be heading. Suddenly, and all too clearly, he realized she could choose somewhere else . . . Helstone, perhaps, where she had been reared as a child. John couldn't let that happen.

* * *

Several days later, Margaret descended the stairs as the housekeeper was admitting a visitor. Since she never had visitors, she continued on her way into the kitchen. A moment later, the housekeeper came into the pantry and told her there was someone to see her.

"Do you know who it is?" She asked."

"Here is his card" she said, as she handed it to Margaret. "It says a Dr. Pritchard."

"Oh, how delightful!" Margaret took the card from the housekeeper and smiled. "He was such a good friend to Booker and me. Please, tell him I'll be right in and then could you bring us some tea and biscuits?" Margaret washed her hands and checked herself in the mirror.

"Dr. Pritchard," she said, as she entered the sitting room. "I'm pleased to see you; I've missed our conversations immensely. Please, have a seat." She pointed to an overstuffed chair by the window. "We will have tea ready in a moment. How have you been?" Margaret said as she settled into a chair next to the piano.

"Fine, Margaret, fine. And how have you been? So, tell me my dear . . . what direction is life taking you?"

"I am bearing up, Professor, thank you for asking. But I don't like London at all, as you know. I want to be where I can be of service. Lately, I have been thinking about Milton, with its impoverished population. I've decided to return there. I have friends there, too. I don't know exactly what I would be able to do, but at least I would be living in a town where some of the people mean a lot to me." Margaret said.

"I'm glad to hear you say that, Margaret," the Professor said with a mysterious smile on his face, "for I have something that might interest you."

"You're looking at me as if I should know to what you are referring." Margaret replied, somewhat quizzically. "What is it that might interest me? No . . . don't tell me! Are you going to Milton to study the Industrial Age like you've mentioned on many occasions? Oh, please say, yes! I would love to know that you were there in Milton with me," she said excitedly, clapping her hands with glee as she saw the smile spread across his face.

"Yes, Margaret. You have it exactly. I am going to have hands-on research this time." He laughed as he continued. "I made up my mind about a month ago to head out at the end of term. These are my last days at the college."

Margaret turned her attention to the tea service which the housekeeper had set on the table. She started to pour the tea, "Oh, Professor, I am indeed happy to hear this. I'm envious of what you are about to do. And to think, we might be living close together. I would have missed you very much. I've always enjoyed your company and our chats. And now, I might not have to give them up. I am well pleased."

"Before we talk more about my plans, I really want to know how you are doing since Booker's accident."

"I seem to be doing well, which I find surprising compared to when I lost my parents. Despite loving Booker differently, I think it has seemed easier because I only knew him for a short number of years. That must sound terrible, but I know I can talk openly with you. I feel guilty about it." Margaret said, as tears seeped out of the corners of her eyes, catching her off guard. She started to wring her hands in her lap, as she began to sniffle.

The professor leaned over and patted her on the knee, saying, "Judging by your tears," he said gently, "you aren't doing as well as you pretend. I was afraid of that, and that's one of the reasons I have come today. Child, you should have no guilt over anything and it was *not* different because of the length of time you knew him. You were the best wife he could ever have had, and he was extremely lucky to find you, but for you, it was also unfortunate. You endured much so he could live his academic life style. I believe you were discomfited in that marriage, as I never saw what I considered to be true happiness in you. It was hard to tell with Booker because he was such a composed individual and always in his element at school. I was wondering if you had ever realized that he had shown too much interest in his students, primarily his male students?"

"I don't think I know what you mean," Margaret said. "There were many times that some male students would come to study and I did wonder why he didn't allow them to study with him in our quarters. They seemed to go somewhere else to study. I think I assumed it was the library. Why?"

The Professor could see the confliction settling on her face. "First let me say, there is no fault here, on anyone's part. There was nothing that either of you could foresee and probably you never did see. You were thrust into his world on campus which was all new to you. And you bore it well, despite all that you had to hide. I could see this . . . he never could.

"You felt I was hiding something in my marriage?" She questioned, realizing with embarrassment, where he might be headed.

"Margaret, I'm sure of it. You were a strong independent woman, but I could see your spirited nature, and the self confidence that I had always admired in you, slowly beginning to wane. I am sure Booker caused that, although, perhaps not intentionally. I'm very sorry he is gone, but I hope you can move on to a life you want, one which will benefit your talents and your heart."

"I am going to try," Margaret said, "but why do you say, Booker caused it?" Before he could answer, she continued. "I felt sometimes I did not give him all the love I could. I didn't feel the passion of love, or what I had expected it to be like, from him. I'm filled with confusion and guilt."

The Professor inhaled deeply before proceeding. "I've come by today, concerned that you might be feeling that way, burdened with guilt. Relieve yourself of that right now. I feel I am the only one in the world who knows why and where your life has taken you the past two years."

"Why? Where? If anything, I was too naive in my feminine ways. I bored him, I'm sure of it. He quickly lost interest in me and I was ashamed of myself, and didn't know what to do about it." Margaret spoke softly in between silent sobs.

"Yes, Booker did lose interest in you, Margaret, and it was natural that he did so."

Margaret was dabbing her eyes with her lace hanky when the Professor's words suddenly took her aback. Shocked, she looked into his eyes and asked, "Professor, what are you saying to me?"

"I think Booker was hiding something of himself from both of us and perhaps even from himself, too. I am sure he was suppressing a strong propensity for young males in his life. And I mean that in the most emotional and sexual way. Feeling certain this was the case, he must have come face to face with his own deep preference immediately after he married you. I will venture to say that the two of you had no pre-marital relations. Had you, possibly the marriage never would have gone forward. But, who's to say? Yes, pine the loss of someone you knew, but do not pine the lost love, for you had very little. Please take my advice and sweep away any self-doubts.

Margaret was crying heavily now. The emotional hardship she had suffered for a year and a half was suddenly lifted from her. She had always known that she had never garnered his full affection. "Professor, I'll never understand how you've come to know me so well. I have forever admired your intellect and insight, but I never knew it was so penetrating. You have just encompassed my entire marriage with Booker. If the truth be known, all my late husband left me was emotional scarring and an utter lack of confidence in myself as a wife and a woman. I didn't think . . . didn't think I'd ever hear myself saying that to anyone." She finished softly, "I was so sure it was me."

"Margaret, early or later in your marriage, you could have done nothing more. I know you thought it was your fault that he lacked deep affection for you, but there never would have been any more from him, and I daresay, what there was, would have slowly faded to the point of friendship. You need to recognize your marriage for what it was rather than what it should have been. I was only able to see this after he married you. I felt quite sorry for you, as I gradually came to realize that the love you were looking for would never come to you."

"Professor, I never suspected anything like that," Margaret spoke earnestly, "but I wouldn't have recognized it in any regard. I know why Booker couldn't help me, now. He was too ashamed to talk about it with me, knowing he'd let us both down. I hope that I can come to terms with what I feel inside. I've been devastated for a long time about my inability to please him."

"Child, the only fault, lies with Booker in the grave. He should have done the proper thing and freed you, once he was sure. Leaving you to suffer his disgrace was unpardonable," said the Professor. "You know, that makes me wonder how you knew you had a lot more love to give. There must have been someone in your past for whom you had strong feelings; perhaps you were not even aware of those feelings yourself. Somewhere, there must be a man you really cared for, because you sensed a difference with Booker. You had the emotional depth and capacity to know there should have been more affection or passion in your marriage. Do you know who this person from your past might be?"

Margaret was slightly nodding her head, as if in agreement. "I've just recently begun to wonder about that myself." she said. "There was . . . is... a gentleman I once thought I might want to get to know better, but all of that got swept away before I could fully grasp what those feelings were. But love . . . I don't really know . . . I was young." She continued, wistfully, "Perhaps it was merely youthful infatuation."

"Margaret, you should revisit that in your mind. Look back . . . over your life. I think you might find that you have left your ultimate destiny behind you, somewhere."

"I have been giving that a lot of thought, because I am headed in his direction to live," Margaret said with an impish smile.

"You must do that." He declared "No more guilt! Go out and enjoy the world, while you're still young. You are a beautiful woman. Find that confidence again. I am sure that real love awaits you somewhere in your future. Ok, enough of the life and times of Margaret Reed." They shared a moment of mutual laughter.

Charmed by seeing, once again, her adorable half smile, the Professor cleared his throat, preparing for the ultimate question. "Margaret, when I get to Milton and begin my research, I will need an educated person, let's call this person a 'partner', someone who can keep me organized, scribe my work to paper for eventual publication and be there to share conversation and challenge my thoughts . . . Margaret, I would like you to be that person."

Margaret felt herself flush from head to toe. She was startled into silence and was trying to embrace his words, and their meaning to her future life.

He's just answered my prayer.

"Margaret, you can take time to think it over, you don't have to answer now. I know I am being presumptuous walking in here like this, asking you to come away with me to Milton and be my research partner."

Margaret stood up and walked over to where the Professor was seated across from her. She threw her arms around his neck. "I don't need to think," she told him, enthusiastically. "I accept! There is no question in my mind that I would love working with you more than anything. "Dr. Pritchard," . . . she continued, but was interrupted.

"Trevor, please call me Trevor or Professor. We no longer have to adhere to the formalities impressed upon us by the academic world and we are good friends after all. Are you absolutely sure you don't want to think this over?"

"As sure as I've ever been about anything."

"But Margaret . . ."

"There are no -buts-, Professor. When do we leave?" She asked merrily, clapping her hands like a school girl. Margaret was breathless with excitement; she couldn't remember being this happy in her life. She sensed the black cloud that had followed her since Bessie's death, was now dissipating into smoke, never to reform again. "Professor, I feel the sun on my face. Do you see it?" She asked, smiling broadly.

"Margaret, you are certainly beaming, that's for sure." The Professor smiled. He was joyful, too . . . both for him and for her. "Let's talk about this a bit before you totally set your mind to it, shall we? First, I will be moving within a couple weeks, before Christmas gets here. I already have a home picked out."

Margaret countered, "I will have John Thornton find a nice place for me to live near where you will be living and depending on that, I may be there before Christmas myself. You don't know how much I want this," Margaret declared.

"Thornton? Wasn't that the man . . . the mill owner you told me you knew when you lived there previously? I wanted to ask you about him before I left, but I didn't think you would accept so quickly."

"The man you seek in Milton is John Thornton of Marlborough Mills. He will have all the history you will need to get you well started.

"Thank you, Margaret, I must write that down. By the way, I insist on paying you a wage, even though I am calling it a partnership. There really is no monetary value in research, but I have plenty of money and must insist on paying you a wage and expenses to get there."

"I'll think about it," Margaret said, knowing she would not accept any such wage, but she didn't want to throw a stone into the glassy pond now.

"Well Margaret, what about the matter of your family and leaving them behind?"

"I think you know how I feel about that without me telling you and there's even more that you don't know. I was already planning my escape," she said, still in her giddy mood.

The professor smiled then continued. "My plans are to go to Milton the day after tomorrow, Friday, to finalize the sale of the house I have selected. I'll return home on Sunday, pack, exit the college and be gone by the end of two weeks."

"Fine. Margaret replied, with no hesitation in her voice. "That suits me just fine. I'm coming with you. I can communicate with Mr. Thornton far more effectively in person, than if I were to send him a letter. When do we leave?"

"Margaret, you are scaring me with your enthusiasm," the Professor laughed. "I . . . we will be taking a late train to Milton on Friday evening. Meet me at the station at 5:00 p.m.; our arrival should be close to 9:30. Are you sure that is not too late for someone to be expecting you?"

Laughing unfettered, Margaret said, "Well, they won't be expecting me because they won't know about it. But, I know I can stay in a hotel, if my surprise doesn't work out. You see, my mother's former housekeeper, she's been in our family since before my birth, is up in Milton, too; she's employed by Mr. Thornton."

"I guess there is nothing more to say right now. We will have plenty of time on the train to talk over things before you are totally committed to the move. You have made me a very happy old codger, and I hope it's the right decision for you, too. I'd better be off, now. Good afternoon, Margaret. See you in about forty-eight hours."

"Good bye Professor. Whether you know it or not, you and your boat have rescued me from my deserted rocky island. And though I am looking forward to the great times ahead, I must thank you, most of all, for lifting the burden since my marriage to Booker. I can understand the 'why' of his actions now, but time and circumstances will have to guide me the rest of the way. I have been in exile . . . now, I feel a bit freer."

They hugged each other at the door and then the Professor left.

Earlier that same evening, John went into his study to complete some work that needed his attention. Sitting in the center of his green felt desk top was the diamond wedding ring he had carried with him since his mother died. He gave it little thought and placed it back in his pocket. He assumed Dixon or Jane must have found it, where it had fallen from his clothing in his bedroom, and placed it on his desk.

Before dinner was served, John returned to the sitting room to read his paper. Dixon was setting the table. "Dixon, where did you find the diamond ring? In my bedroom?"

Dixon turned around to face him as she spoke, "I'm sorry, sir. What ring is that?"

John pulled it from his trouser pocket, walked over, and showed her the ring.

"Sir, I've never seen that ring before." Dixon said, shaking her head. "Should I ask Jane? She's about ready to leave."

"Yes, Dixon, if you don't mind." He was beginning to sense that something wasn't quite right... "I don't want to take a chance on losing it again, so I need to know where it was found. It must have dropped out of my clothes that needed to be cleaned."

Dixon went back down the kitchen steps to find Jane and bring more dinner items to the table. Returning a few moments later, she said to John, "Master, Jane has never seen a diamond ring, either. You must have forgotten and set it there, yourself. None of us has ever seen a diamond ring in this house, and that included Cook."

John pulled the ring back out of his pocket and stared at it as if seeing it for the first time. He knew where that ring was every minute, and knew he hadn't placed it on his desk. "How could that possibly have happened? With a rush of air escaping his lungs, John whispered to himself . . .

Mother ? . . . Is this your sign? It is unmistakable, just as you promised. Please let this be possible. There is no other explanation for where I found it.

Sensing a change was soon to come into his life, John cautiously allowed his spirit to soar.

Chapter 9

 John and Margaret's Reunion

Maxwell and Edith Lennox took Margaret to the train station to meet the Professor for their visit to Milton.

"You know, Margaret," Edith teased her, "it is quite scandalous of you to take off to Milton so early in your bereavement, but I must say that I envy your courage. We're very happy to see you settle into something that you really will enjoy. You've been unhappy for so long. I think you have found a very agreeable place working alongside the Professor. I'll miss you, so when you move to Milton permanently; look for a house with guestrooms."

"Thank you, Edith." Margaret smiled at her cousin affectionately. "I agree, I think I have found a good purpose in my life, one that will bring me joy and takes me away from London. Sometimes, I envied you for your willingness to live within such strict guidelines and proper societal etiquette demands. That has never been tolerable for me as a way of life. Oh . . . there's the Professor, now. I will say goodbye to you and will see you on my return Sunday. Take care."

"Goodbye, Margaret. Enjoy yourself," Maxwell said, as he handed over her overnight bag and he and Edith gave her a quick hug.

Dr. Pritchard and Margaret strolled towards each other, carrying their small bags which would see them through the next two days.

"Excited, Margaret?" The Professor asked, without even saying hello.

"YES! I am full of questions and ideas and I am already decorating my home in my head. I find myself laughing over the silliest things; you have changed my life, Doctor. I feel reborn into someone new. Do you think that a bad thing?"

"Contrary to what your family probably thinks," said the Professor, "I think it the best medicine for you. If anyone needed a life change, it was you. I think of you as a rosebud, once wilting on the vine from lack of care, but now you're like a bloom ready to open itself to the sun, beckoning the bee to taste its nectar," he finished, laughing and raising his eyebrows up and down, like a letch.

Feeling her face redden, Margaret couldn't help but burst out laughing. "I do like you too much, I think," she said, lavishing him with attention. They both roared, almost doubling over with laughter.

"Ah . . . here's our train. Ready, Mrs. Reed?" the Professor asked as he extended his arm for her to take.

"Ready! Dr. Pritchard."

They stepped into the crowded coach and discovered they had to sit separately for several more London stops. When it finally cleared out, they sat side by side leaving only one other person traveling north to Milton. Darkness was creeping into the coach and the third rider lit the gas lights, not waiting for the porter to come by. The man seemed to prefer his own company and newspaper, so the Professor and Margaret settled into quite a long and involved discussion about how to proceed with his reference work and getting settled into Milton. He told Margaret to expect only two or three days work a week, at the most.

"Margaret," he said finally, "the one thing that I am not looking forward to is hiring the housekeeping staff. Do you have any experience with that?"

"Professor, I've very little, but I do know someone who can help us, so don't worry yourself. We can start that task while we're there this weekend," she assured him. The Professor could have talked hours longer because he taught classes all day, but he could hear Margaret's voice starting to get hoarse. "Margaret, I think I shall let you rest before you lose your voice entirely."

Margaret smiled and let her head rest on the Professor's shoulder, knowing Milton was only another hour away.

John had just settled down to write a letter to Margaret when he heard his big mill gate rolling open. He set his pen down and walked over to the window to see who could be visiting him, unannounced at this time of night - and in a carriage, no less. "Dixon," John called out, uncertain as to where she was that the moment, "someone is coming to the front door, I will see who it is, don't bother yourself." He hurriedly threw on his waistcoat, leaving his top coat and cravat lay where they were. Descending the steps, he opened the door and saw the most unbelievable vision of his entire life. A coachman was handing Margaret out of a carriage. His breath left him, although he was sure any minute now, he would remember how to breathe. The driver grabbed her carpet bag and handed it to John. He was so overwhelmed at the sight of her; he couldn't get one single word out.

I know I am dreaming this.

"John, please close your mouth. Yes, it's me," Margaret laughed as her breath plumed in the frigid air. "Surprise!"

She jests! I am definitely asleep.

John, picking up on Margaret's playful mood, replied, "Who are you? You look incredibly like someone I used to know, but I've never heard her jest, so obviously you cannot be her."

"How are you, John?" Margaret asked in all seriousness.

"Do you mean generally or at this very moment?" John laughed, not believing what was transpiring. It felt surreal. He knew he was trembling inside. "I was just sitting down to write you a letter. How kind of you to spare me the trouble."

Could this really be happening?

As John and Margaret entered the sitting room, he called for Dixon to come to the parlor. John set down Margaret's bag as he waited for Dixon to arrive. He was very interested in knowing why she was carrying it tonight, to his home, at this hour. As he removed her coat and hung it in the hall, his heart was pounding hard in his chest. Just then Dixon came into the room and, seeing Margaret, ran straight over to her with her arms outstretched, almost hysterical with glee to see her lifelong charge. They hugged briefly and exchanged a few pleasant words. Dixon asked Margaret if she would like a cup of tea, tea being Dixon's answer for everything.

"Not tonight, Dixon, thank you." Margaret said, as she cast her glance toward John, who was already on his way to the bar. "I think I prefer something a little stronger, for this is a celebration indeed."

"Margaret seated herself on the cushioned settee, feeling relief from hours of sitting on hard train benches.

"Brandy, whiskey or port, Milady?" John asked, bowing to her, mockingly. "What would you desire?"

To anyone who knew them well, John and Margaret's performance would have seemed unbelievable. They were so giddy with delight, beyond happy, both throwing themselves headlong into some joyous abyss. Margaret knew why she was acting this way, but she was shocked to see that John . . . John Thornton . . . THE John Thornton had such a sense of humor and was joining into the farce with her. She had never seen this side of him before and doubted that anyone ever had. His capacity for high spirits enthralled her.

Continuing on with their performance, Margaret stood and curtsied saying, "Port, sir. If you will."

Dixon was baffled by the amusement taking place before her. Eventually, they all laughed and settled into chairs with their refreshments: John, in his usual chair by the fireplace, with Margaret on the couch at his right, and Dixon sat nearby on a small chair opposite John.

John smiled and shook his head from side to side, still unable to comprehend the playfulness that had overtaken him. "Margaret," he said, "thank you for that. I haven't laughed this much since . . . well, I don't if I have ever laughed like this. I can't believe you are sitting here in this room without our having known of your impending visit. Please tell us what it is you're celebrating." John seemed to be holding his breath; judging from the mood she was in, he was expecting some good news. He wanted to pinch himself to verify he wasn't dreaming.

Margaret burst out giggling again, "John, are you pinching yourself?" She asked. "It looks like you just pinched your thigh. I do think you are awake and yes, I am really sitting here, and . . . I will be spending tonight and tomorrow night here before returning to London."

John, now totally embarrassed, normally an almost impossible accomplishment, said, "So you will spend two days with us. I'm happy to hear that." He was still stunned and could only offer courteous, stilted parroted words for this unexpected miracle. He wanted to lift her off the floor and whirl her around in a circle. Finding a ray of sense, he asked, "Who accompanied you here? Surely you were not alone?"

"Miss Margaret," Dixon interrupted, "could you please tell us what is going on? I can't wait any longer," she insisted stubbornly.

"Well," Margaret said, looking at them both and smiling, "I've made a very important decision in my life. I know where my future lies, now, and it's right here, in Milton. I'll be moving here almost as soon as I can."

An audible gasp came from John's direction. He became silent, inwardly reeling from Margaret's declaration which seemed to breathe life into his abandoned soul. It was all he could do to listen to whatever followed. Four years, he had wanted to hear those very precious words.

"John," Margaret continued, "you may remember the Professor who gave Booker's eulogy . . . ?" John nodded yes, just barely. "He has asked if I would partner with him in writing his research book about the Industrial Age, and its beginning, which is here in Milton. He's been a great friend to me. He is helping me overcome some rather serious matters in my life, and I have a long way to go, yet. I had already decided to move back here where I knew I had friends, but two days ago, the Professor visited me, told me of his plans, and asked if I would like to help him. I couldn't agree fast enough."

"Oh, Miss Margaret," Dixon clapped her hands together, enthusiastically, "we're so pleased. I've hoped for this day and now it has come. How long before you move here?"

"Well, that will depend on John, I think."

"Me? Tell me how I can help." John inquired, trying to form his words and allow them to flow out, above a whisper.

I can't believe what I am hearing. Is it really happening?

"I've come here this weekend with the Professor," Margaret explained, "so he could finalize the purchase of a home that he's already selected. Instead of writing to you, John, to ask for help in finding a residence, I thought I would accompany the Professor and ask you personally, so it would be easier to discuss what I would need. The Professor will move here permanently within a couple weeks, and I hope to be here before Christmas, which is only a month away. I don't need the time myself, but John you might, looking for a place, that is." Margaret finished. She was watching John while she spoke. He looked as though he had been hit by a runaway coach. He seemed to be growing paler by the minute.

Only a month away? I am delivered from my hell . . .

"Margaret, count on me to do whatever it takes to get you here. Like Dixon said, we have all waited for this day. I was only a few weeks away from visiting you, myself. This news is beyond belief. Please excuse me for a moment." John walked down the hall to his room and quietly closed the door. He sat on the edge of his bed literally trying to breathe. He was caught in a deluge of happiness that just kept pouring over him and over him, not allowing him to catch a breath before the next blissful torrent assailed him. This must be what pure bliss feels like, he told himself. He cursed the tears that had sprung to his eyes.

I can't face her like this.

Sensing John was overcome with happiness similar to hers, (it felt as if she had been walking on clouds for two days), Margaret told Dixon to go on to bed and they would talk more in the morning.

A few moments later, John heard a light tap on his door and before he could answer it, Margaret entered his room. He quickly turned his face from her with deep embarrassment.

Catching sight of his tear-filled eyes, she walked over to him, and sat by his feet, allowing him to hide his masculine sensitivity.

"John?" Margaret whispered. She heard no answer.

"John, happiness is overwhelming, isn't it? I know what you're feeling right now. I cried, too, when I was finally alone."

John swiftly pulled her up to a sitting position on his bed beside him, holding both of her hands in his. He looked into her face and saw tears matching his own looking back at him.

God, let me find the strength to do what is right at this moment.

He bent towards her and slowly brushed his lips against hers. Feeling no denial from Margaret, he wanted to crush her to him; but then, calling on all his reserve as a gentleman, he quickly pulled away and stood up. "I think its best that we return to the parlor, don't you?"

"Yes, John. Perhaps someday, though." She whispered enticingly, as she walked away.

Her statement staggered him to a halt; he couldn't believe what he had just heard.

She's remembered my words and has held to them . . .

They talked well into the night about her move: the type of home she would like to own and what she could afford. She had the address of the Professor's new home, and was hoping that she could find a home within walking distance to him. Purposely, there was no mention of any ardent feelings between them. Much later, Margaret admitted she was tired and wished to go to bed, but was unsure as to where she was expected to sleep. John showed her the way to Fanny's old room, which was always kept fresh by Dixon. He escorted her to the door and he stopped outside. She looked up into his steel blue eyes and he embraced her tightly, stealing her heat and her scent. He held her as she put her arms around his waist. A kiss was hanging in the air, but did not rush itself. There were no inhibitions on either part, leaving each with a suspended expectation of things to come. They no longer had to hide their feelings from each other, or from others.

Margaret's reaction had shocked him. It was pure. No emotional burden being the cause. It was true and it was right. John returned to the parlor, turned down the lights and sat back down in his chair by the fire. Staring at the embers fading to a soft glow, John drifted through all the past years: the initial meeting at the mill, the misunderstandings, his rejected proposal, the man at the station, the separation, the absence of communication, her marriage, the veranda, the funeral, and now . . . she was sleeping in a bed in the next room. After four years, Margaret was returning home, to his love, a love which he had never given up. John told himself long ago, that he would wait forever. Forever was now here and he had no earthly idea where to start, but he wept with happiness for it had finally come, setting him free from the loneliness.

When he finally retired to his room, he was afraid to sleep, fearing he would wake to find it all had been a dream.

Dawn broke the next morning, signaling the beginning of a new outlook on life for John and Margaret. Slipping over to the office, he invited Higgins over for a talk, but kept the surprise a secret. "I'll be right behind you, Master" Higgins told him, "let me just finish giving directions to our foreman."

John returned to the house and saw Dixon busy setting the table. Margaret's door was still closed but he could hear her moving around and knew she'd be out momentarily. "Dixon please set the table for four this morning and tell Cook. I want you to join us this time."

Moments later, Higgins hollered up the steps and John told him to come ahead. Not having any hint as to what this talk was about, Higgins was surprised at the four place settings on the dining room table.

"You wanted to talk to me, Master?" Higgins asked.

"Yes, Higgins, I want you to join me for breakfast. I have something to show you."

"I see there are four settings? You have my curiosity well and truly piqued." Higgins said as he placed his hat in the hall and removed his coat, wishing he'd washed his hands before coming over.

Dixon entered the room, and told John that Cook would bring the food in a few moments. She began to pour the tea for four. John invited Higgins to the table and they both sat. Seeing Dixon sit down to the table with them really unsettled Nicholas and as he looked at the forth place, he began to wonder. Before he could get very far in his thinking, he heard a voice.

"Nicholas!" Emerging from her room, Margaret shouted with glee upon finding her old friend seated at the table. Higgins had hardly stood before Margaret had her arms around his neck, kissing him on the cheek. "Oh, I am so happy to see you this trip. How is Mary?"

While Margaret was hugging him, Higgins looked up at John for his reaction and saw a beaming smile; he then felt comfortable in hugging her back. "Miss Margaret," he said, "I can hardly believe this. The Master didn't tell me you were coming."

"Actually, John didn't know himself until I showed up on his doorstep late last night, begging lodging," she laughed.

As they all sat down to the table and the food was passed around, Margaret briefly related her story to Nicholas about her return to Milton. Higgins occasionally watched John's face as she spoke, noticing his eyes never left Margaret; Higgins was happy for the two of them.

It was past 9:30 and the breakfast party was just starting to break when there was a knock on the door. Walking over to the window, John saw a carriage waiting outside. Dixon had gone to greet the visitor, and returned, shortly escorting Dr. Pritchard into the parlor. Margaret hugged him and happily introduced him to everyone, suddenly realizing she was surrounded by her loving and only friends, in the whole world. This is what she wanted, she felt it immensely at that moment and knew she'd found her home. To everyone's bafflement, she was suddenly overcome by the warmth and relief that surrounded her and she started to cry. In an effort to regain her control, she turned and headed for her room.

Everyone looked at each other in bewilderment. Dixon was on her way in to see Margaret, when Margaret returned with her hanky.

"I'm sorry for being so silly," she told them, still slightly teary-eyed, "I just became aware that all my favorite people in the world are with me right now, a moment that I have dreamt about for so long. I was overcome with the comfort of it all.

As he listened to her comments, John's knees had weakened at her happiness. He recognized, even with his great passion for her, he could never have brought such a significant moment to her life. He wondered how often that ever happened to anyone.

Rather than standing around speechless, Higgins decided he had to get back to work. "Master, I couldn't be happier for the two of you and for us," he said, and turning to the Professor, "It's been a pleasure to meet you, sir. Miss Margaret," he added with a twinkle in his eye, "I couldn't be more pleased to know that you will be living here soon. If I can be of any help in anyway, please call on me. You know where I work," he finished laughingly as he grabbed his coat and cap and left with Margaret escorting him to the door, leaving John and the Professor alone.

"Won't you sit down, Professor," John asked, pointing to a chair near the fireplace.

The Professor sat, crossed his legs, and pulled out a pipe from his vest pocket. "Do you mind?" He asked, indicating the pipe to John.

"Please," John replied with a slight wave to his hand.

There was a moment of silence while he struck the wooden match and puffed life into his pipe. "So . . . you're the one." The Professor said, more as a statement than a question.

"I'm sorry. I'm what?" John asked in total surprise.

"You're the man in Margaret's life," the Professor said. "Someday, I will explain why I know that, and why I know that Margaret is coming to know, too. Also, you're the man who's making the history around here. You will be very prominent in my book, with all that you have done here in Milton. I won't go into that now either, for I will be moving here in two weeks and it will be several months before I come to you asking for your whole story."

John shifted in his seat. "I will be glad to work with you when the time comes," he said. "Do you and Margaret have appointments today?"

"Well, yes and no."

Just then Margaret returned to the room still looking a bit embarrassed but she sat down on the couch to listen to their conversation.

The Professor continued puffing on his pipe as smoke swirled overhead, said, "Glad to have you back Margaret," he said. "Your heart rendering proclamation warmed us all. Do not feel embarrassed. It is something you've needed probably your entire life. It must have been the equivalent of a person totally blind from birth, having his sight restored. It was an epiphany for you and I am envious."

John was watching Margaret intently, stunned by the personal way in which the Professor was talking to her . . . and speaking that way in front of him. But he saw a smile break out on her face that took his breath away.

There is closeness here, that I don't understand.

"As I was about to tell Mr. Thornton, here," Professor Pritchard continued, "I have come by to see if the two of you would like to see where I will live, so plans can begin for your own residence, Margaret."

"Yes, surely. I would like that," Margaret said as she looked questioningly at John.

"I'd be most interested myself, Dr. Pritchard," John said smiling. "By the way, would you care to have dinner with us this evening?"

"Yes, thank you. I'd like that very much."

Margaret jumped up and said she would find Dixon and tell her, as she also wanted to ask Dixon about a housekeeping staff for the Professor.

While Margaret was gone, John and Dr. Pritchard discussed where he would be locating, and the possibility of finding something suitable nearby for Margaret. John remembered a quaint little house that was being refurbished weeks ago, close by and told the Professor about it.

"Excellent," the Professor was saying as Margaret re-entered the room. "If there is nothing left to do, I have a hired coach outside. Should we take our leave?" That remark was a small joke between Margaret and the Professor, as a sort of nose-thumbing to the vanities of Londoners.

"Oh yes, let's do." Margaret said, as John retrieved her coat, and placed it around her shoulders.

John slipped into his own great coat, grabbed his top hat and they all set off for 840 Queens Lane. As they were being driven there, on what was formerly known as Main Street, John noted the distance from the gingerbread cottage that sat across from the courthouse to the Professor's residence. Upon arriving at the residence, John saw the same Property Agent sign in the window as the cottage. Providence was still holding sway, he thought.

As they entered the dwelling, Margaret began looking around the old refurbished store front home, remarking that it had downstairs quarters for a housekeeper. "By the way, Professor," Margaret told him, "I've spoken with Dixon and she is sure that she can accommodate you with a suitable staff, just as I thought she could."

The Property Agent arrived shortly after, with the necessary paperwork prepared for Dr. Pritchard. "Hello, Dr. Pritchard," he said, "nice to see you again. Oh, and hello Mr. Thornton, I'm surprised to see you here."

John introduced Mrs. Reed to the agent and asked him if he happened to have with him, the key to the cottage across from the courthouse. He replied that he did and handed it to Mr. Thornton, without a care.

"We shall let you two do your paperwork, while I escort Mrs. Reed to the cottage. We will return shortly." John said with a smile.

Surprising Margaret and catching her totally off guard, John wrapped her arm around his and whisked her out the door saying, "Come, I want to show you something."

Chapter 10

 *The Cottage*

They walked arm in arm down the tree lined street, towards the cottage that John hoped someday would be Margaret's. He was thrust into a feeling of incredible contentment welling up inside of him. He didn't care to analyze it; he just wanted to hold this tender sensation inside him forever. John had noticed the little house several times on his courthouse days. He was still finding it hard to believe that they were strolling toward a possible residence for Margaret's return to Milton. John suspected she might like it. Its appearance seemed to be well suited for her, he thought. To him, it looked like a tiny white fantasy house. It had intricately carved ornamental trim, dragon scale wood siding, and a spindled banister porch on three sides. If a house could be male or female, this house would most definitely be female.

As they neared the cottage, Margaret excitedly pointed to it. "John," she asked, "is that it? Is that what you wanted to show me? It looks precious from here. Oh, I hope that's the one."

"Yes, that's it," John reassured her. "With all the fancy woodwork and white paint, I think I should be cutting a piece and having it on my plate. It appears to have icing," he added jokingly.

"Oh yes, hurry! Oh, it's enchanting."

Laughing to himself, John increased the pace of his stride. Earlier, he had to fall in step with Margaret's little strides and now he couldn't keep up with her. Life was heavenly at this moment, bringing him hope along with Margaret's many enjoyable surprises and her endearing feminine ways. It seemed as if the years that had torn them apart, had actually brought them closer. How odd when one considered how they had parted ways.

Where did it all go right?

Before John could locate the key in his pocket, Margaret was already running along the wrap-around porch, from window to window, peeking inside. As he opened the door, they were struck with the stringent smell of paint; undeterred, they proceeded to cover every square meter of the "little darling," as Margaret called it. Occasionally she would say, "Oh, look at this," as John studied the house from a totally different perspective: possible construction weaknesses, leaks, problems with the roof, dry cellar, faulty plumbing and more. He was pleased to see the little cottage had been refurbished with the most modern conveniences, such as indoor gas lights and an indoor lavatory with tub, all of which Margaret was familiar with, having lived in London. Leaving her to her decorating whims, John headed to the rear of the house. On the ground floor, he noted, with interest, there was a nice mud room with a drain and a secondary lavatory without a tub. Glad to see the back building, he walked to the small carriage house and noted it could stable one horse, with room for a small buggy, a tack room, and quarters overhead. He walked the outside observing the painted wood siding and other facets of the restored buildings. John remembered it when it was a home, but for many years it had been a bookstore that he had visited often. Since the expansion of Milton, many of the older main street small businesses sold out, making extremely nice profits. He was pleased to see the Property Agent had enough vision to restore the house to its original state. Satisfied with all that he had seen, he went looking for Margaret.

As John entered through the back door, he caught a glimpse of Margaret twirling around the empty kitchen like a ballerina. She was looking up at the ceiling, as she turned around and around with her arms outstretched. He stood there and watched the woman he loved more than life: seemingly enraptured by the probability that she would be living here soon. How precious these unguarded moments were, he thought.

Finally, realizing that John was at a distance watching her spin, she surprised him by saying, "Do you think I can afford it?"

John walked forward, catching her in his arms, and held her while her twirling dizziness subsided. Heat quickly rose within him. He tilted her chin up, looking deep into her eyes, then at her lips and back to her eyes for any sign of uncertainty. Finding none, his lips found hers, drawing her breath into him, kissing her fully for the first time. His kiss was warm and tender, possessed of passion and longing. John couldn't help the moan that escaped between his lips. Margaret felt his lips soft in touch but firm in deliverance and her knees gave way to a swoon. John immediately caught her, delighted by her response. No other women had ever reacted like that when he had kissed them, but then he knew kissing Margaret was different; his heart was in his kiss. Pleased that she had not backed away like she had on the veranda, he gently released her. Having waited and dreamt of this moment for four years, John felt overwhelmed and he feared he might prompt an action that could have consequences she was not ready to face so quickly. Reluctantly, he stopped it there, allowing the anticipation of the future to linger. Still cradling her to him, he finally answered her question, "Afford it? It shall be yours at any price."

Margaret wrestled herself away from John and stepped back, slightly annoyed and a bit dizzy from the kiss. "John Thornton, I'm renting this house, I don't need any help. If I can't afford it, I will find somewhere else."

Still . . . as independent as ever.

"Well, I can tell how you love this white frosted cake of a house and I think it's sound and solid. Let's go see the agent, Mr. McBride, shall we?" John asked, as he extended his arm and completely ignored her little tantrum.

They walked back in silence, each dazzled in the moment they had just shared: their first kiss; a cherished moment to stow away in a chest of remembrances.

Arriving back at the Professor's place, the Professor and McBride were settling on pieces of furniture that remained in the house: these which would also be purchased by the Doctor. John and Margaret looked around at the furniture that was being discussed, waiting for an opportunity to talk with Mr. McBride.

Eventually it came, John began to ask, "We would . . . " but Margaret interrupted him saying, "I would . . . like to speak with you for a moment, Mr. McBride, privately," looking directly at John as she emphasized the word *privately*.

"Yes, Mrs. Reed, anything you like," he said as John handed the key back to him and he walked her to the back yard.

As much as he wanted to ensure a good price for her, John knew he was seeing what he loved most about Margaret, and that was her spirit. Smiling, he paced the room, watching from the window as he observed their conversation outside. First Margaret would frown, speak, and then smile. Next McBride would shake his head no, and then frown, speak and smile. It took some time but John thought the smiles had it by a slim margin. Twenty minutes after god knew what, John saw them shake hands, both smiling at the same time. "She's coming to live here, and soon," he said to himself.

Margaret had struck her own deal and she seemed quite proud. Good, bad, or indifferent, John could see by her face that she was pleased with whatever decision was agreed upon. Perhaps she would share that conversation with him later. Since the Professor was momentarily nowhere to be found, Margaret asked the agent if he had already purchased the very large upholstered wing chair in the future office room. Being told, no, she then asked that she be allowed to purchase it and have it delivered to her new cottage. She thought the chair looked large and comfortable enough for John, so she purchased it for his anticipated visits.

Following a lovely meal and a thoroughly enjoyable conversation at the Marlborough Mills home, Professor Pritchard excused himself about two hours later, leaving John and Margaret to sit and talk. The three of them had been together most of the day, looking all over the city for furnishings. The Professor had bought most of the pieces that were left in the house, as he had no particular preferences other than the two desks and floor-to-ceiling bookshelves he was having made. Margaret, on the other hand, was looking for contents that would go well with the age of the house and had arranged to have several pieces custom made. John and Margaret had both agreed, since he was well known in the city, they would run the billing through him, and Margaret would reimburse him, when her finances were transferred to Milton. They had accomplished much in just a one day period and Margaret was excited about their progress. Dixon had a cook already lined up and John was to see about a chore man / driver.

It had grown late and Dixon came into the room and announced that she was going to bed and asked if they needed anything before she retired. Receiving "no thank you," she went back downstairs for the night.

John sat slouched down in his chair, arms across his chest, long legs extended in front of the fire. Margaret lounged on the couch. Both felt full and tired, and especially pleased with themselves for their accomplishments of the day.

"John," Margaret said, after a few moments of quiet, "one week ago, I was depressed, confused, and rushing towards flight out of London, and now my world has completely turned around. How is that possible?" she asked, somewhat puzzled, as she stared off through the window into the dark night, still deep in thought.

John came over and sat beside her on the couch, not facing her, but relaxed against its upholstered back, as he took one of her hands in his. "Margaret," he said, softly, "I am sure you know how I have felt about you since I first met you. Someday I shall tell you about my first impression of you, shouting at me in the mill." John smiled, remembering that, "I have thought about you every day for almost four years and suffered the loss of you, twice. I have dreamed of every possible way to win you, to love you, to make love to you and to possess you, forever. I am taking nothing for granted and I am not making any assumptions at this point, but you have to know how my life has changed in the last twenty four hours." He gently squeezed her hand.

Margaret looked up at his handsome profile and spoke softly, "John, thank you for loving me all this time. You may find this hard to understand or perhaps may think it's woman's intuition, but I could always feel you there . . . waiting . . . and I can't explain how. You were always hovering somewhere in the twilight of my life and that brought me comfort, which I can hardly explain even to myself. It has seen me through many difficult times. I still have . . ."

John interrupted her, "Wait . . . please, let me speak first while I can," he said, as he turned to face her, choking back the lump in his throat. "I have always loved you. I have waited a long time to have you near again, and I will wait forever if that's what it takes for you to accept me. I think you have some feelings for me, but I do not want you to feel compelled in any way to express them, at least not for a while. You have only been widowed for three months, and must have many conflicts within yourself to resolve, and a proper bereavement period to conclude. I know you are joyful right now, but a different reality could settle on you once you are comfortably situated in Milton. As much as I would like to carry you off to my bed right now, I know that would be wrong in so many ways. I do not want to scare you, pressure you, influence, or smother you. I'm going to keep my emotions reined as well as I possibly can, and I'll wait for you to come to me. If I get carried away, just say no. I hope I don't get to the point to embarrass us both, but my body doesn't always listen to my brain whenever you are near."

"John . . ." Margaret said, as she stroked his cheek.

Not wanting to lose his train of thought, he pulled her hand from his cheek to his lips and kissed her palm. "Margaret, let me finish, please. I love and desire you beyond all reason. I want to be everything to you, your friend, your lover, your husband, and the father of our children. I will always be at your side to protect you, to cheer you, to comfort you and to love you. But along with my depth of devotion to you, there must come honesty in your feelings. I do not want pity, or any sense of obligation, and I do not want to wear you down. I could not live with that. I will keep my self-respect, for if you turn from me, it is all I will have left. I can take a lot of rejection before it's all too apparent that you do not care for me in the same regard. Just don't say you love me until you are sure of your words, but I do love you and will all my life." John leaned in and gave her a light kiss, then licked the drops, now, falling from her eyes.

Margaret closed her eyes; a hushed sigh escaped her lips, as John drank in the salt of her tears. With a silly incandescent smile, she said, "I wish I had more tears to shed right now."

Snuggling deep into John's strong arms, and resting her head on his broad shoulder, Margaret began her tale.

"I think I am in love with you; I am almost sure of it." You ask me not to say those words just yet, because you fear I don't know myself, I think. However, I will wait, as you ask, until I am sure that you know that I love you. You seem to need proof."

John, smiled as he pulled her closer to his chest, encasing her with both arms, while his cheek rested against the top of her head.

"It is true," Margaret continued, "that I have conflicts within me to resolve, mostly confidence. Not with regards to my independence, as you might think, but my confidence as a woman. With the Professor's guidance and relentless soul searching, I now know why my marriage was a disaster."

Margaret paused, wondering how to say what needed to be said.

"If you are to love me fully, you must know where my conflicts lie. I do not want to tell you this, but lying or holding back from you is worse. I now understand what I never saw before, and what the Professor discovered after my marriage to Booker. He has opened my eyes to the fact that my husband was strongly attracted to his male pupils. Perhaps, he never realized this until he married me, but young men were his preference. I will never know if he married me out of love or as a cover for his dark desires. We had no premarital relationships, so nothing was realized beforehand. Once he discovered the truth about himself, which must have been almost immediately, I knew little love and no passion at all. Unaware of any of this, I began to think it was my fault; I was too naive and inexperienced in the ways of passion. He never desired me, not even the pretense of desire. I lived with guilt over not being enough of a woman for him. In his eyes I was defective, or so I thought. This created deep scars and a total loss of confidence in feeling desirable to a man. We quickly grew apart, barely even touching. No good bye kiss in the morning, nothing - but worst of all, there was no explanation given as to why. I just continued in my misery. In all other ways, he was a decent husband, I guess, but for me, not where it counted - in my heart. I had moved from one setback in my life to another. I had reached the bottom of my existence. After my parents died, I didn't think life could have gotten worse, but the misery became compounded with the feeling that I was being cast off, thrown away. I was of no use. This is the most terrible thing I will ever say: . . . I don't know what would have happened to me, had I stayed in that marriage for a life time . . . and I am grateful, I won't have to know.

So she could liberate all her sorrow and clear her soul, John let her finish without making any comments. He just held her even tighter and kissed her forehead. He wanted to know all of her story. "Go on, my love."

"It became painstakingly clear to me," she continued, "that day on the veranda that Booker's affection for me was far from what it should be, and I had taken it to heart as guilt. Then you said those words to me that I will never forget - "Oh, God, how I love you." You said it in such a way that it tore my heart out because I felt you wouldn't feel that way if you knew me as Booker did. I had often thought about you. I would pull you out of the twilight and I talk with you whenever I was alone. When I saw you a year later at the funeral, it was like someone turned on the light to my soul. At first, I felt ashamed thinking I was happy to be free of Booker, but then I realized it wasn't him, it was *you* entering my life again, descending from my twilight. You weren't there for him, you were there for me. It was my 'someday', and you rescued me that day. The Professor has tried to free me from my guilt. He told me how sorry he felt for me, as he watched the two of us, and saw the relationship spiraling down almost from the beginning. He knew it would get worse. He hadn't been sure about Booker himself, but after we married it was confirmed, to him, in his mind.

John stroked her cheek and kissed the hollow of her neck, still holding her fast to him. Inside, he wanted to explode and put his fist through a wall or a face of anyone who could have treated her with such indifference, enough to make her despise herself. What she must have endured that year and half married and perhaps seemingly still felt. She believed she had married a real man only to discover disappointment; then she took the blame on herself for his lack of interest in her. This was more than John could stomach. Margaret was all the woman that any normal male could ever want and John knew she was everything to him. Wanting to find a way to reverse her wavering confidence and begin to dispel any self doubts, John initiated a delicate but passionate move. He gently picked up her hand, which he was holding and placed it lightly in his lap allowing her to feel his arousal for her.

"Margaret . . . know that you are a very desirable woman and never doubt that again." John whispered, looking into her tear-filled eyes.

She startled herself, as she realized she wanted to know him in that way, but she hesitantly retracted her hand with a forced embarrassed look. Inside, Margaret was glowing from John's physical reaction to her; it had lifted her. She scoffed to herself that propriety deemed this closeness was too soon. Awaiting the end of her bereavement period was going to be more difficult than she had anticipated. Margaret was blushing and feeling the warmth of that sensual moment from head to toe.

John did not miss a breath of her reaction.

She brought both hands to John's face, holding him, as she initiated a light but firm kiss. John responded the same while he slowly licked her lips apart and tried to enter her mouth. Naivety surfaced, and she pulled back unsure of what he was doing.

Now radiating inwardly, and sensing her bewildered innocence of such a kiss, John pulled her back to his shoulder. He was exhilarated to find that this passionate act was new to her. Perhaps, he would be the first in her life for many other sensual pleasures. He selfishly hoped so.

"John," Margaret said, "I want us to take our time. I want to, need to, know that I am what you want in a complete woman. Though I know about Booker, now, I do not feel strongly about myself, yet." Starting to laugh, she said, "I know you are anxious to help me find myself, but we must proceed at my pace. Can you bear with me?"

"Margaret, I can wait forever, because you are my life. I have no other options and wouldn't want them even if there were. Being who you are, at your core, made that choice for me a long time ago. And yes, I . . . together . . . we will find you, you can be sure of that. But let me just say, I would still love you for the rest of my life even if real intimacy wasn't possible. Never, ever think I love you only for carnal reasons, alone. I have had experience in that area of life, and still I have waited for only you. I have had sex, but I have never made love. I have wanted only you, Margaret, to release what I know waits inside of me."

They nestled in each other's arms for a long time before retiring for bed. Again, a brief embrace was the only affection shown before going to their rooms. The air was heavy with unspent passion.

Separately, they each lay awake a long time, ardently cherishing the openness and honesty of the words imparted that evening. Words straight from their heart were starting to tie the bindings of love.

Dixon's assignment was to gather a housekeeping staff for the Professor, which was to consist of a live-in housekeeper, a full time cook and a daily char person, whose duties included setting the fire and clearing the fireplace, scrubbing floors and a few more menial tasks. Dixon had already selected Margaret's cook. She was also in charge of purchasing linen for the home, along with food, cooking utensils and daily chinaware for the kitchen; she would send Margaret the measurements for the window sizes. Margaret would take care of the fine china and silver later. If all of the furniture arrived, Dixon would be allowed to move in at any time.

John was in charge of finding a chore man / driver, who would be assigned all outside duties, such as cutting and stacking firewood, in addition to tending the fireplaces inside, general repairs and inconsequential yard duties. If needed, a part time gardener would be hired on a less frequent basis. The chore man would also be a coach driver, when and if that time arose, as Margaret was already planning on this for some time in the future. In the event that any major pieces of furniture didn't arrive on schedule, Margaret and Dixon would remain at John's residence until they were delivered. The chore man, however, was to begin as soon as he was found, and Margaret's cook would begin next week at Thornton's home. She had recently retired but didn't find it to her liking. Eager to return to the kitchen, she would be preparing meals alongside John's cook, in order to hone her old skills in preparation for her Mistress's arrival if everything went according to plan. Margaret would return in three weeks, the week before Christmas, to her new home and life. John had promised to post to her every couple of days, and keep her informed of their progress.

As they waited for the Professor to come fetch Margaret for the train, John and Margaret stood at his parlor window, looking out at the workers going about their business.

"Margaret," he asked, "Do you remember the last time we stood together looking out this window?"

It only took Margaret a moment to cast her mind back to the day of the riot. "Yes, John, that was quite a memorable day, as I recall."

"In more ways than you know, Margaret." John lifted her hair to see if there was any remaining mark from the stone that had felled her that day. There wasn't, but John leaned down and kissed the spot where she had bled. "I haven't spoken to you much about the mills; I didn't care to waste words, with so little time, but when the strikers were at the door, the words you said to me that day changed my life and the life of everyone who works for me. Those words have been the very cornerstone of my success. I owe much of my success to you, you know."

"Don't talk piffle, John. I did no such thing. Don't credit me for what you have accomplished."

"Somehow, I knew you would say that, but one day I hope to prove to you, what that day inspired in me after your departure from Milton."

John saw the carriage coming through the mill gate and pulled Margaret away from the window. "Margaret, I love you, and I will never tire of telling you so. I will live in anticipation until you are safely returned to Milton in a few weeks' time. I will not have a moments rest while you are away. For you and me, our *tomorrow* has finally come." John pulled her into his arms, kissed her lightly but firmly, and held her until they heard the knock on the door.

Dixon escorted Dr. Pritchard into the room and went straight to Margaret for a goodbye hug. "Miss Margaret, we will have everything ready and waiting for you. I'm so excited."

John retrieved Margaret's coat as he bid the Professor a cordial "hello."

The Professor picked up Margaret's bag, saying, "Hello all...so, Margaret... are you ready? Your carriage awaits, Milady," and bowed from the waist.

Margaret laughed, as she told the Professor, "You're stealing John's lines." Margaret and John smiled broadly at each other.

John accompanied Dr. Pritchard and Margaret outside, and handed Margaret into the carriage. He closed the door and Margaret leaned out of the window, "See you soon," she said. John covered her hand, which was resting on the door frame, and squeezed hard on it , mouthing the words, "I love you" as the driver told the horses to 'walk on'.

John returned to the top of his steps. Once again he was witnessing Margaret being borne away from him. His stomach roiled at the remembrance, but he was uplifted, as she looked back at him, dispelling one horrid memory with a brilliant new one, balancing the scales. He stood there thinking, long after the coach had departed the gates, how the memory of the two worst days of his life had been replaced with two new beautiful memories: This one, that had just happened, replaced the day Margaret left Milton four years ago; the other, Margaret's appearance at his door two days ago, replaced the day he read that she had married.

Chapter 11

 The Neighbor on the Train

The Professor and Margaret's return trip into London was earlier in the day. The train had mostly full coaches; the Professor scouted out the least full cabin and beckoned Margaret over. Handing her inside, Margaret counted three other riders, and surprisingly, noticed the man that had ridden with them two days previous. He sat smartly dressed in his grey coat with a tidy black cravat, arms crossed, unable to stretch out with his newspaper, but he did nod his head to acknowledge that he remembered them. The Professor and Margaret were able to sit together allowing for plenty of conversation to wile away the time of the four hour trip. The Professor told her how he admired Mr. Thornton just from their brief meeting and dinner together, and could well understand why Milton had grown into such a dedicated mill city with someone, such as he, leading much of the way.

About an hour into the trip, the train stopped at one of its two stops between Milton and London, allowing two passengers to disembark and leaving only the "unknown rider," as Margaret had begun calling him in her mind. The train pulled out of the station making its usual chugging noises until it finally reached maximum speed and settled into a more tolerable noise level.

"Excuse me," said the unknown rider. "I couldn't help overhearing the two of you speaking today, so I thought I would introduce myself. My name is Blake Cavanaugh. Mrs.?" he asked looking at Margaret.

"Reed." she said.

"Mrs. Reed, I just wanted to tell you that we will be neighbors. You apparently are going to rent, or buy, the little refurbished cottage across from the courthouse and I work in the law office next to your new home. Quite by chance, we find ourselves on this train, again."

Margaret felt some relief, having unconsciously attached some macabre darkness to the man. "Yes, this is quite a coincidence and a fortunate one for us, since you can probably answer some questions we might have. I never noticed what was next door when I visited the cottage on Saturday. What is it that you do at your law office?"

"I work for a London based firm called Bailer and Banks Law Firm. I'm a lawyer specializing in deeds, titles, and property. I'm not an illustrious crime fighter in the courts, but my job does have its mysteries, occasionally. I happened to be at work on Saturday, my window overlooks your side of our building, and I noticed you. I thought to myself - 'I think that's woman on the train.' Did I see Mr. Thornton with you?"

"Yes, he is an old friend of the family from when I came to live in Milton four years ago. He was a student of literature, who studied with my father, and came to our home weekly for private lessons."

"I know John well. I have done work for him when he bought land to build his second mill. He and I, with his magistrate duties and my deed recordings, pass each other in the courthouse often." He glanced towards the Professor, who was sitting quietly, listening, and observing. "I am sorry to interrupt your conversation, I only wanted to introduce myself to my new neighbor" he said smiling.

"Mr. Cavanaugh, I am happy to know you. This is my dear friend Dr. Pritchard, a former history professor, who is now coming to Milton, to write about its Industrial growth. I am fortunate that he has extended a courtesy to me, in helping him."

The two men leaned across the coach and shook hands. "Yes, I did hear a lot of that conversation on our previous trip. I had been trying to read my paper but the research into Milton's burgeoning city, had quite taken my interest. Our firm has located to Milton for much the same reason. The expansion of the city is enormous and it is not nearly completed."

"I remember it as a town, a rather large town, but the face has disappeared quickly even in so short a time as four years," Margaret continued with cordiality.

The conversation flowed on for quite some time; they talked about many subjects including the mills and the labor force. Eventually, Margaret realized that he had been talking strictly to her the entire time, always mannerly and pleasant. She sensed his attentions were going from neighborly to something more. She was surprised at her own inner reaction to such attention being lavished upon her.

As Margaret and the Professor were disembarking before Mr. Cavanaugh, they promised to meet when in Milton, and the three eventually said their goodbyes. The Professor hailed a coach at the front of the station to take them home.

"Margaret," asked the Professor, as they settled into the coach, "tell me what you thought of Mr. Cavanaugh. What were your emotions?"

"I think I know what you're getting at since I am becoming more familiar with your ways," Margaret laughed. "Is it the fact that it appears that he may be interested in me, more than he might be interested in just being neighborly?"

"Yes, exactly. It was obvious to me, but I could see you didn't realize it for a long time. You kept drawing him into conversation, lots of smiling back and forth, and then suddenly you seemed to pull on the reins. You had some type of realization there, didn't you?" the Professor asked.

"Dear me, how you know me so well. You read me like a book!" Margaret said, as the Professor laughed. "Yes, that is quite how it happened. Before I met Booker, I had three proposals, aside from other times when I had to turn a gentleman down for some other less innocuous reason. I never thought I handled any of them well. I find it very difficult to disappoint someone. While talking with Mr. Cavanaugh, those old remembrances came back to me. I haven't thought about a situation like that for many years. It was very disconcerting and I don't know how I will get on if that occurs again. I've never spoken of this to you, but Booker has left me with emotional scars. Most likely unintended, he caused me to feel undesirable, unfeminine and well . . . and more. I know I must find that confidence before I can feel whole again. Can I find, within myself, a love to give, or passion to express? Can I commit to another man, again? To me, I am a defective woman. I'm sure you have deduced that John has an interest in me. I had turned down his proposal almost four years ago, and you are right, he may be my destiny, left behind. Now, we might have another chance, but I cannot feel right about myself just yet. I don't want him to find himself in a marriage with a woman fighting self doubts and other problems."

"And Cavanaugh?" the Professor asked.

"When I became aware that he appeared to look . . . fascinated, I experienced a very strange reaction. His interest lessened my doubts in being a desirable female but the problem of rejecting him came back to me. First I was slightly elated, then I became worried that his interest could possibly grow more serious, which is something for which I would have no intention.

"Margaret," said the Professor, always the fatherly figure, as he placed his hand on her knee, "Child, you will always have the problem of rejection. Men will forever be drawn to you, and rightly so, until age steals most of your youth and beauty.

You must resign yourself to that fact, even when you marry John Thornton, which I know will happen, that you will still be desired, perhaps, just not by John's close friends. Rejection, rebuff, dismiss, they are all facts of life and unpleasant as they may seem, we each must work out our own way to deal with it. No one has committed suicide on your behalf, have they?"

"No," Margaret laughed, relieved.

"Well then, you must be handling it as well as you can then. And as for the other, the larger problem of your own sense of self and confidence in your natural womanly nature, I don't see that being a problem for long. I will never know your intimate side, nor do I care to even speak of it, but I do know you. You are a warm and caring person with love and passion bursting to take that first breath. You have an intelligent and solid outlook on the world, so I promise you that you will not be a cold or undesirable woman. What you have missed in your marriage to Booker, was a man to make you feel your womanly side, your worth as a wife and a lover. Personally, with what I am beginning to see of John Thornton's love for you, he will certainly not allow you to ever feel that way."

Margaret leaned into the Professor's shoulder and cried. "Thank you. Even though I knew that you could probably soothe my thoughts in that regard, I still found it too difficult to bring up, but I'm glad I did. I spoke to John about it Saturday night. We had quite a heart to heart talk about a lot of things. Of course, he told me almost what you have, but I knew he was tremendously biased." She stifled a small laugh.

"Believe him, Margaret. He doesn't say much but what he does is spoken from deep within. He doesn't speak to hear himself or to impress others, he speaks from his heart. He may be curt sometimes, but he'll always be honest. If you two have had such a conversation as that, you are turning a corner in your life and are well on your way back to your destiny."

"Yes, I think so, too. It was the most unusual two days I ever experienced. I'm not ashamed to admit to you that when I left Milton years ago, John and I were not on the best of terms.

This weekend has been almost as if our relationship grew closer while we were apart."

"I'm sure it has for Mr. Thornton, that is quite obvious," reflected the Professor. "You, my child, are just finding your way back to the love of a real man, one who you deserve."

"The only thing he has really insisted upon is that I not speak to him about my feelings for him until I'm positive that I love him. He said he will wait forever. Why don't you have any monumental personal problems we can talk about? I feel cheated," Margaret laughed, righting herself on the carriage seat.

"That's a good question, one that we may ponder some day, but not now, as you are home. I do not look for anything to deter me in my coming plans, but if it should, I will contact you. So, I will say adieu and see you when you arrive in Milton."

"Thank you Professor, for everything; saving my life being only one for which I'm grateful." Margaret exited the coach at the hand of the driver. He followed, carrying her bag to the door.

A fortnight later, Margaret had her few pieces of furniture, books, personal belongings, and all but some of her clothes, shipped to the Mill's address. John had written that all was going as planned, with the exception of some of her pre-ordered, custom made furniture pieces, which were going a little slowly. It was probable that they would be arriving later than she, but she could stay at his home until hers was completely outfitted. He had hired a middle-aged single man named Adrian Thompson to tend to the outside and other chores. John had gone back several years checking his references, even though he'd been recommended by his own driver, Branson. John also suggested that in the future, Margaret might consider letting him live on property in the rooms over the carriage house.

Dixon posted a note to Margaret, telling her that the kitchen was stocked with all they would need to get started.

The linens were purchased and Dixon's own room was now habitable. Their cook was already working with Mr. Thornton's cook and all her responsibilities were coming together. She also wrote that Margaret was going to love the house and being able to watch the courthouse comings and goings would be interesting. The home next door had some very nice people living there, and Dixon was sure Margaret would easily become friends with them. She was a teacher and he still worked for the railroad.

Margaret also received a hand delivered letter from the Professor saying he was on his way and wishing her good luck with her move. His plans were going smoothly, except for saying goodbye to his colleagues and students which wasn't quite as easy as he had anticipated, but he was happy to be setting out for Milton. "See you next week after your arrival," he had ended the note.

Chapter 12

 Welcome Home, Margaret

The London station platform was filled with people, but at least she had missed the early surge of London workers. Margaret had ensured that her baggage was properly stowed onto the huffing train and glanced down the long line of coaches on the track, recognizing that they led to paradise, to her destiny once left behind.

Booker's family said goodbye to her and had just left the station. It was a sad time, for she liked them very much and they loved her. They promised to come visit her and asked her to do the same. Aunt Shaw, Edith, and Maxwell stayed there to see her off. Lots of well wishes, hugs, and kisses passed between them as Margaret boarded her train to freedom. Edith cried and waved her lace handkerchief to Margaret, as she stepped into her coach.

As the train pulled away from the station, Margaret waved goodbye to her only family and felt everything falling into place. She was endeavoring to set sail into a brand new life, ready to find direction and purpose to her existence, and perhaps, her greatest love.

She looked around at her companions in the coach. She gazed at the young couple who were seated in the corner and the gentleman across from her. The couple appeared to Margaret to be newly married, possibly on their honeymoon. The young man had propped himself diagonally in a corner and the young woman rested between his legs with her back against his chest while he kissed her hair and whispered endearments to her. It was a scandalously improper scene, but she could feel their love and envied them.

She tucked away any thoughts of romance as she reminded herself that she was going to love her freedom. She wanted to twirl in a circle with her hands over her head and let the whole world know that this was a new beginning for her. Again though, her trip was slightly disturbed as the new unknown rider, a very handsome, elegantly clothed gentleman, kept glancing her way. Even as she read her book, she could see him through her peripheral vision and could feel his eyes burning into her, but at least he had the decency to look away whenever she would look up.

John was getting all of his business affairs out of the way and clearing his desk, foreseeing every detail that could interrupt the lovely time he would be spending with Margaret on her first days in Milton. She would be staying at his home for several days, until the rest of her household furnishings arrived. He still was in a dream world anticipating her return, and there he would remain until he saw her step off the train.

As he spoke to John, Higgins could see that, today, his friend's enthusiasm knew no bounds. Higgins was amazed by the change in John over the past few weeks. In all the years of their friendship, Higgins had never seen John so full of life. He had asked a question but noticed John was now staring out the office window and hadn't heard a word he said to him. Clearing his throat rather loudly, Higgins smiled and said to John, "Ahem. "I said when is Miss Margaret due to arrive?"

John was thinking about the face in the crowd that he would soon see. All those passengers leaving their coaches, yet he knew he would spot her instantly. Hearing Higgins clear his throat, he turned and said, "I'm sorry, I was lost in thought. What was it, you said?"

"Master," he said, "I can well understand what this day must mean to you, and I understand you're lost in thought. I, myself, am anxious for Margaret to return. I wish you all the success that one man can wish another. What I said was, when is Miss Margaret due to arrive?"

"I believe she will arrive at 2:00 this afternoon." John replied." Are you sure there is nothing that I need to be doing?"

Higgins shook his head, stating that both mills were running at top performance and no large imports or exports were expected for several more days. He understood that the Master already knew this, but he was only asking out of nervousness. Higgins could see John didn't know what to do with himself as he moved around the room, looking at books and papers, totally unfocused to any purpose at hand. He had both hands wedged in his pockets, tumbling coins, which was something he never did. In fact, John had remarked in the past how ungentlemanly and annoying it was when one of his gentleman friends did the same thing. "Master," Higgins said, smiling, "do you see what you are doing?"

Without saying the words, as he wanted the sound of the jingling coins to become apparent, Higgins pointed to John's hands in his pockets.

"What? Higgins, what are you pointing at?" John quipped, frowning as he began checking the clothes he'd put on that morning.

Higgins started to chuckle as John became aware of the sound he was making.

John's face lit with a smile and he immediately withdrew his hands from his pockets and crossed his arms in front of his chest.

"Fine then, Higgins." John laughed. "If you need nothing from me then I will be off. Should something arise, send a runner with a note. I should be home for a short while and then I'll head to the depot a little early in case the train is ahead of schedule. Make sure the helpers are there by 1:30, and thanks."

"M - i - l - t - o - n, Milton INBOUND," came the call of the porter, who was walking the swaying train aisle.

John had arrived at the station almost a full half hour before the train was due, and told his driver to wait for him in the front. His two helpers, with the cart, where down at the far end of the platform, where the large baggage was unloaded. He passed his time pacing the platform, checking his watch and looking down the tracks. Aware that he was smiling too much, he wondered what people must think of his behavior. He was shaking with anticipation. John had been nervous other times, whenever he spoke to large congregations of his peers, but now that seemed like nothing compared to this moment. This . . . this was the rest of his life about to arrive on these tracks. John could hear the long pull on the train's whistle coming from around the bend. He moved to the back of the crowd that was waiting to board, and stood on a bench, hoping to easily see more clearly, through the crowd of departing passengers, the person who was returning with his heart and soul.

The train came to a stop and John saw a porter open Margaret's door - the door to his future - a vision he'd been dreaming about for many years. Margaret was handed out by the porter, her cloak whipping in the wind and a bit of snow blowing past her face. To John, it was as if she was stepping out of a Great Master's painting. She wore no bonnet this day; scattered tendrils blew about her face and her hair was pulled back in a braided knot, which accentuated the arch of her neck. John had another exquisite vision to remember for his treasure chest. He knew he had to hold on tight for all of the *firsts* that were headed his way. He was undone at the prospect. Her lovely vision smote him like a fist to his stomach. Noticing all the gentlemen turning their heads her way, he hurried along before too many men could offer her their assistance.

When Margaret saw John standing on the crowded platform, cheeks flushed from the cold, she smiled his way. As she watched him approach, she thought him even more handsome then a mere three weeks ago. Aching to be with him, his approach seemed as if it was in slow motion, she became aware of his every movement, every fraction of a second that he strode towards her, smiling. To assist her with her trunks, which seemed to have come out of nowhere at the end of her packing, he had brought two helpers with him. John met her, doffing his hat and tipping his head.

"Welcome home, Margaret. It is wonderful to have you back to stay." He wanted to kiss her, but instead he asked, "Would you mind showing my men which are your trunks so they can be loaded onto the wagon?"

John offered his arm to Margaret as they strolled down to the baggage area and Margaret maneuvered through the piles, pointing out her possessions. The men tipped their heads in recognition and proceeded to load them onto the wagon.

Turning to Margaret and extending his arm again, John said, "Shall we?" As soon as she had stepped off that train, his heart started hammering through his veins. He was sure Margaret could see it pounding through his coat and vest.

She is finally walking out of my dreams and into my life.

"How was your trip?" John asked, nervously, smiling at her.

As Margaret began her tale about her trip, he could see the glow emanating from her rosy cheeks. Her eyes were sparkling just the way he imagined they would, even while blinking the snow away, as she looked up to him. Margaret was still the most beautiful creature in his universe, but now happiness blossomed out of her lit face and made him quiver inside. John didn't think this moment could have gotten any better, but it just did. He steered her toward the coach but could hardly hear what she was saying, he was so enraptured by her presence and the feel of her arm around his, knowing this was just the beginning.

"John? John, did you hear what I asked you?"

Looking a bit shocked, John managed to stammer, "No . . . No, I am sorry, I was lost in you," He allowed himself to say, "I'm afraid that is the second time today that I have been guilty of that. I humbly apologize."

What a total disaster, I am.

"Let's start over again," he said. "Margaret, how was your trip?" This time John paid attention to her story.

As she finished her account of the young couple, they had arrived at the carriage. Atop was a handsome young blond coachman wearing a nice fitted black tunic with brass buttons and a cap. Pulling the carriage, were four shiny black horses, called a "hour-in-hand," who had braided tails and were fitted out with highly polished brass buckles. Margaret looked at her conveyance and felt like she was entering a fairytale coach. She didn't think Milton had such beauty for hire. As John handed her into the carriage, he could see the question on her face, and he smiled to himself. He had to sit beside her rather than across, or else he would only stare and not hear her again.

"John, this is a very handsome coach and horses. You needn't have gone to such expense on my behalf." She looked at him and saw a small smirk in the corners of his mouth.

"Nothing is too good for you, Margaret." His smirked widened.

"What's that look for? Why this expense?" Margaret couldn't help smiling back at John's grin; it was infectious seeing him happy.

John tapped the roof of the coach and Branson reined the horses forward. "Margaret, this is not an expense for me. I own this traveling coach, another small one and these fine horses. Branson, the driver up in the box, works for me. The

Mills have done quite well within the past three years. As Dixon has probably written you, I travel and speak about what we've done in Milton as mill and factory owners. I speak to the issues which we have resolved and how we are still working together, as varied manufacturers, to get our product to the masses and improve the living of our workforce. You will be amazed at Milton when you finally get a good look at the city; even I haven't seen it all. I've been selected as President of our Merchant Chamber of Commerce, and like I said before, you had a lot to do with this."

"I what? You've said that before and I don't know why and don't want to hear it. Please, stop saying so." She turned to look at him in wonder. John noticed she was making the cutest little *'o'* with her lips.

"Well, if you'll close your mouth, I'll tell you why," John said, reminiscing the fun they had, just weeks ago. Margaret stared at him and then they laughed together as he launched into what she had taught him about his own workers and their care and living conditions. "Because of you, along came great change to the mills . . ."

"Oh John, I am so relieved to hear this. Your success and wealth are very nice for you, but to think that the workers are far better off than when I last lived here just makes my heart sing."

John's own heart was singing.

"I will take no credit for any of this," Margaret continued, "do not mention such things to others, either. You were getting there, I know you were. You were finding it very hard to accept their crisis, along with your own, back then. You just needed the most subtle of shoves. I am just so excited. I can't say how many times I've thought of the strife here. When things went badly for me and I would get upset, I would think of the workers here in Milton and see my problem set in the picture with theirs. I was always coming out ahead."

"Margaret, you can say what you will about the people here and what they've suffered, but you must know that you have suffered far more. I know of no one else who has gone through one tragedy after another, and yours were such that no one could fix them. Margaret, you are incredibly strong. Stronger than I, I am sure. To be here, happy and bright, and to know that within the past four years, you had lost everyone, is nothing short of a miracle. Let's change the subject; it depresses me to know of what you've endured."

John was taking in her lovely sweet feminine scent. His heart wouldn't stop its heavy pounding. Unable to resist any longer, he turned and kissed her, covering her mouth with his, holding her head, and chin. Slowly, he pulled back, looking down at her perfect face with her eyes closed. He kissed her eyelids and held her tight.

A poignant moment marked its place in time.

Smiling, Margaret said, "Thank you, John. I've been counting the days until that kiss. Here I am today, looking forward to a new life, one of my own choosing. I am very happy already and I've barely begun it.

As John listened, he knew Margaret was singing the lyrics of a love song straight to his heart. "Margaret, before we get to my home, I want to take you through greater Milton. You didn't have a good look before. Since we have plenty of time, now, I want you to see the uptown section where you and the Professor will live; it's about two to three years old. For just a few minutes, sit back, relax, and enjoy the splendor that has bewitched Milton." They were both silent. Margaret was looking out the carriage window in total awe, while John was looking at her. He slid across the seat facing her and moved towards the window so he could see what she was seeing, in case she had questions. Her scent was the one thing he had missed the most. He could always be aroused by her scent: the smell of her hair, the light fragrance she wore, or the soap in which she bathed. He could hardly restrain himself from reaching out to her this instant. John found that he had to adjust the position of his great coat or things might become embarrassingly obvious. He did not want her to be aware of *his* awkward moment. Apparently, these rare delicate difficulties were becoming all too frequent, which he didn't seem to mind, except for his mortification of being noticed.

"Your nice little cottage is ready for you but without all the furnishings. Dixon is at my home still, she will be your chaperone for the coming nights. I believe Dixon will have dinner ready for all three of us by the time we get there. I have asked her to join us this evening. As much as I have enjoyed having Dixon in my home, she still has had a habit of *mothering me*, too much. She dotes on me like I was her son. She's even learned to sass me on occasion, all in fun, I assure you. It upsets me when I have to tell her that I am the boss, and she always realizes that, but little seems to deter her from doing it again. I have to smile thinking about it. It's very kind of her to watch over my well being, but I think she crosses the line too often." Turning slightly in his seat, John leaned over and spoke into the voice box, "Branson, stop at the cottage.'"

The carriage came to a stop and John saw Margaret's eyes open wide with wonder; she was still in love with her home.

She inhaled loudly, "John, I think it is enchanted, like a fairy tale. It's like a big doll house. I do love it, so. I think that I shall never want to leave this lovely little place." She jumped across the seat, hugged him around the neck, and kissed him on the cheek. "How long do you think before I can move in?"

John felt like he had a little girl on his hands and she had just opened her birthday present and found her favorite doll. "It'll only be a few days, less than a week, I should think." He saw the pout on her face. It was one of those play pouts. None-the-less, she was disappointed, which pleased him very much because it meant she already loved being here. From nowhere, came the thought that he wanted his first child to be a daughter.

"John, thank you for your help with my move."

John leaned out the window, "Home, Branson!" and turning to face her, he answered, "my pleasure."

Someday I will tell her of the pleasure I felt, seeing her step off that train.

"I will be your ride and guide all this week for I have cleared my work for the next five days to be at your disposal, with the exception of one evening meeting. We should be at Marlborough Mills in just a few minutes. It's quite close to this end of town. You will hardly recognize where you are, from looking at the buildings. As a frame of reference, your cottage used to be the little book store, you frequented."

"It was? Oh, how well I remember that little quiet book store, always filled with new things to read. I was at it often and so was father. The book store is my new home! I loved that shop, but I am grateful that it has been restored to what it is now."

John could hear the smile in her pleasant sigh. They were pulling through the mill gates. Dixon was waiting on the front porch when the carriage rolled up to it. Branson came down from his box, opened the door, and let down the steps to peals of delighted sounds. John watched Margaret and Dixon fuss over each other and out of the corner of his eye, he saw Higgins heading out of the office door and trotting over. They hugged each other like old friends would.

"Higgins, close up the office and come on up to the house. Come stay for dinner.

Margaret noticed her carpet bag in the downstairs foyer; she assumed her trunks must have been taken on to her cottage. Everyone ascended the stairs into the sitting room as Margaret and Dixon talked steadily. When they got into the sitting room, John told Dixon to set another place for dinner. Dixon knew he meant Higgins, and headed off to the kitchen.

John removed Margaret's coat and Higgins hung his coat and cap on a peg. John shed his great coat and waited for Margaret to enter the parlor first. Higgins found a chair opposite where John usually sat near the fireplace, while Margaret slowly glanced around the room and then comforted her buttocks, once again on the couch.

John stood at the bar and asked for drink orders.

"Oh John, say it again, please!" Margaret prompted mischievously.

"I'd rather not," John said looking a bit embarrassed.

"What's this then?" Higgins asked, seeing John looking rather uncomfortable.

"Pleeeeeeeease," Margaret donned her pouty face.

"Brandy, whiskey or port, Milady? What would you prefer?" John asked, doing a mock bow to her again, but this time coming up with a red face. No one had ever seen a red face on John like this.

Higgins, Margaret and John, howled with laughter, mainly over John's embarrassment of acting silly. This was totally unheard of for him to act in such a manner.

"Miss Margaret, I have seen great and wonderful changes in the Master here, since the news of your returning, but nothing like this. How . . . did you get him to do that?" Higgins asked, still laughing so hard, he had to wipe the spittle foaming at the corners of his mouth.

Higgins's remark prompted more laughter all over again, as it made John seem like a performing animal act.

"Higgins, if you value your job, you will forget what you saw here," John said, followed by another round of laughter.

Higgins asked for a whiskey while Margaret asked for a port. John poured the drinks and handed them around.

Higgins said, "Well, is anyone going to tell me what that was all about?"

"I can hardly explain my own self," John began. "When Margaret showed up here unexpectedly a few weeks ago, she strolled in here with all the brevity of a stage performer, announcing the *new* Margaret. She was so happy, and full of exuberance that somehow she pulled me onto her stage of merriment. We were being simple, which actually felt good for a change, but I'm sure I've never been that free with myself before. Abandoning all my pride, doesn't seem like it has been enough for her, though. She apparently wanted you to see the act. She shall pour her own drinks in the future."

Margaret leaned toward Higgins and whispered loudly, "I think I should feel complimented, because I actually saw him pinch himself that night."

For the first time ever, John was the center of humiliation. He couldn't stop laughing, he couldn't stop blushing, and apparently he couldn't stop Margaret. He had never felt such joy before, even if it was at the expense of his pride and self-respect. Peals of laughter echoed throughout the house, as Dixon, rolling her eyes at Cook, remarked, "There they go again, just like the last time Margaret arrived."

Cook nodded her approval. "This house has needed that sound since the day it was built," she replied.

A nice dinner was served and conversation flowed on and on about Higgins' marriage, Margaret's new work, the cottage, the changes to Milton and even the rumors about Slickson's retirement and sale of the mill. Everyone enjoyed themselves, especially John, as he glanced in Margaret's direction, often.

Higgins rose to leave, telling Margaret once again how glad he was she was home in Milton. He'd wanted her to see Mary, who was very excited about her return, and to meet his betrothed, Peggy.

"Thank you Nicholas, for the warm welcome back. I'm anxious to see everyone as soon as I am able."

Higgins left, leaving John and Margaret alone.

They sat and talked comfortably until dark about the past three weeks and their preparations for this day. Both Margaret and John seemed unable to keep the smiles from their faces. Each knew they were leaving their sadness behind and embarking on a new and wondrous path in their life.

"You've never seen through the whole house, would you be interested in a tour?"

"Yes, John, I would like that," Margaret said.

To begin the tour, the two went down the kitchen steps and out the back door. Although there was plenty of ground running back behind the mills, there was no porch on the back, to speak of, as the enlarged carriage house had taken up most of the yard. They walked over to the carriage house and

Margaret was introduced to Branson. "How do you do, Branson? It's nice to meet you," she said, as she shivered in the frosty air.

"Thank you Miss," Branson replied as he tipped his cap.

Margaret, eyeing John, said to Branson, "How is it, working for Mr. Thornton?"

"It's swell, Miss. He's a very fair Master. He's taught me things, trusts me with his horses that he loves, especially Plato. He's let me live over the stable. And now that I have a lady friend, he gives me nights off so I can be with her. I wouldn't change this job for any other."

"Thank you Branson, I am sure that is a very accurate assessment of Mr. Thornton, although it was far from my first impression, which I won't go into as I was in error. I'm sure we will see each other a lot in the future. Good Evening, Branson."

"Good evening, Miss, . . . Sir," tipping his cap.

As they walked back into the house, John told Margaret how he had admired the downstairs lavatory and the mud room in her cottage. He would have to consider both of those additions in the future. Entering the kitchen, all was quiet. Cook had gone home and Dixon was in her room. "I'm afraid I can't show you Dixon's room tonight, but maybe another time. There were several other rooms, such as a scullery, pantry, back cellar and a door that lead to a cold room below ground, plus a second lower parlor, or staff dining room, that was rarely used. Lately it had been mainly used by Dixon, for her small business, as an area for training housekeeping personnel. Coming up the front stairs from the downstairs parlor, John led Margaret to his Mother's room, which had been completely refurbished. "I've had this room changed," and that was all John said about that room. They passed Margaret's guestroom, which had once been Fanny's old room, and proceeded through the parlor, to his library. "I work a lot in this room," John said.

Margaret looked about the room, walking around the huge unadorned desk, taking in all his books in the glass fronted cases which had been designed for the room. There was a comfortable upholstered guest chair, near the front of the desk, a window off to the left of the desk, the desk chair and one other small chair placed against the wall. There was an unlit fireplace. "John, this is a nice room. It feels warm and cozy even without the fire going. It's quite manly looking," she remarked. Then Margaret laughed, "Which I think is the point in here." John smiled.

The final room they came to was John's large bedroom with its huge bed; Margaret had entered it briefly on her previous visit. At first, she was startled again at the size of the bed, but soon realized that with John's height, he would need something much larger than average. She walked the room, while John leaned against the door frame with his arms folded. There was a highboy for his undergarments, socks, cravats, and the like; there was a wardrobe for his outerwear; there were two side tables, one holding a gas light, and the other a guttered candle. A bowl and pitcher stand, with a shaving mirror, was off in one corner and two windows flanked the bed. The room smelled masculine and seemed stark, a lot like John himself. Margaret looked at the bed and wondered; could John have any lasting memories in that bed? "John," she began somewhat cautiously, "if I ask you a personal question, will you tell me the truth?"

"Forever," John assured her, "always know that."

Continuing to gaze at the huge bed, Margaret went over, sat on the edge, and ran her hand across the top counterpane cover. "Do you ever entertain guests in here?"

"Entertain?" He was dumbfounded at the word. John straightened his frame in the doorway. This was not a question he had expected from her. He wasn't sure if he should joke with her, or not. Either way, he was not embarrassed to answer. He realized quickly, however, that she could be thinking that he might be carrying long lasting memories of another woman. "I have had only one woman in this *room*, other than my family, and that was someone named Margaret Reed; she was here about three weeks ago."

"John, I'm serious," Margaret told him, thinking he was attempting to humor her.

"I am too, Margaret. I have never brought a woman into this room. I think you are the first to even see into this room. Do you have any other . . . questions in that regard?" he asked, as he walked into the room and sat beside Margaret. "Let's clear up any concern you have there. I don't want you wondering what I am thinking while we both might be in this room."

"No, I don't think I have any questions, at least not now, perhaps never, but it's really none of my business," she finished quietly.

John took Margaret by the shoulders and turned her towards him. "Margaret, I will never lie to you, ever. I am a normal, sexually adept, active male. I have always kept that part of my life private and have always been a gentleman, but if you have any questions about me in that regard, I will answer them. I have sown my wild oats long ago. I am very understanding of the female body and a woman's wants and desires, but I have never loved anyone except you. Like I said, and told you a few weeks ago, I have had sex, but never made love. Every time I've lain with a woman, I have thought of only you. My passion was withheld waiting for YOU." As he spoke, he rubbed Margaret's arms up and down trying to soothe her. "After you told me about your husband and your lack of intimacy, I dared hope to think that I might bring you new pleasures for the first time in your life. I am a passionate man, where you are concerned, Margaret, and it's been waiting in the dark corners of my soul for a long time."

Margaret rose from the bed and started towards the parlor. She had begun this conversation but no longer did she want to hear of it.

John remained seated on the bed, looking at the floor, wondering if he had said too much. He knew instantly, like a fool, that he had. It wasn't what he said, but it was the pressure that he had probably placed on her. He realized that Margaret might feel obliged to show him more than what were her truest feelings. As much as he wanted her, he did not want that. John rose slowly, his mind still reeling at the moment. He turned off his light and walked back into the parlor, only to hear Margaret's door closing.

God, what I have I done? I've been nothing but honest. Was I a fool? I never want her to wonder and feel the jealous torment that I felt.

John paced the floor for a while wondering if she would come out. She didn't. He went to her door and tapped lightly.

"We'll talk tomorrow, John," Margaret said through the door. "I'm tired and I would like to sleep now."

John walked through the sitting room, turned out the gas lights and went to his room.

He sat on the edge of his bed, going over everything he had said to her. What could have upset her like that? Everything, he thought . . . everything could have stepped on her confidence. He was trying too hard, rushing the relationship he wanted so much to build. He wanted to do everything for her, tell her everything, touch her, and most of all show his great passion for her, something which, he realized now, was too much too soon. She knew how he felt about her. Previously, he had convinced himself he would let her come to him, yet he had not done that. He was charging at her, forgetting she had just lost a husband, only to discover, soon after his death, some very unsettling news about him. She had made the move to Milton. She had his feelings to handle, as well as her own feelings and a new house. She was going to be overwhelmed very soon, and John knew he had to be cautious and step back. It was a bitter pill to swallow.

Margaret dressed in her nightwear, sat on the bed, wondering what had made her ask such a question. She was surprised when she heard her own words coming out of her mouth. She berated herself for not having realized that John, being the gentleman that he was, was still an ordinary man with ordinary needs, and it was wrong of her to have questioned him. Growing up, thinking of young men had never been much in her thoughts, but of course, that was her own naivety surfacing once again. She should be thankful that John would have no awakening to other desires, as she experienced in her past marriage. It was ludicrous for her to think she would have been the only one in his life, yet, he had never married. How was she going to apologize for her intrusion into the personal life he had before her, and then for her disappointment in his honesty? Sometimes, she wondered if life was fair. She certainly felt that she wasn't fair, at least in this regard. How naive, she really was, and here it was manifesting itself. Working through these new times and discovering what life really held for her was alarming at best, but she knew John would hold her hand through it all.

Chapter 13

Staying Away

John awakened to the new day, having spent a miserable night, wondering if Margaret would recover from the knowledge of his previous carnal experiences. Had he ruined everything in a moment of openness? She had initially asked the question, which had taken him quite by surprise, and led to his confession. Whatever made her ask that? However, he would have to do his best to restrain his passion, in both words and deeds.

Slightly apprehensive, he took a deep breath and left his room. He found Margaret helping Dixon set the table for breakfast.

"Good morning all," John courteously said.

"Good morning to you, John," Margaret replied, not looking at him as she set the knives and forks down.

"Same to you, Master," Dixon replied. "Do you want your paper?"

"I'll get it," John said, bouncing back out of his chair, glad to have something to do. He usually didn't read it this early because he would be in his office by now, but he took the steps down and retrieved it from outside. He knew he'd need something to keep him occupied, as he tried to avoid the heavy atmosphere in the room.

"John, would you care for a cup of tea before breakfast is ready," Margaret asked, now looking at him.

"Thank you, no. I'll wait." John replied, starting to flip through the pages.

Minutes later, breakfast was brought to the table and Margaret and John followed. As John pulled out Margaret's chair before seating himself, he wondered what to say. The conversation throughout the meal was stilted, and they spoke only about the plans for the day. Margaret planned to visit the Professor first and then was anxious to spend most of the day in her new place.

Desirous to be on their way to the cottage, Margaret and Dixon prepared to leave with John, as soon as breakfast was completed and the dishes were cleared. He had said very little. He didn't know how to make small talk and, sure as not, he'd overstep himself again if he opened his mouth. That only left silence.

Outside, the snow was starting to lie on the ground; it looked as though a white Christmas was on its way. John assisted both women into the carriage, as he urged them to be careful of the slippery conditions they found at their feet. For a brief moment, Margaret had a passing vision of the inside of the milling rooms she had once glimpsed: white fluff hanging in the air, never seeming to reach the floor.

The carriage headed into town where people were crowded on the walkways, shopping for gifts, as the snow started to impede their progress. During their slow ride to the Professor's home, John pulled out three house keys. "Margaret, here are your keys to the house. They are all the same. I wanted to ask if I could keep one and you have the other two?"

"Yes, John, please keep it. I should be glad to know that you have one." Margaret took two keys from John, handing one to Dixon for that day and she slipped the other into her small handbag. Until she was comfortable with everything, she would give Dixon a house key on a 'need by need' basis.

Dixon was let off at the cottage, and John and Margaret proceeded to Dr. Pritchard's. It wasn't far and John was grateful that there was little time for conversation. Margaret, herself, didn't know what to say. She knew she needed more time, than the few minutes they had, to talk with John about the previous night and her selfish reaction, which had been so hurtful to him. Beyond her thoughts on that, she sensed something different about John. He was too quiet and not smiling at all. It felt like a shield had been placed between them.

When the housekeeper opened the door, John thought it was a family re-union as Margaret ran to Professor Pritchard. They hugged several times, kissed cheeks and both wanted to speak at the same time.

"Certainly, you two have much to say to each other." John said, as he observed their spontaneous greeting. I will leave for a time to go to the Merchant's Chamber. I have a meeting and a speech scheduled there for tonight. I shall only be gone a short while." As John departed, he realized that for some reason he was feeling nervous. He had never feared anything before, but now, Margaret's attitude was all too prevalent in his thoughts.

For the next half hour, Margaret and the Professor talked quite a bit about what the Professor was doing and how he was setting up the office. He inquired about her getting settled in and was surprised to find that she was still awaiting furnishings. He showed her through the two rooms that were to be the office, and asked if she would like her desk at the front window, but Margaret had no preference either way.

They talked about the books that were piled to the ceiling in the dining room and the carpenter that would soon arrive to build his custom bookshelves. He had worked out that he might be eating in the kitchen unless his office room could hold all of his work. At least he should be able to manage a small table, if his dining room had been turned into a library.

"Margaret, when you get a chance, could you come and organize the housekeeper and cook here. I am so used to the college's trained staff, that I don't know how to handle the outside world of housekeeping, yet." He laughed.

"Of course," Margaret assured him, "Dixon and I will come by tomorrow. We need to get them underway before Christmas arrives in a few days."

"Oh, is that here already?" the professor asked in all seriousness. "Margaret take a seat, will you please?"

Margaret sat.

"How goes your problem?" He smiled affectionately at her.

"Professor, I have had no time to give that any thought," she lied.

"Well, don't forget what I said about John. I am sure things will work out, however you want them to, and I hope it works out for him, too."

"What do you mean?" Margaret asked.

"Why the man has loved you for many years, since you met, I believe. Surely you know that at least?"

"How can you know that? You hardly know him." Margaret was puzzled.

"There is no doubt in my mind," the Professor continued, "he wears his love for you across his face like a badge of honor. His posture changes when you are around. That serious face, he's apparently always worn, is replaced by a gentle smile whenever you are in the room. You cannot see that?" The Professor laughed at his inane logic – how could she know his look when she wasn't there. "How did I know so much about you? You, yourself, commented on my insight. Let's just leave things the way they are and let nature takes its course. I just want you to find that real happiness and passion that goes with a good marriage."

"But . . . ," Margaret stopped in mid sentence as John opened the door to the office.

"Oh, we'll settle all that once you are here permanently," the Professor said, covering over their conversation. "So, what are your plans from here?"

Margaret turned and looked at John. "We are going to the cottage. Having just arrived yesterday, I haven't been in it since I was here last."

John nodded.

Margaret turned to the Professor and inquired about the two books that he'd wanted her to study to get a sense of his writing and documenting style.

"Margaret, don't trouble yourself now," he assured her. "You're going to be very busy. Just relax and if you find yourself with little to do until things start piling up on you, take the time to see Milton. I've seen drawings and plans from earlier years and the face of the original landscape can barely be recognized. The growth in only a few years time is nothing short of amazing. You two run along and only come back in the next few days to see to the staff here, otherwise, take care of your errands, and get settled. Do not worry about me. I won't need you until the end of January."

"Thank you for everything, Professor. I will catch you up very soon, then. Goodbye Professor," said Margaret as she kissed him on the cheek like a father.

John bid the Professor a 'good day'. He escorted her out to the carriage and handed her in, as the snow continued to come down heavier.

"Margaret," John began, as the carriage made its way to her cottage. "I'm going to introduce you to Adrian and there will be another chap from the mill at your cottage today, for additional muscle. Between Adrian and Danny, they can do heavy lifting or anything you desire. I know you'll see lots of things to be done. I will then get out of your way and let you have the day in your new home."

"You're not in the way. Why aren't you going to stay?" Margaret asked with some alarm in her voice.

"No, I don't see where you need me and I should prepare for my meeting tonight," John lied. "Branson! . . . Around back!"

Branson pulled the carriage around to the back entrance. Adrian came running to the coach and opened the door to hand down his new mistress. Margaret took his hand to exit the coach and then took his arm, steadying herself on the slippery surface as they walked to the back door.

"Thank you. You must be Adrian?"

"Yes, Miss."

"Would you bring Danny, I think his name is, and Branson into the house, for all around introductions?"

"Yes, Miss."

John followed Margaret into the house and waited to see what she had in mind by gathering them all together. As the three men filed through the door, John introduced Danny to everyone, then taking a cue from Margaret, proceeded to make introductions all round.

"Thank you, John. Cook, it's very nice to meet you, and I hope you're ready for us because I would like you to prepare a small lunch for five of us at 1:00, and that will include yourself. I think we can eat off this huge prep table here in the kitchen. Adrian and Danny, I would like you both to remain in the house until I have gone through it, but I am sure you will be inside all day." Margaret smiled. "John, are you sure you won't stay?

"I am sure." John said, rather abruptly. "What time would you like to be collected?"

A small shiver ran down Margaret's back as she picked up on the distinction between 'to be collected' rather than 'for me to collect you'. Something was definitely wrong. She assumed to know what it pertained to, yet at the same time she didn't like the distance that was growing between them.

"I guess Dixon and I will be ready by 5:00 this evening. If nothing else, we'll certainly be tired by then."

"5:00 o'clock, it is then." John turned to leave.

"John, could I speak with you a moment?"

146

"Certainly," John said, as he followed Margaret into her half empty parlor.

"John what is it, what is wrong? I don't like what I am feeling. I know it must be about last night. I need to talk with you."

"Nothing is wrong, Margaret. I just have some issues, I need to work out."

"Can we talk about them together?" Margaret prompted.

"I don't think so, not this time. I will not be having dinner at home tonight. I will be at the meeting. Perhaps, I will see you later this evening. I don't know how long the meeting will last. Branson will be here to collect you. Enjoy the day, Margaret."

Donning his hat and gloves, John called for Branson as he turned and walked away. He was nauseated by his deportment towards Margaret, but he didn't see any other way. He would wait forever, he had always known that, and right now he had to give Margaret space.

Margaret and company had a very active day and accomplished much: What furniture there was, got moved to their proper positions; carpets were rolled out, drapes hung, trunks unpacked and stored and books were shelved. She had her first visitor, Mr. Cavanaugh, the next door neighbor, who stopped by to greet her and wish her luck. He offered his assistance if she would need it, but finding no purchase, bid her 'good day'.

Branson arrived promptly at 5:00 o'clock that afternoon, and came to the door to escort the ladies to his coach. As they drove away that evening, Margaret thought that the house looked lonely and dark, easily reflecting her underlying mood of the day.

Arriving at John's home, the only person to meet them was Cook. Due to the deepening snow, Jane had gone home early. Margaret sat at the dinner table alone, while Dixon ate with Cook downstairs. It was too quiet, she thought. She wondered how John had endured the solitude since his mother passed away. Realizing that she had never lived alone, she thought it almost unbearable. Being hidden away in her London room was horrible, but it didn't compare to this feeling of absolute isolation. She could hardly fathom that John endured this, night after night; it wasn't like he would call Dixon for company, as she herself might do. He must be a very strong man inside, she thought, to sit alone every night, trying to keep his life going as he loved and waited for her, with no real hope, yet managing to run two mills successfully. She knew no other man that could have shouldered all of that under his emotional burden.

With the quiet time, she reflected on the previous evening's conversation. She had been rude and ultimately too forward with her question, and she stunned herself, when she knew why she did it. She had thought that someday she might lay with John in that bed and she wondered if he held memories, but she never anticipated speaking it aloud. All John did was answer her own inquisition and explained himself. Why did she really need to know anyway? Several possible explanations drifted to mind. First of all, there was the question itself. Perhaps it was a form of jealousy, an entirely new emotion for her, and one that is only borne from resentment to rivals. What an odd unsettling emotion it was. Reading the word was one thing, but the power behind experiencing the word came close to earth moving. Secondly, and, now, she didn't know what issue was larger, was the passionate promises he had made to her. How could she ever match her love for him as she was discovering the bottomless depths of his love for her? She had doubts about her own ability to ever love that deeply. From their conversation, she had realized that his need to touch her and kiss her, came from his purest, most basic love for her and not from some near celibate primitive male urge. She had never thought of John in that context before, being with other women. Without realizing it, he had exposed her to the boundaries of her own naivety. She still lived in a cloistered societal cage, oblivious to the real world, where such things were never discussed about, man to woman. She wanted to be a real woman and now here it was, staring her in the face and she had shied from it. All she could give John was her honesty and let him judge her weaknesses for himself.

In an attempt to change her own mood, she decided to write Edith and tell her all that had happened since they said goodbye at the station, omitting last night's debacle. She found Dixon and asked her for some writing paper. Dixon had taken the stationery to her new quarters, but told Margaret she was sure the Master kept some in his desk. Thanking her, Margaret momentarily debated about going through John's desk, but then assumed he wouldn't mind if she took a sheaf of paper.

As she went into his den, Margaret turned up the gas lights and sat at the broad walnut desk. She drew in John's scent. A couple of the drawers were locked; the center one was not. She opened it and found some blank sheaves of paper, but something caught her eye. Gently removing the small pile of written letters, she sighed as she gazed at the words 'Dearest Margaret' at the top of each one of the pages.

Chapter 14

 A Gentleman's Agreement

Margaret strolled over and closed the door to his library, wanting privacy, while she read the letters. "Why am I doing this?" she wondered. The boldness that seemed to come along with her new freedoms was starting to scare her.

Sitting down, she pulled out the little pile of letters from the drawer, all addressed to her. She noticed a mixture of dates and wondered why John had never sent them. Two were before their London meeting on the veranda and the rest were after that day. None of them were finished. Why had they lain in wait to be completed?

The ink on two of the earlier ones seemed to have been smeared, and she assumed this was the reason he had never sent them. But, as she began reading, she realized they had been wet with his tears and he had poured out his devastated life, and his need of her, with his pen and paper. Her eyes filled in spite of herself, adding additional tear stains to the inked words.

John Thornton, Look Back at Me

Dearest Margaret
. . . . that snowy day. . . . .
if you looked back. . . . . took my heart . . . .
. . . . alone with only memories . . . .
love you more than . . . . . . breath of my life . . . . able
to go on . . .

John's heart and soul had been wrung from his body onto those pages. Margaret lost herself in his words of love and emotional disaster. She wept, adding more of her own tears, to the words describing the desecration that she had caused in John's life.

The next two letters were equally forlorn, but showed a ray of hope. She remembered that day on the veranda when she discovered that there was more between them than she had realized before, but he, apparently, had known it for a very long time. He had written that he understood nothing could be done, and that she could not speak to anything, but he left that day, happy that she had come into his arms. He felt he could cope with a life based only on that one memory. Still, these letters spoke so much of his heart and his hopes, they would never have been sent. Continuing to weep, she sought out the last two.

The final letters, written after Booker's passing, showed a tempered joy, no tears, and much hope for the future with her. There were many references to his intimate and sensual desires, some of which she had heard about last night. She almost had to put them down, but she continued reading as she fidgeted in the chair. Margaret doubted these were ever meant to be sent, as he was speaking most passionately from his heart and body. She came across a strange reference to a *sign* from his mother. "Whatever could that mean, with his mother now being gone?"

Still thinking about John's strife, Margaret stowed the letters back where they came from and pulled out a sheaf of paper. Suddenly, he came through the door.

They looked at each other, startled, and Margaret wondered if the guilt was prevalent on her face.

151

"Good evening, John. I wasn't looking for you this early. I wanted to post a note to Edith; Dixon thought you had paper in your desk. I hope it was all right to take a piece."

"Yes, yes, of course. Take all you like. I'm sorry to disturb you. I thought you had retired, so I was coming to look for some correspondence that is stored in my filing cabinets. It's of no importance; I shall leave you to your letter. Would you like the fire lit?"

"No, thank you. I shall be brief in my writing."

John walked back to the parlor. He had sensed a stiffness in Margaret, and wondered why the closed door. That room was freezing with no fire lit. Feeling a bit uneasy, he picked up the partially read paper from this morning. Opening the pages, his mind elsewhere . . .

The letters! She must have found the letters.

John did not immediately know what to do about it. He never wanted her to know the catastrophe that had been his life without her. She might think him weak, but it was in every one of those letters. Why hadn't he destroyed them since learning of her return to Milton? As he heard her footsteps coming into the room, John began to pay more attention to his paper. Eventually, he looked over at Margaret's quiet form, sitting across the room from him. She was perched on the couch, looking a bit awkward, as though she wanted to speak, but didn't know how to begin.

"You look like you have something to say. Is anything bothering you, Margaret?" Now, he thought, was as good a time as any to discuss last night.

"Yes, there is John, but first I must summon my courage."

"Summon courage?" John thought. He was certain she was going to bring up the letters. Aside from the matter of harboring her brother when he was in the country and under an arrest warrant, which he, himself, never understood at the time, she was almost totally defenseless in the use of deception. But how was he to explain them, he wondered.

They sat in silence for a few more minutes, clearing throats and shifting in their seats, when John, not being able to wait any longer, said, "Margaret, if it's about the letters in my desk, you need no courage to summon. They should have been destroyed a month ago when I knew you were returning. I am quite ashamed and embarrassed for you to know the state of mind that I have been in since you left Milton. They do not matter. Those are all water under the bridge. They are just ramblings of a man who loved and lost. And the latter letters are the delusions of a man in love still, never for your eyes or anyone's but my own. They were like a catharsis for me; instead of reliving all those moments of hopes and dreams, putting them to paper helped me not dwell on my situation every minute." He could not bring himself to look directly at her.

"John, how can I apologize for looking at your private writings? I, too, am ashamed about what I did and I knew I had to speak to you right away, but I wanted to form my response with some thought. It was accidently done. I was looking for paper, but when I opened the drawer, I saw papers addressed 'Dearest Margaret' and I wondered why you had never sent them. I can understand the why in each one of them, now. I will not speak to the contents, but I want to talk with you about me . . . and you."

Silence was suspended in the room; the wait for Margaret to begin was almost intolerable for John. He had much to say tonight, himself.

"Foremost, let me say that I am sorrier than you will ever know, for the misery I have caused in your life. It's been devastating to read. I have never known of such love from one person to another as you expressed in those letters and last night. I didn't see, or know, of that depth with my parents, or in my own marriage, but I am slowly coming to know of it on my own. You and I have fought our own demons and were lost, but now, we may be found. My demons were self-imposed, and yours were also imposed by me - unforeseen circumstances and deception by my family - all of your private hell is on my shoulders.

"No, Margaret . . ." John tried to interrupt but Margaret continued.

"Please, John . . ." John sat back, but found himself gripping the claw carved hand rest on his chair, with white knuckles.

She cannot take all this blame. It is behind us, now.

"John, please forgive my intrusive question and abrupt conduct of last night. I am sure I surprised myself more than I did you. It was unforgivably rude of me. I laid awake most of the night thinking about our conversation, but came to some realizations while eating alone at your table this evening. Firstly, I asked the question and you gave me your honest answer. I've wondered why I asked it, it seemed to come out on its own. I think it was in my thoughts because I hope to be part of your life someday and I guess I wanted to know where the memories might be buried. As for your answer, because of your deep love for me, you felt compelled to explain yourself, and I think it was a conscious decision you made that ran very deep. It was a tremendous sacrifice you made and a risk you took for both of us, in admitting those intimate events, you knew would hurt me. But, you trusted me to see my way through all that hurt, coming out on the other side knowing you have experienced all in life and still you chose me, unknowing of the woman I may be.

She -did- understand.

"You did this because you wanted me to know all of you and have faith in your love for me. I am prostrate at your feet for the great trust you have placed in me to find my way through that, and for the confidence you knew I needed to recover."

John was soon going to need to be strapped down in order to keep from coming out his chair.

"That was not my only revelation that came out of last night, "Margaret continued. "When you talked about your passionate promises . . ."

Bolting out of his chair, John took to the center of the room, "Margaret, I must insist that you stop there."

"But . . ."

"No . . . please, no buts. I, too, have had a lot of thoughts and it relates in a way to that which you are about to speak."

"If you feel you must speak now John, then, by all means, go ahead."

"Please try to listen with your head and not your heart."

The moment was suspended as John paced the floor, running his fingers through his hair, endeavoring to form the hardest words of his life.

"Margaret, I have been very selfish. You know I love you, but that should only be my concern right now. Somehow, I've adopted the attitude that you are mine, or soon will be, and I have been very possessive in my thoughts, and maybe some of my actions. You have never discouraged my advances, but that isn't good enough. You have lived in innocence all of your life. You do not know the world outside your husband and me. I cannot be totally comfortable with your lack of discouragement to me, because you have had nothing to base my affections on, except for your marriage, which you know was never a real marriage of love. You are allowing me close, perhaps because of your touching naivety, or some obligation you may feel because of how I feel about you, or any number of other reasons. It may be love, but we don't know for sure, do we?"

"I think my heart does. John, I don't think I understand where you are going with this."

"I am going to step back and try not to insist myself upon you so quickly. As difficult as this is to say, I would like you to accept invitations from other gentlemen. I would want you to compare all of your suitors, so I know when you turn to me, that you do so with a confident heart. Just think about it, please. When I thought about those words I spoke last evening, as much as I wanted you to know my heart, I realized I was laying an encumbrance upon you. I don't want you to turn to me unless you have chosen me for the one you want to spend your life with, and how can you choose without choices? You must experience more of life. For my sake, use your mind and see all the way through this, to the other side, for both of us," John said, in a very agonizing but serious voice.

"John, I want to scream and yell and beat my fists against your chest, but if that's what it takes for you to be sure of my decision, then I will do it. I can understand you seeing it that way with my naivety, but I already know the result. I know where I'll be when I reach the other side. As much as I do not want to be put through this charade, I will accept other invitations, including yours - I will not let you step back that far. How will you handle my advancements to you? Am I allowed that?"

"Only in moderation, until you have spent time with other men." John replied, almost smiling now.

"Can the Professor count as one?" Margaret asked with that pouty face.

John, now laughing said, "No. Spending time with your father figure does not count toward experiences of the heart."

"You know John, I started out thinking of him as a father figure, but he is closer than that. Strange, but he's more like a close brother or sister to me, one who I can really open up to and talk about things that one would never speak to a parent, yet he has the intelligence and life experience to guide me, better than a parent, really."

"Margaret, I am glad you have such a confidant in your life. I've never had that, even with my Mother, and I envy you. Perhaps, someday your husband will take on that responsibility.

"Can I ask a final question?"

"Margaret, always know that you can. What is it?"

"In those letters in your drawer, there was a reference about your mother working on your behalf. What did that mean?"

156

"Margaret, that is for another time to explain, but I promise I will some day."

"So when does this game begin?"

"There is nothing like the present, I suppose, or whenever you feel you are passed your bereavement time, which I think should be about now." John said.

Margaret, breaking the tension that had saturated the air, presented her hand for a handshake. "We have a gentleman's agreement, then?" she asked.

John, smiling, took her hand and shook it, "I dare say it's better than pistols at dawn."

They both laughed. Every laugh between them was drawing them closer.

Chapter 15

Sacrificial Altar

As the evening grew late, they both said goodnight in the parlor and went their separate ways, with John striving to treat Margaret as a guest. Morning was much the same; casual conversation about Margaret's plans for the day and John being her ride and guide. A big part of her furniture was due today and she had promised to visit the Professor's staff with Dixon at her side. John was starting to realize how difficult it was going to be to step back from Margaret.

This was my idea and I'd better find a way to do it.

Outside, the snow had stopped, but nearly a foot had fallen overnight. The mill workers were pushing snow off the docks, trying to get stranded carts and wagons loaded with cotton bales, moved around the yard. While Dixon and Margaret were getting ready, John went off in search of Higgins to find out what was being done about other snow issues they had between the two mills.

Finding Higgins talking with the foreman about the snow, John asked about Mill 2. "I haven't gotten out there, yet, Master. I'm not sure what we're looking at in Mill 2. I've just now got most of the people here assigned to get the yard in passable order and get most of the looms up. I let the third shift go early so they could get home at least, shutting down the looms about midnight. It was the same thing at Mill 2."

"I'll take care of Mill 2, myself. You work here." John turned and walked away trying to step into footprints already made in the snow. He went around to the back of the house and found Branson, harnessing the carriage. "Branson, can two horses pull the smaller carriage in this deep snow?"

"Yes, sir, two horses for the small and four for the traveling one. What do you want me to do?"

"Hitch two horses to the smaller buggy. You'll be taking Miss Margaret and Dixon, first to the Professor's house and then to her home for the rest of the day. I'd like you to stay with them and bring them home when they wish. Also, saddle Aristotle for me. I need to get out to Mill 2."

"Yes, guv, right away."

Within 20 minutes, the smaller buggy and the saddled Aristotle were waiting in front of the house. John was busy, walking the yard to see what Higgins had in progress. He found everything was running as it should be for the emergency they had on their hands. Margaret and Dixon had come out of the house and were waiting on the porch, Margaret wondering about the saddled horse. Did John ride? John was nowhere to be seen, but Branson was up on the steps, in no time, explaining his instructions for the day.

"Where's Mr. Thornton?" Margaret asked of Branson.

"With this snow, Miss, he needs to check the operations of Mill 2. They shut down the machines last night so people could go home early, and this morning they are dealing with getting the yards cleared and passable. You have the smaller carriage today, because Mr. Thornton needed his horse to get over there. Who's first down the steps?" Branson asked, as he extended an arm in the air to assist them.

John made it to Mill 2, but it took twice as long reining Aristotle in a more sure-footed path. The foreman there had started to organize their snow efforts, but John knew he'd never been trained for this. He instructed him through all the phases of snow clearing. Certain procedures were usually done before others. John took the opportunity to walk the entire mill and talk with the workers, thanking them for making it to work today. He encouraged the foreman to make sure each worker received cups of hot tea today, and instructed him to feel free to offer such things whenever he felt it would help.

Dixon and Margaret made it to the Professor's home with little speed, themselves. Upon her arrival, Margaret set off for the kitchen. Dixon asked the Professor if he had any particular requests for his comfort, to which he replied he did not. She then headed for the staff to ensure they knew the basics and ask how they had been managing so far. Branson made himself useful and carried in some firewood, stacking all the grates and refilling the inside wood storage area.

Margaret asked the cook to prepare some tea and toast, while she sat and rested. She specifically did this to observe the cook's, speed, cleanliness, and thought process. All seemed well there. She talked with the Cook about portion control and the science of ordering meats and other foods. There should always be enough for unexpected guests, but only so much waste was allowed. The cook seemed to be way ahead of her and Margaret was grateful for that. Certifying that Dixon had done a good job in a cook selection, she went in search of the professor.

"I think you're fortunate with your cook. She is clean, there is little waste, and she seems to be able to handle a lot going on at once. My question is, 'how does her food taste'?"

"Quite adequate, I must say, Margaret. I did have some favorites from the college that, perhaps, someday we can get around to discussing, but mostly I am very satisfied."

"Do you have a moment to give me some advice, Professor?"

"Always, Margaret; what is it?"

160

Margaret settled into the chair closest to the Professor and acquainted him with the serious conversation she had with John the previous evening. "Do you think he's being fair?"

"Fair?" The Professor laughed. "What a word to be using when you are in love. I think you mean 'is he asking too much of you'; does that sound about right?"

"I don't think so. I think I mean . . . does he have the right to question my regard for him?" Margaret said.

"How do you feel about that?"

"I think he should . . . he should trust me to know my own heart."

"And do you?"

Margaret thought there was some underlying point to the question that the Professor had proposed to her. Curious as to his tone in the question, she stood and paced over to the big display window. The Professor sat back in his big desk chair and lit his pipe, watching the wheels turn in Margaret's head as she worked something through. "You're thinking about Booker, aren't you?" Margaret said. "Don't you consider that far different, though?"

"In some ways, yes, it was different, but not at its most basic level."

"I don't understand."

"Margaret, you found Booker when you were in a very depressed state. You had no one that loved you, or so you thought. You were lonely and unprotected, so to speak. You wanted a different environment than the London scene in which you were being encouraged to participate. He showed you love. You had very few, if any, close relationships with other men before him. I think unconsciously you married him to escape your lonely world. He showed you love, but he was not necessarily someone *you* loved. Have you never thought of this before?" the Professor questioned.

"To be honest, when our marriage started to quickly unravel, that was one place that I thought I should find blame in myself."

"Do you not see the same underlying naivety in this situation with John? He apparently does."

"Well . . . I am not sure I totally see your meaning." Margaret said, sitting back down.

"John is an extremely intelligent man. I give him a lot of credit for devising this -test- if you will. I know no man that would have the courage to do what he is doing."

"What *is* he doing, Professor?"

"He is forcing you to find your greatest possible happiness at a tremendous personal sacrifice to himself. He knows he could lose you, but he loves you more than his own life and wants you to find the love and passion that he feels you deserve, even if it isn't with him. John is surrendering his entire emotional being, preparing for complete and utter destruction of his life, should you turn from him, all for the sake of you choosing what your heart desires. He knows you have to experience more in life in order to compare him. As much as he loves you, he never wants to think you settled for him; that would be worse to his soul than if you walked away. It's so self sacrificing that books should be written about his courage. I can visualize the book cover. It shows a very dark, gothic gathering room from medieval times. The circular room and floor have carved and cast unknown glyphic figures all around. There is only a sliver of light passing through the thick walls from above. Hooded figures, like monks, are standing in a circle; John lies on the stone Sacrificial Altar in the center of the room. You are a dream over John's head, slightly hidden by a fog of clouds and in the arms of another man. There is a hooded figure, with a partially visible face, standing over him, holding a dagger with both hands, poised to plunge it into John's heart. What's makes the cover interesting, is that the hooded figure standing over him ... is himself. He sacrificed himself for you."

By this time, Margaret was crying; tears and moans - all her emotions - were unleashed.

"If you are mature enough, you must understand this with your head and not your heart, which is vastly difficult to do.

162

John wants you to make decisions based on your own feelings, with no regard for what he feels. And you must do that. Above all, be honest with him; he is basing everything on honesty, if you two are to be together. I truly believe it will happen. What woman couldn't love that man? He must be like candy to the ladies in the city, but you are the world he has chosen for his life, and he will wait forever, until you have decided. With what he has asked of you, I can see why Milton is where it is today: a man of such deep convictions is at the core of its growth."

"Oh Professor, it's all so overwhelming."

"It is powerfully overwhelming for both of you. Only this once, try to see what he is going through. It's going to be hell on earth for him to get through. When you were newly in love with Booker, not married, but might see him out with another woman, how would you have felt? Well . . . take that imaginary emotion and multiply it by a thousand. Only look into that once, and then dismiss it, as John would not have you turn to him in pity. That would be spitting in his face, and he seems like a man that has always protected his self respect."

"As usual, you have opened my eyes," Margaret said, still crying. "I do think I am still naive, but not so much as I once was. Based upon what you have said, I am quite prepared to take your advice. Before I make another mistake in selecting the person I want to spend my life with, I need to have choices, even though my heart has already chosen. I hate the thought of going through this, but I will agree to what is being asked of me."

"Will the two of you be allowed to see each other, like you would with another man? Frankly, Margaret, after John waiting for you this long, I don't see him staying away from you for any length of time, as he thinks he can. His passion will eventually dominate his keen mind. But just the mere thought that he is willing to try this, for your sake, is beyond any emotion I've ever seen of one person for another - whether it works or not."

"He says he wants to step back and let my feelings develop slowly and naturally for him, but I won't allow him to step back as far as he thinks he should."

Margaret walked around the Professor's desk and hugged him around his neck. "Thank you," she whispered. "I am quite fortunate having you to guide me through these difficult times in my life. I'm more grateful than I can say. I must get on with my work at the cottage. I will see you soon."

Branson reined Margaret and Dixon safely to her home. He pulled around to the carriage house in the rear and was escorting Margaret in when she noticed a small sign, now covered with snow, over her back door. Puzzled, she said aloud, "I wonder what that sign says."

"Oh, I know what it says, Miss. The Master had me nail it up. It says, 'Margaret's Enchanted Cottage'.

Margaret's eyes misted over. She hurried into the house before they could freeze on her face. *Stepping back, is he? I don't think I can let that happen,* she thought.

Adrian arrived at the carriage and assisted Dixon up the back steps. He was glad to get inside and get the fires started. The house felt like ice. Margaret talked with Adrian about his experience with horse and carts, and asked if she should purchase one. He was very well acquitted with all of that, he told Miss Margaret. Mr. Thornton had inquired into his experience before he was hired. She would have to speak with Mr. Thornton, though, on how one went about selecting and purchasing such a responsibility.

"I don't know what you are used to where you live, but there is small living quarters over the carriage house. You would be welcome to live here on the property, if that would suit you. I know I would feel somewhat safer with a man on the premises, but, please, don't let that influence you. You would have all kitchen privileges and the use of the downstairs lavatory. But I would certainly understand if you wanted to stay with your friends.

"Miss, I would be glad to come to this property to live. I would enjoy living here, alone, and feel honored to protect you

164

and the property. I can say that living among young children is something I would rather do without," Adrian laughed.

Margaret smiled, saying, "Very good, then. Check the quarters for repairs, or other necessities it needs to be habitable, and let me know what you need. Once you are comfortable with it, you can move in."

"Thank you, Miss."

Margaret and Dixon still found plenty to occupy themselves. The day moved along happily until someone pounded the front door knocker. Dixon answered it and brought back the note, hand delivered by a young child, to Miss Margaret.

Mr. Thornton,
I am sorry to say that we will be unable to deliver the furnishings until after Christmas. With the weight of the wood pieces, we know our wagon cannot make it through this deep snow. It will take a couple days for the snow to melt and that brings us to Christmas Holiday. Please excuse us for being delayed. Jason Hughes, carpenter.

Margaret's initial reaction was disappointment, but upon further reflection, she wasn't all that anxious now to leave John's home. Perhaps, this was a blessing after all, she thought.

By late afternoon, Adrian had the new gas heat flowing throughout the house. The gas heat would be used during the day with additional fires lit for overnight. With that worry settled, Branson returned Margaret and Dixon to the Thornton home, leaving Adrian bunked on the carpeted floor that evening, to ensure he had learned all he needed to know about the heating system.

When Margaret arrived at the Thornton home, the table was set for two. John was in his library studying invoices, it appeared. Margaret wondered if he ever relaxed. She doubted that he did. Relaxing allowed your mind to wander, and where would his wander? Judging by the letters in his drawer, it would have been to his own heartbreak. She walked over to the door, peaked in, and said, "Good evening, John"

John stood. "I'm sorry; I didn't hear you come in. I haven't been home long myself. It's been quite a day out there. I'm sorry I didn't come with you today."

As she stood looking at him, Margaret couldn't get the book cover out of her mind. She realized she was staring at a man who was martyring himself for her love. Stepping into the room, she closed the door behind her and rested against it. John was saying something but stopped when he noticed she had closed the door and was far away, as she often was, he assumed, just lost in her thoughts and dreams.

When she closed the door, he became worried that some unpleasant conversation was about to be broached. She hadn't spoken for several minutes. Had she come to some decision he wouldn't want to hear? As he was about to come from around his desk, Margaret snapped back into reality.

"I'm sorry, John, just dreaming."

Now, still wondering why she had closed the door, he began to approach her, but she walked towards him. She pushed his chest lightly, encouraging him to step back. Again, she pushed, causing him to fall into his desk chair. She looked down at him. John had never seen this face on her. "What was it?" he asked himself.

Margaret, still in her daydream, somewhat, put her hands to his face. This made John smile, but still he was distracted. Putting her hands on his shoulders, Margaret turned slightly and lowered herself to his lap. John, inwardly glorified whatever this was, now, and put his arms around her waist, drawing her close to his chest. She rested her head on his shoulder, as she encircled his neck with her arms.

John rubbed his hand up and down her back, soothing her. "I love this moment, but Margaret, is anything wrong?"

"No, I just wanted to thank you," Margaret said softly, picturing him on a sacrificial altar.

"Thank me all you want, if this is how you do it, but thank me for what?"

"For loving me, John," was all Margaret could say.

John was quiet for several moments, allowing those words to hang in the air. "Margaret, please don't thank me for loving you. There is no effort here; I can't even help myself. I've had several years of trying to stop loving you, but it only became stronger. At this moment, I do need restraint if we are to keep to the gentlemanly rules."

Sighing, Margaret quietly got to her feet, slowly coming out of her visual mood of the sacrifice.

They walked out of his room and into the parlor. "Did your furniture arrive today?" he asked, while indicating the couch to sit on, as he went to the bar. "You look like you could use something to warm your toes."

"Thank you. I think I will have a sherry for now and maybe a brandy after dinner." Margaret said, as she sat on the couch with her feet tucked under her bottom for warmth. "I've had some good news and bad news today. The bad news is that my furniture did not arrive."

She paused, waiting for John to ask the next question.

"Margaret, that is disappointing news for you, I'm sure. What happened to the delivery, and what is the good news?"

"It seems that because of the deep snow, the carpenter cannot deliver until after Christmas Day if the snow has gone away. So, I must beg a few more days of your hospitality."

"Oh, I see. And that is the good news for you, is it?" John asked with a beaming smile on his face.

"Well, it is now, since I will not see you as often as I should like, after last night's proclamation," Margaret said with sarcastic amusement.

John became excited at the thought of being missed by Margaret. There might be a silver lining to all this.

"John?"

"Yes, dear friend?" John said jokingly, pouring her drink.

"John Thornton, stop that right now! You are not backing up that much, even if I have to throw my arms around your leg and hold tight to keep you from stepping back too far."

Sensing fun ahead, John said, "Yes, Margaret?"

"Tell me about your horses," Margaret inquired, "I never knew you to ride a horse."

Crossing the room and handing Margaret her sherry, John proceeded. "When I was a very young lad, before father left us, I had a friend who had horses. He would often let me ride with him. I vowed twenty some years ago, that someday, I would have one. With the second Mill coming, the money was good and I needed some regular transportation. I looked a long time to find two matched pair of horses, but they had to sit a man as well as pull a coach, in tandem. Then I found Branson and his knowledge was of great value to me. I've been fortunate in that investment. Someday I hope to teach you to ride, if you would like that." John finally settled on the couch with Margaret, although not as close as he would have liked.

"I think I should like that very much," Margaret said. "What are the names of your horses?

Smiling, John said, "I have Plato, Aristotle, Arkwright, and Cotton. Plato and Aristotle are a matched set, as are Arkwright and Cotton. Cotton is very gentle and will be your horse if you will have her."

"John, those names sound so John Thornton of you." Margaret laughed. "I have another question."

"Hmm . . ?" John said, smiling at her as he sipped his scotch.

"Since I will be here for the holiday, can we have a Christmas tree to decorate?"

"Yes, if you wish. I'm afraid I don't have anything to hang on it. I'm not sure this house has ever had a tree. Tomorrow we will search for a tree, and find something to hang on it. Then, perhaps, you would like to accompany me on Christmas Eve to both mills and spread cheer at the canteens?"

"Oh yes, John, I would love to do that with you. I am interested to see how your mill works. As you might remember, my first and only visit inside was unpleasant for both of us."

John, knowing this would be the best Christmas in his life, thought about making it even brighter for them. "Since you will not be in your cottage by Christmas Day, would you like to have the Professor, and Higgins, his fiancé and Mary over for Christmas dinner? We could make it a festive Christmas Dinner."

"What a wonderful idea, John. Can we really do that? And I could bring Cook and Adrian to have dinner below stairs with your Cook, Jane, Dixon, and Branson?"

"Maybe we should also invite Branson's lady friend, or he might not be here. I hate to think of Adrian left to all those women," John laughed. "This is turning into an amazing Christmas for me, Margaret," he said humbly, looking down into his glass.

Dixon came into the room, and announced dinner was served.

John seated Margaret at the table. Both were smiling because there was no loneliness tonight. Passed, were the two confrontational nights; the air had been cleared and now it had a sense of holiday spirit. As they ate, it seemed both were holding back smiles; deep inside, each hiding from the other a very real warm feeling of contentment. Even with what lay ahead for both of them, the season was working its miracle, lighting a glow inside their hearts. John had only one concern, how to keep from getting too close to Margaret. The last two nights, going to bed without so much as embracing her, had left him wanting the touch of her, more than he should.

As they sat down to a brandy after dinner, John in his big chair stretched out by the fire and Margaret on the carpeted floor, near his feet, they talked about the day. John looked down at his feet, where Margaret sat, watching her stare into the flames. The reflected shadows of the fire light danced across her porcelain skin. He loudly sucked his breath in through his teeth at the stunning image it was invoking. Margaret looked up at John, bestowing a smile that would have stolen his heart, had it not already belonged to her.

I will make love to her soon, here, by firelight.

"John, do you know Mr. Cavanaugh?"

"Yes, he's done some work for me and just recently, too. We pass in the hall at the courthouse, often. He's a lawyer in Property, Deeds, and Titles. Why do you ask?"

"What do you think of him?

"I guess I've never thought about him that much. He's a gentleman, polite, well spoken, a little quiet, I think. I repeat, why do you ask?"

Margaret told John about meeting him on the train with the Professor, twice, and that he had stopped in from his office next door to welcome her and wish her luck. "He said he knew you through his work. I think he likes me a little more than I am comfortable with." Margaret said, looking away as though she had a guilty conscience.

"Margaret, that interest is something you need to experience like I've begun to tell you. You are going to find gentlemen flocking to your door. Many will vie for your affections, be certain of that. I will be in that line, waiting at your door, too." John noticed Margaret's face took on a sullen expression as she turned it to the fire once more. Neither of them wanted to proceed any further with that conversation, suspecting it would dampen their glow.

"I asked Adrian if he wanted to move into the quarters over the carriage house, and he seemed delighted at the prospect. I think I'll feel comforted with him there. He's also going to stay in the house until I move in, to keep the gas lit."

"Good. I am glad to hear it. I like Adrian, and I like the thought of him being there, too. We'll need to stop by there tomorrow and ask him and your Cook for dinner. What do you think of some of the cotton fluff for decorating the tree, like it has snow?"

"John. I love that idea. I've also thought we could find some cranberries and string them for garland and maybe a little holly for garland across the mantle and a table centerpiece. And then there is the mistletoe, I must insist upon it."

"I'm not sure the mistletoe is such a good idea right now. You're going to kill me if you put that up somewhere," John happily lied, hoping she would not heed him.

John knew all too well, that he would kiss her tomorrow night or go mad.

Chapter 16

 *A Sensual Moment*

Margaret woke with a start, suddenly conscious of the fact that she didn't have a holiday gift for John. She didn't have anything for anyone. She was sure it wasn't expected of her this year, but she must talk to John to ensure he wasn't going to purchase a gift for her.

Finding him dressed for the day, already reading his paper, Margaret said, "John, I want to talk about gift exchanging. I know there is a Thornton Proclamation in effect, but I would have liked to have gotten you a small gift, but I haven't had time. Please tell me you are not going to purchase anything for me."

"I cannot promise that, because the first thing we will do this morning is to procure a pair of snow boots for you, unless you have some at your home."

"Why, yes, John. I do. We'll visit my home first and talk with Adrian. And I've realized another person we forgot to invite, Mr. Granger, Dixon's gentleman. Maybe she should be given this evening to visit him. Could Branson take her over to see him tonight?"

"Yes, if she'd like that, it is fine with me for the carriage use. How many would that make below stairs if everyone attends? We may have to find a second goose today.

Margaret started prattling off the names, flipping her fingers in the counting. "Let's see, two Cooks, two Housekeepers, two Drivers/Chore men, Mr. Granger, and Branson's lady friend. That's eight below stairs. Upstairs, we'll have . . . let me think . . . six. Dear me, that is 14 people for dinner and your cook was probably only expecting 3 or 4. I'll go talk with her, now, and ask what she might need in the way of food." Margaret disappeared down the stairs before John could tell her where he was about to go.

John waited, putting the day together in his mind. They would be at Margaret's home, and the Professors; they needed to purchase the liquors, along with the tree and trimmings. He went to the back stairs and hollered to Margaret that he was going to get Branson started and talk to Nicholas about the invitation. "I shall return shortly."

The day progressed easily even in the deep snow. Jane was the only one to decline her invitation, as she was expected at her family's this year. Nicholas was excited to have Margaret and Peggy together. He knew they would fit well as good friends. The Professor tried to beg off, but when he realized that his own Cook would not be cooking for him that day, he acquiesced. A second goose was located, and a box of assorted liquors and a box of champagne were purchased; that left only the tree, cranberries, holly, and mistletoe. John told Branson to drive around until he found some street merchants selling the holiday greenery. He wasn't about to go tree chopping. John reached for Margaret's gloved hand. He massaged her fingers and then pulled her hand to his face and kissed the underside of her wrist, forgetting himself. Startled at what he was doing, he said, "I'm just getting a head start on the other gentlemen. We'll have an early dinner when we get home. I'll have Branson mount the tree and bring it inside with the other greenery and the liquor. I guess we can leave the goose in the stable overnight. While he's doing that, we can walk to the mill and get the cotton snow."

"John, I'm so excited. It all feels so contented and homey. It feels so right. I've had a wonderful day today and am looking forward to decorating the tree with you tonight. Do you keep any old lamp parts around?"

Puzzled, John said, "I think there might be a box of assorted pieces in the back cellar. What are we looking for now?"

"It's possible you have saved some of the crystal prisms that hang from chandeliers. They would catch the light from the fireplace and almost twinkle."

"I do remember seeing some of those. I don't know how many, but we'll use all we find. They'll need washing, I suspect." John was carried away by the day, being able to share this holiday with his beloved. They would be married by this time next year, he hoped.

She said the words – "It all feels so contented and homey. It feels so right." That is the best gift I can receive.

John and Margaret arrived home and walked over to the mill, instead of taking dinner, while they were still dressed for the cold. As she walked into the mill office, Margaret couldn't help but reminisce about her only other time there. Seeing the white cotton waste hang and drift through the air had been beautiful, almost as inspiring as her first impression of John, standing tall in his black coat as he oversaw the workers. He was truly a vision at first glimpse that day. But the image had faded quickly when she saw John administer his own form of discipline to a worker that had lit a flame in a combustible area. That was the beginning of her misgivings towards him; a day she came to regret. It took time for her to be convinced that he had been right in his actions.

"All right, we are here. Just stay by me. I am going to take you up on 'the cat walk', so you can see the whole operation from a high, safe area. Everyone will look at you and me, but I know you are not shy." John laughed. He paused, wondering if he should take her hand. Rolling the wide door open, he hadn't made a decision.

"John, it's positively beautiful," she whispered. John handed her his handkerchief to cover her mouth and nose as they stepped through the door. "I'm sure you don't see it that way anymore. If it wasn't for the noise, I would think I was in a fairytale."

John had to lean down to hear what she was saying. For no other reason than safety, he grabbed her by the hand and pulled her down the narrow aisle and up the six steps to the cat walk. He released her hand. Immediately, he turned his attention to Margaret, wanting the time to study her initial reactions. She was fascinated. He knew they would need another time when he could give her a good deal of information about everything. He leaned in to her ear. "This has been my life and livelihood for many years. My wife will be part of this, too." John could barely be heard over the noise.

Turning to him, Margaret smiled with her eyes, and still holding the cloth to her face, she said, "I think I shall love being part of this."

He hadn't expected that. John felt his knees buckle beneath him as he had to catch his own weight on the hand railing. The room was as noisy as it always had been, but he was sure he heard what she had said. He couldn't dare ask her to repeat it, but he smiled broadly, as her attention was elsewhere. "How can she say something like that and then go on as if nothing had been said?" John wondered. He started to doubt that he heard what he thought he did.

She would love being part of this. Could she really have said that?

They spent a few minutes as Margaret pointed and asked John questions, all the while the whole workforce was watching. John felt so proud inside, showing off his lady to them. He had never brought another female acquaintance into this first room, or any of the mill sheds. John left her on the cat walk, while he walked the main aisle to retrieve a hemp bag of the cotton waste. Margaret thought him almost majestic, as she watched the sight of her tall John striding down through the floating cotton. The workers nodded as he passed, offering their greetings. John was like a God to them. They all smiled when he neared. He stopped to talk with someone in charge and then proceeded down to the end of the room. To think that he provided all these people with safe work, enabling them to live, eat, and raise families, was a hard thing for Margaret to take in. Returning to the cat walk, John motioned her towards the steps and handed her down to the floor. Still clutching her hand and the bag, he led her out, leaving the noise behind them.

"They are in awe of you John, as am I." Margaret said, returning his handkerchief.

"You? After my confession, followed by my proclamation, you can still say that?" John smiled.

With a serious face, Margaret continued, "Don't laugh at me. I mean what I say. I looked over the . . . what . . . fifty people in there and thought about how you provide sustenance for these people and their families. How many people work for you?"

"Close to 800, I believe."

"What? 800? Really, 800 people work for you? I am most astonished. How many other mill owners have that many people working for them?"

"No other; I am the only one. I am in the planning stages of buying a third mill, possibly, which would add another 350."

Margaret was beyond stunned, never having had any idea of the amount of his responsibility. All of a sudden, she felt so very small and inconsequential. For the first time, she had self doubts about whether or not she was good enough for him.

She was perplexed as to how her attitude had so radically shifted in an instant. She was once so sure of the reverse of that emotion, years ago.

"Let us go eat and decorate our tree." John said, embarrassed that he was sensing some unmerited esteem emanating from her.

Our tree. Margaret liked the sound of that.

Dixon was in the kitchen helping Cook wash the dinner dishes, waiting for Branson to take her to see Mr. Granger, when Branson came through the back door with a tall Christmas tree. "Oh goody," she said, like a school girl. "Look, Cook, a tree to decorate. I guess Miss Margaret and the Master are going to do that this evening. I think it's wonderful that they are getting along so well, so quickly."

John was down the backstairs next, heading into a back room. Returning, he handed Dixon a box of prisms and asked her to wash them and bring them upstairs when she was done. Taking two steps at a time, he was back standing next to Margaret. The other furniture had been moved around the room and they stood and gazed at the naked tree, sitting in a corner by the fireplace.

"Where do we start?" John asked, as he looked over the shape of the tree. He turned it several times and stepped back, trying to get the straightest and fullest look possible.

"I guess we don't have anything for the top, but that's all right," Margaret replied. "We will not put any candles on it, either, like some families do. With the cotton, it would not work, and I like the cotton better anyway. So, we start stringing the cranberries first. Next will be the cotton snow, followed by the prisms. Is there a sewing basket in the house?"

John thought he remembered one over in the buffet in the dining room. "Yes, it's still here," he said, walking over to retrieve it.

Handing it to Margaret, she removed what she needed and proceeded to show John how the strings were made, and then attached. During the cranberry garland construction hour,

Branson had brought up the other greenery and Dixon brought the prisms. The pair left, saying goodnight as they disappeared down the back steps to the kitchen.

With garland strewn in swags about the boughs, they pulled out the cotton snow next. Margaret taught John how to make nice little tufts on the branches to make it look like piled snow, then she tried to see how much fluff she could pile on his head before he felt it. John decorated the top branches, and Margaret decorated John until he discovered what she was up to. He grabbed her around her waist playfully, pinning her arms down, and then stepped back. They both encountered an uneasy moment as the merriment had stalled.

Margaret brought over the clean crystal prisms handing them to John. "Since you are the tall one, you hang them and I'll tell you where. We want it to have a balanced look."

The prisms were spectacular, a menagerie of long, and short, pointed or tear dropped shapes of cut or faceted glass that refracted the firelight around the room. Looking like moving stars in the sky, Margaret watched the room evolve into the heavens as John placed them. After a half hour of 'little more to the left and right', the tree was done. They turned to each other and smiled, proud of their creation. John held her around her waist and pulled her back to get a full view of their handiwork. The white snow really enhanced the tree in its dark corner, while the constellation exhibition overhead on the dark ceiling walls danced and held them breathless.

John was on the verge of losing himself until he looked over at Margaret and saw her glassy eyes, too. Turning her to look at their tree, he stood behind her, wrapping his strong arms around her and resting his chin lightly upon her head. No words needed to be said as they both got caught up in this uninhibited moment of contentment. Their mirrored emotions took root and Margaret turned in his arms to face him. John looked down into her fire lit face as she lifted her hands against his shoulders, encouraging him forward.

"Unless you say no, I am going to kiss you, Margaret."

178

John pulled back slightly to look into her eyes for his answer. He took her head in his hands and instinctively brushed his lips lightly over hers, letting her respond in her own measure. Margaret reacted softly in a return kiss, allowing his lips to find more firmness. The taste of his lips and breath stirred within her, and she was intoxicated by his tenderness and warm body, now moving against hers. She parted her lips to taste more of him, and that was all the encouragement that John needed. Holding her fast, he let his tongue glide across her lips, savoring her flavor. He deepened his kiss by slipping his tongue into her parted lips. It prowled hungrily, sweetly, wantonly, until he was certain that she felt he had a right to be there. Stealing her naiveté, he could feel when she was momentarily startled and then relented, accepting him, yielding her innocence.

Margaret shivered with delight, surprised at the sensation she felt as his tongue searched her mouth lightly and then he began probing her depths. She moaned quietly. The sensual kisses continued with Margaret participating more until she slipped her tongue through his lips. He took her tongue and suckled it lightly, not wanting to let her have it back, which elicited a moan from each of them. Margaret knew that Booker's bland kisses were like soft rain compared to John's delicious storm. Booker kissed lightly with his lips; John kissed with his entire body. This was love.

John knew he was dangerously close to the most intimate of acts and he eased back, exacting every bit of his control. Margaret became well aware that this new experience, would lead to other things. Their runaway passion could ignite, and she welcomed the forbearance that he showed.

"John?"

"Yes, Margaret," John whispered.

"I have never been kissed like that. I feel dizzy from the sweet pleasure of it. I can even feel . . ." but she paused realizing where she was headed.

Where were these words coming from that suddenly wanted to spring from her mouth when she was with John?

"Margaret, I know how and where you can feel it, it's the same for us, both. I've waited for this, for us. You can't know how I have been turned inside out, thinking of someone else giving you these pleasures. I am overcome, as a man, knowing I, most likely, will be the one to dispatch you to another place, another sphere of existence. I want to kiss you like that all over, every centimeter of you. I want to kiss you forever, but I think we should return to our tree or I will carry this too far. I think I'm doing a fine job of backing away, don't you?" John said laughing sarcastically.

John went to his chair by the fire to study their tree. Margaret walked over to him and sat on his lap, putting her arms around his neck and snuggling her head on his shoulder. Not looking at him, she said, "Thank you, John."

As he held her and kissed her softly at the top of her forehead, he asked, "You're thanking me again; what for? Margaret, you never need to thank me."

"I am just having a weak moment. I am finding a new depth of my ability for love. It is for you John, and I was thinking how different it is from my past. I need your closeness. I have been so adrift. Regardless of your edict, I know that you are by my side; your sheltering arms are there to pull me in, should I need it; I will dare to be free of the ghosts that have haunted me these past years. I'll no longer feel that I cannot come to you for fear of you expecting more from me, right now. I recognize your passion is being held at bay, because you are a gentleman and want me to be sure of myself. I thank you for that. I'm sure it's costing you all your reserve, but still I thank you."

John continued to hold her tightly, rubbing her back and kissing her temple. "Margaret, all will be right someday, and to me every minute with you is perfect, no matter the cost. Have you forgotten I am your guardian angel, that you once thought me? Please, just let me always comfort you at your difficult times . . . reach out to me. And I do know that you will be the woman, and have the life that you want someday, which will include loving me. I know this in my heart. You are my woman, Margaret. And I know this from a higher authority, too." John smiled.

"Margaret shifted on his lap, looking more into his face. I think you have been in my heart a lot longer than I knew. Having been only briefly married, that day on the veranda, when you stood to leave, I thought, *'I can never be closer to him than I am right now'*. I could not accept that. That frightened me, not knowing where that emotion was coming from, and what I would do with it when you left. I needed to spend it, or carry it forever. Already, I thought myself a failure in my marriage and thinking of you just added to my guilt."

John held her tightly and kissed her from her ear lobes, lightly down her creamy neck to the top of her breasts. Margaret pulled him closer to her, enjoying this most intimate sensation. Margaret became quite aware of John's own intimate sensation. Before she could rise from his lap, he lifted his head and covered her mouth again with his probing tongue, causing deep moans from both of them. He pulled his tongue from her mouth and let it slide down to the hollow of her neck, kissing and licking there. Margaret put her hands in his hair and pulled his head lower, allowing him to taste the swell of her breasts. She could feel the sweat in his damp hair, and knew his control was straining him. She knew John wanted to remain there, stroking the deep curves of her cleavage with his tongue, as she herself wanted . . . but she must find the strength to put a stop to it now. These sensations were all so new. She was so lost in his love; she didn't know what she should be doing. She pulled his hair back until he raised his face to her, and she kissed him lightly, signaling it was over. She rose to her feet, and swept her hand under his chin, forcing him to look higher, into her eyes. She bent and kissed his eyes closed and then walked to her room, shaking.

Margaret sat on the edge of her bed, feeling the heat settle in her tender areas. "Oh, dear God, how naive I really am.

181

How can I be this age, previously married, educated, and not know that such deep sensations even existed, forgetting experienced?" She realized it for what it was. The passion of loving someone . . . no, not someone . . . the passion of loving John. When John said he loved her beyond all reason, she felt she could now understand what that meant. She readied for bed, thinking of all the years that John had carried this same love for her with no hope. Margaret cried herself to sleep, plagued by John's misery, which both John and the Professor had told her not to dwell on.

John continued to sit in his chair looking down, replaying the moment. She had come to him. He raised his hands to see how badly he was shaking, never having felt like this before. His pulse was racing and his heart felt like a wild bird, trapped, banging itself on the sides of its cage, trying to escape. He had never needed control with other women. He knew loving every exquisite moment with Margaret was going to be agonizing pleasure. These passionate encounters would eventually take a toll on him if he had many more like this one. But he would take them all and damn the toll.

He banked the fire, turned out the lights, and sat in the dark for another hour. His body finally subsided, and he wondered how he would get through the next couple of days with Margaret being so close.

Chapter 17

 Christmas Eve Day and Night

The first rays of the sun were glistening off of the re-frozen snow crust. Christmas Eve day dawned brightly with no apologies or explanations or new edicts expected. Coming out of her room, Margaret inhaled a wonderful pine scent, and found John standing in front of the tree. He was looking at the cranberry strands, which now stood out as red swags, in the sunlit room. She watched him as he leaned against the back of a chair, long legs crossed at the ankles, arms folded, looking at the tree without knowledge of her presence. Margaret knew she was seeing him in an unguarded moment. Her heart raced.

"Good morning John," she said, startling him slightly, "do you see something wrong with our tree?"

"Good morning. I was looking at the cranberries, which make the tree look nice with the light of day, and wondering what to put at the top." John was partially lying; he already knew what he was going to put there. "Are you excited about today, visiting the mills and talking among the workers?"

"I doubt I'll be talking all that much. I'll be a strange face to them, but I shall enjoy it all the same. Good morning Dixon."

"Good morning Miss. I see you and the Master did a right nice job on that tree. I love coming upstairs to the smell of pine. It makes it cheery."

"How is it below stairs?

"It's already busy. The Master's Cook is discussing food preparation and timing with our Cook. Cooking for six above and seven below stairs is a challenge they are both eager to do. There's a lot of laughing; they must have the cooking sherry hidden someplace down there because they sure have the holiday spirit, as I think we all do," Dixon laughed. "And they're dragging poor Branson in on the serving tomorrow. He's just hauled in the huge goose, and they are uncertain how to fit two large birds in the oven."

Margaret replied, "That sounds wonderful. Be sure that Adrian is worked into your plans, as well."

John escorted Margaret to the breakfast table and seated her, saying, "Yes. Branson needs to pick him up early."

As they sat down to eat, Margaret suddenly remembered Nicholas's children. "What about Nicholas' children tomorrow?"

"I've discussed that with him. They will have their Christmas dinner tonight and arrive a little later tomorrow, allowing time for gifts to be opened. I am pleased that Higgins' ability to give to them has grown through his hard work for me. I truly am appreciative of that day you sent him to me. As for today's plans, normally there are three shifts working around the clock, except for Sunday. Tomorrow they will all be off, and today's work is a bit different, with each shift working for four hours instead of eight, with the last one ending at 2:00 p.m. Hopefully, today you and I can catch two shifts as they change, because the night shift left two hours ago. Do you need anything from your home today that can't wait a couple more days?"

"Yes, John. I need some fresh clothes. Can I take a bath here?"

"Can you!! . . . ?" John said, raising his eyebrows in mock excitement. "I'm sorry," he said, laughing, "I'm afraid a little mischievous spirit imp has invaded my senses today."

Margaret burst out laughing, unable to hide her own joy of this holiday. Yesterday and last night, she had turned a definite corner in her life. She was positive that she wanted to spend the rest of her life with John. She was getting to know a John that probably no one had ever seen, and more likely, not John, himself. Had he ever been a happy person? Thinking about what she knew of his past, she didn't believe he ever was. He'd had a young life full of terrible hardships, then there was the toil and strife of managing the mills and her absence from his life, some of which she read about in those dark letters in his desk. No, he had never known happiness, and now he was happy . . . more than happy... and she was, too. She knew he was caring, intelligent, honest, and loving, but Margaret was reveling in the humor she found he possessed. What new delights still awaited her, she wondered? He was amazing her at every turn. She realized she'd never really known this John Thornton, and she loved every moment of him. How could she possibly go on with his proclamation? But she promised she'd try.

"Margaret?" John said, laying his hand on her arm. "You're off in that strange land where you go so often. I've noticed this several times. Where is this place in your mind?"

Embarrassed about drifting off, she said, "Oh, I have several lands. Mostly, I put to shore on my Hopes and Dreams Island, my favorite place. There are other islands, too. There is Rocky Island, which is my least favorite; I was stranded there for a long time."

"And just now, which island was that?"

"I was on my Reality Island. That is a newly charted island for me. I am spending a lot of time there, lately. But last night," Margaret began with a smile, "I glimpsed an entirely new land on the horizon; I think I am going to name it Passion Island."

John looked at Margaret, loving her little islands. "Margaret, I am your safe harbor; when you are in a storm, sail to me. You can always find me on Passion Island, waiting for you."

"John, don't start with those loving words," Margaret said. "You'll have me crying before the day begins."

And she smiled."Aye, me matey, Captain Thornton, at your service." John saluted her.

Laughing again, they both discovered another moment, birthed from humor, as each recognized it as a new experience in their lives. Every laugh seemed to tie the bindings tighter.

"Captain, is it? We'll see about that!" The laughter continued, as John dwelled in the sparkle of her eyes.

"John, did we forget to invite Fanny and her husband? It would be so awful to overlook them."

"As much as I love our intended guest list, I did talk with Watson and they are headed away for the Holiday; so, relieve your mind there."

Branson brought around the smaller two-horse carriage, and the day began at Margaret's. Adrian was outside chopping wood, but he had a banked fire inside, keeping away the coldness. Branson came down from his box, and after opening his master's door, he went around the other side of the carriage house to talk with Adrian. John handed Margaret out and up the slick back steps and followed behind. He stopped in the dining room, watching her pass through the parlor.

"Oh look, a piece of furniture must have arrived after all. I wonder which one it is," Margaret said, walking over and pulling the cover off it. "Dear me, I wish I'd been here when this beautiful piece came; it's been delivered to the wrong house."

John walked up to Margaret and wrapped his arms around her from behind. Leaning down, he rested his cheek next to hers and said, "Happy Christmas, my love."

Margaret stood there paralyzed. She couldn't speak. John could feel her beginning to slide through his arms, once again, but then she found her legs. "I'm sorry, John. My knees became weak." Finally, after many long moments of silence, in a soft low voice, she asked, "This is for me?" John could feel her start to shake with quiet sobs. Sobs, he knew, of delight.

"Yes, Margaret. That is for you, my love."

Margaret slowly lifted the cover to reveal the black and white ivory keys of her new piano.

"Someday you shall have a grand piano, if you wish it, but I knew your cottage would be too small for that now," John said, holding her quiet shivering body in his arms. He turned her to face him.

Margaret's face was a mask of pure disbelief. She looked into John's face with tears beaded on her lashes, unable to speak, and mouthed the words, "Thank you, John." She reached up, put her arms around his neck, and laid her head against his chest, still dazed.

He held her momentarily, and then pulled her back to kiss her, but found she had sailed to one of her islands. She was totally unfocused. She wasn't pulling out of her state of disbelief. John closed the lid on the piano and pulled the cover back over it. "We can talk about this later," he said. "Get your clothes. I'll wait outside, or I'm afraid we'll be here all day." He walked her over to the steps that led upstairs then left the house and went out to his horses to pat them down. He was happy with Margaret's response to his gift. He wanted to give her everything. He wanted to spoil her. Someday . . . perhaps...

Margaret was back within ten minutes, still dazed, and John went over to fetch her.

Before he could get to her, she started down the steps. As she turned around to point up to her "Margaret's Enchanted Cottage" sign, she slipped from the step, pitching forward. John caught her and lifted her off the step, setting her down on the ground. He released her slightly, so she could free her arms, but he wouldn't let go of his hold, since she appeared to be allowing him that closeness.

John thought how small she was next to him; he could crush her so easily, if he hugged her too tightly. He desperately wanted to always protect her fragileness.

Silence reigned between them. Margaret slipped her hands from his chest, up to each side of his face, and held his head in her hands, beckoning.

John whispered, "If you don't say no right now, I am going to kiss you again, my love.

"I would like that." Margaret said softly.

John let her go long enough to throw his top hat to the ground and took her fiercely into his arms, properly, almost bending her backward. He looked at her ivory throat, her ruby lips and then into her eyes, slowly moving to cover her mouth with his. He was tender and slow, licking her lips and gently parting them. The stroking seduction of his tongue took away her senses and blocked any slight resistance she might be thinking was improper. She wrapped her arms around his neck and pulled him closer, trying to reach his mouth more fully. Margaret made a low, utterly female sound and relaxed into him. She had been innocently tentative on their first kiss, but not so now. She met him hotly with hunger that fed his own. John's uninhibited feral groan undid her. Her head fell backwards as his mouth claimed her throat. Reacting passionately, he moved one of his arms lower, just near her buttocks, and drew her more tautly to him. He wanted her so badly. He was burning up. The caged animal wanted to assert its prowess over its mate. Margaret could feel John's longing, liking it more than she should, as it was ardently presenting itself. He wanted her to know his desire for her as a woman and he pressed her closer to him feeling her heaving bosom upon his chest. Margaret, starting to understand passion, pressed herself to John's erection.

"Margaret, please let me love you," John whispered, as he started to kiss down her neck; behind them, one of the horses suddenly whinnied, startling Margaret. She backed away out of propriety, mortified that she had been swept away, forgetting that John's driver was back there. As she timidly peered around John, she could see that Branson and Adrian had politely turned away.

"Oh dear, I am so embarrassed, " Margaret said, suddenly turning crimson.

"Not I," said John. I am not ashamed of the love I feel for my woman. I've waited too long to show the world my love for you." He stooped to retrieve his hat and cleared his throat which seemed to signal Branson to open the door. Highly embarrassed and red faced, Margaret was handed into the coach, John following with her bag.

"Thank you, thrice, John. Once for saving me from a very uncomfortable accident on the steps, and thank you for my adorable little sign," as she pointed to it, "which I know is your doing. I love it. And how can I thank you for my exquisite pianoforte. I have so longed for one. I think you are getting far ahead of our gentlemen's agreement. And I think you did tell me that you were not buying anything for Christmas?"

"Margaret, first of all, if you remember our conversation about gift giving for the holiday, I never agreed to any such thing; we only talked about your boots. Secondly, that was ordered several days after your return to London because I knew you had left one in Helstone and wanted you to have one, no matter where our relationship went. And finally, there was nothing in our agreement about a gift for my love only that you needed choices, and that hasn't changed. But most of all, I cannot help myself." John kissed her lightly and then shouted to Branson, "Mill 2."

Arriving after 10:00 o'clock, they had missed the second shift change for both Mills. John knew that Higgins was spreading his own form of cheer through all the shifts today.

Margaret remarked on the vast difference in layout between the two mills and their sizes. John explained that Mill 2 had 450 workers, whereas Mill 1 had 350. The changed layout had come from 10 years of learning what would expedite movement around the yard. It was built like a fortress, with 20 loading docks, 10 to each side facing each other, uniting all the buildings into a U shape with the canteen at the far end, between the two sides. The office was located at the entrance.

"The canteen," John shouted to Branson who began threading his way between the loading wagons on each side of him. "One side is for importing and the other side is for exporting," John told her. "This design is more efficient than Mill 1."

They enjoyed two hours there, with Margaret following John around, saying little, - mostly nodding hello when introduced. The workers came to get their free dinner that John had provided for everyone, as a token of holiday cheer. Oranges would be passed out when the shift ended; John had ordered almost a boat full of imported oranges to be given to his people. They were a real treat anytime of the year. Margaret was delighted to see Mary, but they would talk tomorrow as she was busy serving. Higgins was there, traveling a different route around the canteen, shaking hands, thanking and talking. Margaret was so happy to see that Nicholas was appreciated and finally finding his merited status as a hard worker and overseer. But once again, she felt overtaken upon viewing John's responsibilities: the mass of faces, the wagons with all the horses, and the size of these huge buildings and the sound of machinery running somewhere in the distance. As she observed the way they all respected him and looked up to him, she didn't feel herself fairing very equal as his partner in life.

How is it he's picked me, of so little significance, to love?

The same scene repeated itself in Mill 1. Most of these workers had been with John the longest; some, Margaret thought, might even remember her. She felt more comfortable there as she walked among the tables, even without John, wishing the workers a Happy Holiday, and thanking them for all they do for Marlborough Mills. John stood off in the kitchen area, fascinated, watching Margaret conduct herself down the rows of workers, alone, shaking hands, and talking with them. With him not at her side, he wondered how she was explaining who she was. This was a beautiful sight to behold, and caught him off guard with the emotions it brought forth in him. This was another exquisite remembrance for their treasure chest of love. Every moment he watched her, he felt her beauty, her scent, and the touch of her. Second, only to Margaret, were his mills and his people. John knew in his heart that she would fit in perfectly, better than his own mother. He knew his people would absolutely love her.

When they arrived back home in the late afternoon, Margaret asked that a bath be prepared for her before Jane left. Dixon found her and had her own request, "Miss Margaret, we are as ready as we can be downstairs. As you can see, the upstairs has been prepared and most of the table is set, with the exception of your dinner places. Could I be allowed the evening off?"

"Yes, of course, Dixon. I won't ask, but I hope it has something to do with Mr. Granger."

"Yes, Miss Margaret. He bought a small tree and we will decorate it tonight. And if I could have tomorrow evening off after the dinner has been cleaned away; we will be exchanging gifts then."

"Yes, yes, of course, please take both nights off." Margaret said, happy for Dixon.

"Thank you Miss Margaret, and one last thing; since you will be going home the day after Christmas, is it all right if I just return home instead of coming back here?"

"Yes, I guess. Yes, but only because Adrian's there. You still have a key for now. He will be there, probably sleeping on the carpeted floor in the parlor."

Margaret went for her bath. John left the house and went to his office to look over the Slickson mill offer again. He felt that it was better to be away from where Margaret was right now. The yard was empty, but he saw that Higgins was still here somewhere. Higgins had long ago moved out of the Princeton District and found a small cottage just a little way out of town. He had a horse and small buggy for getting to work and it was still on the property.

"Higgins," John said, as Nicholas stepped into the office, "I think I am going to go talk directly to Slickson next week and stop relying on rumors. Our only questions seem to lie in the condition of the mill itself and its machinery, does it not?"

"That's about it, Master. Their productivity level is only slightly below our own, but the people that he has, look good."

"Good . . . then why don't you get yourself on home? Our security men are all working and rotating this holiday, are they not?" John inquired.

"Yes, that's where I've just been, checking at both mills, that all the machinery has been shut down properly and security is in place. They know to contact you first and me second, should an emergency arise."

"Well then, it sounds that all is as it should be. Take yourself away from here and come back for dinner tomorrow about 1:00 or so in the afternoon"

"See you tomorrow, have a good eve tonight," Higgins said, waving his cap as he left.

After dinner, John realized that they were left alone, as Dixon would be gone for several hours. He was not sure he had the strength to get through the next few hours alone with Margaret without stepping past his own line, especially with the way she looked tonight. She was wearing a burgandy frock and her scent was eminently alluring. He thought she must have brought her own bath soap.

John went to the bar and got a brandy for both he and Margaret, while she had gone to her room for something. He stoked the fire, added a log, lowered the gas lights, and folded himself down onto the carpet in front of the fireplace.

As Margaret came from her room, carrying a book for the evening, she said, "Ah . . . What's this? No lights, only firelight? Mr. Thornton Proclamation, you are not arranging a romantic evening, are you? Excuse me while I send someone for the Proclamation Police. Someone needs to come and enforce procedure here."

John was quietly shaking with laughter and could only manage to beckon her over to him with his hand. Margaret looked around the room and remembered the sewing basket was in the buffet. Finding what she wanted, she returned to John and sat down on the carpet, placing a piece of yarn between them, effectively giving them sides on which to stay.

"There! You have your side and I have mine. Unless you want pistols at dawn, the gentlemen's agreement stated that I could only make moderate advances to you until I have seen other men. Are they not, in fact, your very words, sir?

John loved this game, but he had sure outsmarted himself this time. This could have been a perfect evening, almost too perfect, and here he was with a dividing line between them.

"I am a gentleman; that was a gentleman's agreement, and I will keep my word." John picked up his brandy glass. "You see this brandy glass, Margaret?" She nodded. "One of my favorite pastimes is to sit in my chair, holding a glass such as this, and swirl the contents. The best part about it is watching it coat the inside of the glass while watching it through to the fire." John demonstrated for her. As he was taking his first swallow of it, he saw Margaret start to lean for her glass that sat on the floor in front of him. He slowly, and deliberately, pushed it out of her reach with his booted foot. "I'm sorry, did you want something?"

"Yes, I would like my brandy, please" Margaret said.

"And how to you propose to get it, my love?" John smirked, looking at the dividing line.

Undaunted, Margaret did not answer John or pursue her brandy. She started this little game tonight and had to see it through.

John couldn't help but love the look on her face as she contemplated some reciprocal act. She had such a fierce look on her face, like a mad little kitten.

Margaret decided to raise the stakes. She thought she had figured something out. So, hiking the hem of her dress to the knee, she reached down to remove her shoes.

John was aroused seeing her legs. He knew a real game was afoot, now. John pulled off his boots, hoping this game was headed where he thought it might.

Margaret didn't know how long she could keep doing this with a straight face. She sat for a minute as if in thought. She swiveled so her back was to John and hiked up her dress much farther to catch the top of one stocking.

John quickly lay down on the carpet, so his body extended back, and he caught Margaret with her dress to the top of her thighs.

Margaret, said, "No fair!"

John took off one sock, laughing.

Margaret took off the other stocking, ensuring he didn't sneak a peek.

John removed his other sock. He was beaming the whole time.

Margaret, still with her back facing John, removed a garter that held a stocking.

John started to sweat. Was it the fire in the fireplace, or the fire in his body? He removed his cravat and his shirt fell open.

Margaret tried to twist around to see his open shirt. What she wouldn't give to be lying next to that bare chest. She would work the game until his shirt was off and then stop. She removed her last garter and returned to sitting next to him.

Just before he removed his waistcoat, John took stock for a minute and counted items left for each of them. He was anxious to go straight to his trousers and undergarment to see what she would do, but this was too much fun, so he removed his pocket watch.

Margaret inhaled deeply, she hadn't expected that. She thought she had things counted correctly. Think . . . think . . . she removed her earrings.

John went for his waistcoat.

After each piece of clothing was removed, they would stare into each other's eyes, smiling, having survived another round, daring each other to go on. Still no words had been spoken. John knew he would have no embarrassment, so he wasn't nervous, but he'd like to win the game, rather than lose it.

Margaret was getting nervous about how this was going to end. John had three more items to go, if it should ever go that far, which she was sure it would not. She had her dress, full slip, half slip, corset, and undergarment. She didn't like this, but she could not blink now. Her dress was the next likely item, but she stood and slid down her half slip, pooling it at her feet, and then kicked it away.

John knew he was going to lose, which he didn't really want to do, because it was so heart rendering having Margaret figure this all out, probably feeling frightened about now; he decided to call her bluff.

He stood up beside her and instead of pulling off his shirt, for which Margaret had patiently been waiting; John proceeded to reach for the buttons on his trousers.

Margaret's eyes got as big as saucers as she shouted, "You Win! Stop! You CHEATED!!"

"How do you arrive at that conclusion?" he asked, choking back the laughter and the joy at her surprise. Oh well, he thought, these were days they could never recapture and were worth every second to have as memories, just like the first night she had arrived, their first kiss, and the tree decorating. These were all firsts to cherish their whole life.

Still laughing, John leaned down and picked up the yarn, tossed it into the fireplace and reached for Margaret.

Just then, they heard the downstairs door open. Dixon was home early.

Chapter 18

 *The Gift*

Hearing Dixon coming through the door downstairs, John and Margaret grabbed their clothes and scattered to their own rooms, laughing hilariously, like school children putting a frog in the teacher's desk. John quickly dressed and returned to the parlor, just as Dixon came up from the kitchen.

"Hello Dixon, I didn't think you would be back this early. Did you have a nice time?"

"Yes, I did. Master, I don't know if you noticed but it's snowing again, not nearly as hard as before, but I thought I'd better get back in case it got bad. I just came up to tell you I was home and about the snow. Goodnight Master."

"Thank you, Dixon, and goodnight." John went to the window; the snow didn't seem like it would amount to much. He waited for Margaret to return, but she didn't. It was after 10:00, so he decided to turn in. Still crowing to himself over the game, he turned the lights off and went to his bedroom, delighting in his new treasure. He wondered if life could possibly get any better than this, but he knew it could. Before retiring, John returned to the Christmas tree and hung his mother's ruby pendant, her gift to Margaret, at the top of the tree. It wouldn't be easily seen, but he would wait for her to notice it.

The morning broke with a beautiful pristine vista, as far as one could see. No one was coming to the mill; there were no sounds, nothing to disturb the light dusting of the snow that had fallen last night, painting the entire landscape in white, with tiny sparkling diamonds, whenever the sun caught it. John woke at his usual early time, but the house was already alive with many voices coming from downstairs. He went down the backstairs into the bustling kitchen and was taken aback by five people trying to get around each other, as they headed in different directions. With a rather loud voice, he said, "Happy Christmas to all." Everyone echoed back the same and went about their work. Dixon asked if Miss Margaret was awake; John answered, he didn't think so.

"Would you care for a cup of tea while you wait on Miss Margaret?" Dixon asked the Master.

"Yes, bring a pot upstairs, if you don't mind."

John had just finished adding a dab of rum into the teapot, when Margaret emerged in an exquisite emerald green frock, very dressy and festive.

He inhaled deeply and went to her. Pulling her into his arms, he started to waltz her around the room. "You are dazzling, this morning, Miss Margaret. Happy Christmas, my love," John whispered to her.

"And a Happy Christmas to you, John. I see that you waltz, sir. Is there no end to your talents? I cannot find the whole of you."

"Do you mean like last night? You were very close to finding the whole of me," John whispered boldly, with a big grin, still waltzing her around the room.

What has come over me? Why did I say that? Where is this coming from? Where are my manners?

Margaret blushed over that comment, sensing it had an air of inevitability.

As he continued to waltz her in a circle, he pressed his lips to hers, giving her a firm but light kiss. Opening her eyes as they parted, Margaret noticed that the mistletoe had been hung from the chandelier. "I see you put up the mistletoe."

"Me? I saw it and thought you did it. That's where we were when I just kissed you. Let me fix you my spiced hot tea and give you a warning . . . do not go downstairs," John said, as he walked over to the teapot on the dining table.

"I think I can hear why." As Margaret strolled over to the fireplace, she was remembering last night. She found a small length of yarn that had not burned, and placed it in her book that still sat on the table. What a precious keepsake, she thought. On some distant anniversary, she would present it to John and remind him how he cheated.

The heightened excitement seemed to make the day go by quickly. John had set the bar with everything except champagne, which would come later. He talked Adrian into tending the liquors. Margaret checked the table and the upper floor for tidiness, as if she was lady of the house. This did not escape John's elated, rapt attention.

The smell of the meal cooking drifted upstairs. The bar was ready and the table properly prepared to Margaret's liking. There was only an hour left to go before Branson would pick up his lady friend, the Professor and Mr. Granger. John was browsing a book, but kept one eye on Margaret as she walked back into the room checking that everything was in its place. She was standing looking at the tree from a distance. She moved closer as John continued watching her. As her eyes drifted away, she thought she glimpsed something glittering near the top of the tree. She stopped and tried to see it again, but she couldn't find it. She walked back and forth, looking up, trying to catch the light on it at just the right angle.

John thought what a wonderful portrait that would make. This was an extraordinary Christmas.

Margaret stopped and stared. It looked like a chain of some kind. John had intentionally tucked the pendant behind a bough, so it couldn't be seen. He watched as she tried to reach for it, but she was too small. He didn't think she realized he was in the room, because she hadn't asked for his help.

"Darn him," John heard her mutter, "we agreed to no gifts. That looks like a very beautiful gold chain to me. Where is he? Wait until I get my hands on him!" She turned and found him standing directly behind her as she walked straight in to his chest. "Oh, there you are, sorry." John looked down at her, giving nothing away. "I thought we agreed not to buy anything for each other this year."

"I'm here so you can get your hands on me, like I just heard you say. What are you talking about Margaret?" John said smiling, still wondering about the piffle that was springing from his mouth.

"This!" she said, as she jumped, pointing to the gold chain. "I guess that got there like the mistletoe."

John started laughing. "I did NOT hang the mistletoe on the chandelier, and I did NOT buy you that, whatever it is." He now wondered who DID hang the mistletoe.

"Well, what is it, then? Where did it come from? John Thornton, I do not believe you."

John reached up on his own toes to lift the necklace very slowly off the top branch, finally exposing the large heart pendant, swinging from the heavy gold chain.

As he lowered the gem to Margaret, she gasped when he put it in her hands. "John, this is absolutely stunning. It's the prettiest thing I've ever seen . . . a beautiful ruby heart." She smiled up at him and pulled his lapels down for a kiss, a deep kiss.

John wrapped his arms all the way around her, crushing her to him and kissed her fiercely, slowly thrusting his tongue around and in and out. It was a very carnal kiss; he was making love to her with his mouth and tongue. Margaret's knees weakened, and once again, she fainted. John carried her to her room and laid her on her bed. He sat beside her, and hollered for Dixon.

Dixon arrived promptly and before she could become hysterical, John said, "She's fainted. Please get me a cool wet cloth." Dixon rushed out of the room returning in less than a minute.

Handing the cloth to the Master, she asked what happened. "She was given a nice gift and it overwhelmed her. I gave her the heart pendant that my mother wanted her to have. She's coming around; would you mind leaving us?" Dixon backed out of the room as she saw Margaret's eyes begin to flutter open.

Margaret slowly sat up trying to focus her vision. John moved enough so she could swing her legs over the side of the bed. She kept staring at the gem in her hand, realizing that it was an antique, or a family heirloom. "John, tell me about it."

John told Margaret the story and ended with telling her how his mother had wanted her to have the necklace. On her death bed, she had accepted Margaret as John's love, and wanted to apologize for how she had treated her. John put his arm around her waist while she cried heavily into his shoulder. She couldn't stop the flood of tears. She had always known that she was not well received by John's mother, and for that, she also carried guilt. John took the pendant from her and placed it around her neck, noticing how beautifully the red heart hung against her ivory skin and emerald neckline. Once fastened, she grabbed the large gem immediately and held the heart tightly in her fist. It was as if she was "willing" the stone to mend the distance between herself and his mother, for John's sake.

The first guests were arriving, and John handed her his handkerchief as he rose to greet them in the hall, just outside Margaret's bedroom door. It was Higgins and his family.

Upon seeing Margaret come out from her bedroom with red eyes and a runny nose, a sense of sadness wilted the moment. Margaret quickly said they were –tears of joy- and showed them the necklace. Higgins looked over at John.

"That was an heirloom gift specifically to Margaret from my Mother, before she died. That's why all the tears. I'm lucky you came in when you did, or I might not have escaped the same fate, myself." Higgins clapped John on the shoulder, saying nothing but giving him a smile.

Margaret gave Nicholas a hug and turned to Peggy. Nicholas introduced Peggy to Margaret and the ladies held hands, as they bid each other hello and made the appropriate greetings. Margaret turned to greet Mary next. She looked so pretty without her work clothes and severe hair style. Margaret could see a beautiful young woman emerging.

Adrian arrived to take the drink orders. Everyone found a place to sit and they all became caught up in the spirit of the holiday.

With Margaret's guidance, the conversation flowed cheerfully for a half an hour and soon the Professor arrived and was escorted upstairs by Branson. Margaret introduced him to everyone. Both Nicholas and Peggy were interested to hear about his work. John was content to sit back and let the others talk while he studied his 'once shy' Margaret, blossoming into the happy woman she was becoming. She had a beautiful profile, which he rarely seemed to see. How could such a small demur woman, with ivory skin, blue eyes, light brown hair, and an independent temperament sweep him off his feet so completely? He was always off balance around her, never feeling his feet touch the ground.

God . . . how deeply, I love her.

Dinner was then served, with Nicholas and John seated at the ends of the table. There was lively conversation throughout the meal; the food was excellent and plentiful, and everyone was partaking of the holiday spirit. The goose dinner was cooked to perfection, along with all the trimmings that accompanied a traditional holiday dinner. The Professor regaled them with Christmas celebrations in other lands, while

Margaret spoke of their cotton waste snow trimmings and the magnificent pianoforte that awaited her.

Later, Margaret thought she heard something from far off. Not quite knowing what it could be, she said, "Quiet everyone," as she stood and tried to listen. With the silence in the room, it quickly became clear that they were being serenaded with Christmas carols, from below stairs. All seven folks from the kitchen came up the stairs singing and stood behind everyone at the table. They sang, "The First Noel," and the tabled clapped with pleasure. As they sang a second carol, each of the seven filled their hands and trays with dishes from the upstairs table, and had it cleaned off in one quick swoop.

John stood and thanked all of them. "Before you leave, and I know your arms are full, but I wanted to thank all of you for the lovely dinner today. I know everyone worked very hard, even our two guests downstairs, who seemed to have been enlisted. Branson and Dixon, please introduce your guests."

Branson and Dixon did as they were told, to the embarrassment of their guests. Margaret introduced Adrian and the two cooks. The merry singers returned to the kitchen, laden with dishes and trays.

With the dishes cleared, John asked everyone to remain at the table a little longer. Margaret and Peggy were enjoying talking to each other. They were going to be close friends; Margaret could feel it. She was a gentleman's daughter, but did not regard herself that way, just as Margaret herself felt. She was warm, intelligent and no airs. She was perfect for Nicholas.

John excused himself for a minute, while Adrian brought out champagne glasses and poured a glass for everyone. John returned to the table, as five faces looked at him in bewilderment because of his absence. It appeared they were waiting for something else to happen.

The Professor, looking at John, anticipated a toast of some sort. "If I could be so bold as to say something right here?" he asked.

John motioned for him to continue, and took his seat.

"Nicholas, I wanted to tell you that you were given a very nice compliment. I haven't told John this either; I wanted to tell you both. Mr. Bryan McNeil stopped by the office yesterday. I had to decline a dinner invitation with him for this evening because I wanted to be here. I told him that I would be at Mr. Thornton's home, with his overseer and betrothed, but I didn't mention you by name. He asked me if your name was Higgins, and I said yes. He said he did not know you, but in his past 10 weeks here in Milton, he had made inquiries and had heard a lot about Marlborough Mills. It seems that whenever Marlborough Mills was mentioned, your name would come up as a highly regarded overseer. Mr. McNeil had heard about your ingenuity in helping the people of Marlborough Mills, and the owners, come together. He's also quite interested in hearing why John hired you after you almost forced the loss of his business." Ending there, the Professor smiled and sat back down. There was a smattering of applause.

As everyone politely laughed, Higgins felt quite embarrassed. Mary and Peggy looked at him proudly, while John and Margaret looked at each other as if to say, "I've never seen him embarrassed before."

Higgins finally spoke, "Professor Pritchard, I don't know what to say."

Standing with a champagne glass raised in his hand, John said, "Well . . . I do."

John paused to let the words settle in and to raise the anticipation of what he was about to say. Clearing his throat, John began.

"Nicholas, as you know, you have not only become my best friend over these last few years, but a very good part of Marlborough Mill's more recent success is driven directly by you. I don't think I have ever thanked you enough for all you have done for the mills and for me. The Mills owe you a great debt, and so do I. I want to settle that debt, right now. I hope you are comfortable in gentleman's clothes, because for your wedding present, I am giving you and Peggy a 15 percent partnership in all of Marlborough Mills. Nicholas, you are now an owner in the business and no longer an overseer. I have paperwork for you to sign," John said, as he pulled a folded deed out of his coat pocket.

"Of course, this means that you have to come up with your share when *we* purchase Slickson Mills." John smiled.

Silence hung in the air with disbelief. There was a pause, as everyone came to grips with what he had just announced.

"Nicholas, you are going to have to find a Higgins for us. Welcome to the land of property and the rank of a gentlemen. Thank you for everything. A toast: To Nicholas Higgins, now a partner in Marlborough Mills. Oh, here are your two tickets to the Chamber's Ball coming in early spring."

Everyone stood, except Higgins, and raised their glasses. He was so overcome with emotion, his eyes misted. Slowly he got to his feet and lifted his head toward John. His eyes were glassy, now. He lifted his champagne glass and everyone clinked their crystal together over the center of the table. Margaret, Mary, and Peggy had huge smiles on their faces, John had a broad smile on his face, and Nicholas was speechless.

John added, "No one deserves it more than you, my friend."

John caught Margaret looking at him with the most endearing look on her face.

Nicholas cleared his throat, barely able to stutter out the words, "Master, I don't know how to thank you for this. I am speechless; I mean, I really am speechless. Thank you, thank you very much from myself, Peggy and the rest of the family. How does one thank someone for giving them such a magnanimous gift as a partnership?"

"Nicholas, it is I who needed to say thank you. Not you. Things are going to change very rapidly for you. I have already set the paperwork in motion as you see here, so you better buy yourself a whole new gentlemen's working wardrobe. And henceforth, you call me John, no matter who is around. No more Boss or Master. That title now belongs to you, too."

Peggy leaned over and embraced Nicholas and turning to John, said, "Thank you from me, as well." Mary kissed him on the cheek.

Margaret came to John's end of the table. She looked up into his happy face as he looked down into hers. She was in awe of this man once again, the one who said he loved her. She looked into his face for a long time before finally saying, "John, that was the nicest, most sincere gesture I have ever seen. I am so proud of you for what you just did. As I've said in the past, there is no end of you. You gave Nicholas the respect he deserved at a great personal cost to yourself. That was a beautiful show of passion for your conviction and belief in him. You are passionate in more ways than one," she said with a smile.

Margaret, you hardly know the beginning of my passion.

Little did anyone know that John was getting the better reward hearing her words of praise for him. He had wanted her love, but gaining her respect and having heard her say those words was another miracle in his life. He smiled down into her face, wanting to thank her lips for what they had just spoken.

Margaret, sensing the same feelings, quickly went to the other end of the table to hug Nicholas and Peggy. John followed her. John put his hand out to Nicholas who grabbed it with both hands, firmly. The men hugged each other like old friends, while the women did the same. The Professor walked to the end of the table, too, and offered his congratulations, saying, "You will have a large part in my book as well, but that was planned for you even before this great night."

The evening eventually ended with Nicholas, once again, thanking John for everything. Margaret said goodbye to all of them. The Professor accepted a ride home with Nicholas, thus freeing Branson for the evening with his lady.

A sense of merriment mixed with pine scent, and holiday cheer filled the spirited evening. Now, being totally alone until dawn, John and Margaret settled into the comfort of enjoying each other's company.

Chapter 19

 *More Then Joy*

Finding John unwinding from the excitement of the day, lounging across the couch, Margaret curled up beside him.

"Today was so wonderful. I can't think of any other day that I have enjoyed more. Sadly, I think I shall have to be going home tomorrow. John, thank you for these past days; they've meant more than you could know. They have been the loveliest and happiest days, ever, in my life."

"Do not thank me. I need no thanks from the one I love. I cannot tell you how it has pleased me to my very soul to have you here. I've laughed more in a few days than, literally, my entire life. And like you, our time together has meant more to me than all my life experiences."

Margaret smiled at John. "You're going to have to be on your best behavior tonight because sooner or later you will discover that Dixon is out for the entire evening. She will return to my house instead of here. So we are totally alone all night."

His body flooded with warmth at her words. He knew his control would not last through the night. His mind started whirling and he could feel the heat rising in body. Damn the proclamation; this chance may never happen for a long time, he thought. He more than thought - he wanted to act. He dreamed and hoped that the night would bring him the opportunity to allow Margaret to know herself and feel like a real woman. John wanted that more for her than anything. His own ecstasy was secondary. "Hmm . . . this presents a dilemma," he said.

Again, Margaret began experiencing sensual stirrings that were causing her body to feel warm all over. She was not so naive as to misconstrue them as anything other than passion for John. Against all propriety and a pious upbringing, she wanted him to make love to her. She knew he could make her feel like the woman she wanted to be for him. Margaret still held doubts about herself, as she had never known anything different with Booker. But sensing the differences that her body was telling her, she knew that John was the one to clear all doubts. Although, just coming out of her bereavement period and already feeling a commitment to John, there was no chance of intimacy tonight. The possibility of conception was at its peak. She knew she had to move away from being so near him. She rose and went to sit by the fire. "What do you mean by a dilemma?" she asked, refocusing her mind.

"Excuse me just a minute; I will return, momentarily," John said, as he walked into his bedroom. He turned up the gas heater so the room was warm and pulled back the sheets. He came back, passing through the parlor into Margaret's room. He ruffled her sheets so it might appear that she had slept in her bed and then leaving, closed the door.

"John, what are you doing?" Margaret asked in bewilderment.

As John sat down next to her in front of the fire, he said, "I am preparing for a dilemma."

"What dilemma?"

"I think we are out of yarn," he laughed.

Margaret broke into a smile, but it further deepened her knowledge of the disappointment she knew was coming. She started to rise from the carpet to sit in the chair when John grabbed her arm.

John sensed she was pulling away from him, but this time it seemed serious. "Please, sit with me, here. What is wrong, my love? Are you apprehensive about what you perceive this night could bring to us? I can remain the perfect gentleman if that's what you truly want, but please let me be near you." John looked over and saw tears welling in her eyes. Was she frightened of him? He couldn't bear it, if she was. "Please don't be afraid of me. Nothing will happen unless you allow it."

Margaret didn't know anything else than to be honest with John. "I am not afraid of you; it's quite the reverse. I am afraid of myself." Margaret paused, wondering how to explain the rest. "I am well aware that the Thornton Proclamation is not in effect tonight. I am sitting here . . . very . . . much desirous of you. But it cannot happen tonight. I am quite sure that I'm near or at the peak of conception. I'm sorry." Margaret exhaled loudly, finally getting those words out of her mouth. She was embarrassed about sounding so unladylike, or being too forward and expectant.

John fell back on the carpet, reeling at her words, not so much about the conception, but that she desired him enough to let him love her. Every day of heartbreak for the past four years dissolved in those words that she had just spoken. He put his arm over his face and only pride kept his tears from falling. It was the epitome of his hopes and dreams. A word had not been invented that expressed his emotions at that moment. He was not sure he could withstand the rush of four years of unrequited love, now reversing its course. If Margaret's feelings for him in the past had been a drop of water upon his face, he was now standing under a delirious waterfall.

He sat up quickly, took her hands in his, as her tears fell, and studied her. He looked at her face, her eyes, her lips, her hair, missing nothing of her beauty. She was his world, his universe, his everything.

Can this moment really be here?

Margaret couldn't understand all that was showing on his face, but he now expressed the most intimate smile she had ever seen, if there was such a thing. He was in awe. "John, you've said nothing in the last five minutes. Please speak to me."

John didn't know where to begin. "Those words that you just spoke, and I know they were from your heart, just fulfilled a hope and dream I've had for many years. You are giving me the chance to love you, because you desire ME, John Thornton, a person you hated at one time in your life."

Margaret flinched at the remembrance.

"I have not only waited for you, but I have waited for a happiness in my life. I've known that I would never find it without you by my side. I, now, know that it is achievable and within reach. As for the Thornton proclamation, it is now null and void because I know that you love me, even if you are not completely and utterly sure for yourself, yet. Still, I do not want you to say the words. And least of all, about your conception worries, let me love you tonight without any concern there.

"But . . ." Margaret started to say.

"No buts . . . Do you trust me?" John asked solemnly.

"Of course, I do. I just don't see how . . . "Margaret trailed off.

John searched her fire-lit face for any signs of dissent. All he saw was a weak smile. He slowly stood, pulling Margaret up with him. He looked into her eyes, his heart still hammering through his chest. "Margaret, are you sure?" John asked, very tenderly.

"Yes, John. I am sure. I've never been this sure about anything."

His passion and want of her lost its long suffering control. The brake was released. He took her passionately in his arms and kissed her sensuously, for a long time. Margaret clung to him, clutching his shirt, and then finally trusting the night, encircled her arms around his neck. Without taking his lips from hers, he lifted her to his chest, carried her to his bed, and closed the door with his foot.

"John . . .?" Margaret said, holding her glance steady in his eyes as their lips parted.

"Shhh, Margaret," John said softly. "These moments of our love are going to happen between you and me. They have been waiting in the shadows of our dreams for a very long time. I will be extremely gentle with you. If you say stop, I will. I will be slow until you show me differently. He looked deeply into her eyes for any sign of fear; the light was dim, but he saw none. John gently set her down allowing her to stand.

"Margaret, I love you."

He lightly moved his finger tips up her arms to her shoulders and neck. Touching his lips to hers, his fingers slowly traced her cheeks, down her throat and finally to the nape of her neck; he pulled the ribbons and pins from the back of her hair, letting her light brown curls cascade. His dreams and fantasies were no longer in his mind. They were in his hands. She had beautiful, long, full tresses that wound about her neck and down her back. He gently began to acquaint her to his touch. John raked his fingers through her hair, feeling its silkiness, and pulled it to his face to inhale her stimulating scent. He held her face and hair in his hands and drew her to him for another long sensual kiss, probing all, stroking the inside of her mouth, searching for her tongue. Margaret hesitatingly entwined her arms around his waist. John pulled away just enough to look into her eyes, for any signs of discomfort, one final time.

"Are you very sure?"

"I am very sure. But . . ."

John smothered her mouth with devouring hunger before she could finish. His lips were warm and wet and they covered her mouth. He lightly nipped and sucked on her bottom lip before parting her lips with his tongue. John was pulling her face hard against his. He tightened her to his frame so they could each feel every soft curve and rigidness of the other.

"Margaret?" He could see her eyes were closed but she was responding sensually, whether she was aware of it or not.

"John, I am anxious and frightened at the same time. This has been a very long time for me. There was very little intimacy in my marriage. So . . . please John, take care with me. I've had a very sheltered and sparse physical relationship and don't know what to expect. I am already more overwhelmed than I ever was in my marriage. I don't think I will know what to do. I feel so different; this heat that is traveling through me is new to me," Margaret said, with a hushed voice that trembled as she spoke.

"Margaret, I love you more than life itself. You will not have to know what to do. I will guide our passionate journey, my love." John whispered these words as he wrapped his arms around her and held her for a long time, letting the fear lessen and the anticipation grow. John knew he didn't want to scare or spare her. He swayed and rocked her, there, where they stood. He would not let it end too soon.

The gas light from the mill yard cast shadows and spilled angles of light into the room.

Still standing by the bed, John began kissing her again. He teased her with his tongue. Long slow probes that were making Margaret's knees weak. He held her tightly realizing he was overwhelming her, which he had intended. He slowly turned her toward the light streaming in the window and unbuttoned the clothing that bound her. He did this as he kissed her, stopping only to place her hands on his shirt, encouraging the same sensual act of removing his clothes.

Margaret began to unbutton his shirt at the neck, exposing his dark chest hair across his broad frame. His maleness was unfolding in the dimness of the night. The slowness of this passionate act was building the anticipation, stronger than it had been only a moment before. She unbuttoned his shirt further, pulling it out of his trousers. Only recently, she had envisioned this moment.

John pulled it over his head and then turned to Margaret, completing all the fasteners of her clothing.

His body was beautiful, muscular, and so . . . masculine. She rubbed her hands, over his broad shoulders and through his chest hair, circling his flat nipples, stimulating them into a hard bead with the light touch of her finger tips. He closed his eyes and sighed, almost bringing his own movements to a standstill while he felt her delicate touch to his body. He couldn't *ever* remember being *this* hard. Opening his eyes and looking into hers, he slowly slid the dress off of her shoulders and let it drop to the floor, revealing lovely, pristine, translucent shoulders. He pulled her forward and kissed each shoulder, her neck, and throat, moving back to her lips as he let her corset and petticoat slip from her body.

Margaret was standing there, only in her undergarment, in shyness, with naked bosoms. John looked down and cupped both of her well rounded breasts with his warm hands, as he leaned down and gently kissed each one, running his tongue around her nipples. He loved the fact they were already responding like lush berries, pink, pebbling, and sweet. He breathed in the scent of her. He was on fire. He could feel her feminine shivers as he moved from her breasts.

He took Margaret's hands and brought them back to his trouser opening. She found all the closures, and she could not miss the hard ridge that was lying beneath. She trembled at his size. His manhood was . . . He was a big man in all his attributes. She wasn't sure how . . .

His trousers dropped to the floor. He stood in his undergarment and she stood in hers. John gently removed her undergarment slowly and then his own, freeing his erection. He sat on the edge of the bed, and drew her in front of him. With the pale light of the outside gaslight casting its light upon her, with her ivory cream skin that revealed translucent blue veins running to her breasts; she was the most beautiful creature his eyes had beheld. He moved her back a few inches so he could take in the whole radiant image of her femininity.

Margaret was quaking with her own shyness. "What does he think of me?" She trembled.

Holding her arms out to the sides for her, he said, "Margaret, you are exquisite. You are perfect and lovely, and soft. You are more beautiful than I dreamed. You are the closest I can get to heaven, while here on earth. I have imagined this moment for years. God help me to be the man worthy of the woman who stands before me."

Margaret, having been holding her breath, now exhaled a soft sigh. She felt relief from John's most beautiful words. "I am here because I want to be with you, she told him. "I want to know you; I want you to hold me, and I want to feel your body and to feel your breath upon my face."

He kissed her almost translucent skin, circling her nipple with his tongue before drawing her into his mouth with a strong but gentle suckling. The taste of her was sweet as honey, and she started to sigh softly, while wavering on her feet.

He reached for her and pulled her down on top of him, as he lay back on the bed.

Lying on top of John, she was very aware of his erection. Margaret felt the heat stirring in her own womanly area as he pressed against her. He adjusted her so that his hardness was pressing into the notch of her thighs. She was always inhibited with Booker when they were naked, even in the dark. The way John had positioned her had started rippling sensations that she didn't know how to handle. She now felt nothing but the need of John and his firm lean body touching hers. Two naked lovers were casting shadows against the wall for the very first time.

John sensing that his own firmness was losing control, rolled her onto her back, so he could look into her face and kiss her again, but he knew he had very little time left before he would erupt.

"Are you sure about the conception?" Margaret asked softly, still unsure. "I trust you, but how can you stop now, or me, either? I've never felt these sensations. I don't know how to bring them down."

"You won't have to, and I certainly won't let you. Give yourself to me without any fear. I have waited an eternity for this moment."

"I want to give myself to you, but it's the wrong . . ."

"No, my love, there are no wrong times. These 'times', that you seem embarrassed about, make you a woman, and I love you because you are this woman. God has brought you back to me. We will be united as one in the future, but not tonight, and neither of us will be disappointed." He turned her wet simpering face towards his. "Look at me." He knew she would soon find solace.

"Give me your hand, my love . . . Keep looking at me. I want to look into your face."

John took her hand and slowly guided her toward his erect penis. "With your warm hand, just hold me and feel me. That is the only passion that I need right now."

Margaret, timidly, took John into her hand, grasping the firmness of his manhood.

John inhaled loudly. "Oh dear God, Margaret," he barely whispered.

Feeling his length and girth, and smoothness, she slowly started to stroke him, even though he hadn't asked for that. She sighed at first and then trembled over his size. John, struggling for concentration, was looking at the uninhibited innocence in her face as she touched and caressed him. Margaret watched as he slowly closed his eyes and shuttered heavily against her, gasping deeply with completion. She felt the flood of his warm release.

With misted eyes, John hugged her tightly. "How I've longed for you to touch me in that way. Thank you," he reverently whispered into her ear.

Margaret wrapped her arms around John, loving the fact that he reacted to her with his manhood. "Thank you, John, for responding to me in that way. I feel . . . well . . . I don't know how to explain how I feel . . . needed. Perhaps, I feel needed or wanted, as a woman, to bring you to that act. It was so fast. Could I do better next time?"

"That was fast for both of us, but it's only because I have wanted you and needed you for four years. There was love on both sides, and that never warrants regrets. We will learn together, since I will need and want you for the rest of my life; this will happen again."

Margaret kissed him, but he pulled her over on top of him again and they kissed for a long time. He slid his hands up and down her smooth back and buttocks, just feeling her fevered skin and soothing her emotions. She could feel that John's arousal was returning. She lifted herself up on her elbows and said, "Maybe, it's best if we stop now."

John held her fast, not letting her go. "Oh, no . . . not yet. I've only just begun. You are staying in this bed all night." He gently turned and laid her on her back. He lingered over her, kissing and licking her face, while he parted her legs gently with his knee, determined to show her pleasure. He was going to explore and enjoy every part of her body. "I want to know all of you, Margaret, the feel of you, the scent of you, and the taste of you. My hands and tongue have been waiting for the discovery of every texture of you, from head to toe."

John began very slowly letting his hands and tongue, cover all of her. Margaret started wincing beneath his touch, partly from embarrassment and the partly from ecstasy. Her sheltered life had never prepared her for this. "Oh John," she murmured. She felt like a thunderbolt was starting to travel through her body, searching for a release to the outside, as his hands roamed.

He began his soft kisses around her neck and down to her breasts, already hard with anticipation. After licking and suckling at her breasts, he continued down to her abdomen, circling her navel, while his hands now glided from her breasts to her inner thighs. He encouraged her slim thighs to open for him, to welcome him into their embrace.

216

Timidly responding, she felt exposed and helpless, about to burst into flames.

"How long can I bear this . . . this . . . ?" she moaned. It did not matter, for he was not going to stop.

"Just let the sensations happen; just let go," John whispered.

Still kissing her lower abdomen, his gentle hand stopped at her soft mound. His finger entered her. First one and then another. He loved hearing her moans and her rapid breathing. His slid his wet fingers out of her sheath and found that most sensitive area of her, and started to massage her delicately, like butterfly wings'. He knew this was going to cause the greatest response. Her legs started to tremble. She was too close, so he stopped for a moment, watching her body yearn to go on. She started to arch her back. John wanted to sustain her pleasurable torment a bit longer. He could feel her sensual desire rising, so he held her writhing hips and legs tenderly, readying them for his sensual assault.

Her consciousness started to reel out of control. She was shuddering on the brink of . . . what... she didn't know. "What's happening to me?" John heard her gasp.

"I am loving you, Margaret."

She quieted down but John could feel her body shaking violently.

"Margaret, don't hold yourself back from me, release your feelings. I love this as much as you do." He had wanted to give, only her, this pleasure.

John lightly parted her soft mound with his tongue. He had waited a long time to pay this sweet tribute to her femininity.

A startled cry tore through her when he claimed her with his mouth. He knew to be as gentle as possible now. Tenderly exploring her folds, his slow tongue swirled and licked, and stroked and savored the sensitive area at the top of her cleft, wanting to send her over the edge. He gently circled the outer rim of the soft entrance to her body. Returning to her sweet erect womanly nub, he could feel light throbs there as he

217

paused; they matched her rapid heartbeat. He knew she was there, teetering, where he wanted her.

Margaret would have screamed from the wildfire running through her if she had any breath, as everything seemed to center on that one single spot. She could feel his wet hair lightly brushing the insides of her thighs. Her back bowed in agonizing pleasure. She was the tempest to his calm.

"Joh . . ."

John knew she was existing only through her physical sense at this moment and he was controlling her. She was heavenly in her responsiveness. She was fire beneath him.

He was dispatching her to luscious torment. "John," she cried out, piercing the silence, as she was consumed in sensual swirls sweeping her upward to the pulsating darkness at the top of the unknown. Her body clenched unbearably and tightened, and John held her down with his mouth. She cried for mercy, but John had none. The sensual tension became tighter and tighter. She couldn't breathe, and her heart was beating so rapidly, she was beyond caring whether she lived or died through this. She could not hold on any longer and it suddenly snapped. She heard her own blatant cries and moans, disbelieving they were coming from herself.

Margaret split the silence again with her exquisite sounds of euphoria. "Dear God, John!"

John heard her loud cry and felt her body quake and her muscles quiver. He allowed himself a smile and only a few brief moments of breath before he started again. He did not want to stop. He felt her hands tighten on his shoulders and her nails dig into his skin. This moment was so spectacular; he loved giving her this pleasure. She found his hair and pulled it, trying to coax him away, but he wouldn't stop. He wanted so much to hear her sounds, to listen to her continued moans, to feel her legs tremor and spasm. He climaxed again only from the pleasure of feeling and listening to her. John wanted to enter her so badly, but he knew he could not.

"Joh . . . Joh . . . John . . . I'm . . . going to . . . faint . . .

He pulled himself up to kiss her neck and shoulders, and cheek, and held her while she quivered and cried as her orgasm floated her back to consciousness. He almost cried himself for this most precious of moments.

"I didn't know . . . I had the capability to feel whatever that was, in every muscle, and nerve ending, "Margaret said between gasps for air. "I can't stop crying and I can't stop smiling from the miraculous feelings. John, you have brought the dawn of an awakening to my womanhood. I thought I was being driven mad until . . . until I . . .

"You climaxed, Margaret. It's called an orgasm, apparently your first, and you don't know how happy, as a man, it makes me feel to be the one to bring that to you. I had once hoped to be first in your life for that experience, and now I find that I am. I'm afraid I am going to weep, myself," John said ardently to her.

"I have never experienced this, or anything close to it, before. And just when I thought I was falling gently back to earth, you brought it back again, leaving me unable to breathe. I think I was on the verge of a delirious faint. John, I felt your passion run all the way through my body; every fiber was on fire, all worry and embarrassment was gone, until I just burst inside. I didn't want you to stop, but I just couldn't take the pleasure anymore without fainting. I feel so selfish.

"Margaret, you are a woman in every way possible and thank you for allowing me to show you that. I was taken away with your rapture, by your response to me."

John held her close, both their hearts racing because of the physical action, but more obviously from the emotional connection they had just shared. These were the most wonderful moments of both of their lives. It ended all too soon, though. It wasn't all it would be someday for both of them, but it was everything right now. He had taken Margaret to the edge and caused her to fall into ecstasy. He had never wanted this kind of exalted pleasure with anyone else, and had never felt this gratification, so overwhelming to him. John realized that this union, this evening, had brought to him the most aspired moment in his manhood: His ability to carry Margaret to the zenith of her orgasm and hold her there, giving all her she could take.

She is a woman and she is mine.

"John, I don't have the words to describe what you caused to happen to me. I'm sorry that you could not engage in it the way you would have wanted to do," Margaret said, feeling her breasts heave as she struggled for air. I'm not sure I would have permitted it, had I known the immeasurable pleasure that I would be receiving, and you with none.

"Margaret, I would not have exchanged my own pleasure in this for anything in the world, except more of it. You cannot know the emotional climax I have experienced." John held her tightly. "Someday, we will have a life full of this, you know. I just want you in my arms every minute of the day."

They lay together in silence letting their luxuriant feelings ebb.

"Margaret, you are positively glowing," John said, as he watched the light streaming in on her face. "And we still have the whole night ahead of us." Although she couldn't see it, she could hear the smile in his voice.

"I wonder how long this floating feeling will last. I feel like I have wings. I would have it forever if I could, but John, can I ask you something?"

"Of course you can. Never ask if you can ask me. Whatever is on your mind, I want to know all about it. And yes, you can have it forever. That's certainly my intention."

Margaret looked rather embarrassed and in hushed tones asked, "Was that legal?"

John, trying to be a gentlemen and a sensitive passionate man, couldn't help himself, but nearly came off the bed, bursting with laughter. He should not laugh but he was so happy and it was the perfect finish to their first hour of the night. "Oh Margaret, my love, how innocent you are. Magistrate as I am, let me put it this way: Whatever two consenting adults want to do in their own privacy is legal. The key word, of course, is consenting. Why? Do you wish to file a complaint to someone?"

"Yes," she said.

"Yes? ... You do?" John almost gulped.

"Yes. Why have we waited this long to be together like this? I wish you were the first man to take my virtue, but then again, I wouldn't have known what an extraordinary lover that you are.

"And Margaret?"

"Yes, John?"

"It gets better!"

Chapter 20

 A Dinner and a Rose

The following week, John visited Slickson to talk about the rumors of his retirement from the cotton business.

"John, I admit that I've been giving it some thought and somehow a rumor has spread that I'm getting ready to sell. That part is not exactly true because I've not made a firm decision. However, my wife is in a state of health that will not allow us to travel for many more years.

"I'm very sorry to hear that." John said.

"Thank you, I know that you mean that, John. Over the years we've been fierce competitors and good friends. You are to be commended for all the advancements you've brought, not only to the mill owners, but this new industry, itself. If I only learned one thing about you after all this time, it's that you are a compassionate and honest man."

"Thank you, Slickson," John said as he reached out to firmly grasp Slickson's extended hand, surprised at his sincerity.

Slickson recommended a chair to him and then sat himself. "Brandy, John?"

John waved it off.

"So, I take it John that you are considering adding another mill to that spread you have going over there."

"Well . . . my thoughts are not completely formed on this idea yet. New interests are rising that may take up my time."

Slickson interrupted. "Yes, I see Miss Hale is back living in Milton." He smiled at John while he lit his cigar. Oh, Thornton, don't look so surprised. I think all the Masters were aware of your feelings back then. I must say, we were pulling for you, but you are such a private man, that none of us wanted to bring it up. We were sorry when she left so suddenly and have since been aware of your masked self-imposed loneliness. You dated the ladies, and who wouldn't, but you always seemed to return to the solitary confinement in your mind. It became apparent what was happening to you, but only from those of us that new you best. It's none of my business now, but I wish you good luck this time.

John lowered his head, as if in embarrassment, but remained silent, while twirling the brim of his top hat. He finally looked back into Slickson's face, giving no indication whether Slickson's words were true or not, but his lack of rebuttal said volumes, he feared.

Slickson, looking for some comment or gesture from John was cheated of it once again, which was no surprise, but he chuckled. "John, I admire that you've come straight to me to ask about this mill. That shows me some respect and respect for my workers. I'm going to let you have total access to the buildings and I'll have my overseer show you around. Talk to the workers, look at the machinery, check the repair logs, and inspect the building. Take what you find home with you and give it thought. Of all the Masters in Milton, if I decide to sell, I'll hope that you'll be able to make a decent offer. I feel like my workers would be well taken care of and that has become important to me over the years, as it has you. I admire the other Masters and I think most of them run their mills just fine, but I envy your way of doing business the most. When I set a date and make an announcement, I will open my books to all prospective buyers. I hope maybe we can shake hands over a sale in the future, if both you and I see eye-to-eye and your other interests are also agreeable." He smiled at John.

John thanked Slickson for his time and the opportunity to see everything first hand. John left with a handshake and followed Slickson's overseer to the mill.

* * *

Margaret was quite busy the following two months, after getting her new home set up properly, and then spending all her days at the Professor's office.

Working with the Professor proved to be very interesting but it had become some form of literary torture, she was sure. Margaret was certain he knew where he put everything but there was no organization that she could see. He was either going to have to learn her way or he was going to teach her his way. She started making piles of similarities until the Professor could find those books that he wanted her to see. She would use that system as a guideline for storage of research, waiting to be penned.

The Professor would have one or two visitors a day, who he would spend a long time discussing their connection to Milton. Dr. Pritchard, while scribing his notes, wanted to know what role they played in the science of the industry and machinery. Several manufactures were interested in only knowing Margaret more thoroughly, to her dismay. Everyone was charming, she thought, but she wasn't prepared for their advances. One particular gentleman, named Mr. Albert, who was mature, but most particular in his mannerisms and distinguished in his dress, preferred to overtly observe Margaret while he was there. She was becoming somewhat uncomfortable about his and other's attentions. The first week Margaret worked there, Mr. Albert seemed to find reasons to return to the Professor another two times, and he didn't run a mill, but was part of the Milton growth. She felt like a bug under glass. He was a very polite gentleman, tall, fine body and a handsome face, but was possibly forty years her senior.

"Professor, I do not know how to ask you for advice on this but I am becoming aware of . . . the . . ."

". . . The interest that these fine gentlemen have in you?" Asked the Professor, raising his eyebrows and smiling broadly.

"Well . . . yes. I don't know how to react. I've never encountered this very often and it seems almost daily here."

The Professor laughed, "That does not surprise me. Before, you were among very young men and the older men knew that you were married to a friend of theirs. That is another fault that Booker had; he never let you know of your beauty and attraction to men; he never gave you that confidence in yourself."

"Professor, you are trying to embarrass me."

"Margaret, I am only stating fact." He laughed.

"What am I to do about it?" Margaret asked.

"What do you feel like doing about it? I mean really feel?"

Margaret blushed again, "As embarrassing as it is, I like the feeling of being complimented in that way. It makes me feel very feminine, a little sanguine, and courageous, too. But I don't know how to react to it."

"Margaret, your thoughts are valid and healthy and I am glad to see them rising from the ash. I cannot tell you how to react. That must come from your heart. You will do what is right for you. Measure each approach for what it is. It would probably do you good to be in the company of other men occasionally, to absorb that confidence that you seem to need."

The following week, John invited Margaret out for diner in the city. He had picked out an elegant restaurant called The Dove, one of Milton's finest. They had seen very little of each other since that exotic Christmas night. She had been busy with home and work, while John was reacting to the potential movement of managerial workers, should he successfully win the Slickson mill bid. After the preliminary conversation on how things were going in their lives, John launched into some unpleasant news. "Next month is the Chamber's semi-annual ball and I am afraid I have an unavoidable commitment. I wanted so much to dance with you all night at the ball, but I have an engagement with the Bristol Commerce Association. I will be gone four to five days as the travel is quite long from here.

"John, please, do not worry yourself. I won't miss attending the ball."

"Margaret, I would like you to go with whoever asks you. Even though we no longer have the proclamation in effect, I would like you to experience something like that. I have enough confidence in our relationship to want you to go. Nicholas and Peggy will be there as well as Fanny and Watson. Most especially for me wanting you to go is that the Chamber is inviting the Professor and will introduce him at the podium, which he knows nothing about. I know he's been trying very hard to speak to the Members briefly and I want to give him his chance. I want to expose him to many more than he would see at a normal meeting. If, and I seriously doubt this will happen, if no one invites you because you are not yet known to them, then you can be the guest of the Professor. Also, I would like to have you and the Professor over for dinner next week and I will extend the invitation to him, myself.

"Actually, John, I've had four invitations. I'll be so pleased for the Professor, but not so pleased about the other, but I will do it. How formal is the ball?" Margaret asked, already wondering what she had in her wardrobe.

"Four! Four? May I ask who they are?" John said, feeling the bottom fall out of his confidence about which he had just boldly boasted.

"Yes, let's see. There is Mr. Cavanaugh from next door, the lawyer that you know. Mr. Albert, a man that comes to the Professor's often; he's the one who likes to stare at me a lot, and a Mr. Cribb, and a Mr. Steen. The latter having something to do with guns, I believe. Mr. McGregor seems like he's trying to find the courage to ask, too.

Do you know any of these gentlemen besides Mr. Cavanaugh?"

"I know all of them. Gentleman, all. Mr. Steen, Mr. Cribb, and Mr. Albert are quite familiar to the Chamber. Mr. Albert owns the 'The Sterling Theater' in the city. He's a very fine distinguished mature gentleman, much older than you, but I understand he is bringing nice cultural entertainment to the city. We must go sometime; at least it isn't opera. Mr. Cribb is the owner of the Milton Grand Hotel and holds a financial office in the Chamber. Mr. Steen. He's probably been in Milton less than two years. He manufactures gun barrels for small hand guns. Most gun making is done in pieces mainly in Birmingham, but they ship here, Steen tools the barrels and assembles them for export to the latest war around the globe. I guess he's a nice enough chap. I feel he'll be a gentleman with you. Mr. McGregor is relatively new to the area. He has a small looming mill that weaves the different tartans for the Scots. He only came here to learn the machinery, but has stayed, I think, longer than he anticipated. You know, this is hard for me to watch you go to a ball with another man, but I think you could choose any of them."

"Well, not knowing I might have to choose someone, other than yourself, I have given it very little thought. I'll talk with the Professor about who he thinks, since he's interviewed them all. Tell me about this ball," Margaret asked.

"Please do not think Milton as having a gala as you may have seen in London. Formal wear is required, but not the latest fashions or dances, except maybe the waltz."

"I shall like to dance, but I will miss being with you." Margaret said.

Their evening came to an eventual end and John was relieved that Margaret would approach it as he had hoped. He placed Margaret's wrap around her shoulders and escorted her out of the, still busy, restaurant. Branson waited with the coach and John handed her in. All the way to her house, John kissed her and hugged her tightly, and whispered endearments into her ear. It had been too long since he could touch her. He escorted her to her door and opened it with her key.

"I would invite you in for a cup of tea, but it is getting late, and I don't think Dixon is home yet."

"Would that be so bad?" John asked with a soft voice and nice smile.

"Thank you for such a lovely evening." Margaret said, ignoring his blatant grin.

"I will see you next week for dinner with the Professor."

John waited while Margaret entered her home and then said goodnight, kissing her inside the doorstep.

Margaret closed the door and rested herself against it. She was in dreamy mood thinking about John, how wonderful he was, and how she had missed him.

Leaving a light on for Dixon, she climbed the stairs to her room feeling the sleepiness starting to take her. Turning on the gaslight, she noticed something on her pillow. She walked over to see that it was a white rose with a note attached. *How did this get here?* She opened the note but did not recognize the handwriting, as it was printed and not written. The note said,

I WILL HAVE YOU SOON AND I KNOW YOU WANT ME.

No signature. She sighed and smiled wondering what type of tricks John was up to. She knew he had a key and must have had Branson do this while they were at dinner. If the rose was still nice by John's dinner, she would wear in her hair.

Chapter 21

John's Alarm

The rest of the week, John and Higgins went over some serious planning for the probability of purchasing Slickson's mill. John needed to make some people moves for the strategic positions and Higgins needed a replacement, as overseer. It was determined that three overseers would be instituted, one for each mill. The organizational format was going to have to change with having three mills and Higgins in a whole new capacity. John wanted all the training started immediately, because he was sure Slickson's mill would be his. He understood very well that he could handle the added work with the top people he had. John was very confident in the men that Slickson had in place and knew the top overseer there and several other top men. He was impressed to find what he did at Slickson's Mill. The building was in good condition. The machinery was kept in top shape, serviced, and inspected often. Speaking with several of the lay people, John found they had a wonderfully satisfied attitude. As hard as he tried to get them to confess to problems there, it seemed no one had any. Most of the workers knew of John Thornton and his mill workings and were hopeful that he would be their new master some day.

Finished winding her braids, Margaret found the white rose that was almost past its bloom and pinned it in her hair. Her gown was appropriate for a small home gathering diner, Margaret thought. She had acquired many such dresses from all the functions that she and Booker had to attend at the college.

Dixon called up the steps that Mr. Thornton and the Professor were arriving. Margaret took a final look in the mirror and then hurried down the stairs as Dixon was opening the door to John.

"Good evening Margaret, you look splendid. Are you ready to leave? I see you have a lovely rose in your hair tonight." John remarked.

"Yes, I am ready," Margaret replied. "You are quite the man with flowers," she said showing a small gleam in her eye and handing John her wrap for him to place on her shoulders.

What could she mean by that? . . . Quite the man with flowers. I have never brought her flowers. And why haven't I?

The three enjoyed a nice meal at Marlborough Mills that evening. John and the Professor talked mostly about Milton, and the Chamber Ball invitation, and John promised to set a date to talk with him when he returned from Brighton, about his beginnings in the milling industry. To Margaret's chagrin, the Professor told John of all the interest Margaret was garnering from his visitors. "Thank you for the invitation to the Ball. I will love to attend. I hope I can sit with Margaret and her gentleman," said the Professor.

Her gentleman . . .

John was trying to cast aside his green demon that had so recently made itself known. His stomach roiled every time he thought of another man approaching Margaret for any reason. "I'm sorry I will be unable to be there, myself. I am sure you will enjoy it, Professor, and Margaret tells me she likes to dance. Maybe you can accommodate her," John smirked.

John escorted Margaret and the Professor to his traveling coach with his fine four horses, carrying them to their homes in fashion.

Branson dropped off the Professor first, and then reined the carriage for Margaret's house.

Margaret asked, "Would you like to come in for a cup of tea or a brandy?" John replied that he would indeed, a little too hastily.

He spoke into the speak box, inside the carriage, and told Branson to pull around back where they would exit the coach. With smothered excitement in his voice, John asked if Dixon was home, for if she was not, he might have to give Branson some different instructions. Unfortunately, Dixon was home and Branson was encouraged to visit Adrian if he was home.

Dixon brought tea as John reclined in *his* chair that Margaret had purchased for him, telling her that the size of it made a very comfortable seat. They were discussing the Professor and the ball when she mentioned, "He has a pretty thick folder on you, already, John. I read it today." Margaret said with a twinkle in her eye.

"He does, does he? I am sure it is full of fanciful exaggerations."

"It is a large folder and he hasn't even started yet on your documentation. I am most seriously impressed with what you have accomplished while I've been away. You have been far too modest to let me know about the status you hold in this new age. I'm so proud for you, John. Why didn't you speak to me of this?"

John shifted in his big chair. "Margaret, first of all, I care for none of that heraldry. I wish I could change my name some days. Nothing came difficult to me. And secondly, none of it would have happened when it did if it were not for you. I want you to fully realize that my success came from your ideas, your passion."

"That is as may be, John, but YOU took my ideas, which were only a few words, YOU took the risks, and YOU almost lost everything. YOU depleted nearly all you owned to make it work. YOU saw it through to a successfully smooth transition. YOU need to accept the fact that YOU are a man for the history books, like it or not."

John watched her face as she spoke with such earnestness. Although, he did not care to hear about his successes, he was more amazed at Margaret's insight and perspicacity. She was driving her point. Her vitality was stunning. He was hugely pleased to see what working with the Professor was doing to her confidence. Or could it be, all the interest that gentlemen were finding in her was giving her this assurance? Although, he didn't want to think of that as the reason, but it was what she needed, and he knew that.

"Can we not talk about that for now?" John asked. "Have you accepted an invitation to the ball, yet?" It didn't matter who she said, he was not going to like it.

"Yes, I have accepted Mr. Steen's offer. I believe he is fond of dancing."

"Well, at least you will be safe with him, I think he always has a gun on his person," John said.

"Since you're putting me through this at least I would enjoy dancing."

John laughed to himself, "Margaret, you will have many offers to dance. Men will flock to you. If I were taking you, I could shield you from that, if it made you uncomfortable."

"How do you know this?" Margaret asked.

"One day you will find your complete inner self again. And you will like what you see. I think you are too naive, still, to believe in your own beauty, even with all these potential suitors that come to your office. Margaret . . . divorced, widowed or single; you are a very alluring woman. Many men there, that night, will want to be close and to hold you in their arms . . . I don't think I can talk about this any longer. You will dance all night. I'm glad that I'll not be there to see it, honestly. If I took you, I wouldn't share you."

"I think you are a bit biased, Mr. Thornton."

"Say what you will. Yes, I am very biased, but I know the attraction that you will unintentionally cause. I have watched other men turn to look at you. I wish you could have seen the heads turning your way as you stepped off the train that day."

Now Margaret wanted to change the subject. "That was quite a trick. How did you do it?" Margaret said to John.

"What is this trick you speak about, Margaret?"

Margaret pointed to the rose in her hair. "Oh John, don't play coy. I know you know,"

John sensing trouble, but not wanting to alarm Margaret played along with it to find out what she was talking about. "So tell me, what did you think?"

"Coming home from our diner out the other night and seeing that note and rose on my pillow had me alarmed at first until I remembered you had a key. You must have put Branson up to it, didn't you?"

In a calm voice, he said, "Well, I don't know if it was mine or not. What did the note say?"

"John! Stop being funny."

"Actually I went through several versions, which one did I actually send?"

"Oh, you know . . . the one that said - I WILL HAVE YOU ONE DAY AND I KNOW YOU WANT ME, or something like that."

"John immediately was reminded of the kidnapping note. Yes, I remember now. Well . . . you've known that haven't you?"

"I wasn't sure it was from you immediately because I've never seen you print before, but then I remembered the key. It might not be a good idea for the neighbors seeing a strange young man, like Branson, entering my dark house," Margaret laughed.

"Margaret, how long is it before Adrian will be able to move here?"

"Ahhhh . . . yes . . . wondering how long you have to do this, are you?"

"I'm not saying a word, just wondering when he'll be on premises."

"Actually, he moved in a month ago. I am glad he'll be here when you are so far away in Brighton."

Brighton! John remembered how he would be away next week. He would have to put some plans into action without Margaret's notice. It could be an admirer, or something unthinkable. He was taking no chances. And whoever it was had found a way into her home.

"It is getting late, I must let you have your rest," John said rising, immediately wanting to see Mason.

Margaret followed him to the door, disappointed in his abrupt departure, wondering why the sudden change in his attitude.

Having his hand on the doorknob, "I will see you before I leave for Brighton." Goodnight, Margaret." John said as he opened the door and then turned back to kiss her, almost as an afterthought. His mind preoccupied, he climbed into the carriage, telling Branson to take him to the back of the courthouse.

Filling with fear for Margaret, John hurried through the rear doors and proceeded to the police station on the first floor, looking for Mason; he hoped he was on duty. Chief Mason was in his office. He knocked on his door and entered.

"Mason, I am glad to see you working late tonight. I think I may have a problem and will need your help," John blurted out with an anxious tone in his voice.

"Anything, Mr. Thornton. It just happens to be my shift this week to be here now. What's the problem, sir?"

John told Mason all about the note and rose that had appeared on Margaret's pillow. He, also, told him that he left Margaret thinking it was his idea, so she wouldn't be upset.

"How long ago did this a happen, Mr. Thornton?"

"This is Tuesday and we had dinner at The Dove last Friday between 7:00 p.m. and 10:00. I have a spare key, she has one for herself and a third, which she may have given to her housekeeper, but I don't know that for sure."

Mason looking at his notes, said, "Are you sure you want to keep it from her? We should ask her questions about the keys, and has she noticed any other strange things?"

"You're right, Mason. I'm afraid I am likely to over react on this. I just know that I'm terribly worried and might not be the best judge of the situation."

"I understand Mr. Thornton. With your seniority as a Magistrate, I am relieved to know you understand that."

"Could you put someone on the house for now, until we can talk with her in the morning? If it's an admirer that will be bad enough, but I'm concerned it could be more than that. Remember the kidnapping note?

Mason replied, "Yes, I remember very well." He told John to go on home and he would assign two officers and watch the back and front of the house, without raising suspicion.

＊　　＊　　＊

Dixon ambled to the front door muttering, "Who could be calling this early in the morning?" Opening the door she was shocked to see Chief Mason along with Mr. Thornton. "Won't you come in sirs? I'll get Miss Margaret. If you would like to sit at the dining room table I will bring tea for all of you."

Dixon went upstairs, where Margaret was just finishing her hair for the day. "Who was it, Dixon?"

"Miss, it is Mr. Thornton, but he has Chief Mason with him."

"Oh dear, that sounds a bit ominous. I'll be right there."

Margaret entered the dining room and both men stood. John spoke first, "Margaret, we are sorry to bother you so early but we think we may have a situation that we need to speak to you about."

John looked at Mason, who encouraged John to go on with the story.

"Please go on," Margaret said, while she took a seat at the table. Both men sat.

"You do remember last night telling me about the rose and the note left on your pillow last week after our dinner?"

"Yes, of course. I thought it quite clever of you. What's wrong?"

"Margaret, I did not send that note and rose."

"But you said last night . . ."

John interrupted, "I didn't want to worry you until I had some things sorted. Your house has been watched all night and now Mason is here to ask some questions, so we can get to the bottom of this. It could be an admirer, or . . . we don't know what else."

Dixon brought in the tea.

"Miss Dixon," Mason asked, "Do you have a key to this house?"

"No, sir, I don't."

Margaret interjected saying, "I lend Dixon the second key, when she needs it. I should have two keys and Mr. Thornton, one key."

"Would you mind finding both keys, Mrs. Reed," asked Mason.

Margaret said, "Certainly," and headed for her small handbag. "I should have both of them in here." Digging in her purse, she could only find one, so she dumped the contents on the table. "Well . . . where is it, the second key? Dixon have you seen a key around the house that was set down?"

"No Miss Margaret."

"Mr. Thornton, do you have your key?" Mason asked.

John produced it from his big key ring. "These keys are to my home, my mills, and this house. They are always on my person, except for sleep."

Mason asked if someone would summon Adrian into the room.

Margaret, looking worried said, "I kept both keys in my purse. With having two and only using one, I cannot tell you how long it's been gone. It could be at Dr. Pritchard's or lost somewhere in the house. I doubt if it would be in John's coach."

John said that he had already thought of that. With the little sleep he had last night, he had gone over a lot in his mind.

"I will check my bedroom once again and bring down the note."

Adrian appeared in the room. "Someone wanted to see me?"

Mason said, "Yes. We have an issue of unlawful entry into this house and are asking everyone here what they may have seen or know. Where were you last Thursday evening between 7:00 p.m. and 10:00 p.m.?"

"I was visiting my old friend and his family."

"And they were at home with you the whole time?"

"Yes."

"Have you seen anyone suspicious around this house or watching this house since coming here? Someone who might be paying a little more attention to the house than would seem normal to you?"

"No, I don't think so . . . wait . . . I remember working out front sometime last week and there was a man, a gentleman that was sitting over there - under that tree on the bench, in the court yard." Adrian said, as he pointed to the courthouse lawn. "He was looking this way, but I just thought he was watching me while he was waiting for someone. I didn't pay him any mind, so I don't know what happened to him."

"About what time of day was this?"

"I believe it was around 4:30 p.m. because Miss Margaret came home from work about then and she stopped and talked to me."

"Would you recognize him, if you saw him again?"

"I don't think so. Like I said I didn't pay him any mind."

"How do you know he was looking this way?"

"Well, you see how that bench is angled, you would have to turn your head to look this way, as it is not dead on. The couple times I looked over there, his head was turned this way."

"Was there anything remarkable about him that you can remember?"

"Just that he was a gentleman. He had a top hat on. I think he was wearing something grey. He looked average size, maybe twenty five to thirty five years old. I didn't see the color of his hair, though."

"Thank you Adrian, you've been a big help."

John stopped Adrian before he left, giving him some money out of his pocket. "I want you to get two new door locks for this house today and have three keys made. Give me the three keys when you return. I will be in and out of here today."

"Yes, sir, Mr. Thornton, right away sir." He left the room.

Margaret had returned with the note as Adrian walked away. "Why give you the three keys, John?"

John waited until he was sure Adrian was out of the house. "I want to go back to where he bought the locks today and talk with the lock maker to be sure he didn't make four of them. I think Adrian is a good man and telling the truth, but I am leaving nothing to chance."

"Here is the note and no sign of the third key." Margaret said.

Mason and John looked at it. It was very nicely printed but they couldn't tell if it was from an admirer or some type of impending sexual warning, which turned out to be the case with the last kidnappers, who were never caught. John was beside himself. "You'll keep someone watching her, right Mason?"

"Sir, I am going to have an officer in the house during the day and two at night, out of sight. I don't want it to appear she's being protected. It appears whoever entered did use a key and that you are resolving today. And . . . we will also have someone watching her go to and from work and another inside her work place."

"Thank you, Mason. I cannot think of anything else except to move her out and that will never catch this guy. I just wish I didn't have to go to Brighton in a few days. I am very worried.

Chapter 22

Constable Wilson and The

Threatening Notes

It was two days before John left for Brighton. He kept in touch with Mason daily, but nothing new had surfaced except the note had an impression from the page written before it. The labs had determined the letters to be: _ _ U _ T MON_ _ _   BAR _ _ _ _ _ R (something scratched over) _ _ N E. Mason had everyone looking at it from the labs to the Bobbies and even John tried to decipher what had been written. Everyone seemed to be in agreement that the MON was for MONDAY, but nothing else would come together and Monday got them nowhere.

Knocking on Margaret's door felt good to John. He hadn't seen her for two days.

"John, you've arrived just in time, look!"

He was handed a second note. **I AM WATCHING YOU,** was all that it said. "Where was this one found?" John was upset and not hiding it. He was going to explode on whoever was doing this to her.

"I just opened this envelope and it was inside. It came through the post today."

"Let's walk it across to Mason. Bring the envelope and we'll give it to the lab. At least this one was not inside the house. That is some small relief."

Margaret took John's arm and they walked over to the courthouse.

They found Mason down stairs and all the questions began. Mason took the paper to the lab immediately and wanted to know if there were any impressions on the paper. A quick appraisal seemed to reveal the letter H. The lab kept the note to go over it further.

Mason said that he still had the same men watching the house and her place of work. Having come through the post, there wasn't anything further that they could deduce. Very discomfited, John walked Margaret to her home.

"Let's go out back, so we can talk." John urged.

When they had walked past the carriage house, John asked her, "Margaret, how are you doing with all of this? For some unexplainable reason, you seem to be doing better than myself. I cannot even think anymore."

"I'm really all right, John. I'm tiring a little of the police being around all the time. I do think it must be an admirer and more of a nuisance than anything. This second note gives me the shivers though. I don't feel in danger, but now, he says he's watching me."

"That could be true or just words of annoyance as the first note could have also been. I've tried to postpone my Brighton trip, but there are too many irons in the fire down there, so I must go, but I hate leaving you. I will worry. I will be thinking of you instead of why I am there. The two other Masters that are available to do this sort of work are either laid up sick or out of town. I would . . . though . . . absolutely refuse to go if I thought you were in any danger. I wish I could take you with me, but I know you have the ball, now.

"John, do not worry. I'll be fine. I'm spending a little more time with the professor rather than coming home. Dixon hasn't left my side and Mr. Granger has come here to visit, which is lovely of him to do. You have two keys and I have the other one which I keep in my bodice all the time. My handbag may be out of my sight at work, but my clothes aren't." She laughed. "Adrian has offered to sleep in the house, but I said no to that, knowing there are officers watching the house.

"How is Higgins doing with his promotion, by the way?"

"Well . . . he hasn't made the big jump to new clothes, but he's probably waiting for my announcement, after I get the deeds back. He and Peggy should be at the Ball, too. I hope he doesn't relent. I am going to tell him of my worry for you and insist he does go, just in case. I should be going, but I will come by tomorrow before I leave."

John and Margaret walked back to the house holding hands, saying nothing. Touching her anywhere felt so intimate that John did not want it interrupted with talk. He waved to the officer stationed out back, as he walked Margaret to her door and said goodbye.

John returned home and sat down to open his own mail. He was sent a note, too. **YOU DON'T DESERVE HER**. John immediately hollered to Branson not to stable the horses and bounded down the back steps to go see Mason again. The note went to the lab, while John and Mason talked about this new twist. Someone *was* watching her, but John was not going to tell her about his note.

"Mason, in case you find anything under the microscopes, send for me, otherwise I am going home to pack."

"Do you want us to put some men on your house?"

"No, I've got security around the mill. I'm not worried. See you tomorrow before I leave."

John went home to his dinner, his favorite chair, and the brandy he needed to help settle his nerves. He pulled out a tattered piece of paper with the impressions from the first note and looked at it once more. Nothing. He paced the floor worrying about Margaret; he wanted to hit something. John couldn't stomach this feeling that he was not in control.

What if something happens to her?

Still seething with frustration, he thought about the worst that could happen. Should it happen, he knew he would follow her to the grave. He wasn't going to live without her; there was no doubt in his mind that he'd go with her immediately. Putting the worst case scenario aside, he tried to think about what type of fixation this man had for her. They were not dealing with a normal person. This person had mental problems, which made him unpredictable, and that's what John feared. This man knew that he had feelings for Margaret, so he might know that he was going to be away. It must be someone that he knows. He decided to take the late train tomorrow evening and sleep the eight hours of the trip arriving in the morning. He could cut off almost a half day that way. Every protective, primitive instinct that John possessed was brought to bear on Margaret's safety.

John went to the office the next morning and took a few hours to review all the documented Brighton studies he would carry. Later he talked with Higgins about what had been transpiring for the past few days.

"Nicholas, if you don't mind, could you stay on the mill property while I'm gone. I will leave the house to you. I just don't know who we're dealing with and since I've had a note, I don't want someone sneaking in here and burning the house down while it's empty. Were you planning on going to the Ball? If so, would you mind sitting with Margaret and Mr. Steen and the Professor.

"Of course, John. I'll be glad to stay there *and* go to the Ball."

"I saw Cavanaugh yesterday and he'll have the deed ready when I get back, so prepare for our Marlborough Mills celebrations, and I mean that literally. I want both Mills to

243

have refreshments and small cakes. Let's plan it for next Monday, a week."

"All right, John." Higgins smiled. "And thank you once more from Peggy and I. You've made a tremendous change in our lives."

"I can't imagine how my life would have been without you around this place, my friend."

John had a bit of lunch at home before heading off. Gathering his travel bag and satchel, he called for Branson to take him to the courthouse. He spent most of the afternoon with Mason and Constable Wilson, who was most anxious to help.

"So, Constable Wilson, do you have any thoughts on this case."

"Yes, sir. I do," the young Constable replied.

John continued, "Have you discussed them with the Chief, here?"

"Actually, not yet, sir. I've been formulating the ideas like a detective would and, although, I see a lot of signs, I haven't put them altogether to form any specific concept, as of yet."

"Would you mind sharing them with the Chief and I?" John said as he looked over to Mason, anticipating a very basic outline of things, here-to-for known.

"You really want to hear what I have come up with?" Wilson asked in surprise.

"Have you discussed much of this with Mason?"

"Not much. I know about the notes. I know that there are impressions on the notes. I know what her chore man thought he saw. I know we have officers watching Mrs. Reed around the clock. I think that is about it, isn't Chief?"

"That's probably pretty close."

Wilson was handed the notes and studied them once again, while John smiled at Mason, eager to hear the youngster's report.

After a minute or two, Wilson looked up and said, "I'm ready, sir."

"Go ahead then," said John.

"We are certainly working with a mentally disturbed man with a fixation on Mrs. Reed. He is aware that there is something between, you sir and Mrs. Reed or knows that you are interested in her in more than a simple friendly relationship. He writes clearly and decisively, with little words. He knows not to write too much because he could be giving something away and that shows either intelligence or a higher education. He's wealthy. He is definitely watching her and I think he is going to be someone known to all of us. His time is probably his own if he can watch often, meaning he's most likely not a laborer, merchant or shop owner, constricted by time schedules. You are going to know him, Mr. Thornton. He has most likely spoken with Mrs. Reed, either passing on the street as she walks to and from work or in her place of work itself, because he's been close enough to know he wants to have her. You are probably looking for a man between the ages of 25 and 40. He feels sexually powerful and wants to fulfill his desire with her, which may push him into brutality if she resists. Mr. Thornton, he doesn't like you butting in his way, but he is afraid of you, due to either your size or your importance. He is probably a man who most women would not look at more than once, therefore the fierce, sexual desire. He's single. I think the impressed words start with Court Monday. How's that?"

John and Mason were looking at him with their mouths gaping.

John said, "I am exceedingly amazed at your insight or whatever it is that drives your thinking. You have a real gift there, Constable. And you have apparently been studying detective material. I think I can speak for Mason and myself when I say, we are quite taken aback. Mason, bring this lad along quickly; let's not waste his mind while it's able to absorb so much.

"Very well, sir."

"I would like to ask you how you arrived at some of your conclusions because you have gone far beyond our thoughts. Why do you say he's wealthy?"

"That was one of the easier ones. There are two clues. He is educated or intelligent, and I feel his is educated, meaning money, because of his clear printing. The other is a little less obvious. Having a note that made an impression from another paper above it indicates that he may have a tablet of paper. There are few, if any, impoverished people that have tablets of paper."

"Excellent theory." John said. The age?"

"That's just statistical. If he is feeling sexually powerful, he'll be within those ages.

"How about the theory that he is watching her and he'll be known to us?"

"He's not standing out as a stranger to anyone, while he watches her."

"Why is he afraid of me?"

"I'm not sure if afraid is the correct word in this care. He sees you standing between himself and Mrs. Reed. He doesn't know how to attack you physically or professionally, so he's taken to words to torment you. He would like to tear you down in Mrs. Reed's eyes. He thinks that would smooth the way for her affection for him. He is delusional, and mentally unstable. It worries me that we have an educated mentally unstable man out there seeking sexual favors with Mrs. Reed."

"I cannot argue with that or any of your logic. You are astounding. How do you come up with COURT as the first word?"

There aren't too many words that will fit those letters. There is COUNT, BLUNT and maybe a few others, but COURT MONDAY sounds like something someone may write down. If I can add a little more?

"Please do."

"First I would find out anything having to do with any court session on a Monday, who were the participants, judges, witnesses etc. Furthermore, I think this man is going to be caught by Mrs. Reed's chore man. Not literally, but he'll spot that man again that was watching that day and tell someone. I think her chore man needs to be inside the front of the house watching the courtyard all day until he's caught. COURTYARD also fits in with the word COURT. And as for using a house key the first time, which we are not sure of, yet . . . but Mrs. Reed could have mistakenly left her key in the door when coming home. If he's been watching her, he could have spotted that and retrieved it without her knowledge of it even being lost. And finally, and this is a real long shot, but I think he might be our kidnapper, although he has a new twist to his method. We know what happened to last young lady with a note and I see nothing here with which to indicate the same won't happen. Sending you a note, sir, is the twist which indicates an escalation since he feels successful from the other time. He's almost playing a game, daring you to catch him. With an attitude like that, nothing will stand in his way."

Reeling from Constable Wilson's words, John tried to compose himself. He just shook his head wondering what they had with this perceptive young man. "Mason, if what Wilson says turns out to be true, I want him sent to London for further training as a detective. He thinks we're going to need a detective agency in the future and I'm inclined to agree. I would like him to head it up and work closely with you. Once he's trained, I'd like you to go for the same training."

"Yes, Mr. Thornton. Thank you, most kindly. I will do exactly as you say. We've been wondering how to work that training into the budget."

"If the city does not have the money, I will go to the Merchant's Chamber for it. Worst case, I will pay for the two of you to train myself, if what he says is true. I will see Margaret shortly and have Adrian brought into the house to watch the courtyard. Wilson, I want you to work on how many professional jobs and or gentlemen out there who can fit into your analogy."

"Yes, guv! Thank you, sir."

"Wilson, you are dismissed," Mason said. Wilson left the room.

"Mason, you have some wizard on your hands. What do you think?"

"I've known he had great potential and I have given him a little more responsibility, like allowing him to go to London that day. But what I just witnessed was beyond anything I have seen, ever. It almost makes me feel small."

"Mason, you are not alone. He's out shown us all. I know you are a better man than this, but some bosses would feel threatened by such a brilliant worker. Just drive him, challenge him, be his mentor, and certainly acknowledge him to the others. Be proud to have him."

"Have no worries there, Mr. Thornton. I wouldn't be where I am today, if I didn't have someone like yourself to bring me along and have confidence in me, driving me to do better. I know what that means. Someday, I may work for this young man, nothing is ever forever."

"I knew you would see it like that, Mason. I'm proud of you."

John and the Chief sat down and began scrutinizing all that Wilson had said. Plans were made.

"I am going over to Mrs. Reed's home for a while and then I will leave for the train for Brighton. I shall be gone . . . four days instead of five, I hope. I don't know exactly when I will be return on Friday night, but it will be very late. Mason, she means a lot to me. Take care of her for me. One last thought, and this may not be possible, so don't hesitate if you need to take action, but if you find out who it is and can watch him until I return, I would like to be there when we catch him."

"Yes, Mr. Thornton, I know she means a lot to you. I think everyone knows that and so does our bad guy. We will do everything possible to watch her. No shortcuts, nothing taken for granted, ever, and if we can wait, we will. Have a good trip."

"See you when I return, Mason." John shook Mason's hand with both of his and said, "Good luck. My future is in your hands now."

Branson carried John around the block to park on Margaret's side of the street. John told him what time to return for his trip to the train station.

"Would you mind if I went around back and talked with Adrian?"

"Yes, that would be fine. I will want to talk with Adrian, too. Tether the horses and coach out front. I want the coach easily seen here."

John was welcomed into Margaret's house and he greeted the police officer. "Officer, how long have you on duty in here this evening?"

"I only have but half an hour before the night shift comes to the back of the house."

"I wish you to go out back and send Adrian in here, and then you're excused for your last half hour because I will be here."

"Right you are, sir."

John asked if Dixon was here. Margaret said not this evening. "She's been so wound up and sticking solid by me that I insisted she get out for several hours. She left only moments ago."

"I think we're perfectly safe, even if our culprit saw Dixon leave. We have Adrian and Branson in the back yard talking. I need to speak with Adrian. Peggy's clever brother has offered us some insight into this madman and we're going to catch him soon."

"Hello Adrian, how are you doing?"

"Fine, sir. What can I do for you?"

"For the next week, I want you to sit in this front parlor and just watch the courtyard across the street for any signs of the same man you thought you might have seen that one day. If you see him, you will point him out to the officer that is here. He will leave through the back and go around the block, and contact the Chief. He will point out to Mason, who you pointed out to him. Are there any questions?"

"No, sir. Clear as a bell."

"Thank you, Adrian. That's all."

John sat down heavily, rubbing his forehead, mentally exhausted. His nerves were taught with fear. John slid down so his head rested on the back of the couch and propped his feet on a nearby chair. "Margaret, will you come sit next to me."

Margaret, worried by the look on his face, eagerly went to John. As she sat, John took her hand and held it to his chest, without even turning to look at her. Staring at nothing across the room, he said, "We're going to get through this. There are a lot of new plans in place, now. I will worry for you, most certainly unnecessarily, but I can't help it. I will tell you now, since we have a lot more in place to keep you surrounded, but I got a note yesterday too, in my post. It said YOU DON'T DESERVE HER."

"Oh John, are you worried at that?"

"I'm only worried about you. Since my home will be empty, Higgins is going to stay there to keep an eye on it. Let me tell you what young Wilson has come up with, you will be amazed."

John told Margaret all that Wilson had said and his reasons for it. Margaret could feel something forming in her mind. Wheels were turning and clicking into place. John noticed she was staring off into space, her mouth slightly agape. He sat up to watch her. He could tell what he said had meant something to her. She was appraising all his words. He didn't disturb her.

Margaret, still staring said in a calm low voice. "I know who it is. It all fits."

"Who? ... Who, Margaret?"

Chapter 23

 The Plan and the Spring Ball

"Please, John, I need to be sure. Please repeat all you said a moment ago."

John slowly went down the list, not leaving anything out, while watching every suspicion pass across her face. "Yes," Margaret said, "I think I know who it is."

"Would you care to tell me, or should I guess?" John asked, speaking firmly to her for the first time. He was starting to lose patience.

"But what if I am wrong?"

"Before we arrest whoever it is, there will be many others who will find the proof of your assumption that you are *not telling me about*," he said in a rising voice.

"It all sounds like Mr. Cavanaugh next door," Margaret said in a light half-hearted tone.

John, stunned, promptly flopped back against the couch. Now he was running down the list himself, almost too disturbed to think it could be him. He pulled the crinkled paper impression from his vest pocket. Barrister would fit. COURT MONDAY BARRISTER . . . KANE? That could easily have been written on a tablet in the office. John ran to the back door and called to see if the officer was still on the property. He was.

"Don't leave, officer. I want you to carry a note to your Chief immediately and wait for a reply." John quickly scribbled something down on a paper and folded it in quarters, handing it to the officer. "Take this to Mason, now. Thank you."

"Margaret, you may be right. It does fit, with the exception that he's never given me any impression of being mentally disturbed, but all the rest works. I hope you are right. I can leave now, with a great burden lifted, that he is being watched while I am away. It should not be long before he tries something new and plays into the Chief's hands, especially if he knows I am going to be absent for a few days.

There was silence for a long time and each of them proceeded through all the scenarios. Even if Adrian recognized Cavanaugh as being the person he thought he saw, it was not proof enough. But it was a start.

Shortly, a message was returned by the officer, via the back door, and handed to John.

Mr. Thornton.

We will heed Mrs. Reed's intuition. A lot fits there. I will continue with all coverage of Mrs. Reed and add an additional detail to watch Cavanaugh at all times. He will make a mistake and we will catch him, but we will still not lose focus on others whose names are now on a list being formed by Wilson. Travel with peace of mind that it may all be over when you return, or perhaps he'll be waiting for your own justice.

Margaret huddled closer to John, sensing relief might be in their future and this nightmare would soon end. She could see that John was still far away in his mind. She hated what all this was doing to him more than she feared for herself. Observing his internal grief, she had seen his concern for her pour out these past few days.

"What are you thinking about, John . . . Cavanaugh?"

"Well . . . yes, that and the thought of anyone harming you. It isn't over until he's put away, if it is him. I'll worry until it is proved. And to think he'll be right next door to you while I'm gone. I can barely stand the thought."

"John, it sounds as though I will have many people watching me, and him as well. Nothing can possibly go wrong. Don't leave worrying about me."

"Speaking of leaving . . ." John pulled out his watch to check the time. "I thought I'd have more time with you, but it has slipped away. I must go."

"John, may I ride with you to the station?"

"It's either that or I carry you there . . . Of course, I want you to ride with me. Where is your shawl? It's a bit cool this evening."

John whistled out the back door to alert Branson he was ready to leave and for him to assume his post.

"Adrian!" called John. "Would you guard the house until Miss Margaret returns? The other officer should be here by then. She's just going for a brief ride with me to the train station."

"Yes, sir, I'll wait right here." He indicated the back step.

"No, it's better if you wait in the house so you can hear if anyone comes to the front door."

"Very good, sir."

John accompanied Margaret through the front door, watching her as she locked it.

Handing her in, he slid in beside her and once again took her hand as he sat thinking, his mind churning. Nausea was going to claim him before this night was over.

Sensing his worry, Margaret asked, "So exactly what are you doing on this trip?

"I'm sorry. What did you say?"

Margaret repeated her question; John gave her a brief outline of his schedule and what all the meetings entailed. She added a few other questions to the conversation to prevent John from relapsing into worry.

John continued to stare out the window. "Margaret," he said, "I know what you are trying to do, but it won't work. I will not ever stop worrying about you when you are out of my sight, not for the rest of my life. You must know that whatever happens to you happens to me. Please take care of me, while I'm away."

John heard her sigh. The station was coming into sight and he had turned within himself, knowing the moment to depart was drawing near. He was consumed with regret for leaving her behind, in possible danger. All approaches were well covered and he would have to rely on Mason, and everyone else involved, to watch over his beloved. The coach came to a stop. John turned to Margaret. He hugged her tightly and kissed her a very long time, as if it could be his last. He fought to release her and hesitated taking the initial steps to leave her side.

"I will be back as soon as I can possibly get away. Take care, my love. God, how I love you," John said, in a harsh agonized whisper, as he kissed her neck.

He grabbed his travel bag and satchel and stepped out of the coach. Looking back over his shoulder at Margaret, one last time, before he disappeared into the station depot.

John was almost sick with anxiety. He had held Cavanaugh in high esteem, but who knows what dwells deep within someone's mind. Well, he must focus on something else. It may not even be him. But telling himself not to think about it was like trying to stop a wave from crashing on shore. He was alone in the train coach and decided to try to settle in and doze, if he could. It was going to be an eight hour journey from almost one end of the country to the other. Several hours later, forced into total mental exhaustion, he drifted off into a nightmare.

It took three days for proof to finally present itself. Adrian had already confirmed that Cavanaugh looked very much like the man he had seen watching the house, but could not be entirely positive. Per her normal schedule, Margaret left her home to walk to the Professor's for her daily work. Several hours later, Dixon left the house with her market basket.

Cavanaugh, watching from his office window that faced Margaret's home, thought the house to be empty, so he decided to deliver his next note. He had to be careful not to be seen by that man she had working for her, who was usually always around the back of the house. He easily slipped outside and walked a few feet to Margaret's front door. He delivered the note through the mail slot and began walking back to his office, in a casual manner. The officer inside heard the brass hinge banging closed, and immediately went to the window and saw Cavanaugh walking away. If what he had slipped through the door was another note, they had him.

The officer was a little unsure if he was permitted to open the note to confirm it, so he got Adrian's attention to come inside. The officer gave Adrian both his note and the delivered note; he asked him to take it the long way around to the precinct and see Chief Mason, only. Adrian put the notes in his pocket and hurried around the back block, so as not to be seen from any of the law office windows.

Margaret and the Professor were discussing some of his recent interviews, but Margaret eventually asked him about coming to the Ball. The Professor beamed with delight

"I am most excited, Margaret. To see the original Mill Masters and the future generation of machinery masters, in one place, is a thrill for me. I hope I learn a few names and can talk with them about having a more in-depth interview at another time. There will be some, should they attend, whom I have already met. I am very sorry that John cannot be with us tonight."

"As am I; I'm attending with Mr. Steen, you know."

"Is your table full?" the Professor asked.

"Oh . . . I have no idea. Nothing has been explained to me, but I want you to sit with us. I need you there for support."

"Does John know of this Mr. Steen?"

"Yes, John knows. He is familiar with Mr. Steen. He put on a very brave face, but I knew he was bothered. I think jealous is the word, but he's certain this is a step I should be taking. I am very hesitant, but knowing that you and Nicholas will be there has eased my mind considerably."

Just then Chief Mason came through Pritchard's office door, looking very excited. "Mrs. Reed, I think we may have the proof we need to verify Cavanaugh is our man, but we need your help."

"Yes, of course. Professor, will you excuse me?"

"Margaret, take the rest of the day. I will see you this evening at the Ball."

"Thank you. All right, Chief Mason, shall we go?"

"I'll tell you what has happened on the way to your house," Mason said.

*   *   *

"Oh Dixon, please stop fussing with my hair. It must be quite lovely by now. Mr. Steen will be arriving soon and I still have my gown to put on."

"Miss Margaret, that sure is a lovely dress, with all that lace and ribbon. If it weren't so low on the shoulders, I think it would look like a wedding dress, even if it is a peach color."

Margaret and Dixon slipped the gown carefully over the ribbons and flowers in Margaret's braided hair. Dixon fastened all the fittings to her dress and steered her toward the floor mirror.

"It is lovely, is it not, Dixon? I think it will go well here in Milton even though it was last year's fashion in London. Would you get my matching shoes and bag from the wardrobe?"

Margaret sat at her vanity and applied the few light paints that she rarely used: a bit of color for her cheeks and lips, and a small dab of perfume. Finishing that, she popped the paints and a comb into her bag and took one last look in the mirror. She picked up her lace shawl and headed downstairs with Dixon.

As she waited in the parlor, she began to pace, thinking about the man next door, and wondering why they were going to wait for John to return home tomorrow. The proof was definitely there.

The officer came from the kitchen and almost dropped his tea cup when he saw Margaret. "Ma'am, you look very lovely this evening. You will turn heads tonight."

Oh dear, Margaret thought, she didn't want that much attention. She remembered John saying a lot of men would ask her to dance. Now, she wished she hadn't accepted, but the Professor was proud of her and that was enough to see her through this. It was nearing 7:00 p.m. when Margaret heard Mr. Steen's carriage arrive.

Watching him exit, she thought he looked most handsome, in his forest green velvet coat, cream color embroidered vest, and matching forest green breeches with white stockings and a nice pair of black dance slippers, made especially for men in formal wear. His top hat matched his vest, and he carried a gold-headed cane in one hand and a nosegay for her to wear, in the other. She'd wage anything that it would match his boutonniere. She realized she was excited to be going. John had been right. He was always right. Why did she ever feel distress over his suggestions? This was good for her, and down deep she knew it, herself.

Dixon answered the door. She greeted and led Mr. Steen into the parlor. Looking at Margaret, and stunned by the sight of her, his face radiated approval. He knew her to be beautiful, but her gown added another glow; one that wasn't ever apparent at her workplace.

"Mrs. Reed, you are the loveliest vision I have ever seen. I will have to fight the men off with my cane this evening," he smiled.

He had Margaret laughing. "Thank you."

"Here is a small bouquet for your wrist, but it now pales against your own bloom."

Dixon took the flowers from Mr. Steen and began to slide them over Margaret's hand. No way, was she going to let that man touch Margaret, forgetting they would be dancing together that evening. Dixon liked him well enough, but not where his interest in Miss Margaret was concerned.

"Thank you, Dixon, and thank you Mr. Steen for the pretty nosegay and nice compliment."

"If you are ready, milady . . . shall we?" Mr. Steen asked, extending his arm. "Would you mind calling me, Craig? I'm not sure I could stand Mr. Steen all night as we dance."

Laughing, Margaret replied, "Craig it is, if you will call me Margaret."

"Margaret, we have an accord. Would you mind inflating my self confidence by allowing me to know how many other suitors asked you to the Ball this evening?"

Margaret saw his smiling, laughing face and could not deny him. "That would be three others, apart from you."

"Oh, I am the most fortunate of men. I have even impressed myself. Thank you, Margaret, for allowing me to escort you to a grand evening of dining and dancing. I'm looking forward to dancing. It has been a while."

They walked across the street and arrived at the courthouse's entrance where Margaret surrendered her wrap. They proceeded up the wide staircase to the top floor, a climb which nearly exhausted everyone that evening. As they approached the main entrance into the ballroom where many were gathered, Margaret could see people standing in the wide door frame, talking to each other. She could see it was lovely inside the main ballroom. There were many round tables with white linen (or was it cotton?) tablecloths, shimmering with fine china, crystal, and sterling flatware. Once their tickets were taken, they were permitted to seat themselves wherever they chose.

Craig heard Margaret gasp. He quickly turned to look at her, barely seeing the huge smile on her face as she took off across the room.

"Margaret?" Craig muttered, quickly following her.

"Nicholas, Peggy! What a joy to see you here. John was hoping you would come. You both look marvelous. Although somehow, Nicholas, you look uncomfortable in that formal attire, but you do look most handsome." Nicholas' face reddened.

Craig caught up with Margaret as she excitedly introduced Nicholas and Peggy.

"Oh, are you the Higgins from Marlborough Mills?"

"Yes," Margaret responded before Higgins could. "This is Nicholas Higgins and his wife to be, Peggy. John has recently made Nicholas a partner in Marlborough Mills, so he is no longer the respected overseer that you, perhaps, have heard about. He is an owner now," Margaret remarked with pride.

Nicholas was already standing, and reached across the table to shake the man's hand. "Nice to meet you."

"I am Craig Steen and please call me Craig."

Margaret looked around the table, resolving the seating arrangements so that the Professor could sit on one side of her. Craig Steen waited until she decided and then seated her. Dr. Pritchard entered a few minutes later and Margaret glided across the floor, to the main entrance, so she could accompany him to their table.

Mr. Steen wasn't sure if he could keep up with Margaret if she kept running away from him all evening.

"Oh, Professor, thank you for coming."

A few minutes later Fanny and Watson appeared. Margaret introduced Mr. Steen around again, but Watson seemed to know him and a conversation ensued. Margaret was smiling and looking around the room at the gowns and faces and all the men in their finery. Their table was full with only one empty chair. She looked at Nicholas and knew he felt the significance of the empty chair.

Margaret soon launched into a discussion about Dr. Pritchard, who he was, and what his project was in Milton. While dinner was being served, there was much talk around the table about the Professor, Nicholas' partnership, and his upcoming marriage. Everyone was getting along splendidly. A nice dinner was served and eventually the dishes were cleared of the dessert plates. While the wait staff circulated the brandy and wine decanters to each table, a podium was pulled up to the center room in front of the wide entrance.

Watson stood. "Excuse me," he said, "if John were here tonight, he would be doing this." As he proceeded to the podium, he pulled a note from his pocket. He never cared for talking to crowds, but this would be short; he was thankful for that.

He welcomed everyone, adding a few words, but nothing of much importance, except to say "enjoy the evening." Then it was time to introduce the Professor; Watson waited for silence in the room before he continued.

"I am very privileged, tonight, to introduce to you someone who most of you will get to know very soon, if you have not already met him by now. As our mills and industries have grown here in Milton, I think most of us know the impact that we have made over the years, not only nation-wide, but world-wide. Tonight, I would like to introduce the man that is going to literally put us in the history books. He has made his home here, living among us, and is writing about the growth of Milton and the beginnings of the Industrial Age. Please welcome, Professor, Dr. Trevor Pritchard.

A very great round of applause was heard as the surprised Professor walked to the podium. Margaret was so happy for him; she looked around at all the people acknowledging him with their applause. Suddenly, she caught sight of Mr. Cavanaugh looking at her. He nodded his head as if to say "hello" and she demurely nodded back. She knew not to give anything away.

All through the Professor's speech she could feel his eyes burning into her. She did not mention it to anyone, for fear they may look his way and alert him to something. As the Professor concluded his short talk on his plans for the future, there was a very large round of applause and people began standing as they clapped.

Watson's final words were, "Let's dance, everyone," as the applause began to die down. He walked the Professor back to the table.

Upon being seated, the professor turned to Margaret, "Margaret, did you know about this?"

With a chagrined look on her face, she nodded yes.

Many congratulations were offered from around the table and several factory owners came over to introduce themselves to him; one was Mr. McGregor, the tartan mill owner.

After speaking with the Professor, Mr. Albert asked across the table, "I hope you save a dance for me, Mrs. Reed."

A liquor bar was set up at one end of the banquet hall, with the orchestra at the other. The musicians started to tune their instruments and the crowd grew loud in anticipation of the entertainment ahead. The orchestra leader conducted his musicians into the first dance of the evening.

Craig asked Margaret to dance and then escorted her to the floor. Margaret trembled a little but soon fell into the rhythm of the steps. He turned out to be an exceptionally smooth dance partner. They danced several more, before the other gentlemen found their way to Margaret's table. She danced with Mr. McNeil, Mr. Albert, Watson, and other unknowns; even Mr. Cavanaugh asked to dance. She hesitatingly accepted, afraid of what he might want to talk about, but he was a gentleman the entire dance. She invited the Professor to dance and he finally gave in. Craig claimed dances whenever he could, before the orchestra rested around 10:00 p.m.

Margaret finally noticed, whenever she would look up, she would be aware of heads that turned her way as she walked to and from the dance floor, and she couldn't help but feel a little nervous. Many times she had to turn down dances from unknowns, strictly out of politeness to Craig. The evening was turning out to be very pleasant and Margaret finally began to feel comfortable with other gentlemen, but she missed John being there . . . *or so she thought.*

Chapter 24

 *I Will Kill You*

The orchestra came back for their final set and had just finished their tuning up when a commotion seemed to ripple through the crowd, interrupting conversations and redirecting gazes. It seemed to Margaret as though something was happening, and it was catching everyone's attention. Hearing whispers and gasps, she started to look around to see what everyone was looking at, when she noticed heads were turned toward the wide entrance.

She saw him: He took her breath away. John Thornton was standing in the doorway, radiating the pure masculine beauty that she had once studied as he slept. Margaret thought he was so handsome, it almost hurt. Her knees weakened as he filled the entrance with his considerable air and poise. The man's very presence seemed to suck all of the air out of the room. She didn't know if he was looking for her, but he hesitated, modestly. Unknowingly, he was being admired by every woman in the room and a lot of the men, too. Their admiration of him, between the men and the women, was for entirely different reasons.

Higgins said, "There's our John and doesn't he look . . ."

". . . resplendent . . . I think, is the word you are looking for," Margaret whispered, overwhelmed with the beauty of the man.

There he stood: tall, dark haired, austere, and stately in a rich heavy black linen coat with long tails. He wore a white crisp shirt, ivory waistcoat and an ivory cravat adorned with a gold stickpin. On his lapel was a single red rose. John was so exquisitely male, that other gentlemen could easily feel jealous. Margaret noticed that he had on dancing slippers, too. His elegance was in his narrow cut, classically understated attire. No frilly cuffs or frilly shirt, no gloves, little jewelry, even his watch and chain were not showing. His cravat was neat, nicely knotted and not billowy and frilly like most gentlemen were wearing that evening. He needed no fine accoutrements to enhance his splendor. He was impeccable. She felt warm all over and blood rushed to her cheeks. She was going to have to look away soon, or run to claim him as her own. He looked magnificent. He drew everyone's attention as he passed through the rows of tables, talking with people. Many wanted to come to him and shake his hand. To the younger men, he looked as if he was a god. Margaret was dumbstruck with the amount of respect that he was being shown. Again, she felt small. All the women had their heads turned his way, unable to keep from staring and smiling. Suddenly, there was that feeling in her stomach again as jealousy welled. She caught the Professor looking at her; he knew exactly what she was going through. John eventually sat down with Slickson at his table. Margaret wondered why he wasn't looking for her.

Craig took Margaret to the dance floor, and while twirling her around, she saw John looking her way. He gave her a beautiful smile that filled her with his love. She suspected that he was showing respect for the fact that Mr. Steen had brought her there tonight.

Eventually, John walked down to the bar end of the room to fetch himself a drink. On his way back, the handshakes began again, so he stood and spoke to many people, never looking in Margaret's direction. When the second song began, Mr. Latimer, who she hadn't seen since her last time living in Milton, asked her to dance. She obliged him and he escorted her to the dance floor. Margaret thought him an extremely fine dancer.

She took the opportunity to inquire about his daughter. "How is Miss Ann?" she asked.

"Oh . . . she's fine. She eventually grew tired of waiting for John to propose, and she married an architect who was here in Milton, designing the early stages of the city. They live in London now. You look wonderful tonight. I understand that you are working for Dr. Pritchard?"

"Yes, I am. He's an intelligent man and we have been close friends for about three years now. I'm sure he will do Milton proud with his book. He has written many books and was very well respected at the college."

They danced in silence for the last minute of the music and Mr. Latimer walked her back to the table, thanked, and seated her. She looked around for John and could not see him, but Cavanaugh was still looking at her. Craig had just asked her for the next dance, when John appeared. He said hello and shook hands with Craig.

"Higgins, I'm glad you found the courage," John laughed. "Would you mind if I ask Peggy to dance?"

Peggy had not been on the dance floor yet, and Margaret had felt sorry for her. She was glad he asked Peggy to dance, and she hoped he would stay at their table when the dance was over.

After a rather lively dance, John brought a smiling Peggy back to the table, and immediately turned and walked over to the orchestra. He spoke briefly to the conductor. The orchestra started up and John returned to the table and asked Margaret, "Could I have this waltz, Mrs. Reed?"

On their way to the floor, the music began and Margaret could hear some groans from the audience. Apparently, the waltz, previously thought scandalous but now coming into fashion, had not been entirely introduced to Milton, as yet. Only a handful took to the floor.

John, standing tall, held out his left hand for Margaret to take. She could feel his body heat radiating on her face from his chest. She drew in his manly scent and wanted to melt right there, into him. Her bosoms were heaving from the excitement, which did not escape John's notice. He then slipped his right hand around the back of Margaret's waist, placing it properly, square in the center, leaving a small amount of proper airspace between them. Margaret put her left hand on his shoulder. John took in her breathtaking scent, as he always did, and enjoyed the presence of her in his arms. Her breasts surging up and down where making his loins ache. He looked directly at her with his steel blue eyes. They both smiled at each other.

"Do you know the waltz, Mrs. Reed?"

"Yes, I do, Mr. Thornton," she said with an air of amused sophistication.

"Then let us dazzle everyone here and regale them with a waltz."

John and Margaret slipped easily into the 1 - 2 - 3 rhythm that was the waltz. John whirled her all around the dance floor with such grace as one would think it was one person dancing. All eyes were on them, but their eyes were only for each other.

Margaret realized the moment for what it was. She was oblivious to the watching eyes, the two other swirling couples, the glow of the candles, even the music. This was the moment she knew, beyond all doubt, that she wanted to be with him, forever in his arms. John noticed a new gleam in her eye and the thumping of her heart had hastened. He thought she might be having 'a moment' on one of her islands.

"John?"

"Yes, Margaret?"

"Are my feet still touching the floor?" She asked, with all the love she could give him showing on her face.

"I hope they never touch the ground when you are in my arms," John whispered to her.

John's tails flared gracefully away from his body as he twirled Margaret, and her gown swept out to the movement of the dance with a light whisper of ribbons and linens and lace. The two other couples left the dance floor to watch the spectacular show that now appeared in the center of the huge room. John and Margaret were an exquisitely mirrored couple, dancing close together in perfect harmony. Not once did John look away from Margaret's eyes; he always had a sense of their position on the floor. There should have been no doubt, by anyone watching, that those two were deeply in love. The orchestra, recognizing the display as almost a performance, played longer than was usual.

"Margaret?"

"Yes, John?"

"You are an exquisite sight tonight."

"Thank you. And you are most dazzling, yourself."

"Thank you, Margaret." He paused briefly.

"Margaret?"

"Yes, John?"

"You are going to marry me someday."

"I think I will, too," Margaret said.

"You will tell me when that will be. And I fully understand your reasons for being free from me and finding yourself. When you are sure, you will come to me and tell me that you love me. You have not spoken the words yet, you know, but I will wait forever."

Margaret's eyes were misting over and John felt it was time to refrain his words of love. He had just heard Margaret utter the very words he had wanted to hear, ever since he'd met her. If only he could kiss her right now. He remembered the diamond ring that he always carried with him. Someday, he thought. Someday soon, he hoped.

One last turn around the dance floor and the music ended. Even though John was only aware of Margaret on the floor, and she only aware of him, everyone else was aware they were a pair, and gave them a huge round of applause. They broke from their entranced state to realize they had been the only couple dancing the exotic waltz.

John escorted a red faced Margaret back to her seat, next to Craig.

As they approached the table, Margaret asked John, "Where did you learn to waltz, Mr. Thornton?"

"I found it of benefit to learn due to all the banquets I had to attend on my trips. Thank you, Mrs. Reed," John said, and continued around the room meeting people.

Everyone at the table remarked upon the magnificent display of dancing that she and John had performed. The two of them appeared to dance as one person, every move meticulously reflected by the other. The Professor had a very broad smile on his face. Margaret noticed and lowered her eyes, wanting to elude the compliments. Mr. Steen commented that he must learn this new waltz soon.

Nearing midnight, the evening began to draw to a close with the announcement of the final dance. Craig escorted Margaret to the dance floor. There were butterflies in her stomach, as she watched John take another woman in his arms and smile at her. Margaret felt the curse of jealousy, but realized that John had been through the same ordeal since arriving tonight. With the final bow and curtsey, Margaret thanked Mr. Steen for a truly enjoyable evening, and remarked on his exceptional mastery of the dance.

With the evening concluded, people were gathering their things and filing out the wide door.

Suddenly, everyone stopped. A disturbance had broken out at the door entrance. People murmured among themselves and tried to step backwards from the frightening scene. Margaret could hear John's raised voice. She ran around people to the front of the line and there was John, enraged, holding Cavanaugh by the lapels, shouting at him. John swung at

Cavanaugh with his fist; it landed on Cavanaugh's chin, knocking him to the floor. The crowd stood watching and wondering what could have incited such anger in John Thornton.

Cavanaugh tried to kick and claw, but John pulled him up by his shoulders and punched him again. Cavanaugh put up little defense after that, and people began to pull John off of him.

Higgins grabbed John from behind, whispering loudly to him, "John! John! He's done. Don't do anything to ruin your future."

John shook Higgins off and turned to Cavanaugh, shouting for all to hear, "If you *EVER* do that to her again, I will *KILL* you."

Mason's men came charging through door and hauled Cavanaugh to his feet. They pulled his arms behind him and handcuffed him, leading him down stairs to the bottom floor precinct.

John stood there as people began asking, "What did Cavanaugh do to whom?" He was sucking big gulps of air as he ran his fingers through his hair and straightened his waistcoat and cravat. He did not talk, or look at anyone. He was trying to get his rage under control. Margaret approached him, he turned, looked at her, then walked away and rapidly descended the stairs. Margaret saw him pass through the outer doors and leave the building.

Craig caught up with Margaret and took her arm to guide her down the stairs. She was visibly shaking. "Margaret, it's over."

"I have seen John's temper only once, but it didn't compare to what I saw tonight. He was obsessed."

"Margaret, that is because of his love for you; even I can see that. What did this fellow Cavanaugh do to you?"

Higgins hurried to her side. "Margaret, you know he's been worried sick about this man hurting you. He had every right to do what he did. That man has very badly brutalized another woman, something they had not suspected of him until this recent incident. Don't hold John responsible for his temper this evening. He knew a lot more about this man then you were ever led to know."

"I'd like to go home, if you don't mind. I need to be alone."

"Of course, Margaret, whatever you want," Craig said.

Margaret paused at his statement, thinking . . .

"Do you really mean that?"

"Mean what?" Craig asked.

"Whatever I want?"

"Yes, of course."

"Could you drive me to Marlborough Mills? I want to talk to John."

"All right, I will be glad to, and I understand your need to see him right now."

Margaret asked Higgins to tell Dixon that she would be at John's tonight.

"Thank you, Craig. You are a fine gentleman and friend. I did enjoy the evening with you much more than I anticipated. By that, I mean that I am quite shy around men. I was rather intimidated at first, but had no reason to be. Thank you for bringing me."

Ten minutes later, Steen's coach pulled up to the Mill's gate. Craig handed Margaret out of the coach and waited while she spoke to the gateman.

"Is Mr. Thornton at home?"

"Why yes, Miss."

"I would like to see him."

"Yes, Miss."

He started to roll back the gate and Margaret reached up and gave Craig a kiss on the cheek.

"I'll find a way home. Thank you again for everything."

Craig doffed his hat and entered the coach. Margaret stood there waving until he was out of sight.

John was sitting in his chair watching his hands shake as the liquid sloshed in his brandy glass. He had removed his tails, waistcoat, for more comfort. He was looking down at the floor, still trying to calm down from his earlier confrontation. John had been overcome, thinking of what might have happened to Margaret at the hands of that man, and he had let control slip away. He was livid and sick to his stomach. He could now understand "insanity pleas." He was certain he was close to going insane tonight, blinded by sheer hatred and having lost all sense of self. Where would he and Margaret be, if he had killed the man like he had wanted to do? As he held his brandy in one hand, and ran the other through his hair and across his brow, he worried about how it could have ended. He recalled how Higgins, once again, had come through for him. Suddenly, as he was about to undo his cravat, he heard a small voice call up the stairs.

"John?"

"Margaret? . . . Is that you?"

Chapter 25

 A Passionate Treasure

"Yes, John. It's me."

John ran to the hall and saw Margaret closing the door behind her. He watched her come to the top of the steps and into the parlor. After removing her wrap, he pulled her hard against him and kissed every part of her face, trying to wipe away his own fears for her.

"I'm sorry you had to see me in that state, Margaret. I don't have the words to explain what that man has done to me. He has torn out my insides. I couldn't get it out of my mind that he might find a way to get to you. We now believe he is responsible for another unspeakable horror. You can't know how, in my mind, I saw you suffering that same despicable act, while I was away. I went mad with worry and returned home before my work was done. I knew before walking in there tonight that there was proof against him. Knowing him like I thought I did, I just had to see him for myself. I walked the room, which I usually do anyway, but I wanted to watch him watching you. He watched you constantly, never taking his eyes from you. His obsession was clear. Hate is not a strong enough word, for what I felt. I can hardly believe it's all over, I had become obsessed, myself, I think."

John continued talking as he handed Margaret a brandy and paced the floor not looking at her, sipping at his own glass. "Because he is mentally disturbed, I don't know if we'll ever find out the reasons for his actions or if there is a second person behind him."

"John, with me not ever feeling the weight of this entire situation, as you did, I was never really afraid. I'm sorry you endured so much pain and anguish on my behalf."

John could not countenance Margaret's misplaced but well-intentioned apology. She was so completely and utterly blameless. Yet, somehow, he knew she'd take some absurd responsibility for driving him to his own rebellious actions.

He put down his glass, swept Margaret into his arms, and carried her to his room. Waiting through the past few days for terror to strike his life, John had exposed a savage soul living within him. His most basic, fundamental nature was driving him to brand her as his own. The gentleman was struggling to survive and do the right thing, but something much deeper and more primordial needed to stake its territory; it was far stronger than his great love for her.

Moonlight was streaming through the windows, softly lighting the room with its faint glow.

He let her stand and put his hands to her face, holding her steady for a deep probing kiss. Margaret flung her arms around his neck, meeting the intensity of John's tongue as he searched her with fierce passion. With every measure of restraint, he softened his approach, not wanting to dominate. He wanted glorious pleasure ahead for them tonight. He had to have her.

He pulled back and looked into her eyes. "Margaret," he said, "God, how I love you so. I don't care if this is the right time or not for us, but I am going to make love to you. I am going to savor you with all of my senses. I cannot wait any longer. "

"Neither can I, John." Margaret crooned softly, as she began to unknot his cravat. She could feel his heat searing her hands.

The sensual, slow ritual of disrobing each other began to unfold, but quickly escalated. John was too anxious and she was nervous. Margaret trembled remembering the size of him, something which worried her their first night.

As the final pieces of clothing fell to the floor, John kissed her tenderly and carried her to his bed, placing her on her back.

"You're trembling, Margaret? What is it? Tell me."

With tears in her eyes, Margaret reluctantly confessed, "I'm worried we won't fit together. You are very . . . well . . . and I don't think . . ."

John leaned in and stifled her words with his lips, savoring her sweetness. "Have no concerns there. I will take it very slowly. How I love your innocence."

Lying beside her, he soothed her with soft whispers of love and kissed her deeply as she ran her fingers through his hair and down his back. He could feel her body was tight as a bow string. He became aware of how anxious he was, which might be scaring her as well as her concern for their compatibility. Responding to her needs, he gently stroked her and kissed her until her muscles relaxed and her fears turned to longing. His hands found all of her body. He softly stroked her nipples already pebbled and waiting. The smooth moistness of his tongue found the hollow of her neck and John could feel her rapid pulse beating against his lips. As he moved down to her breasts, he became aware of her heavy breathing, which was matching his own. He suckled at her, pressing her nipple hard against the roof of his mouth, while his tongue worked at her plumpness. She began to writhe under his touch. John knew her body was calling for his. His hand found the moistness that lay within her womanly folds. She was exquisitely wet, ready to take him into her. John knew this beginning would be far too fast for what he wanted her to experience.

"Margaret, I must tell you that this first time will be uncomfortable for you, unlike any other time after this. I will gently expand you to accept me, and it will be fast because I am about to erupt now. I will *take you.* I will not be making love to you because my needs are beyond my control now and it won't be what I want for both of us. But that is only for this first moment. Our lives will be forever enriched with what we will share tonight."

"John, I don't care that it will hurt. I want you to fill me, please." Margaret said, as she stroked his face. "You have to believe that."

Hearing this from Margaret's lips, John smothered her mouth, silencing any other words she might have said. Being as gentle and thoughtful as he could, he wiped saliva from his mouth to his finger tips and wet his penis, as he wanted to ease this anyway he could for her. He proceeded to guide himself into her small opening. Exerting the first small thrust, he heard Margaret inhale slowly.

"Shall I stop? I won't be able to, much longer."

"No, don't stop no matter what I say. I want this."

John thrust deeper and waited while her sheath adjusted to him. He could feel her womanhood responding with contractions around him, her body was embracing him from within. For John, taking these first steps in small intervals was both pleasurable and tortuous. He drove deeper, holding back some of his length, and then started the slow strokes that brought him to shuddering completion within seconds.

Margaret heard a soft, low husky sigh. His life jetted into her, seemingly without end. She felt the flow of his seed and held him tightly while he panted for breath. She knew he withheld the all of him, denying his own ultimate sensation. He made it so gentle for her, relieving her of any fear, but his strained control had cost him, she knew.

He buried his head in her neck and laid there for a few seconds, experiencing every movement of her inner passage. "Margaret. I've never felt like this." He lingered over her, savoring the scent of her aroused body and feeling her moist skin against his. John withdrew from her and rolled to his side, pulling Margaret onto his shoulder and holding her tightly. He kissed her.

"We have not fulfilled our passion as one yet, but we will. You are staying all night in my bed."

He kissed her again. "Are you all right?" John whispered.

"I'm more than all right, John. I want you again. You make me feel like a woman."

"No, I haven't, not completely. Soon, we will both go there together."

John went to his basin of water, washed himself, and brought back the wet cloth to the bed. Margaret reached for it and John said, "No, let me bath you."

Margaret started to protest.

John laid her back down on the bed saying, "I will bath you."

At John's urging, Margaret timidly opened her thighs to him; he nudged them a bit wider. With the utmost delicacy, he washed her folds before spreading her further open with his other hand. Using his lightest touch, he washed all of her sensitive parts.

"This is an incredible pleasure for me, "John whispered reverently. Finished, he returned the cloth to the basin.
Returning to the bed, he was already aroused again. As he laid back down by her, pulling her to him, she reached down to hold his erect penis. She caressed all of his maleness and enjoyed the sound of his accelerated heartbeats.

"God, how I love you touching me like this, but I'm not so sure you should be doing that Margaret, not now anyway. Are you not a bit tender? You are slightly swollen."

"I just want to know you, John. You have torn down walls I had built around myself. I don't want this night to end. Let me hold you." Margaret caressed and stroked John.

John nestled her closer and allowed himself to be lost in her unhindered innocence, but that lasted a very short time.

Before she knew what happened, Margaret felt a delicate suckling at her breast. John's musky scent filled the air.

"John?"

"Ummm . . ." John hummed, not wanting to leave her nipple.

"The first time tonight . . . when you said you would take me and not make love to me . . ."

"Yes?"

"That's all the lovemaking that I've ever experienced, except you were more gentle and caring and explained things to me. On the rare occasions when he wanted to have sex, and that's the only way that I can think of it now, it was very brief. No real pleasure for me, but I thought that was how it was supposed to be, because that's all I ever knew."

In John's quiet, deep voice he said, "Margaret, he was not making love to you. That was just a physical release for him, like I just went through. I think a lot of married couples go through life that way because they don't love each other as passionately as we love each other. They don't know how, or are too modest, to share their intimacy. They don't communicate and share their needs and desires. We will never let that happen to us. I cannot be thankful enough to be the only man to *make love* to you, and bring you the full feeling of womanhood that you and I deserve. And it will be my first time for making love, too, for I have *loved* no other. Like you, I have only experienced sex. You and I are the same in that respect. Whether realizing it or not, we have waited for each other in our hearts across time and space. I could feel you speaking out to me through your silence. It was almost like our souls were linked without our minds knowing of the connection. From the day we were parted, we have fought our way back to each other, somehow crushing the walls thrown between us. We have survived all the hardships, the disappointments, the test of time and the detours, but our love held strong and pulled us through. You held me somewhere in your heart, and I loved you more than life. We've been waiting many years for our time, and it is here . . . it is here, now."

John lovingly returned to her breasts that were awaiting his touch. He slowly kissed all of her body from her neck to the back of her knees, his hand returning to her soft mound, while he urged her thighs open. Margaret was circling his nipples with her finger tips, making him momentarily slow his own actions and emit a soft moan. He drew up to kiss her hard and deep and she welcomed him. While probing her mouth with his tongue, he was probing her sensitive cleft with his fingers. He started to fondle her small nub delicately, but only for a few moments, heightening her sensation and expectations, loving the change in her body as she shook, and the intake of her breath every time he touched her like that. Leaving her mouth, he once more looked into her eyes before she closed them, leaving unshed tears seeping out from the corners. Smooth, soft, caressing kisses and licks traveled her neck and collarbone, until finally they made their way down to her breasts, where John suckled from her once more. Her heart was beating a soft tattoo that pulsated against his mouth as he suckled each sweet nipple. Becoming unexpectedly bold, Margaret slid his hand back down to her small opening. He loved her sensual impatience; smiling inwardly, he found the dew of her entry. Heralding her readiness, he moved down and stroked her with his tongue, emboldening her response as her hips wanted to lift off the bed, seeking more of him. Again he wetted himself and cradled within her soft trembling thighs.

He could hear her soft whimpering breaths, as she anticipated his entry into her. Her movements became a live wire in his arms, reaching up for more of him. He smoothly thrust forward as she tried to draw him in further and deeper. "Are you sure?" John asked, barely above a whisper, as he felt Margaret's insistence of raising her hips up, desiring all he could give her.

"Yes, all of you, John," she panted softly.

John easily lifted her buttocks, positioning her for her pleasure and his. Every thrust was going deeper and deeper. Margaret's body was accepting the all of him. She held on tightly to John's upper arms. He thrust further and faster, sheathing his erection to its hilt. He was lost in the sensation of burying himself deep within her, branding her as his own. He had wanted this. *This.* Not just the pleasure, but the joining with her, the intimate bonding of one to the other.

By some instinct she didn't quite understand, she wrapped her legs around John's waist, not wanting to let him go.

The wonder of it caught at his heart, and he held deep inside her, savoring every one of her internal contractions. He slowed it down, withdrawing slowly, and pressing inward again and again.

Margaret's moaning mirrored her own arching rhythm. John was delirious with her craving for him. She was starting to spiral below him.

"John . . . I love . . . "

"Shhh . . . Margaret, we're almost there."

John began increasing his speed and powerful thrusts. She began to claw at his back. Their souls were connecting through the torment of the rising pleasure. He plunged deep inside and held himself completely sheathed, for a moment, so he would not spill himself into her, yet. They would share their ecstasy of this moment as one. Feeling her body beginning to shake violently, John moved higher on to her so that each thrust and withdrawal caused the base of his penis to rub against the top of her cleft, massaging her most sensitive area.

Margaret's wet face gazed into John's eyes, pleading. She tried to speak but John swallowed her sound. His hair was wet with sweat from the effort of his perfect control. Her breaths came fast and shallow. John was driving deep and fast now, there was no holding back anything. Margaret closed her eyes as she was being drawn higher and higher into a celestial world. She was moaning his name. Suddenly all of her nerve endings and muscles collided into a burst of release.

In a gush of air, John loudly whispered Margaret's name as he writhed against her, milked dry by the rhythmic muscle contractions of her sweet sheath, bringing them both to dazzling bliss. Burying himself deep, John convulsed and then lay still within her. He embraced her shuddering descent and held her close through her sounds of pleasure; he wanted to be part of her continuing orgasm. His intentional movements against her womanhood sustained her spasms, which kept him aroused. He was enraptured as he watched her discover what she was capable of experiencing. He knew they had found the euphoria he had sought for them; their oneness was beyond belief. He thrilled to her continued descent for many moments, experiencing incredible bliss, until, finally exhausted, she lay breathless; but one stroke, he knew, would continue her journey.

As he hesitatingly withdrew, John regarded her for several moments, marveling at Margaret on his bed in the moonlight. His woman . . . her eyes were closed, tears seeping from the corners, her sensual furrowed brow trying to find solace, she was wet from his sweat, her nipples were pebbled, her hands were just starting to unclench, her breasts were heaving, her legs, still quaking. He would never forget the sight of her at that moment. She was the epitome of the visions his manhood sought. He was all man and she was all woman. And they were one.

John rolled to her side, enabling them both to pull air into their lungs. The overwhelming joy brought tears of happiness, again, to Margaret.

Margaret sobbed to him," It's too . . . there's not a big enough word . . . to tell how you make me feel."
John faced towards her, "It will be forever like this for us, love."

He rose up to look into her face. "Was it all you had hoped for, Margaret?"

"John, there was never any hope for anything like this. It didn't exist in my world until now. I felt like I was floating away, being drawn to an ethereal plane in the dark sky. The entire experience shatters the sanity from the tormented pleasure of the buildup, breaking through the barrier of relief, and then gently floats you back to earth with all its tremors and spasms and shudders until you are completely spent."

"Margaret, you might be interested in knowing that I can take you to your ethereal plane over and over, until you faint, whereas I cannot experience that. I need rest stops along the way. Care to try?" John smiled into the dark, thinking . . . perhaps someday.

"I do not have enough air for such another trip, just now."

"Yes, I know. That's what would cause you to faint and wouldn't that be lovely?"

"How was I, for you, John?"

Pausing to find words that would only begin to say how he felt, John answered her. "There are no words. It was far more than I imagined . . . the sweet anticipation . . . the sensual reciprocation, the nurturing of each other. Those were the loveliest moments of my life, having you beneath me. I felt our souls touch. It was so much more than the physical release as I've known before. I cannot explain the depth of love that filled me when we were united as one. You are mine and always will be. I felt like I wanted to bury myself in you and crush you to me so that you are part of me."

Margaret began to weep quietly at John's beautiful words. He pulled her close, nestling his mouth in her hair and kissing her, while lightly stroking her smooth skin. She was his to possess and protect.

They cuddled close and slept, waking twice more over the hours to enjoy each other's passionate embraces. John knew he was one step away from his greatest goal. He knew that when Margaret married him, he would be at the pinnacle of his life.

Chapter 26

 *The Mill Fire*

Branson returned a slightly embarrassed, but totally euphoric, Margaret back to her cottage later that morning. She hardly knew herself after last night. She felt consummated with John, who had lovingly and tenderly delivered her to womanly rapture. Again she had witnessed him in a different light. Another awe inspiring moment revealed the passionate, sensual man that lay hidden, and he had waited only for her. Margaret felt she had witnessed the two extremes of male love, and she was certain that John, like in most things concerning him, was the exception to the normal. The evening before had affected Margaret like none other. The sensual pleasure was almost more than she was capable of holding. The depth of love that she felt for John last night was too engulfing, even more so than the physical pleasure.

She felt flustered over her reckless abandon and having given herself up to him so eagerly. She knew she had cut every proprietary string that had bound her all her life, and this was as big a revelation to her as the pleasure of it. She was finding a new Margaret that, until these past two months, had lain fallow. In the light of day, it was too much reality to look into his face and realize that he knew every intimate part of her, having listened to her moans and her pleadings and felt her spasms. She would not want to see him too soon, again, as her sensibilities and new awakenings were raw.

She decided to write John a note, explaining as best she could, about her feelings.

My dearest love,

I find this note very difficult to write, but I must express my feelings to you, for I am not strong enough to look into your face and say these things. Last night . . . your tenderness and love for me was what allowed me to completely trust you and deliver my entire being into your hands. You not only brought me the greatest pleasure I have ever known, but exposed me to a part of myself which took me far from the rigid proprietary that has bound me all my life. I'm having severe awakenings, and it's all so hard to grasp at one time. Looking back over our entire time together, I now realize the exact moment when I took you into my heart. I am sure you are probably thinking that you know when that moment was, but I think you would be wrong. Someday, I will tell you about it; I think you will be surprised.

You were my champion last night, in all aspects, and will forever be. I am still floating above the clouds today, and have to find my way to earth; please give me time. I feel overwhelmed and a bit disconcerted over my own blatant sexuality. I know you brought that out in me, but the realization of it has stunned me. I am rather embarrassed to see you for a while. Please understand.

Soon, my love...

Margaret

Margaret closed the note, sealed it, and asked Adrian to run it up to John's home, taking the buggy she had acquired several weeks previous.

It was no less than 30 minutes after Adrian returned, when a carriage pulled up in the back of her home. John exited the carriage and walked briskly to the back door, opened it without knocking, and saw Margaret there. He picked her up, grabbed her shawl, and carried her outside and into his carriage. He was having none of this, "*I am rather embarrassed to see you, for a while.*"

Branson ruffled the reins and set the horses toward a path outside of town. His instructions were to go nowhere, specifically, but out of town where it was peaceful. He didn't need to stop anywhere, just keep driving.

Dixon saw part of what took place, so she knew Margaret would be out.

John immediately took Margaret into his arms and kissed her very long and hard. If he held her as tight as he wanted to, she would suffocate. Margaret returned the welcome embrace.

Finally retreating, John held her face between his hands as Margaret tried to look away. She was shy at this moment. "There will be no hiding from me ever again. If you feel embarrassed, then I want to share that with you." He pulled her to him for another long kiss. Finally allowing her to breathe, he said, "Margaret, you are experiencing love, love for me, and I can almost die from my own emotional ecstasy. Do you think I have lived all these years in hope of you, and would not want to desperately see that in you? You gave yourself to me, and wanted me, as I did you. That wasn't sex; it was touching each other's souls, deep down, where only we can share. Don't hide or shy away from the experience of our own private moments. There's no embarrassment to each other. It's love Margaret, real love, far beyond the words that could express it."

John pulled her in for another long kiss, parting her lips with his tongue. She anxiously awaited this. John could feel her shyness starting to melt away. He pulled his arms from around her and held her shoulders, while he kissed below her ears down to her breast. Her arms being free, she took her hand and massaged his arousal, without being prompted. He lightly slipped her dress down her shoulders and kissed the swell of her breasts. He licked his way back to her neck and up to her chin, finally finding her mouth. He kissed her closed eyes and feathered her face with more kisses.

"I love you touching me," John moaned. "Don't ever stop."

They rode in silence for a while, John holding her tightly around her shoulders as she sat back against his chest. "Someday soon, all of our nights will be as we have now shared."

John signaled to Branson that it was time for home; otherwise, he was likely to take her in the coach. Those fun games would come later. These new tender moments needed nurturing.

"So . . . you are going to make me guess the moment you decided to love me? I must know when that moment was, so I can chastise myself for not doing whatever it was I should have done, years ago."

Margaret smiled at John. "I wouldn't say it was the moment I fell in love with you, but the moment that tore at me like I'd never felt before. I was awestruck at my own feelings, never having recognized those feelings ever in my life. It was later when I realized that was the moment I knew you had found a place in my heart. I shall not tell you now."

"You know that will be on my mind until the day you do?"

"That's my plan," Margaret said, laughing.

"Margaret, I love you so much that you have been in my head for over four years. I've dreamed every possible way of loving you and you loving me. I do not think I can separate fact from fantasy anymore. Could I ask at least one question?"

"You can ask, but I'm not promising to answer."

"Fair enough. When you had this epiphany, was I there with you?"

"You were there."

John paused.

"I sense that we were not together, by the sly way you answered that. All right, I'll just have to give that a lot of thought, or wait for the day when you decide to tell me. I'm quite interested to know."

A week later, John was invited to Margaret's home for dinner. She was excited about the dinner because she had prepared the meal herself. John arrived promptly, with a bouquet of flowers this time, having berated himself for not doing that in the past. He kissed her without a care if Dixon was near. Margaret did not shy away from that fact, either.

"Thank you, John," she said, as she searched for a glass vase she wasn't sure she owned. She went into the kitchen and returned with the flowers in a large canning jar, setting them center table.

John had wrapped his arms around Margaret and was asking her to play the piano for him, when suddenly he stiffened.

"What is it John?"

"Can you hear the bell ringing?"

"Yes, what does it mean?"

"There's a fire at a mill somewhere. I must go. I'll see you as soon as I can." With that, John fled out the back door to his carriage. He whistled for Branson and they pulled away as fast as Branson could take his seat.

"Oh no!" Margaret cast her memory back to a conversation she had had with John: He clearly painted a picture of 300 corpses, lying on a hillside, the result of a mill fire. Those kinds of fires consumed everything in their path, almost instantaneously, he had told her.

Margaret worried for John and anyone who would be in harm's way. She paced the floor wondering what she should do. She couldn't stand waiting to hear from him, knowing he'd do all he could to help. She decided she had to go, even if it meant the possible horror of staring into the dead eyes of victims. She ran to the back door and called to Adrian for the buggy.

Margaret sat in the front seat holding onto Adrian as he whipped the horse up as fast as it could manage. Horror arose in the night as the sky lit up; the flames were licking the twilight. Margaret sighed in temporary relief that it did not appear to be one of John's mills, but she knew that wouldn't keep John safe.

As they got close, there were many carriages and horses tethered, not allowing them close proximity to the fire. It seemed everyone in the city had turned out to watch or help. Adrian took Margaret by the hand and pulled her through the crowd as fast as Margaret's feet could run. The mill did not belong to anyone she knew, but she frantically started looking for John. The flames were leaping into the air. Margaret saw the incredible speed with which it was moving and suddenly understood John's rage on that day they had met. He had desperately tried to prevent this type of monumental catastrophe. It was a horrifically devastating sight. The top floor appeared to be almost fully engulfed, and it was just beginning to spread to the downstairs. The northern far end was starting to collapse in on itself. *Where is John?* She could see a mass of people huddled over on the south end of the building where the flames were rapidly approaching. She spotted Nicholas and pulled Adrian that way.

"Nicholas, are there many people in there?"

"There a three people, plus John, in those flames on the second floor. John is trying to rescue them at this end; no one else would go. John ran up to the second floor stairs like a fool, before the flames took it. He's been handing them out the window and holding them while he drops them down into the crowd."

"John?"

"Yes, I'm afraid so."

"Oh God, not John."

Margaret saw John come to the end window, black faced and gasping for air. "How many?" he shouted down.

"One more," someone shouted, and John disappeared back into the room where ashes were drifting out and flames were licking at the window, half a room away from where he was. The window exploded out.

"Oh God. Oh God, please let John be all right," Margaret pleaded. She had a premonition of him not making it out. Her black cloud was returning. She began to cry and shake uncontrollably.

Nicholas pulled her to him, trying to hold her as she watched the dreadful scene unfold. "You know John; he'll be all right. Do you think he'd take any chances, now that he has finally found you again?" he asked, trying to reassure her.

"Nicholas, I can't live without him."

"Looks like you won't have to. He's got the last victim and he's about to lower her down."

Margaret's heart stopped as she watched an exhausted John sweating black rivulets and gasping for fresh air, as black smoke rolled out of the window where he stood. He lowered the woman as far as he could. "Such strength," Margaret thought, as he released the woman to the waiting crowd of arms. Whatever she suffered from the fall was nothing compared to the probability of losing her life. Margaret watched as she fell into the crowd.

"No!" Nicholas hollered suddenly, and then took off.

Margaret looked back at John, wondering why Nicholas was hollering. John was overcome by the smoke and exhaustion, he was staggering, unconsciously. Margaret screamed. Like a rag doll, John crumpled to the sill and fell through the window to the ground below; he never felt the impact. In horror Margaret watched him fall, then went screaming and crying in the direction she believed he must lay. She had to push her way through the horde of people watching the fire. She could hear Nicholas calling loudly for Dr. Donaldson.

"Oh, please dear God, save my John. Please God, don't take John, too." Margaret was praying out loud as she pushed and shoved her way to the man who had become the rest of her life.

As she approached, she could see him sprawled on the ground at a torturous angle; his eyes were closed and blood dripped from his mouth and one ear. Dr. Donaldson was hovering over him, while Nicholas yelled for everyone to move back so he could have air.

"Hello Mrs. Reed," Dr. Donaldson said, calmly. "Well, he's certainly got a concussion, but he's alive," He quickly removed John's cravat to bind his ribs. "He's had all the air knocked out of him, too, which isn't a bad thing really, considering that it's all smoke. Higgins, get some men and let's move him away before this side comes down on us. Mrs. Reed, I do know he has a broken arm and maybe a couple ribs, plus a pretty nasty bump on his head; he must have bit the inside of his mouth; that blood doesn't look like internal bleeding. I can tell more once we get him to my surgery. Our main concern will be to watch for the severity of the concussion and internal bleeding, but I don't see any discoloration on his side to the ground, so that is a good sign. I hope they can get that flat wagon here before he wakes up and feels the pain."

Instead of Nicholas bringing men to help move him, he guided the flat cotton wagon back, stopping near John. Several men helped Nicholas lift him gently onto the wagon and Nicholas helped Margaret up to sit beside him, Dr. Donaldson with them. Margaret called to Adrian, instructing him to come to the surgery.

Margaret, not caring who was around, began wiping his face with her petticoat hem. He was soaking wet with sweat and black with soot, but he was alive. She didn't think he could look any more agonizingly beautiful, lying there injured with his closed eyes, blood running from an ear and mouth, black faced, bloodied knuckles and dirty clothes. "So this is what a hero looks like," she thought.

Six hours later, John opened his eyes to a white, unfamiliar room, wondering where, and what, had happened to bring him there. He became aware of a whimpering sound and slowly turned his head, feeling immediate pain. Margaret was there, holding his hand, her head bent down in prayer.

"Margaret?" John said in a very raspy, almost inaudible, voice."

Margaret looked up at him. Her face was full of tears, her eyes red and puffy and errant locks of hair cascading down her sooty face. She hadn't left John's side for a moment, even to clean herself. "Oh John, you're going to be all right. I thought I had lost you. I saw you fall."

"Shhh shhh . . ." John, seeing the tortured look on her face, tried to console her.

"I will never get that out of my mind, ever. I thought I was going to die, myself, until I could get to you."

"Margaret," John whispered, "it's over now."

"You were so brave saving those three people, but it almost cost you your life, and mine, too. If you hadn't fallen through the window and had fallen to the floor, you would have burned to death. There would be no rescue for you, John. You were only out of that window by minutes before the room flashed into flames."

"Did everyone else get out?"

"Yes. You saved the only people that were trapped up there."

"So, what did it cost me . . . and you?" John asked, still trying to swallow the rasp out of his voice.

Margaret handed him some water. "You have a concussion, three broken ribs and a broken left arm, plus lots of abrasions and bruises. Dr. Donaldson said you will be here another day so he can observe the severity of your concussion and ensure you don't have internal bleeding."

She paused for a brief moment, then in a quiet, solemn voice, whispered, "John?"

"Yes, Margaret?"

"I love you. Love doesn't even seem to be a strong enough word for how I feel, deep within my heart. I've wanted to say it so many times, even way back, long ago, but you wouldn't let me. I just can't hold it back any longer."

John pulled her up with his right hand and drew her sooty face towards his mouth, giving her the deepest kiss that he was able. "These are the words I've waited to hear you say. Margaret, you know I love you, too, with all my heart and soul. But please tell me that I don't have to go out of a second story window again, for you to tell me you love me the next time."

"John Thornton! Don't jest. I was hurt more serious than you were, watching it from below.

John tried to laugh but began coughing, as Margaret said, "I had planned to say those words to you tonight, in more expressive tones than in the heat of passion, but you went running off putting yourself in danger for strangers. You have to know that I loved you long before we were intimate, don't you?

"Yes, my heart felt that you loved me, but my mind wanted you to be sure for yourself. I knew I took with me a piece of your heart on that day we met in London. Margaret, are you sure? Do you feel ready to commit to a real courtship? That means not seeing other men, and saying those three words once in a while." He tried to smile, regardless, but he was beaming.

"John, I am at the other side of my quest to find the confidence in myself and my love for only you, as you challenged me to do. I know what will bring me a life of happiness, and it is you. You've steadfastly helped me through my doubts, and I feel good about bringing a whole person to you now."

"Margaret, you were always a whole person, and I've known that since the day I met you. We've had a rough road, but we've both made it to the other side – you finding yourself confidence and I painstakingly hoping you would choose me, to spend the rest of our lives together."

"John, I love you so much."

"Can I ask you a question, since I'm lying here all broken, and have nothing to do but think?"

"It makes me nervous when you ask if you can ask me," Margaret smiled.

"Well, I guess you know how I've felt. You do that to me all the time." John coughed.

"All right, ask then, and get rid of that smarmy look on your face." Margaret grinned.

"God, I love to see you smile. Ever since you left that statement dangling in the air about, 'I was there', when you realized you had some feelings for me - well, thinking I have been *with you* since you've moved back to Milton, and *with you* in London on the veranda, that seems to leave the funeral. I highly doubt it would have been then, because I was *with you,* when you knew I was there." John paused, watching her expression.

Giving nothing away, Margaret asked, "Is there a question in there somewhere?" She was practically gloating.

Rasping his words, John said, "Unless I have misunderstood you and there was no cryptic meaning in your statement, then that leads only to a time before you left Milton." John stared at Margaret's straight face, trying to decipher any hint. "This seems extremely curious to me since you said that, and I am becoming quite obsessed with it now."

"I still don't hear a question in there." Margaret was teetering on outright laughter.

"All right, here it comes. You have just heard me explain my thinking on this. My question is: Am I headed in the right direction?"

Margaret shrugged her shoulders and sighed. "Your logic seems to have a lot of merit, the way *you* seem to see it, being a man, that is. Tell me, when will men ever learn that they will never figure out a woman?"

"Pardon me?" John said, raising his eyebrows. "Who are you? Where is Margaret Reed, my lady? I seem to remember, not so long ago, being rather proficient at showing her how *well* I knew her. And I don't remember having to figure out anything, either. She'll tell you how much I knew of her. Please go find her." John had to cough out the words he was trying to emphasize and laugh at the same time.

Margaret immediately blushed from head to toe, and she could feel the heat rising in her embarrassment. She put her hands over her face and bent over to hide in her lap. She was praying no one heard that. John was inwardly trying not to laugh at Margaret's red ears which were giving away everything. Margaret jumped up from her chair and turned away from John. She was flustered and she was amused at the same time.

John had to add, "Remember, we share everything, Margaret, even embarrassment. Come here and kiss me, unless you want me coming off this bed."

Barely recovering from her red face, she walked back to John's side and happily gave him a kiss. John asked, "So . . . is that the only answer that I'm going to get?"

"Mr. Thornton! You seem to have one unbroken arm. Would you care for a matched set?" With that, Margaret burst out laughing and John tried to do the same.

"But since you are laid up with time to think, I will give you the real answer to your question. Yes."

"Yes?"

"Yes."

"Yes, to all of it?"

"I think that constitutes a second question, does it not?" Margaret laughed.

"Whoever you really are, you are driving me mad. But since Margaret isn't here, would you mind kissing me, again?"

Chapter 27

 *A Fainting Finale*

John and Margaret entered the top floor of the courthouse. They were attending Slickson's retirement party that was being held in the grand ballroom. John was delighted to have Margaret on his arm, and as they milled around speaking to many of the attendees, he introduced her to his business acquaintances. John swelled with pride as he watched all the men taking an interest in her, and knowing she was his. He escorted Margaret to sit with the Professor, along with Nicholas and Peggy, near the front, while he joined the original mill owners on the raised dais.

Everyone eventually found their seats and dinner was served. Slickson finished his meal ahead of most and came down off the stage to walk among the guests, thanking them for coming and briefly discussing his future traveling plans. He approached Margaret's table.

"Good evening Professor Pritchard, and good evening to you Miss Hale... please excuse me . . . Mrs. Reed. I'm not sure I will ever get that right. I hope you enjoy the rest of the evening," he said, as he winked at Margaret. Then he moved on, heading back to the stage.

"Professor, did you see that? Mr. Slickson winked at me. That was rather impertinent, don't you think?" She asked, turning to look at the Professor.

The Professor just beamed a big smile.

"Professor? What is the grin for?"

"Shhh . . . John is getting ready to speak," said the professor, as he skillfully brushed off her question.

Margaret brought her attention back to the front of the room where her elegant John stood, tall and beautiful, preparing to address the audience. As she began to listen to him speak about Mr. Slickson, she was impressed by his illustrious public speaking presence and voice, no doubt honed by all of his Chamber travels. He had so many talents; she found astonishment in him at every turn. He looked at her several times, and she thought she would burst with admiration.

"From a single spinning wheel, to an industry . . . ," John began in earnest, following a few opening remarks. He spoke for about five minutes, ending with an introduction and applause for Mr. Slickson. He sat down in his seat next to Watson, as Slickson took the front stage position.

Slickson spoke for a short time about his past decade in the cotton business. He brought to the audience's attention that competitors can become friends, and although he was going to miss being in his mill every day, thanks to the generosity of his former competitor, John Thornton had promised him he could return, at any time, to visit. He concluded by expressing his appreciation to everyone for coming to wish him and his wife a fond retirement. When he was finished, the audience applauded enthusiastically and gave him a standing ovation.

Once everyone had seated themselves again, Slickson continued.

"Since we are all gathered here this evening, the executive Members of the Chamber thought we would like to take this opportunity to present two new awards. We have created an award to honor someone who is with us tonight. Because of his pursuit of excellence and his determination to set a higher standard for all of us here, this man has been a pillar of the commerce industry for the past decade. He pioneered the inroads in the early days of wage disputes, despite knowing there was very little profit on cotton. He championed his workers and in so doing, almost bankrupted himself."

John was starting to feel like jelly. He had never heard of this award prior to this moment, and his stomach was churning. He felt his worst nightmare was about to claim him, here and now, in front of all these people.

Slickson continued, "He is singled-handedly responsible for turning Milton into the city it is today due to his advancements in employee relationships, from which we all profited and grew. Looking out over this audience, I see members who represent the many new products that have now moved to Milton because of the reputation this town has built, all on the backs of our hard working laborers in the early years, and still, today. The original Mill Masters worked tirelessly, trying to resolve the conflicts, the strife and the poverty that was being inflicted upon our workers who lived in abysmal conditions. One man threw everything he had to the wind, spending long nights, month after month for almost a full year, succeed or fail, he was determined to achieve what the rest of us could not do. This man is appreciated and respected by all of his peers. There have been articles written about him in trade publications; many other burgeoning commerce areas across our kingdom have sought him out for his advice. Most of you probably don't know that, along with all his other achievements, he is a Magistrate for our city. Now as if that isn't enough, several months ago he put his own life in great peril when he rescued three people from a burning cotton mill. As we all know, there is nothing more dangerous than a fire in a cotton mill. He very nearly lost his life that night. I believe he has a guardian angel watching over him. I know that by now he has figured out that we are talking about him, and he is very uneasy. As much as he shuns the limelight, we are not going to allow that tonight. Ladies and gentlemen, allow me to proudly introduce our 'Man of the Decade in Commerce' . . . John Thornton of Marlborough Mills."

Hearing the announcement and witnessing the standing applause that followed, Margaret burst into tears as John's peers cheered him to the front of the stage. She knew this was a wonderfully historical moment for John: Finally he was receiving the tribute for which he never sought, yet so richly deserved.

As Margaret watched, John slowly approached the accolades of his audience. There, standing before her being honored for his achievements, was the man who knew her every intimacy, the man she would marry. John was like a Greek God being paid homage. As the audience came to its feet, he stood looking out over them like a conquering warrior, proud and fearless. He was stately and he was transcendent. Nicholas beamed from ear to ear, clapping as loud as he could. He, too, had not expected this award.

Slickson adorned John with a large gold medallion hanging from a blue ribbon; the Chamber's insignia and the words, "1st Industrial Man of the Decade Award, John Thornton" was embossed on it. He also received a bronze, engraved plaque with a cast of his first mill, which showed the back of him looking towards it, and the inscription, "John Thornton, 1st 'Man of the Decade' for the Industrial Age." After several minutes of more applause, the audience quieted.

Laughingly, Slickson told him, "John, you are expected to say a few words here, you know."

Silence. John was struggling to compose himself. He was engulfed with emotions, the result of the unexpected recognition that they were showing him tonight. He gazed at the floor for a few brief moments then finally raised his head to the audience, displaying the strength of character for which he was known.

"I thank all of you for this gracious honor. I do not feel that I am more worthy of this praise than any man up on the stage tonight. Since I was not prepared for this, let me share

300

with you what I believe is the reason that I am up here, holding this outstanding award."

John paused.

"Aristotle once wrote: *'Pleasure in the job puts perfection in the work'.* Respect for your workforce must ultimately be that first step to perfection. The day there were striking rioters from all the mills in Milton, standing at my front door at Marlborough Mills, I learned that adversity introduces a man to himself. I want to tell you how that day changed my life, the town of Milton, and perhaps even the Cotton Industry itself."

John walked off the dais, took Margaret by the hand, and motioned for Nicholas to join him. Margaret was still shedding tears of pride as John gently pulled her on to the stage. Nicholas followed, looking bewildered.

"I think most of you know my new partner in Marlborough Mills, Nicholas Higgins." John waited while the applause died down. "You might wonder why I hired the man who instigated that strike in the first place."

A smattering of laughter was heard.

"Nicholas Higgins was against the rioting that took place that day, but his interest in driving the strike was for the betterment of his fellow workers."

"In the middle is Margaret Reed, some of you will remember her as Miss Margaret Hale. She and her family came to Milton over four years ago. Miss Hale happened to be visiting my mother the day of the riot. She stood with me by the window, watching the workers clamoring for me to come out. For years I have tried to remember her exact words, but in essence she made me look at them as people, as humans who were starving, and she beseeched me to put myself in their place. Her words on that day haunted me. Miss Hale left Milton shortly thereafter, due to the death of her parents, but her words from that day remained."

John looked over at Margaret; her eyes were looking at the floor. He could see her tears dropping like rain. Nicholas, seeing her discomfort, took her hand and handed her his handkerchief. As he stood beside her, he realized for the first time that it was Margaret who would have been the woman that was hit by the rock that day. She took the handkerchief and dabbed her eyes, but she would not look up into the eyes of the audience.

"Weeks after the strike was over and the mill workers had returned to their machines, I had a visit from Nicholas; he was looking for work. His master had rightly refused to reinstate him."

John looked at Nicholas and they both almost laughed.

"I basically told him I wasn't going to hire him either. But once again Miss Hale entreated me to listen, telling me what a good man he was; this made me give him a second thought. Miss Hale knew him as a friend; I knew him as a smart man. Although I have never told him of my thinking back then, I saw in him a man with intelligence, a man who had conceived and driven a large strike, a man who showed managerial and organizational skills. The riot that ended the strike was never his idea. So, I took the chance and eventually hired him. As you can see, now, he is a partner at Marlborough Mills; it was a good fit for both of us. He's been a tremendous paragon for all workers who wish to succeed. Hard work, respect and honesty, know no bounds with this man. And, once again, Miss Hale had shown her insight into the depths of human souls.

I give most of the credit for this award to these two people up here with me tonight. Margaret opened my eyes and forced me to see problems with the laborers, in a different light; I made the plans, took the financial risk and had faith in her judgment; and Nicholas, here, brought labor and owner together. Nicholas took the plans that I created from Margaret's insight and made it happen. I want to thank Margaret Reed and Nicholas Higgins, who I feel should share this award with me." With that final statement, John stepped back and applauded them.

The audience joined him and rose to their feet. Margaret finally lifted her head, rosy cheeked from embarrassment. She looked over at John and saw him beaming at her. She couldn't seem to turn off her tears.

Still applauding, Slickson appeared next to John holding a second plaque. The audience sensed he was about to speak and slowly sat down.

"John, I doubt many here knew your story back then, but I think most of us original Mill Masters figured that's what happened, and we had our thinking authenticated by Mr. Higgins here. That's why we have a second award to present tonight. It is my privilege to present our first Key to Commerce Award to Margaret Reed . . ."

John and Nicholas now backed away, clapping, as they left Margaret in the spotlight by herself. Once again the audience came to its feet, bestowing their honor for her part in the making of Milton. John smiled broadly, so proud of his woman, standing before his fellow peers; he knew every part of her belonged to him and the people loved her.

Margaret, mouthed, "Thank you."

Slickson handed the award to John to present to Margaret.

The room quieted down and Nicholas took Margaret's hand and began to leave the stage.

John quickly said, "Margaret, could you wait just a minute? I have one last thing to say."

Nicholas continued down to his seat as John turned to Slickson and handed him back the award.

"I see there is a mistake on the plaque and it will have to be corrected."

Slickson looked at the plaque, puzzled. "Where is there an error?" he asked.

"It's the name," John said.

"It is Reed, is it not?"

"Not for long, I hope," John said.

The audience gasped, holding their breath, and a hush fell.

John turned back to Margaret who still seemed in a state of confusion. He took her by her shoulders and turned her around to face him, like a child. He quietly asked if she was ok.

"I . . . I . . . think so. Can I go sit down, now?" she stammered, a little too loudly.

The audience laughed. They had figured out what was going to happen, but could see that Margaret was completely unaware of John's intentions.

John shook her hands a little to get her attention. She finally focused on his eyes. He sensed the audience knew what was coming, even though Margaret didn't. He looked out into the faces of all his friends and said, "You cannot know how much I love this woman."

Someone hollered, "Yes, we can!" Laughter and light applause followed.

John reached into his pocket for the ring that he had carried there for such a long time; he knelt down on one knee. The audience buzzed with anticipation.

"Margaret, I've carried this ring in my pocket for over two years."

Again, he took both of Margaret's hands in his and looked up into her face. The buzzing stopped and the room fell silent like the night.

"Margaret Hale Reed, will you do me the great honor of accepting my hand in marriage?"

Margaret was stunned beyond words. Did he really just propose? She wasn't sure. She wasn't sure of anything.

"W-h- a-t?"

A small laugh from the crowd rippled around the room.

"Margaret Hale Reed, I have loved you since I've known you; will you do me the honor of becoming my wife?"

He did ask.

"Yes . . . Oh yes, I will, John!"

As the audience broke out into loud applause and congratulatory greetings, John rose to a standing position, taking the ring and holding Margaret's hand as he slid it onto her finger. Margaret looked at the ring and then looked at John; tears began to stream once again.

John took her into his arms and kissed her passionately, not caring about his audience. For the third time in his life, he found Margaret sliding down, out of his grasp. He caught her tightly and swung her up to his chest, carrying her off the dais and out into the foyer. The banquet hall went wild. Everyone was glad to honor John with their appreciation, but what a spectacular, unexpected ending for everyone to witness. Nicholas caught Peggy by the arm and hurried to the outer hall with the Professor behind them.

The attendees began to filter out of the room to see what was happening with the happy couple. Peggy was fanning Margaret with her fan as she slowly awakened. She was still lying in John's arms while he sat on a bench with her; her vision began to clear. She looked up at John and his beautiful smile. Becoming aware of the crowd which gathered around her, she swooned once again.

John stood with her in his arms, realizing he had to remove her from the smothering onlookers. To the shouts of *"congratulations"* from the attendees, he thanked everyone, and told Higgins and the Professor, "I'm going to get her home." He carried her down two flights of stairs and across the street to her own home.

John struggled to open the door as he continued holding Margaret firmly in his arms. Dixon, hearing the sound of the door opening, came running.

"Oh Mister John, what has happened to Miss Margaret? She is fainted."

"Dixon, I proposed marriage to her tonight and she accepted; and now you see her," he said with a worried laugh. "I brought her home, but now I think I will take her to my home. We will have a lot to discuss. She will be home when she is home. Do not worry about her."

"No, sir. I know she's all right with you, Mr. John," Dixon said, as she held the door open for John to carry Margaret out to his coach.

Even though Margaret's eyes drifted open, John still held her to his chest as they traveled to his home. He wanted her with him tonight. All night.

"Where am I?" Margaret whispered.
"You're coming home with me."

Chapter 28

 The Game is Afoot

John gently rested Margaret on the couch in his sitting room. He went to the buffet and poured them each a port. He sensed she needed something to strengthen her consciousness.

"Margaret. What am I going to do with you? You will have to warn me when you are about to faint because you startle me before I know it's happening. I'm thankful that all three times you were in my arms when it happened." He smiled as he handed her the wine glass.

John settled next to her on the couch and turned towards her. He put his arm across the backrest and caressed her cheeks with the back of his hand, moving it from her temple and then down her shoulders. He kept stroking her while she began to focus on the recent event.

"John, it's because I am in your arms that causes me to faint. You overwhelm me." Margaret paused. "John . . . I think you proposed to me in front of everyone tonight?"

"That, I did. And you graciously accepted me and then fainted. I have hundreds of witnesses. There is no turning back now." John was glowing, watching her bewildered face as if she was trying to sort things out.

Margaret slipped into an unexpected state of serious reflection. "Tonight, John, I watched as you were honored as *The Man of the Decade* for the Industrial Age. That is ten years worth of sweat, toil, and determination for your caring about the human condition that was Milton. They extolled you as being the hero who sacrificed his life to save the lives of three strangers. I was so passionately proud of you and humbled, my tears came from very deep within, bordering on reverence, I think. To me, you stood there looking like a saint. I felt that you were finally . . . *finally*... accepting the praise that you have so ruthlessly shunned. Your posture was gracious, majestic, even. I almost fainted when the audience came to their feet to bestow their admiration and appreciation for all that you have accomplished.

"Margaret . . ."

"Shhh . . . I need to say these words...."

"I watched as you looked out over the audience, finally receiving the distinction that you justly deserve, and found it hard to believe that you love me . . . me! John Thornton, *Man of the Decade,* loves plain, little Margaret Hale from Helston. I felt so incredibly small and vastly unworthy in the whole scheme of your life.

"SCHEME OF MY LIFE?" John questioned loudly, with incredulity. "Margaret, you ARE my life!"

She continued. "To save your family's name and respect, you spent your teenage years supporting your mother and sister and repaid your father's creditors for his mistakes. With shame, I recalled my initial impression of you. My naivety overwhelms me: From that first day when I met you in your mill and I thought you uncaring and harsh, to your moment of fame that I witnessed, just a short time ago, when people recognized you for the caring man that you are. Along with everything else you affect, you are even a Magistrate for Her Majesty, Queen Victoria's courts. You are responsible for the livelihoods of over . . . now, well over a thousand people.

"And yet . . . you are still the same man I met over four years ago. All your courage, caring and honor has lived within you all of your life. Why could I not see it four years ago . . . this total person who stood on that dais tonight? As dreadful as I was to you, you loved me even back then; you suffered for me all those years since; you hoped and waited for me. . . living a lonely life with a broken heart. On my suggestion, you took a man in and gave him work, who almost bankrupted your business. You interceded on my behalf when you saw me that night at the train station, saying goodbye to my, unknown to you, brother, and I had to lie to the police about being there and witnessing an accident. Because of the late hour and my being alone, you protected my reputation, again, with your discreet reserve, not to mention your first marriage proposal when you attempted to rescue me from totally embarrassing myself. You championed my honor at the Ball. In spite of being normally reticent to stand out in a crowd, you whirled me around the dance floor, gazing lovingly at me with every step, and remained unruffled by the fact that we were the only two being watched by many. And tonight, you knelt down on one knee and proposed to me in front of hundreds of your peers. How am I so honored to have your love?"

John's heart leapt into his throat. "Margaret, I have loved you from the beginning of our acquaintance. I loved everything about you, loved you to your core for who you are inside. You are right; I *am* still the same man as back then, except that I love you beyond all reason, now. If you are proud of me and consider that I am intelligent and caring, what do you think that says about the one I chose to love for the rest of my life? I treasure you, Margaret. I love and lust for you, Margaret. I would give my life for you. God forbid you leave this earth before me; I will follow, for I cannot live in a world where you do not exist. You are so deeply embedded into my spirit and my soul; I just want to be lost in you. I love you Margaret, soon-to-be-Thornton. You are my life, now and forever more; you are my reason for living."

John pulled her to him and they sat in silence as Margaret shed her tears of devotion for the man who loved her.

Wrapped in each other's arms, silence prevailed for many moments, while they absorbed the words spoken by the other.

"I have something that I want to show you," John said softly.

He left the room and came back from his study with a letter in his hand.

"I took some liberty, hoping eventually that you would agree to marry me. You might like to know what's in this letter."

"Before I read this," she took John's hands in hers and pointed to her ring, "thank you for loving me and thank you for this strikingly beautiful ring which proves our love by you offering, and my accepting it. I want everyone to see that I belong to you, and if you must know the truth, if you did not propose to me soon, I was going to do it myself." She smiled into John's eyes.

John perceived the deep love and desire in her face. His own body flooded with passion, magnifying what was already within him; he drew her tightly to him and kissed her hard. He whispered in her ear, "You can read the letter tomorrow. Just give me a moment," he said, as he laid the note down on the table and stood.

John went to his room and returned with a feather blanket that had been in storage. He spread it in front of the roaring fire and turned off all the gas lights. After adding another log and stoking the fire, he took Margaret's hand and guided her to the downy quilt.

"Oh, stay here, I forgot something," he said, as he disappeared into the dark. Returning, he held his hands behind him.

Margaret waited for the unveiling of what he had retrieved and was now hiding behind him.

"Care to guess?" John asked.

"Oh, John, you're not going to make me guess, are you? We'll be here all night, standing like this," she said, putting on her pouty face, which she sensed John loved.

"All right, I doubt you would have guessed, anyway. Now, close your eyes."

Margaret closed her eyes.

"Hold out your hand, palm up, so I can place something in it."

Margaret held out her palm, face up.

John placed something small and soft in her palm.

"Now, don't open your eyes yet, and tell me what it is."

"Can I use my other hand to feel it?"

"Yes."

Margaret started to feel the soft little ball in her hands. She handled the item for a few seconds and then she burst out laughing. "It's YARN!" She opened her eyes. "You cheated last time, as I recall."

"I don't quite remember it that way, myself. I remember outsmarting you, so I am going to give you a chance to redeem yourself. Only this time, I select what you remove and you select what I remove," John said grinning. Ready for the rules?"

"Rules?" Margaret asked, laughingly.

"Yes. Rules. There aren't many. You may not select an item of clothing that has something lying over it that has to be removed to get to it. Say . . . you could not ask me to remove my woolen socks before my boots. That's pretty simple, isn't it? And there, Milady, are the rules."

John had been working on this game for several weeks, in his mind. He was sure he had counted all the garments, and even jewelry, that she could possibly wear, and he had so equipped his pockets with bits of odds and ends to even the score.

"John, this isn't a good week for me to undress," she said with a straight face.

Shaking his finger in her face, John said, "Mrs. Thornton-to-be, that is the first fib you have ever told me and we will have none of that. If you don't think I have that figured out and plotted for the next year, you have seriously underestimated me. "They both fell into roars of laughter. John laid the yarn down between them. "Ready?"

"Who goes first?" Margaret asked.

Withdrawing a coin from his pocket, John said, "Notice that I have a coin in my pocket; you will want to remember that. I will flip it and you will call it." John flipped it and Margaret called tails. "Tails it is. You may choose first whether to TAKE or GIVE."

"I will take first and ask for your boots." John handed Margaret his boots.

John said, "My turn. I will take your shoes." Margaret handed over her shoes.

She stood there starting to work out his clothing, coin and watch, versus her own garments. He had tricked her last time and she wanted to avoid that, or beat him to it. "I will take your watch." It was handed over.

John said, "I will take your undergarment."

Margaret's eyes got really big and she began to protest, until she realized her undergarment had nothing really restricting it. She looked wide eyed at John and saw his shoulders shaking with laughter, but he wasn't making a sound. He put on an air of smug intellect. Margaret turned her back and pulled off her undergarment pitching it to the chair behind John.

John said, "That's a foul, but I forgot to tell you that. You must hand your garment to your opponent." John retrieved her undergarment and slung it over his shoulder.

Margaret was mortified. *I guess I can be grateful that he didn't wear them like a hat,* she thought. "I will take your stick pin."

"And Margaret, I will take your dress. Do you need help with that?"

"No, I can do it, but somehow I don't think you're playing fair."

John looked at her as she stood before him in her corset and half slip. She looked like a short ballerina. She was so adorable, standing there, looking like that; he smiled broadly as he watched her.

Margaret looked down at her predicament and noticed John had hardly removed anything fun. She knew she was in trouble as she realized he'd have her on the floor in three turns. He wouldn't worry about her stockings, garters, hair barrette or jewelry. Yes, this was a different twist, all right. Margaret gave it a lot of thought. An idea came to her; she studied it for a moment and then said, "I will take the contents of your trouser pockets."

"Wait, that wouldn't be fair. You cannot ask for more than one thing," John said with some alacrity.

"Well, you didn't ask me for one shoe, you asked for my shoes. I think that constitutes more than one, don't you?"

"Why . . . you little smart aleck. I didn't count on that; you outsmarted me. If you don't marry me, I will hire you." John handed her his bits and pieces. They both were laughing at each other. John stepped over the yarn and kissed her; that move of hers deserved a reward.

"I will take your half slip thing, whatever that is called."

"It's called a crinoline. Here!" Margaret handed it over, leaving her still in her full slip. "I will take your trousers, please."

John knew he was beat, but he had one last trick up his sleeve. As he unbuttoned his trousers, he watched her face. He tucked his thumbs in both his trousers and undergarment and slowly started to slide both down, watching Margaret every second. The look of realization on Margaret's face was priceless. She inhaled loudly and slapped her hands to her eyes. John was laughing so hard that he almost tripped trying to step out of his own pants.

She was still hiding her face. "John, you cheated AGAIN! Don't you have underwear on?" Margaret asked in her little girl voice.

John stepped across the yarn and pulled her hands from her face. He buried her mouth and stroked her lips and tongue with his. He pulled her closer so she could feel his desire against her. Eventually, he stepped back and started to disrobe her and she did the same with the remainder of his garments.

John brought her down on the blanket, sitting on his knees, and nestled between her thighs. The firelight was throwing its golden light on her exquisite silken skin; he was intoxicated. Looking down at her naked body, awaiting him, he could not touch her enough. He knew that at any minute he would remember, again, how to breathe. He lifted her womanhood to his mouth, robbing her of her senses, almost immediately. John loved doing this to her, and for her, and for him. With all embarrassment and hesitancy gone, she climaxed quickly, as he knew she would. Before her last spasms could subside, he guided himself into her and thrust into her sweet depths, sustaining her climax while he met his. There was no sweeter joy to him, including his own orgasm, than giving and hearing Margaret have hers. To him, that was the culmination of being a man. She would always come first in his life before himself.

"Margaret, I have fallen in love many times . . . always with you." After several more hours of lovemaking, Margaret fell asleep cradled in John arms in front of the fire. As the fire began turning to ash, John picked Margaret up and carried her to his bed, returning for all their clothes before he closed the door behind them.

The workers coming in through the mill yard woke Margaret. She became a little flustered with the full light coming into the room, but she lay in the bed and admired John as he dressed, his body hard and muscular, but slim, without all that thickness of clothes.

"I love you, John Thornton"

"And I love you Margaret, soon-to-be-Thornton. I love every soft centimeter of you. You are so beautiful to watch while you sleep, especially naked. But I think you should dress, unless you want more of the same. I am quite prepared, you know? If you're still in bed by the time I'm shaved, I'll be back on top of you before you can protest.

"Protest? Let me think about that for a moment." Margaret giggled. "Last night you said something about a letter?"

John was beaming at her little joke. "Oh yes, let me get it."

"Here, read it. It is to both of us."

Margaret lifted up on her pillow pulling the sheet above her bare breasts and began to read. "It's from my brother, Fredrick! He is giving his approval for me to marry you."

"John, how did you . . .?"

"I got his address from Dixon and wrote to him. Although you are your own woman, you are still a lady and a gentleman's daughter, so I thought you would appreciate that I have kept to one of the gentry's honorable traditions by asking for your hand.

"Oh John, that was so thoughtful of you." She jumped out of bed, naked, and came over to throw her arms around him and give him a big kiss.

Even though he had lather on his face, he returned her kiss, picked her up, walked to the bed, and sat her on his lap. He wanted his fingertips to roam her warm velvet skin before she covered it.

Margaret insisted that John get to work and allow Branson to drive her home. She didn't care about the propriety of leaving his home early in the morning. These were her people, now.

John called for Branson to bring the carriage to the front. After a final long, hard kiss goodbye at the door, John escorted Margaret outside to the coach, where he claimed another long, erotic kiss, disregarding Branson, before he handed her inside.

Chapter 29

Blissful Beginnings

With all the things John had going on in his life, Nicholas and Peggy still had not had their wedding, but it seemed to now be planned for two weeks before Christmas. Nicholas had adapted to his gentleman's clothes and let his hair grow longer, which allowed for a more distinguished appearance that seemed to suit him rather well. He and John had all three mills running at top performance, and life was good to both of them and their prospective brides.

On a beautiful, crisp autumn day, the town of Milton found itself poised to celebrate the marriage of the decade for their city. John Thornton was to wed Margaret Hale Reed in Milton's largest church.

Nicholas, in his own coach, drove over to John's house to find what preparations he could help with, before setting off for his wedding riders. John was dressed to perfection, as usual, and he handed the ring to Nicholas for safe keeping.

"Are you nervous, John?"

"Actually, no; not severely, anyway. I am struggling to comprehend that my dream will come true today. After all these years, how do I switch it over in my mind to reality? Nicholas, I am sure you know how it must be for me, as you, too, are waiting to marry your lady. Today, all of the lonely tormented years will be vanquished for all time. I gave you the ring, did I not?" John asked as he patted all of his pockets.

"Yes, John, you just handed it to me." Nicholas laughed. "All is ready with you then? I should be picking up Peggy, Margaret, and the Professor any minute now. You need to get to the church, sir. I have traveled beside you, for the most part, on your journey to this day, and my heart is filled with happiness for you and for Margaret. My very best wishes to you, both."

John put out his hand to shake Nicholas's and then pulled him in for a brotherly hug. "I must be on my way," John said.

Branson, having spit polished the carriage and himself, held the door open for his master. He had bathed the horses and braided their tails, polished the brasses, oiled the leathers and straps, and painted the wheels. He was proud to drive his boss to church on his wedding day. He wanted to show his respect with his fairy tale coach, which would sit near the entrance, gleaming in the sun.

"Branson, your carriage is impeccable. Thank you for the compliment to our wedding."

"Right you are, guv, and good luck today."

"Has your other duty been taken care of?"

"Yes, sir. All done."

With great pride, and looking his finest, Branson climbed into his box and reined the four shiny horses and the groom toward the large bell-tower church. Later, he would ferry the married couple back to the mill house to change and collect their luggage for the train headed to parts unknown.

When he arrived, John saw a horde of people milling around outside, talking and waiting for the festivities to begin. As soon as Branson brought the carriage to a stop, he jumped down, opened the door, and lowered the steps. John exited the coach looking breathtakingly splendid in tails and top hat.

John stood outside the church, talking and shaking hands with the invited guests, until the time drew near. His joy knew no bounds today; he wore it proudly. True to the devotion to his workers, many of his mill workers and managers were in attendance, as well as all Chamber members and other business acquaintances from across the motherland.

With nerves beginning to twitch, as the time was drawing close, John pulled out his pocket watch and checked it once again. His stomach did a flip when the organ started playing, inviting the guests to come and be seated. John saw Higgins' coach approaching and he became weak in the knees. He had waited longer for this day than any other day in his life. And the time was now at hand. He turned toward the entrance, feeling like he was about to enter the pearly gates on earth. As he stepped inside the nave of the church, he bowed his head and said a silent prayer:

"Thank you, Mother. I love you. Your work is done."

He turned to speak with someone who was just inside the door and then proceeded toward the altar, holding his hat in his hand. Shaking hands, walking the aisle, oblivious to the faces in front of him, he found his way to the minister and placed his hat on the front pew; he waited for Nicholas, his best man, to come down the aisle, followed by the miracle that had come into his life. John could not help but smile; it was permanently affixed to his face today. His beloved would be by his side very soon and remain there for the rest of their lives. In a few moments, Margaret would be his to possess and protect, sharing his dream, fulfilling his life.

John saw, through the sea of heads, Nicholas helping Margaret out of the carriage with Peggy right behind her. Margaret was stunning in her understated ivory cotton gown, which she had designed herself, wanting it to be cotton, embroidered with ivory flowers and ribbons at the waist and neckline. He was totally mesmerized; he watched as Peggy lifted the veil over Margaret's face and placed the bouquet of roses in her hands.

The organ had stopped playing and the gathering quieted, too, rising to their feet. Nicholas placed the Professor and Margaret in their positions, with Peggy and himself ahead of them, to lead the small procession to the altar. The organist started playing the traditional wedding march, as everyone turned their gaze toward the best man and maid of honor making their way.

Margaret found John with her eyes. She was overcome with his masculinity, dressed in resplendent elegance. Her man, the one waiting for her at the altar, was tall and proud and exquisitely handsome. He wore his black, long tails, an ivory shirt and an ivory waistcoat, but this time he had a red cravat and a single red rose that matched her bouquet, on his lapel.

Margaret was staring at John, who was sending his love back to her, as Peggy and Nicholas began their walk. She knew to count to ten before she and the Professor started their steps. By the time she got to five, the Professor stepped back from her and her brother Fredrick stepped out from the shadows and into his place by her side.

As he put his arm around her, he looked into her eyes and said, "Hello Sis. Did you think I would let you walk down the aisle without me? I love you, dear sister. This is your big day and I wouldn't miss it for anything." Fredrick urged her to take the first step.

"Shall we?" He asked.

"How?" Margaret whispered, as they started their march.

"John arranged everything. I think he pulled in a lot of favors, and I am grateful to him to be here with you at this moment."

Margaret could feel the moisture forming in her eyes. She would be a sight when John lifted her veil, if she didn't pull herself together right now. "Fred . . . ?"

"Shhh," said Fredrick. "Behold, your man, standing at the altar waiting for you. He is dispatching his love for you from where he stands. He is glowing and you are a glorious sight to all of us today." Margaret looked up to see John, in his regal splendor, staring at her with devotion and pride unfolding across his masculine face. His chest was full; he stood impressively erect. She never took her eyes off of him, or he, off hers, until she and her brother reached the altar.

318

Politely shaking John's hand first, Frederick, then, gently placed Margaret's hand in John's. John dared to believe the moment was here.

The look in her eyes . . . The English language is inadequate of words to describe her loveliness, what this woman is today...

The minister began the service. Keeping his eyes on her, John knew he would carry this vision into the world beyond.

Their responses were uttered to each other, and the ceremony continued until John turned to Nicholas and asked for the ring that he was holding safe.

John placed the ring on Margaret's finger and looked into her eyes, as he repeated the words . . . *with this ring I thee wed.* They concluded the remainder of their vows and pledges to each other without taking their eyes away from one another. John could hardly believe that he had overcome almost five years, with all its obstacles, and it had led to this moment.

"And what God has joined together, let no man put asunder," said the minister.

It was done.

John lifted the veil to release the goddess beneath. He inhaled deeply when he realized Margaret was wearing his mother's ruby heart. Tears welled in his eyes, knowing the happiness of this day could never be repeated in his lifetime. As he took Margaret in his arms, he quietly said to her, "You are the completion of me. I will love you beyond our next life."

Before he kissed her, Margaret said, "John, your lips have kissed my soul. Love was just a word to me, until you showed me its real meaning. John... thank you for Fredrick."

They smiled at each other, and to the cheers of the crowd, they kissed passionately

As they walked down the aisle to John's waiting carriage, the guests gathered, tossing flower petals at them, and the church bells pealed to announce that John Thornton and Margaret Hale Thornton were now wed. Margaret tossed her bouquet; it sailed through the air, right into the hands of a blushing Mary Higgins.

Hopping back up into his box, Branson reined the *four-in-hand* set of horses toward the courthouse, as John settled Margaret into his arms.

"Are you happy, Mrs. Thornton?" John asked, endearingly, while looking into her tear-filled eyes, gently rubbing the back of his hand down her cheeks to the base of her throat. "Those were beautiful words you said to me at the end. Thank you for that."

"Mrs. Thornton. That has a wonderful sound. This is the happiest day of my life, dear husband. Knowing that I will always have you to myself, to love you, to be loved by you, to be protected by you, to bear your children... I could not ask for any more out of life. I am blessed with happiness beyond words."

Feathering her face with light kisses, they drove in silence to their reception.

Now that the ceremony was concluded, everyone made their way to the courthouse fourth floor. John, Margaret, Peggy and Nicholas formed a reception line to welcome their guests.

Margaret whispered to John, "Where's Fred?"

He's back at *our* home. He will travel with us on the train. You will get to speak with him for several hours before we part from him."

"Thank you, John. This is unmatched by any gift you could have given me."

"You are welcome, my love. Oh, how nice that sounds to say out loud, now, not worrying who's around the corner."

"Would you like your present from me tonight?" She asked.

"Not in front of all these people, surely," he laughed. "I'm sorry, I am too happy right now. Yes, what is it?"

"I am going to tell you when I knew I was in love with you," said Margaret.

"You don't know how long I have wondered when it happened. To find out now, and the fact that you chose to wear Mother's ruby heart pendant on our wedding day, could not please me more. Thank you, my love."

"I wanted your Mother to be with us today."

"I know she is with us, as this is the culmination of the signs she has been sending me for two years.

John reached over and kissed her, unconcerned of the people waiting to shake their hands.

All of the traditional amenities being observed, the orchestra tuned their instruments and waited to begin their music.

John and Margaret took the floor. The conductor began the first song, a waltz, requested by John, called Brahms Waltz in A-Flat Major, Opus 39 No15, for violin.

The music began. John bowed to Margaret. "This is my dance, I believe?"

"I believe it is, sir." She curtsied to him.

He put out his left hand for her to take. She took his hand with her right. John slid his right hand behind her to the small of her back, but this time he allowed very little proper space between them. She placed her other hand on his shoulder, reaching as far as she could.

The beautiful couple unfolded their mirrored dance of swirls of ribbon and tails, moving about the room as one. John had tremendous grace about him; he glided, rather than stepped, as he moved. His right hand splayed against the small of her back as he conducted her with assured commands into intricate little twirls and wider whirls. The audience was transfixed by their stunning performance and was amazed at how John never took his eyes from Margaret, but sensed his position on the floor at all times. The mill workers were astounded by this man who was their boss, and who displayed such elegant form.

"John?"

"Yes, my love?"

"Do you remember the last time we danced like this?"

"I will always cherish my memory of our first waltz together, as I will this waltz, on our wedding day. This is my favorite classical piece and I have yearned to dance it with you."

"I loved our first waltz because it brought into my mind when I first fell in love with you, even though I wasn't totally aware it was love that I felt. I am going to tell you now, but I would like to hear your thoughts on when that was, first."

As John whirled Margaret around the floor, his eyes never leaving her, he said, "I didn't think I would be asked, but I have thought about it. You remember, while I lay in the hospital, how I

321

figured out something from your words? You somehow wiggled out of a definite answer. You said I was there, but you wouldn't answer if I was there with YOU; I believe that's how it went. I am going to say it was the day at your husband's funeral, when I walked away. I remember so vividly, looking back, and you were still watching me, even though your family was closing in on you. Am I close?"

"No."

"Hmm . . . Now, you really have my curiosity piqued. Earlier?
"Yes."

"Yes?"

Margaret smiled at John's sudden bewilderment. "I'll give you a big hint. It was before I was taken away from Milton."

John almost came to halt in the middle of the floor. "What? BEFORE you left Milton? I loved you then as I do now. I don't understand. I thought you knew my feelings for you. What happened and when was it?

"John, to be honest, I didn't recognize it then, but I felt sick to my stomach all of a sudden. I had never experienced the pangs of jealousy, and didn't realize that moment for what it was. But I know, now, that was the moment I knew I had feelings of love for you."

"Please, love, don't keep me in suspense any longer. I cannot, at all, remember a time when I would ever have made YOU jealous."

"Oh, you didn't do it; it was someone else. And you were quite unaware of it, I think."

"Please, Margaret . . ."

"It was the day of your sister's wedding. You had just exited the church and were shaking hands and talking with people as they filed out. I stood there, watching your serene countenance, thinking how handsome you looked. You extended your arm to shake someone's hand and Ann Latimer entwined her arms around yours. You hadn't offered it, but she took it upon herself to show those gathered that you belonged to her. I became ill just then, and had to look away; I didn't understand why at that moment. You had, by then, and rightly I might add, dismissed me from your life. Of course, after that, I thought you two were interested in each other. Then father died shortly thereafter and you know the rest. I left Milton that day, thinking you were going to find happiness with Ann. I think our letters would have saved us years of misery."

"Oh God, Margaret, you thought I had feelings for her and I thought you had feelings for the man at the station. Let's not spoil our day with any more talk like this. I love you, Margaret, my lovely wife. We shall be happy for the rest of our days and beyond. I can't wait for the rest of my life to begin this bliss that we share."

John bent down and kissed her while they turned and twirled about the room.

With Margaret's lace hem and ribbons swaying away from her, and John's tails floating aside his body, he slipped his hand up her back, pressing her closer to him, and she followed, moving her hand from John's shoulder to the back of his neck. Pulling her right hand to his heart, he cupped her fingers and palm against him. He leaned towards her and pressed his lips to hers again; closing his eyes, he held her close for a final whirl around the dance floor. She had become the woman she wanted to be for him, and with her in his arms, he held the love he had always sought.

Margaret and John: Finally. Their hopes, dreams, passion, and hearts, once existing as two entities, now beat as one.

The End

About the Author

Loyal Wynyard (a pseudonym) is retired, living in Florida.

Being totally swept away by the Elizabeth Gaskell novel, and BBC Production of North and South with the characters of John Thornton and Margaret Hale from the mill town of Milton, Loyal felt she had to keep the dream alive.

Having never written a novel before, she feels her writing is very simplistic, and spends most of her words extending the story. According to Loyal, her writing is "an easy read" with a nice story.

Loyal Wynyard's sole goal is to carry-on more of the story, more romance and more love, without changing the characters. She is not looking for recognition or fame or even profit, she wants North and South fans to have something to embrace the fantasy and advance the love story.

John Thornton, Look Back at Me continues this voyage. It does contain some sensual loves scenes which are included in novels in the Romance Genre. If this type of reading is offensive to you, do not purchase this book. For others, enjoy!

Loyal Wynyard thanks all of the websites that are keeping North and South alive in their hearts and online. She frequents JustPeriodDrama.com and the IMDB.com North and South forum. She can be contacted at LoyalWynyard.com

This book is in excess of 330 pages and considered an auxiliary work to North and South.

Made in the USA
Lexington, KY
10 April 2011